MYSTERY MOST INTERNATIONAL

THE MYSTERY PATRONS PRESENT

MYSTERY MOST INTERNATIONAL

EDITED BY

RITA OWEN
VERENA ROSE
SHAWN REILLY SIMMONS

LEVEL SHORT

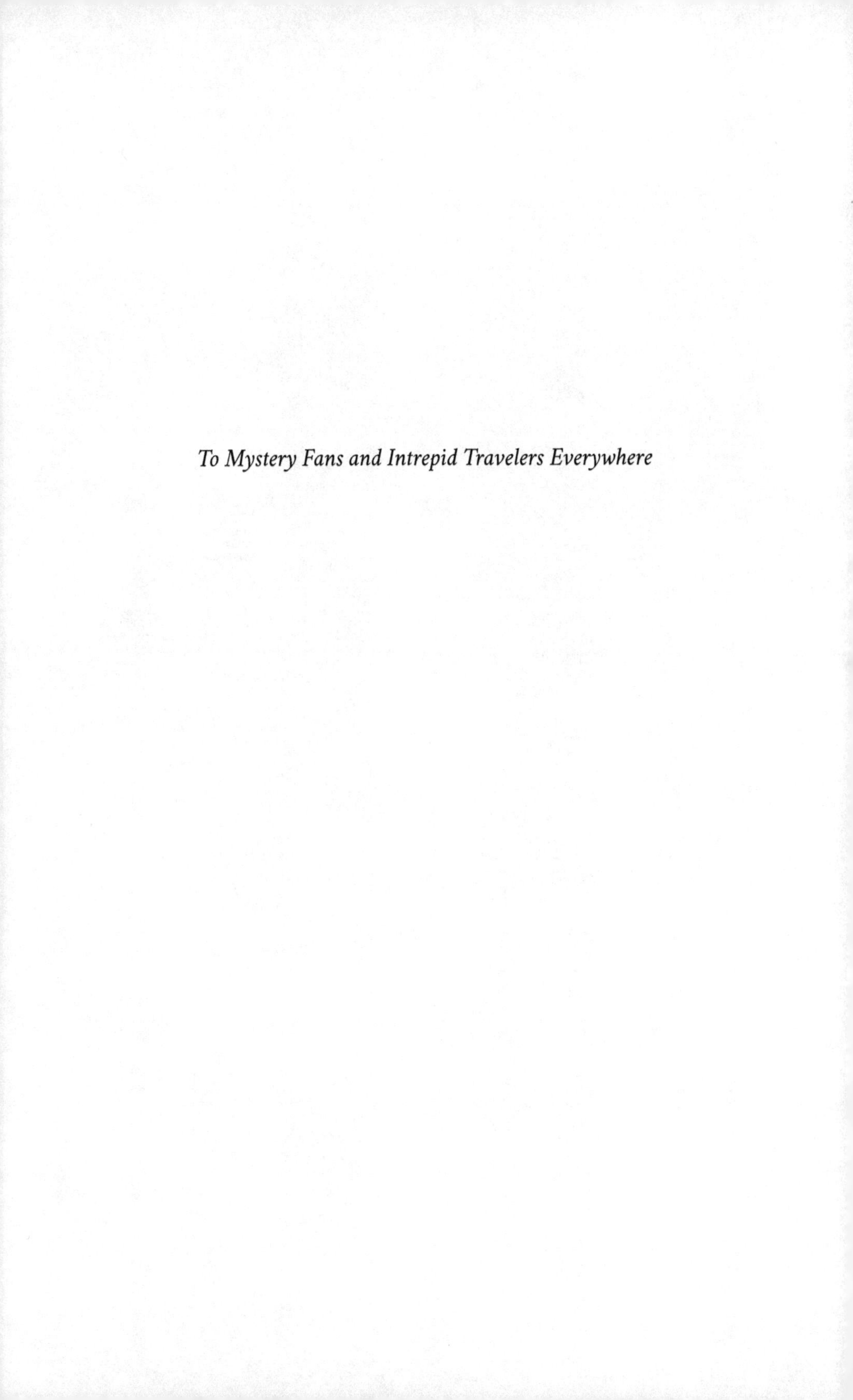

To Mystery Fans and Intrepid Travelers Everywhere

Contents

Mal de Ojo   1
By Liz Milliron

The Last Fado of Ricardo Reis   18
By Gabriel Valjan

The Canadian: Death at a Ghost's Hands   28
By Joseph Benedetto

The Far Shore   43
By Susan Daly

The Road to Limerick   59
By Chris Dreith

Grave Expectations   74
By Marni Graff

White Elephants   90
By Peter W. J. Hayes

Sweet Revenge Hotline   106
By Deborah Lacy

Dragos & Son   118
By Alan Orloff

Death at Dunarven: A Jane Bennet Mystery   134
By Annie R McEwen

The Voynich Manuscript   149
By Bev Vincent

A Warm Moscow October   163
By Nina Mansfield

A Farmhouse in Provence   173
By Merrilee Robson

Swan Song   189
   By donalee Moulton
Murder in the Wine Cellar   206
   By Aimee Kluck
Tent City   223
   By Rob McCartney
Stranger on the Train   238
   By Kate Lansing
Thin Air   250
   By Katherine Ramsland
Lost at Sea   259
   By Cathi Stoler
Big Vuto in Lusaka   273
   By Lorraine Sharma Nelson
Reynisfjara   290
   By Kristopher Zgorski
Arsenic and the Shepherd   302
   By Nev March
The Package   318
   By Anne Hillerman and Dave Tedlock
The Diamond Caper: An Alternate History   334
   By Verena Rose
Sins of the Father   344
   By Kerry Hammond
From Hunger   354
   By Robin Hazard Ray
French Fried   359
   By Lori Robbins
Tears of the Trophy Wife   374
   By Elaine Viets
The Last Dance   391
   By Josh Pachter
No Escape   399

By Robert Lopresti
Death on the Nile   407
  By Jeffrey Marks
Death Comes to Coakley   418
  By Shawn Reilly Simmons

Mal de Ojo

By Liz Milliron

San Juan, Puerto Rico

"You're worn out," they said. "Take a vacation. Get away from it all. Go reconnect with your roots."

Great idea. Except someone missed the memo.

I stood at the base of Yokahu Tower, the popular observation spot in El Yunque National Forest in Puerto Rico. All around, tall trees with heavy foliage kept the steamy air from escaping. Here and there, bright flowers peaked through the green. The only true tropical rainforest in American territory. A place people came to see nature.

Not dead bodies.

Yellow tape kept the gawkers at a distance, but it didn't keep the cell phones away. Pictures would be on Twitter, SnapChat, and Instagram within minutes. Yet "nobody saw nothing." Not much different than home.

"Name?" asked a young cop. His uniform wilted in the sauna-like heat, but he didn't show discomfort. The sound of waterfalls and coquis—the island's signature tree frog—filled the background.

"Juana Esperanza Cruz."

He looked up. "You live in San Juan?"

"New York City." I fell into the language of my childhood. "*Abuela* never forgot her home."

The young cop nodded and switched to Spanish. "What happened?"

"I was at the top of the tower with all the other tourists. There was some jostling behind me, I heard a scream and a thud. Looked down and there he was."

The "he" in question was a man in his middle-fifties. Graying hair that had been neatly combed and parted but was now matted with blood. Deeply tanned skin. Trim, muscular build in khaki shorts and a dark, floral pattered shirt. A straw hat more suited to the Cuban culture than Puerto Rico was nearby.

"Did you see him at the top of the tower?" the young officer asked. "Was he with anyone?"

"He was standing by a woman in her late forties, maybe mid-fifties. Abstract-print dress. Short hair, big floppy hat that obscured most of her face. But I have no clue if they were 'together.' They might have just been near each other."

"You're very observant."

"New York homicide detective."

"Do you see the woman?"

I scanned the crowd. "Sorry. Who's the victim?"

The officer slipped his notebook in his shirt pocket. "I can't say."

"Oh come on. One cop to another."

"Sorry, Detective. If the situation were reversed, you wouldn't tell me."

No, I wouldn't. Fortunately, I knew someone who would.

* * *

I went back to my hotel, the Holiday Inn at the end of the San Juan strip. I admit I was a bit torn. On the one hand, vacation. On the other, dead guy. I'd spent most of my time on the beach and people-watching in the casinos. Exciting for a day, maybe two. I missed the bustle of NYC. But the San Juan police didn't want some outsider detective poking around, even if that detective had a local connection.

I crossed the lobby and the front-desk clerk hailed me. "You have a message, *señorita*. You are to call Detective Gabriel Estrada."

The exact man I wanted to see. His *abuela* and mine were girlhood friends and never lost touch. *Abuela* Estrada had stayed in Puerto Rico. When I visited in the summers of my youth, Gabriel and I played in the surf. We figured our *abuelas* were matchmaking.

I called from my room. "What's up, *mi amigo*?"

"Heads up, Juanita. You're gonna get a phone call."

"From who?"

"Senior detective Paulo Medina."

"Why?" I kicked off my sneakers.

"You were there."

"Oh please. Lots of people were there."

There was a long pause. When Gabriel spoke again, it sounded like he didn't want to be overheard. "Someone said you argued with the victim right before he died."

I did?

Oh mierda. I did.

We'd been at the bottom of the tower. He'd cut in front of me while we'd been at one of the waterfalls and almost made me drop my camera in the water. He hadn't apologized, so when I saw him at Yokahu, I'd pointed out what he'd done. Loudly. Like any good New Yorker. "It was a stupid argument. It didn't even get physical. They—"

"I can't talk about this now. Meet me at La Factoria in an hour." Then he hung up.

* * *

La Factoria was a blaze of people and noise, filled with a seething mass of *touristas* in tropical flower shirts, too-tight short-shorts, tank tops and sandals. Probably what Gabriel was after. He stood out against the crowd. No silver in his hair, he wore neat jeans and a polo. I walked over a tapped him on the shoulder.

"Nita. You look amazing. New York agrees with you." He held me at arm's length, then brought me in for a brotherly hug. "Pick your poison."

"*Un mojito, por favor*," I said to the hovering bartender. "On his tab." I hopped up on the barstool and waited until the bartender moved off. "No call from Detective Medina yet. Fill me in."

Gabriel shook his head and held up one finger. The bartender returned in a few minutes with my drink and Gabriel led me through the crowd to a table in the back corner.

"The story." I sipped.

"The Yokahu Tower victim is Felipe Romero. He's big with the Puerto Rican Independence Party."

"I thought independence was dead."

"There are still a few hard-liners who like to beat the drum." He gazed at the crowd. "What happened between you and Romero?"

"We were down at one of the waterfalls. I was taking a picture. The *pendejo* bumped into me. I almost dropped my camera. I called out to him, but he ignored me and took off. Jerk. One, it's a nice camera and two, it has all my pictures from this trip. But it's not worth killing over."

Gabriel arched an eyebrow. "You're the outsider, Nita. You know how it goes."

I polished off the mojito and asked a passing waitress for another. "I'm no mainlander. I was born here."

"But you live in New York."

My drink came and we sat amidst the noise and lights for a bit. "Is that it?"

He pushed away his empty tumbler. "There's something else, but I don't think anyone is paying much attention."

Except Gabriel. If it pinged on his radar, it would be important. "Go on."

"Two nights ago, the body of Diego Salazar was found on the rocks under San Cristóbal. His surfboard washed up nearby. Coroner said he drowned, probably after falling off the board. It hit his head and knocked him unconscious. He was into risky surfing, like in storms. He had skills, but hurricane winds are unpredictable. I'd buy it, if not for Romero."

"I heard. What's the connection?"

"Both men were leaders of the independence movement. Coincidence?"

Cops hated coincidence. I swirled the ice cubes in my glass. "If it's as dead as you say, why kill two leaders of the party? There must be another motive."

"Romero and Salazar have been leading the charge for years with Maria Arroyo. Independence got five percent of the vote in the last referendum. Romero and Salazar were pushing for a boycott of the next ballot."

"Arroyo didn't want a boycott?"

"She's a true believer if there ever was one. She wasn't in favor and she let them know."

I drank in silence, lost in the chatter of the crowd. Finally, I finished my mojito, set aside the glass. "Suspects?"

"Hard to see how they'd be political targets, but Inez Irizarry comes to mind." Juan leaned back. "She's at the top of the Fifty-First State group. Not affiliated with either the Democrats or the Republicans, but she's rabid about statehood. Got in a big, public blowout with both Romero and Salazar just before the latest referendum."

"Anyone else?"

"Both led pretty clean lives. No illicit sex, drugs, or gambling." He paused. "Call me *loco*, but I'd look at Arroyo."

"I thought she was working with them?"

"I told you. Arroyo hasn't been happy with her partners. She's given interviews where she's made no bones about how she thinks the movement has faltered due to lack of commitment from the top."

"A political rival and a dissatisfied partner. That it?"

He nodded. "Nita, watch out for Medina. He's a bulldog. Romero was a big name. You were on the scene. The others weren't. And Medina doesn't like mainlanders." Gabriel stood, pecked me on the cheek and left.

God, I loved political intrigue.

* * *

My cell buzzed as soon as I left La Factoria. "This is Detective Medina," a rough voice said when I answered. "Where are you?"

I quashed a flash of annoyance. "I went out for a drink. If you wanted me to stay in one place, you should have called sooner."

"Meet me at the Holiday Inn." Medina clicked off.

I could see this relationship was off to a brilliant start.

When I walked in the lobby, I didn't need to ask where the detective was. Medina was older, maybe mid-fifties, dark suit, white shirt, polished shoes. Graying hair with a ruler-straight part, a scowl stamped on his square jaw.

I approached, girding my loins for battle. "You must be Detective Medina. Detective Juanita Cruz." I didn't offer to shake.

"Detective? I don't know you."

"New York City homicide."

His waved my words away. "You were at the Yokahu tower this morning. Did you—"

"Let's go to the patio bar." I headed outside. I knew I sounded rude, but if Medina was already against me, I needed to stay in control. I picked a table off to the side and sat with my back to the wall, facing the beach and the Atlantic waves.

Medina paused. Annoyance flashed in his dark eyes, but he took the opposite chair. "Now, Miss Cruz—"

"Detective Cruz." The lines on his face were getting deeper by the moment, but I didn't care. I grew up with *machismo* and I wasn't going to be run over.

"Detective. Tell me about your argument with the victim at Yokohu Tower."

I walked him through the details. I was thorough, but I didn't offer any exposition or opinion.

"You don't know him?"

"Not even a little."

"Why are you in Puerto Rico?"

I wanted a drink. "Vacation."

"Nothing more?"

"Should there be?"

He fiddled with a pen. "Two deaths in the People's Independence Party and a mainlander on the scene. You can see why I'd be suspicious."

"No, I can't." I uncrossed my legs and leaned on the table.

"You must have an opinion on Puerto Rican statehood."

"Not really. If the people want statehood, awesome. If they don't that's okay too. You can't possibly believe I care."

His expression showed his skepticism. "A lot of mainlanders do."

Where was a waitress when you needed one? "Is that your angle? Someone against independence? Bright man like you, I know you aren't buying this crap about 'accidents.' Or is there something else?" I didn't expect him to share, but it was worth a shot.

He stood and straightened his jacket. "You claim you are on vacation. I suggest you stay on vacation. I do not need the help of a *nuyorican* and a woman on top of that." His disdain for Puerto Ricans who lived in New York came through in his tone when he used the slang term.

I'd earned the respect of my male colleagues in New York. But it looked like the attitude of 'women belong in their place' was still very much alive in San Juan.

"Here's my card. I'll be in touch if I have any further questions." He stalked off.

Medina couldn't possibly consider me a viable suspect. If he wanted to put me in my place, his visit had done the exact opposite. My hackles were up and frankly, so was my curiosity. Vacation, I decided, didn't really suit me.

* * *

When a cop is in another city, she might not have the resources she has at home, but she still has the internet. In very little time, I had contact information for both Maria Arroyo and Inez Irizarry, as well as the phone number and location of each party's office. I decided to tackle Maria—the third independence advocate—first.

The office of the People's Independence Party was a small building in

Old San Juan. Less of an office space, more like a personal apartment transformed into a work spot. I called to make sure someone was there, but claimed I'd dialed the wrong number. I hung up and headed over.

The woman who answered the door was in her mid-fifties. Sleek black hair pulled into a stylish low bun, designer clothes, four-inch heels. Her jewelry was tasteful sterling silver. No wedding band, no engagement ring, just a silver ring with a piece of larimar, the Caribbean's signature stone. "Can I help you?"

"Detective Juanita Cruz." I held up my badge, hoping she didn't look too closely at it. "I need to talk to you about Felipe Romero and Diego Salazar."

"Please, come in." Maria held open the door. The interior was modestly furnished with mostly older furniture. Not shabby, but not plush. She led me to a club chair next to the open window. Sounds of the busy street below, street vendors and tourists, came through it. "Have a seat. It's terrible what happened to Diego and Felipe, but I thought they were accidents."

I could smell the salt water, overlaid with flowers and spicy food, but not see it. "In this kind of situation, we like to cover all the bases." I smoothed my dark gray chinos, the only official-looking pants I'd packed, and sat. "Tell me about the two men. Did you get along?"

Maria crossed her legs at the ankle. "We've worked together for almost ten years. We had our differences, of course, but we all believed in Puerto Rican independence."

"What about outside the office?"

She folded her hands. "We didn't mingle much outside work. Different social circles."

I made a mental note to ask Gabriel about the finances of the victims. "You all believed independence was attainable?"

"Yes."

"The party didn't fare well on the last referendum, though. Seems the people don't quite agree with you. You didn't get enough votes to stay on the ballot."

She twisted her ring. "Our message has not been effectively communicated."

"Is that why you argued?"

"Excuse me?"

"With both victims. Quite vehemently. It's common knowledge."

Icy silence.

"Ms. Arroyo, I'm sure running an operation like this is stressful for everyone. It's natural you'd have differences of opinion with your partners. I'm simply gathering facts."

Her dark eyes glittered. "Diego and Felipe were…disheartened by the latest vote. They thought a boycott would send a message. That unless independence was an option, the people shouldn't vote because their voices would not be heard."

"You disagreed?"

"Yes. Staying away from the polls would only mean we'd be forced to accept a decision by the minority. We need to be out in numbers, arguing our cause, not staying home in silence." Her voice deepened, each word burning with passion and fire lit her eyes.

No question what her beliefs were. "Isn't one of the remaining options a self-determined Puerto Rico? That could be a step toward independence."

"We'd still be aligned with American interests," she snapped.

Interesting, but I wasn't here for a political debate. "I understand Diego was a great surfer. I would expect him to be more careful."

"He was a fool." She sniffed. "Surfing hurricane waves. I told him it would get him killed one day. A surfboard may be made of light foam, but being smacked in the head with one by a forty-foot wave is no joke."

"Felipe's fall. Did that surprise you?"

She clasped her hand so tightly the knuckles turned white. "Yokahu Tower is a popular spot. A pushy American tourist must have shoved him while trying to take a picture, one of those stupid selfies. Those people are arrogant slobs."

"They bring a lot of money to the island."

"So?"

Tense body language, the tightly closed hands, fire in her eye, proud lift of the chin. Americans weren't the only ones with attitude. "Tell me, Ms.

Arroyo, where were you when these accidents occurred?"

"Me, I was—" She narrowed her eyes. "Why do you want to know?"

"As I said, covering the bases."

The sounds of the streets, vendors and visitors, was the only sound as she studied me. "May I see your badge again?"

Damn it. I handed it over.

"New York City. A little far afield, aren't you? What are Puerto Rican issues to you?"

"My *abuela* is from San Juan." I took back my badge.

"Get out. Before I call the police."

I hurried out, before I met Detective Medina again on even less-friendly terms.

* * *

Before I headed for Inez Irizarry's office at the Fifty-First State coalition, I called Gabriel. "Can you get me a financial rundown on the victims?"

"Bad idea, Nita," he said, voice hushed. I heard the typical noises of a police precinct over the line. "Medina is covering that. Plus..."

"What?"

"You didn't make a good impression. Medina is old school. You're a strong woman and from New York City. Figure it out."

The *machismo* thing I could understand as a cultural irritation. But interfering? "Does he honestly think I'm a subversive force here to fight for Puerto Rican statehood?"

"I don't think so. But Medina is proud. We don't talk a lot, and definitely not politics, but I hear him complaining about policy from D.C. made by 'people who don't understand the island.' He may not be one-hundred percent for independence, but he doesn't like you mainlanders, either."

The comment stung. "You mainlanders?"

"I didn't mean it like it sounds." He paused. "I'd like to help, but I could get in a lot of trouble."

"Not as much trouble as the time you smashed a baseball through *Señora*

Dominguez's window."

He sighed. "Go back to your vacation, Nita."

"Those are for tourists. I'm a cop, this is what I do. Even if Medina thinks I'm a woman who can't put two and two together."

"You were always stubborn." He gave a half-hearted laugh. "Just remember. I broke the window. You broke her grandmother's vase. Who got in the most trouble?"

I got the message. That vase had cost me my entire savings. If I got in trouble this time, it would cost me a lot more.

* * *

The offices of the Fifty-First State advocacy group were located in a San Juan high rise with plush carpeting and sleek steel-and-glass furniture. The most eye-popping feature was the view of the ocean. Gray-blue dotted with whitecaps, whirling birds overhead in a deep blue sky. The Atlantic was not as serene as the Caribbean, but no less awe-inspiring. In Manhattan, this kind of real estate cost a pretty penny. I was willing to bet San Juan was no different.

Inez Irizarry was around my age, mid-thirties, with brown hair that brushed her shoulders and deep brown eyes accentuated by tastefully applied makeup. I had expected her to be dressed in designer duds, but her denim pencil skirt was topped by a colorful Puerto Rican peasant blouse. Her jewelry was all ethnically influenced as well. The only modern piece was a modest diamond solitaire on the ring finger of her left hand.

Unlike my last interview, I didn't try to flash my badge. "Ms. Irizarry, thank you for meeting me. My name is Juanita Cruz, I'm a homicide detective with the New York City police."

She puckered her forehead. "Why are you here?"

"I was present the day *Señor* Romero fell from Yokahu Tower. Since then I've learned that Diego Salazar was killed in a surf accident. One hazard of my occupation is being cynical."

"We have police in San Juan, Detective Cruz."

"I know. I met the detective in charge. He was a little condescending. To put it lightly."

"It's the 21st century, but *machismo* still reigns in Puerto Rico." She smiled.

"I realize I have no claim on your time, but I'd very much like to speak with you."

"Please, come in. Coffee?"

"No, thank you." I followed her to a modest office. The glass-topped desk was covered in paper, a black leather swivel chair behind it. I noticed the row of diplomas hung above the black lacquered bookcases stuffed with legal volumes. "Columbia Law. Impressive."

"It's one reason I am very familiar with your reaction to the detective's attitude." She sat behind the desk. The position of power. "America has many faults and women are still nowhere near equal in the workforce. At least many of my male classmates at Columbia respected my intelligence. Here?" She spread her hands. "Let's just say the diplomas don't carry a lot of weight."

"Yet you came back."

"Because I firmly believe Puerto Rico's problems can only be solved by becoming the fifty-first state in the Union."

"That's what I want to talk about." I crossed my legs and clasped my hand around my knee. "Diego Salazar and Felipe Romero didn't share that belief. I've seen some of the debates before the referendum." Before I'd gone to the Fifty-First State offices, I'd done some digging. Thanks to YouTube I'd seen video of the most recent debate. "'Maybe after the dinosaurs are dead, Puerto Rico would become a state.' That's what you said. Were Romeo and Salazar the dinosaurs?"

She leaned back and fiddled with a fountain pen from her desk. "Ah. That. And now they are dead and you are here. Yes, I was talking about them. I understand they wanted what is best for the island, but they were wrong in their approach. We're not equipped to succeed on our own."

Inez was honest. I'd give her that.

"Detective Medina interviewed me this morning. I'll tell you what I told him. It was a rash statement made in the heat of the moment. I apologized to both men after the debate. I regret the words, but I do not regret the sentiment behind them. People like Romero and Salazar are standing in the way of Puerto Rico's path to success."

Inez's voice was measured, light. She might have wished she hadn't phrased it quite like that, but no doubt she wanted both men out of the picture. "What did they say in return?"

"They were gracious, said they remembered the fire of youth." Inez laid down her pen. "More importantly, after the referendum, both men said the people obviously agreed with me. Diego even asked if there was a position for him on our staff."

"Really?" Maria hadn't mentioned this. She couldn't have taken the news that one of her allies was ready to jump ship calmly. "Where were you at the time of the accidents?"

Inez laughed and tilted back her head, sending her silver earrings tinkling. "I should be insulted by that question, but I'm not." She sat up and tapped her computer keyboard. Then she swiveled the screen to me. "When Diego died, I was in New York, meeting with Puerto Ricans there who support the bid for statehood. Yesterday, when Felipe fell, I was at Luquillo Beach with my fiancé. We stopped in Poncé for dinner. Naturally, you'll want to verify all this." She wrote in a notebook and ripped out the page. "Names and phone numbers of my contacts in New York, as well as my fiancé. Information for the restaurant we ate at. I'm sure the wait staff will remember us."

I'd never had a witness be so cooperative. Inez was either one of the best liars I'd ever met, or as innocent as she claimed. I wanted to believe it was the latter and not just because I recognized a kindred soul—a Puerto Rican woman who'd made something of herself. But I knew better than to do that. Yet.

I took the paper. "Thank you, Ms. Irizarry. If I have more questions, I'll let you know."

* * *

No sooner was I on the street when my cell phone rang. Gabriel. "What have you got?"

"You're on to something," he said. "Salazar and Romero both started life in the rough parts of San Juan. That was part of their story. Both have built themselves into successful businessmen. Salazar was in construction, Romero ran a staffing company. But economic times have been hard in Puerto Rico. Both businesses are on the ropes. Because their primary contract is—"

The answer came to me in a flash. "The government of Puerto Rico."

"Correct, *amiga*. The government has no money, or almost no money. In fact, many people argue that the only way the government of Puerto Rico can survive is bankruptcy. We can't do that as a protectorate. We can only declare bankruptcy—"

"By becoming a state."

* * *

Salazar and Romero had been ready to jump ship. Not because they lost the referendum, but because they thought they could line their pockets when Puerto Rico became a state. Maria had not mentioned that little tidbit. I pulled out my phone, called Detective Medina and left a message. Not that I thought he wouldn't eventually get to the same conclusion. To myself, I could acknowledge a smug satisfaction that I'd gotten there first. Or I thought I had.

I returned to the independence party offices. No cop cars. Of course, that might mean Medina had already come and gone. I might not physically be first, but I'd always have the emotional satisfaction.

I missed the weight of my weapon at my waist. I should wait. But Maria was a middle-aged woman. I was a fit police officer in my prime. No contest.

At least it shouldn't be.

The door was cracked open, the only light from the back. I crept toward it and tried to make as little noise as possible. I looked around. Not even a dowel rod to use as a weapon. I pushed open the door.

Maria was in a plush space beyond the reception area. She sat behind a mammoth desk in an executive armchair. Thick carpeting, dark wood bookshelves. Not the smaller, more modest, room she'd been in earlier.

I was willing to bet this office belonged to Salazar or Romero. "Did you get a promotion?"

She barely flinched, even though I had to have caught her by surprise. "I'm the most senior party member left," she snapped. "What are you doing here? I told you to get out. I should call the police."

"They're on their way."

"To arrest you for trespassing?"

"No, to collar you for murder."

She tutted and tossed her head.

I scanned the room, but I didn't see any threats. I didn't know what she had on her. Nothing, I hoped. "Let me tell you a story about three people who started out believing in Puerto Rican independence. Eventually, two of the three started businesses where their main client was the government. A cash-strapped government. They realized that the road to money lay in statehood."

"You're insane."

"The third person, she was a true believer. The cause was losing at the polls, but she hung on. When her compatriots said they were switching sides, she went wild. They ignored her. After all, she was only a woman."

No response.

"It was time to give them the *mal de ojo*, the evil eye. Bring a little misfortune their way. It was easy enough to stage some 'accidents' for her erstwhile friends. She could take over the cause and prove she was right all along. How close am I?"

Maria pressed her lips together. A spot of color appeared on each cheek, her breath hard and fast through her nostrils. "You think you worked it out, have you?"

"I know I have. Salazar and Romero not only couldn't get the job done, they were willing to go over to the statehood cause because they needed the cash for their businesses. You could have carried on, but their influence, and any contributions from it, went with them. That they didn't take you seriously added insult to injury."

"Mercenaries." Her voice was a low hiss. "I told them over and over, we needed to convince the people with our passion. But did they listen to me? Of course not. *Machismo* fools."

She lunged around the desk.

"You didn't call the police. I know your type. So eager to prove the men wrong. Well, I got rid of Diego and Felipe, didn't I? Woman or not, you're a mainlander. It shouldn't be hard to deal with you too."

She clawed like a stray cat, but I'd dealt with worse on the streets of New York. I'd barely grabbed her arm and twisted it into a lock when several uniformed officers crashed through the door, followed by Medina and Gabriel.

"Evening, Detective," I said. "I see you got my message."

He nodded to the officers. "Take Ms. Arroyo, cuff her and put her in the car." They hustled Maria out of the office as she shrieked curses and twisted like a captured chicken. "Miss Cruz—"

"*Detective* Cruz," I said.

Gabriel rolled his eyes.

"Detective Cruz," Medina said. "Didn't I tell you to leave this alone?"

"You did, but I'm not very good at following directions. Not bad for a *nuyorican* woman, huh?"

"Your name isn't going to appear anywhere on my report." Medina smoothed back his hair.

"I know. But every time you think of this case you're going to remember." I walked up and poked him in the chest. "I got here first."

* * *

Liz Milliron is the author of The Laurel Highlands Mysteries series set in the scenic Laurel Highlands, and The Homefront Mysteries set in Buffalo, New York, during the early years of World War II. Liz is a member of

Pennwriters, Sisters in Crime, International Thriller Writers, and The Historical Novel Society. Liz lives in Pittsburgh with her husband and a very spoiled retired-racer greyhound.

The Last Fado of Ricardo Reis

By Gabriel Valjan

Lisbon, Portugal

We were men of mystery, men who made the impossible possible, and we were mortal. Everyone would see the name of a dead man in the morning edition of the *Expresso* and think nothing of the man, or know his real name, his true occupation. Before he was Ricardo he was Raoul from Montreal, and his career highlight was tying the shoelaces for Operation Zorro and relocating Eric Galt to Lisbon.

Protocol dictated that I meet with the station chief. The Company may have officially severed finances to Radio Free Europe in '72, but that didn't mean we left the country. Portugal remained a hotbed for activity, and Lisbon was called the City of Spies for a reason. Those were the days of wine, of fado and roses. For us, then and now, it was and always has been Company, Country, and God, and God didn't mind third place because He was a Company man too.

A phone call confirmed the time and place.

I thought of when I first came to Lisbon and met Ricardo Reis. We'd climbed the city's steep hills together on the Elevador da Glória, and he showed me all the food markets, and introduced me to piri piri, a bold, citrusy and tangy sauce made from African chili peppers. Ricardo and I had spent many a night in the clubs listening to fado music, Portugal's version of the blues. We drank, but I would shy away from his favorite drink, ginja, because I disliked the taste of sweet and tart cherries. He smoked, and we talked, using code only those in the trade might understand.

Like me, when he'd been assigned to Lisbon, he worked with a cobbler, so the diplomas, passports, visas, and other documents all said RICARDO REIS. The inspiration for his identity came from a writer whose wife's maiden name was Reis. Her husband José Saramago was a Communist, a translator, and a journalist.

Today, the news says Ricardo Reis is dead.

I knotted my tie while taking in the city of Lisbon from my balcony. It was a clean and colorful city, the weather pleasant, and the people reserved. A recent rain had, to misappropriate Chaucer, pierced the root of understanding. A breeze swept in from the harbor; the day was overcast, and the sun hid behind a cloud.

Ricardo had started with the OSS in Vienna before the Company became the Company in '48. He'd been the last man out of Iran in August of '53, the first into the Palacio de La Moneda in Chile in September of '73, and now he was dead in Lisbon. His death by drowning shook me like an earthquake, and I waited for the inevitable tsunami.

The paper suggested suicide, the body found in the river Tagus. It seemed that Ricky—I called Ricardo Ricky—had hurled himself from the Vasco da Gama Bridge into the water below. Probably new to the paper and with no say, some ghoul was assigned to write the obituary. The journalist assigned to cover crimes for the same paper theorized that a combination of depression and drink led to the impulsive decision. His article stated that no note had been found anywhere, only carnations.

A bridge. Suicide (alleged). Flowers.

The presence of red carnations was the first clue. The journalist claimed a vendor had dumped flowers he couldn't sell into the river. The flower itself had come to represent the 25 April coup d'état against the Estado Novo, the last gasp of António Salazar's authoritarian regime here in Portugal, in '74. The flowers represented a tacit agreement between the soldiers and protestors. The arrangement was that those who took to the street would place carnations into the muzzles of military rifles, and the soldiers wouldn't shoot them. The journalist did get one thing right: carnations were in season, and they were for everyone everywhere a symbol of change and nonviolence.

Ricardo Reis had drowned in a sea of carnations. I made a call to a friend with a friend in the Office of the Medical Examiner before I left the hotel for the café in the Old Quarter.

I was told carnations had been found in his pockets, in his mouth, and in his throat.

* * *

I checked the time on my watch. I admired the Swiss timepiece, its factory-issued band, and the mechanical craftsmanship that kept me faithful to the hour and on time for my appointment. I had seen Ferdinand Soares before he saw me.

He'd chosen the Café A Brasileira, a famous meeting place for intellectuals and artists. The poet (and Saramago's literary obsession) Pessoa wrote poetry, and drunk absinthe and coffee, here.

Soares called me Finn, and I called him Ferdy.

Neither of us used our real names. We had nothing in common, except for the Company and a certain university in New England, though decades apart. Ferdy was an old-timer, like the late Ricardo Reis, one of the lions in our profession. Ferdy was tenured tweed, a professor of Classics on sabbatical, and the farthest image one could have of a spy.

I imagined that had he been born centuries ago, he would have been a Jesuit, one of the soldiers of Christ during the Inquisition. He'd look smart in a black robe while he towed orthodoxy and pursued the heretics with zeal. These days, the closest he'd get to wearing black wool was if he were cold or imitating Carlos do Carmo and singing fado in the streets.

I raised two fingers as a signal to the waiter. *"Duas bicas, por favor."* I'd ordered two coffees. My eyes scanned buildings and windows.

"Relax, Finn. You're not in Dallas."

"Habit," I said. "I prefer not to remember November."

"Executive action," he said. "You have to admit that it was planned beautifully."

I looked at him, somewhat shocked at how clinical, how matter-of-fact he was about that particular operation. He blinked and then said something peculiar, even to me.

"Advanced and sophisticated, yes, but we didn't arrive overnight at fluency. We had twenty years of Professor Higgins drilling Eliza with, 'The rain in Spain falls mainly on the plain.'"

I shook my head and said something blasé, "Nepotism is dangerous."

"The Dulles brothers. The Kennedys. The Gracchi brothers. Take your pick. 'The measure of a man is what he does with power.'"

"Sun Tzu?" I asked.

"Plato."

The waiter returned and left us our coffee. I sipped mine, while Ferdy discussed current events and quoted aphorisms from Sun Tzu this time. I listened because I wanted to be thought of as either agreeing with what he was saying or appearing as not to have an opinion.

A kid on a Vespa came to a halt in the middle of the street so an elderly lady could cross it. The pop song "Stayin' Alive" blared from a radio that he had jerried to the frame of the scooter. I appreciated the irony that the disco tune had become the theme and soundtrack to our lives.

Ferdy asked me about work. On my papers I was listed as a journalist but the truth is that I created crossword puzzles for a major newspaper. I asked Ferdy how he was enjoying his sabbatical. He answered, "I'm preparing a paper on comparative grammar."

"There's the cure for insomnia."

"Portuguese grammar stands apart among Romance languages. Did you know that?"

"I did not."

"It offers odd verb modes, derived from Latin infinitive forms, to express nuances of causality and eventuality. There's the personal infinitive, which technically is a contradiction in terms."

"I'll stick to crossword puzzles, Professor."

"It's worth some consideration; the distinction, that is. In the case of the impersonal infinitive, the verb refers to the general idea of the action, the subject itself. The phrase 'to err is human' is an example of the impersonal infinitive. The personal infinitive, however, is a different animal altogether because there is a known subject. When you conjugate the infinitive, add the endings, you create context and meaning around the subject."

"It's over my head, but I'll take your word for it, if you say so."

He lowered the cup to the small saucer and placed it there without a sound and asked me, "You know when to use the correct infinitive?"

"The impersonal versus personal? Haven't a clue."

"Clever pun for a crossword man. Think of dialogue."

"As in subtext?"

"As in our departed friend." Ferdy focused his eyes on me, wet and bright from the glare. The shy cloud from earlier in the day could no longer obscure the sun's heat and radiance, nor prevent Ferdy from acting professorial.

"If the focus is on a particular subject doing the action, use the personal infinitive, and if the focus is more on the general action itself, use the impersonal. Nuance is everything."

He looked at me with serious eyes, which troubled me because they could simultaneously express cruelty and leadership. Today, he pointed to linguistics to prove his point, when in the past he would cite historical examples, such as Roman emperors who had members of their family murdered, either to secure their power or demonstrate it. Caracalla had the Praetorian Guard kill his brother; and Nero, his wife and mother. Few emperors died of old age and in their bed, surrounded by family. Hazards of their profession.

My finger tapped the small handle to my cup. The game of chess had begun. A death in the field required a debrief. Ferdy as Lisbon's station chief would ask questions, several or one and my answer determined the next page in the jacket that the Company kept on me. He was playing white and moved first. I always found it perverse that my color was black, which symbolizes evil, when white was the absence of color.

I made my move. "I take it that our friend had made the impersonal personal."

He nodded. "He planned to air subjects best left alone."

"Impersonal or personal?"

"Personal. You write, don't you?"

It sounded like a question but I read it as an accusation.

I countered. "Only crosswords, if you can call that writing."

He waved a finger. "Touché."

"Then the rumors were true."

He shrugged. "Hard to say, but lest we forget: Everything is read."

I nodded. "The golden rule is never to write anything down."

"Or talk on the phone."

It'd been in the wind for some time that Ricky was writing his memoirs. Tell-all books sold. Among our allies John le Carré wrote literary entertainment. Native son E. Howard Hunt had been writing potboilers since before World War 2, but the closest he came to personal was a slim volume about his participation in a failed invasion of Cuba.

Howard, however, was luckier than Ricky. Howard had survived the memo that said certain matters should never be committed to paper or discussed with a spouse. He paid the penalty, though. Howard's wife, a journalist, and a Congressman died in a plane accident. The man responsible for the successful coup in Guatemala liked to brag that he'd received Che Guevara's severed hands in a box. Whether there was any truth to Che and the hands or not, I do know that Félix Rodríguez, who had taken Che's Rolex, liked to show it to reporters. As for Howard, he is sitting in a jail cell at an Air Force base in Florida.

"This weather is something," I said and looked around. "The rain has made the river rise. Water is Nature's way of expressing catharsis."

"'Profit and loss, A current under sea.' T.S. Eliot's *The Wasteland*, part four."

"Death by Water. Poetic."

"Poetic as flowers."

I agreed with him. "I could do without seeing another carnation."

He'd pushed his cup and saucer to the side of the table for the waiter. I kept mine. Portuguese coffee made me think of its Italian cousin, the espresso. They both boasted the same hazelnut crema, except I found the Portuguese version creamier, more balanced, the volume larger, and the kick from the caffeine stronger. I had spent time in Italy, although not as much as Ferdy opposite me.

Ferdy had worked the '48 election in Italy. With a successful Soviet coup in Czechoslovakia in February of that year, Truman ordered that there would be no communists or socialists in western Europe. The Company listened and obeyed. In Italy, there was no way the communists would win the vote.

And they didn't.

Ferdy had made certain the Christian Democrats won, held, and maintained power. Ferdy was the Company's man in Rome, the station chief and the hand inside the gauntlet made of lead. Those who defied him received one warning, a single chrysanthemum, dyed black. Those who ignored the message disappeared.

He asked me, "Where to after Lisbon?"

"Somewhere in South America is my guess. I don't know."

"Typical, isn't it? They don't tell you until the last minute. I don't care much for South America. The whole damn place is the Devil's furnace."

The way his eyes moved said he'd thought about his time in Bolivia, where he had contracted both dengue fever and malaria.

"I need to ask," he said.

"Then ask," I responded.

"When was the last time you saw Ricardo?"

I conveyed the date and time, which he already knew from surveillance reports. I told him that we had enjoyed a night of fado. The evening was dedicated to the glorious songs of the fadista Amália Rodrigues. Where many singers sang of sea and love, of misspent love and heartbreak among the poor, she released the poetry of some of Portugal's greatest poets into the air.

"Did Ricardo drink too much?"

I thought about it. "No more than usual, but not enough to cause concern."

"Did he indicate that he planned to walk away?"

"No."

"What was the last thing he said to you?"

"Nothing really," I said. "It was rather impersonal, an observation."

"What did he say?" he asked, this time the eyes said, 'No more games, answer.'

This was the question he'd come to ask me. It seemed that his man or woman couldn't get close enough to our table that night to overhear our conversation in the club. I'd known that before the body was found, Ricky's place had been ransacked for anything and everything that connected him to the Company. His place was tossed and then reassembled as if nothing had been disturbed. He'd been audited.

I said, "The last thing he said to me?"

"The last thing, yes."

"He said the music couldn't stop."

I nodded and I smiled as if I were Faustus and he was Mephistopheles.

"The music?" he asked, puzzled.

"Observation, like I said. I think what he meant was that if America didn't have an enemy, she'd have to invent one."

He swatted his neck as if a mosquito had landed and bitten him. When his hand moved, I noticed the watch. I asked him for a cigarette. If the request surprised him, he hid it. I wasn't much of a smoker, but indulged on occasion. Cigarettes broke conversations, and there were times when I measured a lifespan in smoke rings. Ferdy reached into his breast pocket. The hand emerged with the familiar red and white hardtop of Português Reds, which were not to be confused with the similar looking pack of Português Suaves or 'Softs.' Reds didn't pack the bite that came with Marlboro Reds or Camels. I'd compare them to the soft and serviceable Winston Reds.

The ritual of cigarette and light bought time.

Fingers on his left hand lifted the lid to the pack of cigarettes and the thumb pushed up a brown filter and then the white cigarette for me to take with my fingers. I tamped the end against the table to pack the tobacco tight while he chose a smoke for himself. It's an unspoken courtesy not to have a guest smoke solo. Men about to be shot smoked alone.

I put the cigarette to my lips. His right hand reached down, out of sight, and returned with a Zippo. I leaned forward, my eyes met his. I heard the metallic click and the wheel turn. The flame jumped. It was natural to look down at the flame as it fired the end of your cigarette.

I saw the watch. I recognized it.

Twenty-five years in and the Company's idea of gratitude was to hand the dutiful and loyal employee a watch, but not just any watch. Corporate types spent serious *escudo* on garish gold timepieces. People think of marquee names, such as Audemars Piguet, Patek Philippe, or Rolex as the pinnacle of success and status.

Not our government. Not the Company. They purchased dead brands.

Japanese quartz technology put over sixty-thousand Swiss watchmakers out of a job, so our government, in its pecuniary wisdom, bought bulk, at a discount, on the taxpayer's dime.

I glanced down and saw a Nivada Grenchen, a Chronomaster that Ricardo called the Chaosmaster. I wore one myself and but kept the original band. The watch itself didn't interest me. I could care less whether it could tell time in the Antarctica or at full fathom five. The custom speckled band interested me more because to this expert of crossword puzzles, the black blocks and white squares hid an identity and initials visible to the knowledgeable eye.

Ricardo Reis was an alias, but I was one of the few people who knew his real name.

I knew his name, in life and death, but not the name of his killer before me.

* * *

Gabriel Valjan is the author of the Roma Series, The Company Files, and the Shane Cleary Mysteries. He has been nominated for the Agatha, Anthony, Derringer, and Silver Falchion Awards, and received the 2021 Macavity Award for Best Short Story. Gabriel is a member of the Historical Novel Society, ITW, MWA, and Sisters in Crime. He lives in Boston and answers to tuxedo cat named Munchkin.

The Canadian: Death at a Ghost's Hands

By Joseph Benedetto

Tientsin, China

The Treaty Port of Tientsin, China

The Autumn of 1901

The murder took place in broad daylight inside the walled Chinese city of Tientsin, halfway between the ancient Temple of Wên Miao and the newly built Telegraph Office. I wasn't there, but a dozen Europeans witnessed it, along with at least 40 Chinese…yet nobody saw the killer.

Two officers of the British Occupation Force were being pulled along in a huang pao ch'e, a 'rickshaw.' It abruptly halted just inside the East gate of the city, blocked by three dirty Chinese muleteers arguing over whose cart had right of way.

With a *WOOMPH!* a violent cloud of dense white smoke billowed up alongside the rickshaw. A spearhead-shaped silver dart with a crimson cloth tail trailing more than 10 feet of fine silver chain flashed out of the smoke and hit the neck of the man sitting on the far side, Lieutenant Williams. Before the other officer, Captain Blackborough, could even take a breath, the killer whipped the silver chain hard and the dart flew back into the white smoke cloud.

Lt. Williams slumped forward, dead.

Beside the rickshaw, the smoke cloud dissipated, revealing only an empty street.

* * *

The Treaty Port of Tientsin consists of two vastly different parts: the walled "native city," a mile on each side and completely surrounded by native shops and houses, and the international settlement at Tzŭ-chu-lin, two miles away on the banks of the Hai River, containing the Foreign Concessions of Great Britain, Germany, France, and Japan.

One-million Chinese live in Tientsin and its attached suburbs, while less than 900 foreigners live in the international settlement. So to say we were alarmed by the killing would be putting it mildly. Yet the next two days passed with no further attacks involving a smoke cloud and a Chinese sheng piao, a 'rope dart,' coated in poison. The general consensus changed from *'This is the first in a string of attacks against random foreigners'* to one of *'What did Lt. Williams do that caused him to be singled out for death?'*

Well, Lt. Williams had been in charge of the planned demolition of the ruined Temple to the City God, just one of countless buildings destroyed during the recent Boxer Rebellion that had left China prostrate before Great Britain and the other 10 foreign countries that had defeated her. Given how much of the temple was broken stone and burned brick, it was only natural that someone in the Occupation Force had marked it for demolition without bothering to ask the natives for permission.

So I had the motive. I didn't know the dead man, but being a former constable of the Canadian North-West Mounted Police, as well as a recently mustered-out Officer of Canadian Scouts in the British Army fighting the Boers, I couldn't help but get caught up in it. An impenetrable cloud, a silver dart, a vanishing assassin? This was the stuff of legend. But all I had to work with were rumors and guesses.

Then the second killing took place.

Captain Blackborough and the new head of the demolition project, Lieutenant Soames, were in a one-horse stanhope gig, the lieutenant driving, the cold-eyed captain sitting on his right. They were a mile and a half from where Lt. Williams had been murdered, but Blackborough still kept his hand on his holster all the same. Just east of the Buddhist Temple of Chieh-yüan, by the banks of the Ta Yün-ho—the Grand Canal— Lt. Soames pulled up short; a Mongolian pony pulling the dung-cart ahead of them had gone down.

WOOMPH! A violent cloud of white smoke billowed up on the captain's side of the buggy and a spearhead-shaped silver dart with a crimson cloth tail trailing a fine silver chain flashed out of the smoke, missing the captain by mere inches and hitting Lt. Soames in the neck. As Captain Blackborough drew his revolver, the killer whipped the poisoned dart back into the smoke. Captain Blackborough desperately fired off three blind shots, then tried to help the lieutenant, but it was already too late. Lt. Soames, like Lt. Williams before him, was dead.

Beside the gig, the white smoke dissipated, revealing only an empty street.

* * *

Both officers had been in charge of demolishing the ruined "City God" temple. And both had been murdered. You won't be surprised to hear that no one else wished to take over the project.

A reward was offered for the identity of the murderer.

No native dared come forward.

As to the unbelievable method of killing, it turned out to be the modus operandi of Meng Chi-Hsien, a master assassin who had been beheaded by order of the Dowager Empress five years ago, an act witnessed by most of the "foreign devil" Diplomatic Corps. Being dead, he was not going to be the most likely suspect in the investigation. But a rumor quickly arose among the natives that it was Meng Chi-Hsien's ghost, come to Earth to wreak vengeance on the foreign invaders trying to eradicate the Temple of the City God.

I was, it seemed, tracking a ghost that killed men.

Such were my thoughts, walking up the *Rue Sin Sheng* in the French Concession toward the Bund on the riverbank, on my way to the shop of the watchmaker Monsieur Moreau. Turning the corner onto the Bund, I ran into someone coming the other way. His face was familiar, but only because it had been in the morning paper: I'd run into Captain Blackborough in mufti. "Excuse me, Captain," I said. "Entirely my fault."

"It most certainly is, you damned zounderkite!" the pith-helmeted captain snarled, his face a marble effigy of contempt as he glared at me.

Narrowing my gaze at him, I automatically sidestepped to allow an overloaded Chinese wheelbarrow to edge past me.

The act saved my life.

WOOMPH! The white smoke cloud billowed up on my left, the silver spearhead-dart flashing between the two of us and hitting a passing top-hatted Frenchman. I drew my .455 Webley revolver as the silver chain jerked taut and the bloody silver dart flew back past me to disappear into the billowing white cloud. I dashed into the smoke but couldn't even see the end of my nose. Off to my left a native woman gave a startled cry. I ran over and found a Chinese serving girl sitting on the ground, yelling after the man who had knocked her over as he fled.

"Which way did he go?" I asked in Chinese.

She gestured, cursing, and I went after him, but it was no good.

He was gone.

My cheeks burning, I stalked back to Captain Blackborough, and grimaced.

Like Lieutenants Soames and Williams before him, the Frenchman was dead.

* * *

I had been the target, and I was still alive only by accident. But there was no reason to kill me, so why was I attacked? I had no connection to Captain

Blackborough. It felt like I had been attacked solely because I was the one standing closest to the captain. And that made no sense.

I fell back on my training and opened the warrant book in my mind. *Make an assumption, Constable, and work from there.*

I got attacked because I was standing near him.

No, lots of people had been just as close to him, all the way from the railway station to where I ran into him on the Bund, and none of them got attacked.

So why choose me? Why would I have been marked for death?

I squared my flat-brimmed "Mountie" Stetson level with my eyes.

Of late I've made the rent by hiring myself out to 'adjust' other people's problems. (Being a former Mountie, I try not to think too hard about the jobs I have to do.) So: maybe my reputation had finally preceded me. What if the killer had gotten word that the foreign devil they called "The Canadian" was trying to find him? That would be the perfect reason for the assassin to target me.

Hmm. It was possible, but how probable was it?

What if I was not the target?

What if Captain Blackborough had been the target?

Again, it was possible, but how probable was it? Three attempts on one man, and each one missed? What kind of assassin could be that bad with his aim?

And what had Captain Blackborough done to merit it? The two lieutenants had been officers under his command in charge of demolishing the City God Temple. I had no connection to either man, let alone the temple, and yet I had been the third target, while Blackborough came through all three attacks unscathed. And both lieutenants had been murdered outside the precincts of a Chinese temple, whereas the attack on me had been made on the Bund, the road dividing the riverbank wharves from the landside warehouses. There were no temples anywhere near where it occurred.

Theory: maybe the killer was taunting Blackborough, trying to terrify him for some reason. Again, why? What had Captain Blackborough done to merit it?

Given that the natives had been saying the dead assassin was still killing people, it looked best to learn everything possible about Meng Chi-Hsien and figure out who was copying him, hopefully finding some connection between the assassin and Blackborough.

Huh. A Chinese assassin. Who else besides he himself would have known the exact details of how he performed his attacks? How close was this new killer following the *modus operandi* of the dead assassin? I needed answers, so I checked that my Webley revolver was loaded, then hailed a rickshaw.

* * *

I learned to play *hsiang ch'i*—the Elephant Game, what some foreigners call "Chinese Chess"—out of need. The bearded, poverty-ridden Sage I had come to see, Tung Tien-fu, would only speak to me if I would play him a game, out front of his hovel, using a well-worn board that had been carved when William the Conqueror was on the throne of England.

As ever, Tung Tien-fu took Red and went first. "Meng Chi-Hsien, very famous assassin," he said, moving one of his Horses one point orthogonally and then one point diagonally. "Last of Great Assassins of Floating Temple." He raised his hand to tell his house maid to bring tea—but she knew him so well she already had it ready and waiting.

Oh yes, the Sage employs a servant. This poverty-ridden old man living in a hovel still has enough money to hire a servant, because here in China there is always someone far poorer than you, who will accept a pittance to do your scullery work.

As she poured our tea, I moved one of my Advisors one point diagonally, staying inside 'the palace' on one of the only five points he could occupy. "What about the way he kills? How close is it to how Meng the Assassin carried out his attacks?"

"Weapon used…silver dart, red cloth, thin silver chain. This Meng's weapon. Others use rope, and dart of iron. Only Meng used thin chain and dart of pure silver. And," he added, his face clouding with uneasiness, "I praying in Chieh-yüan Temple when second attack occur. White smoke there, same as smoke Meng use, made of special ingredients, rare and expensive, and only Meng knew formula. Nothing else smell like it. That how I be sure this same smoke as Meng use."

I moved one of my Chariots five points to the right. "Would he have written down the formula?"

"Never. Grand Assassins never commit anything to paper."

I sipped my tea. "Who was close to him? I mean, someone who would know how he made the smoke. An assistant, an acolyte...or maybe a child? Did he have any children who could be looking for vengeance?"

Tung moved one of his Cannons across the board to match the position of my Chariot. "He last of Great Assassins of Floating Temple. Have no assistant, no acolyte, no student. No one who know how to craft smoke, or use his sheng piao. Perhaps wife or son know, but wife and son also both beheaded, and home burned to ground. No record in ink or in memory lives now, reveal how killing done."

I moved my second Chariot over to protect the first one. "So, you're telling me that the killings each appear to be Meng's work, and his work alone. Nobody else's."

He moved his right-hand Elephant two points diagonally to threaten my intended move across the river to his side of the board. "It impossible, but it also true. There only one answer."

"Which is...?"

"Attacks carried out by kuei."

"A ghost."

"A *ku tu kuei*. Venomous ghost! He disappear from smoke cloud by transforming into insect. That why you not able stop him. You find Buddhist *tao shih* to pray and placate ghost. This only way defeat *ku tu kuei*."

Just then my sixth sense shouted *Danger Above!*

I jumped up to my feet, which surprised a shadowy figure on one of the far rooftops. It might just be some prowler or thief, but there was no point in deluding myself. There could only be one person who would follow me here, climb up onto a rooftop and watch me.

Tung looked up at me, disconcerted. "What—?"

"Get inside," I ordered, stepping out into the street and staring up at the shadowed figure. I put my hand on my holstered .455 Webley, and he disappeared into the darkness.

I stood in the street, a marked man, alone.

***

How certain was I that it had been the killer?

I wasn't. Unlike the last time our paths had crossed, I wasn't attacked.

There could be a host of reasons why he hadn't attacked. Maybe he was just doing a recce. Maybe I'd spotted him before he could get close enough to attack.

Or maybe he wouldn't attack me unless Captain Blackborough was present.

Blackborough. He was the key.

But what did his presence have to do with the killings? He couldn't have been orchestrating them. My running into him on the Bund had been a complete accident. So the attack on me couldn't have been planned ahead of time.

Which suggested he was being followed by the killer.

I needed to find out more about the English captain.

The best way would be to see his personnel file at British GHQ. The problem with that idea was the fact that GHQ is only accessible by military personnel; even when a civilian can get inside, they're escorted the entire time by an armed guard. As I was no longer a British officer, I needed to find a different way in. I had my old uniform, but it was too distinctive, too Canadian: the wide-brimmed Stetson, the CANADIAN SCOUTS shoulder insignia, the maple leaf emblems on my high collar. It was sure to draw attention to me, the last thing I desired.

Still, devoid of emblems, the basic uniform was British, after all. I could lose the Stetson, the spurs, and the Canadian insignia; I had no pith helmet, but my old field service cap, worn at the properly rakish angle on the right side of my head, should suffice. Add in a swagger stick, change my accent, and I'd be just one of countless officers coming and going from GHQ.

One hour later, stick under my arm, uniform pressed, and buttons polished, I looked exactly like a junior lieutenant of some indeterminate regiment as I strode along Victoria Road in the British Concession. I casually used my swagger stick to return a few salutes along the way, surprisingly at ease back in the uniform of one of our late Queen Victoria's officers.

That is, until I saw the building housing British GHQ. No one was being allowed into the building without a pass.

I ambled up near one of the guards and pretended to be waiting for someone to arrive, checking my pocket watch and looking up and down the street, all the while trying to get a good look at the pass. But I couldn't get close enough without drawing attention to myself, and my waiting-for-someone act had already been noted by the guard. It was only a matter of time before he became suspicious.

A horse-drawn carriage clopped up, in which sat a frumpy, walrus-mustached British colonel and a bored-looking major. The carriage came to a halt in front of the HQ, causing the guards to come to attention.

I blinked.

"Sir! Oh sir!" I called out in that high-pitched, supercilious British accent I'd heard from so many new English subalterns in South Africa. Both the major and the colonel turned to look at me as I strode up toward them. "Oh, colonel!" I gushed. "It IS you. I thought it was. Oh, father shall be ever so happy."

The colonel frowned, and opened his mouth to ask who in Hell I was, but I cut him off. "Father spoke so often of you! I cannot wait to tell him that I saw you again."

"Oh? Well, uh—"

"I am SO pleased that you still recognize me, sir. Mind you, I was quite a wee lad the last time you bounced me on your knee, but everyone says I am the very image of my father. You know, father bet me 10 Pounds that you would never recognize me as his son after all these years. Ha! I dare say I won, wouldn't you, sir?"

"Oh, um, yes. Yes, indeed. How could I...not recognize you—?"

I gestured him to go on inside, falling in step alongside him as I continued talking. "You know, father called you his dearest friend. Why, the stories he tells about the two of you—!"

The colonel modestly cleared his throat. "Yes, those were quite... interesting times."

"I should say so!" I declared as we walked in past the guards who, as I suspected, did not ask senior officers like the colonel and his aides for their passes. "I cannot believe my luck in running into you here," I went on as we walked into the building. "And on my first day in T'ien-chin," I said, making sure to mangle the Chinese name of the Treaty Port like a newcomer would.

"Well, you know, your father and I go back quite a long way," the colonel said, beaming as if he remembered me and 'father'—which he did not, of course, but he would surely be far too embarrassed to admit that he had no idea who I was, when I evidently knew him so well.

I grinned. "Indeed, sir. Oh!" I declared as he moved to enter one of the offices. "I shall telegraph father of our meeting and let him know he lost our wager. Oh, I wish I could see his face when he hears of it. Finally, I have won a bet against father! This is such a grand day for me." I stiffened and gave him the snappy salute that only newly minted lieutenants use. "Sir!"

The smiling colonel returned my proud salute and I about-faced and walked off. Behind me, the colonel spoke to the major. "Fine lad. Known his father for years. Oh, yes. We were best of friends, you know."

The moment he was out of sight I strode up the corridor, angrily slapping my swagger stick into my opposite palm. Nine times out of ten, a man who (1) looks like he belongs here, and (2) is terribly angry, will not be questioned by those who wish to avoid being on the receiving end of his wrath.

I stopped a passing private. "You there! Where is the Office of Record?"

He nervously gave me directions and I continued my 'angry march' to the proper office.

I entered, fuming.

The sergeant manning the front desk was all business. "How may I help you, sir?"

I put on an irritated British accent. "You can help me by getting Major General Creagh off my back," I muttered, naming the seniormost British General in China. "Ordering me around like I was his stable-boy—!" I loudly inhaled through my nose, as if forcing myself to remain calm but not entirely succeeding. "I need to see the file on Captain Blackborough, specifically page five, if the general is right in his God-damned presumptions," I said through clenched teeth.

"Of course, sir. Hughes! Fetch the file on Captain Blackborough for this officer." As the corporal left to retrieve it, the sergeant spoke up. "I was given to understand that the captain is leaving for the coast, sir. Been reassigned, to a posting at Tong Ku."

"I know," I lied through my teeth. "They're hoping his being removed from Tientsin will stop these damned attacks." *So that was how they planned to handle it, eh?* Transfer him out of the Treaty Port and see if it all might just blow over. Interesting.

The corporal returned with a file in his hand, and I snatched it away from him. I paged through it, muttering darkly about the general and his crazy ideas, which ensured that both the corporal and the sergeant would do their best to avoid getting caught up in whatever mess I was in. I quickly looked for anything out of the ordinary.

I stopped when I got to the report from Blackborough's commanding officer, regarding the charge of rape made against him a month ago by a Chinese girl called Bian.

I read on, no longer needing to fake my anger. Blackborough's uncle was the Duke of Leeds, so his commanding officer had given him administrative punishment—a fine—and an admonition not to go around raping the natives. That was all. Nothing more. He had assaulted and raped a Chinese girl, and this was his only punishment?!

But justice has a way of catching up with a man. According to the file, the girl, Bian no-last-name, had once been the servant of a Chinese merchant called Meng Chi-Hsien.

Oh, Hell! I slapped the file shut, shoved it at the corporal, and fled the office.

* * *

I had to find Blackborough, and quickly. The fact that any Chinese can afford a servant had escaped me when listing the suspects.

Meng's loyal servant. The only person close enough to him to know how he did things. Maybe she even helped Meng prepare his special smoke, polished his weapons for him, watched him practice day in and day out for God knows how long. She was not an assassin herself, but she knew enough of his ways to emulate her dead master. The raped girl had been using that knowledge to toy with Blackborough, make him feel the kind of fear and helplessness she herself had known at his hands.

But no animal toys with its food forever. At some point, she was going to kill him, probably slowly and cruelly. As a rapist he deserved no less. But the Law made no such distinctions, especially when the girl seeking vengeance had murdered three completely innocent men already.

He was being reassigned to Tong Ku, which for a British officer would mean taking a train 30 miles east to the coast, so if I was to save him, I had to get to the station before Bian did. I hailed a rickshaw and climbed aboard. *"Get me to the train station quickly, and I will pay you double,"* I told the coolie.

He gave me a broken-tooth grin and took off running.

In less than five minutes he pulled into the settlement railway station. I hopped out, paid him double, and scanned the area.

The whole of the railway here had been destroyed during the Rebellion as the Imperial Russian Army and the Imperial Chinese Army fought for control of the station, the international settlement's only link with the outside world. Things were still being rebuilt, the air crowded with the pounding noise of all manner of construction. I hurried into the station, but he wasn't there, so I ran outside onto the platform.

Damn! Too many trains, too many carriages and wagons. An unmanned steam locomotive stood nearby. I climbed up into the cab and clambered up onto the top of the coal piled in the tender. Yes! I could see across into the entire yard...but there was no sign of either Blackborough, or the Chinese girl bent on murdering him. Now what? In the midst of all this pounding noise it would be impossible to hear anything, even if I did have something useful to shout.

A noiseless cloud of white smoke appeared between two lines of carriages away off to my right, near the engine house.

I jumped down and took off, crunching the gravel underfoot as I ran between two of the trains. Captain Blackborough appeared, running away from me. The reason why came into view: Bian had found him.

I tore off after them.

Blackborough ducked into the engine house, the girl following him. I ran into the darkened building and found Blackborough facing the girl, his escape blocked by an inspection pit.

I raised my Webley revolver toward the killer and the rapist—

The man I was fighting to save was a rapist.

I lowered my revolver.

Bian twirled the dart alongside her like a rock on the end of a string and then let it go, and it sailed off to the right of Blackborough, missing him only by inches.

God's nightgown! She hadn't been toying with Blackborough—she'd been aiming straight at him every time. But she had no training. *Every throw she made went off to the right.* Instead of murdering Blackborough, she had unintentionally killed whoever was close to him.

Blackborough jerked away from the dart, causing his foot to slip over the edge of the inspection pit. His terrified cry was cut off when his body hit the floor of the pit with a hideous snapping sound.

Bian grinned a dark smile of revenge.

I stepped out into the open. "Do not move, Bian."

She looked at me in surprise, and our eyes met.

Oh, Hell—!

It was the Chinese serving girl I had seen just after I was attacked, the one I had assumed had been bowled over by the male killer fleeing the scene. But it had all been an act, and I had fallen for it. Yet who would have expected this little Chinese servant to be the vicious killer everyone was looking for?

She whipped the poison-coated silver dart back to her.

"You are under arrest," I said in Chinese.

My words seemed to amuse her. *"Why?"*

"You killed three men."

"Four," she said with easy defiance, gesturing at the open pit as she coiled up the fine silver chain. *"Five,"* she added darkly, her gaze fixing on me.

With a sneer she whipped the dart at me.

It was damned close, but as I expected, her aim was still off.

Mine wasn't.

The roar of the .455 Webley echoed through the Engine House, and Bian crumpled slowly to the ground, as dead as Blackborough.

* * *

"Hang on," I told the doctor. "Blackborough's still alive?!"

"Yes. But he suffered a severe spinal fracture. Complete paralysis from the waist down. He'll never walk again."

Paralyzed from the waist down? I could think of one crime now forever denied Blackborough, and walked away in silence, shaking my head. I'd solved three murders, only to find that both parties involved in it had been the guilty one.

Now you know why I try not to think too hard about the jobs I take.

* * *

J. F. Benedetto is an author, editor, and historian whose fiction covers five different genres: mystery, historical, science fiction, adventure, and steampunk. He is a writing mentor in the NY chapter of the MWA, spent four years as assistant editor of the *Triangulation* SF anthology, and for nine years has been a contributing editor for American Mensa's *Calliope*, a career summed up in his personal motto, *Heus, laboro in eo!* ("Hey, I'm working on it!")

The Far Shore

By Susan Daly

Northern Ontario, Canada

Writing a feature article about Misty Pines Lodge wasn't exactly my idea of hard-hitting journalism. Even so, it had three things going for it.

It was work. Paying magazine work outside the usual lady-writer ghetto of fashion, food and family. It included a four-day stay at the historic wilderness lodge in northern Ontario, courtesy of *Outdoor Leisure* magazine. And getting a foot in the door at one of the new glossies that were dazzling middle-class America in 1953 was an undoubted coup.

I arrived just before cocktail hour. After checking in, I wandered into the big rustic lounge in search of potential sources for both history and local color. And a drink.

The lounge was just right. Long and woodsy, with three walls of windows looking out onto Morningstar Lake. Plenty of log furniture for relaxing, and at the far end, a massive stone fireplace with the requisite moose head overlooking the room.

A few other guests were seated in groups here and there. At the near end, two women sat on a roomy settee among tartan cushions. One, perhaps mid-sixties, in a sky-blue twinset, was knitting something pink and fluffy, and doing all the talking. The other, mid-thirties perhaps, with short dark hair, looked more fit and outdoorsy. She nursed a drink and exuded a pretense of listening.

The bar, just inside the lounge entrance, was cheerful with cultured lights, beer signs and a big vintage map framed with birch branches. A well-weathered, capable looking woman in her forties was ready to serve me.

I surveyed the taps and ordered a Labatt 50, then introduced myself— Jessica Innes from New York—and my mission.

This seemed to come as a surprise.

"A magazine article? First I've heard of it."

"The editor arranged it with the owner, Doug Chrysler."

A *that-explains-it* look came into her eyes. She pulled me a pint.

"Yeah…Well, *I'm* the owner, Peggy Ternbrook. Along with my sister. Doug's my brother-in-law, and assistant manager here." She placed my beer on the bar.

I started to point out the advantages of publicity—

"We don't need any. Every year we're booked solid with Canadians and Americans who appreciate the real wilderness. But Doug's starting to hanker after a different class of guests."

She drew a beer for herself and leaned on the bar, settling in for a chat.

"I've seen *Outdoor Leisure*," she said. "It appeals to the new suburban set: the backyard brick barbeque types, matching pedal-pushers and halter tops for mother and daughter, station wagons filled with pristine camping equipment."

"In a way, yes. But I think the magazine is pushing old-fashioned tradition as well." I didn't add that suburbanites were hankering to recreate the North Woods look in the comfort of their basement rec rooms.

"Tradition has been the lifeblood of this place since my parents built it nearly 50 years ago. My sister Nancy and I were in training to take over ever since we were kids, and a few years ago, my parents all but retired. But now, Nancy's letting her second husband do all the thinking for her, and he says shiny and new is the way to go. He sees fresh blood. With fresh money."

"That would be a shame."

"Yeah. Replace the wooden deck chairs with steel tubes and vinyl strapping, get some high-powered motorboats for the guests to tool around the lake and terrorize the loons. Water-skiing. I ask you...*water-skiing?* Leather furniture for the lounge. Get rid of Theodore." She glanced down to the end of the room to the moose head.

I looked around the comfortable lounge. Perfect. I'd found my theme. Tradition vs. Post-war Modern.

* * *

In the interests of research, I studied the framed photos in the lounge. Early days at the lodge. Peggy had said her mom, armed with her trusty Kodak, was always taking snapshots of the guests.

Male guests posing with strings of dead fish, dead moose, deer and bears. A trio of young women on the dock in 1938, according to the label. Two of them in practical plaid jackets, dungarees and high-laced boots, the third in a light floral dress and city shoes, holding a wide-brimmed sun hat, her face framed with a riot of blonde curls.

A picture of a thirtyish man holding a paddle, a canoe tied up nearby. He wore an old army shirt, sleeves rolled up to the elbows, jodhpurs, no-nonsense boots. Beneath the brim of a battered fedora, his crooked smile seemed to say, *Sure, I'll pose for you.* A Wilderness Man. And none too hard on the eyes.

Peggy had told me there were tons more in the old photo albums in the dining room. I was welcome to use any I wanted for the article.

A second beer in hand, I went out onto the spacious wooden deck to pull some ideas together. Mercifully, the infamous mosquitoes and black flies had abated by mid August. I leaned on the railing to take in the beauty of the lake, the surrounding forest, the misty islands in the distance. The far shore, according to the wall map at the bar, was nothing but endless wilderness.

I inhaled the intoxicating piney woods smell, as a long mournful wail rose off the lake.

"Hey, I heard you arrived." I turned to see a well-nourished middle-aged man in a golf shirt and chinos. Clearly Doug Chrysler. His style, white suburban cool, seemed out of place among faded denim and khaki and plaid.

He introduced himself and proceeded to tell me what to write and how to write it.

"Hold on, Doug. I'm happy to have your input on the history, but don't forget I'm writing this article for *Outdoor Leisure*, not Misty Pines."

A momentary look of taken-abackedness darkened his face, then he gave a would-be good-natured laugh. "Of course, of course. Just want to make sure you don't miss anything important, honey."

"I understand you've got some plans for modernizing the place?" I might as well let him work off his ideas; then I could ignore them or brush them with a hint of ridicule. Payback for the "honey".

"We sure do." On top of what I'd heard from Peggy, he was planning gravel paths through the woods ("nature" trails), tennis courts, a swimming pool.

"Is there space for all that?"

"Oh, we'll have to cut down a few trees. But hey, one thing we got lots of around here is trees."

I was saved from making an appropriate response by another haunting call from the lake. "Is that a loon?"

"Damn birds." Doug frowned in its direction. "You should hear the racket they make in the night. Keep everyone awake."

"Do people complain?" The eerie cry stirred something in my soul.

"Not yet."

I wondered if his new breed of guest might find nature in the raw disturbing.

"Maybe you could shoot them," I suggested. "Make it a paying attraction, hunting loons."

He looked thoughtful, then shook his head. "Naw…there aren't enough to make it worthwhile. Anyway, they're protected."

* * *

After supper, I was back in the lounge, enjoying coffee with some of the guests gathered on the chairs and settees around the pine-slab table near the fireplace. Theodore watched from above, unaware of his possible fate.

"So you're the lady reporter doing a story on the lodge?" This was from Chester Daniels, husband of Betty, the knitting lady. She was still knitting up a storm as we talked.

I confirmed my role, adding the feature was part of a magazine series about historic lodges across North America.

Almost everyone seemed ready to toss their memories into the mix. Chester and Betty had been coming here from Buffalo since their honeymoon in 1914. Thelma and Suzie, two outdoorsy-looking women in their thirties, were making their second visit. The dark-haired woman I'd seen earlier in the lounge said nothing from her corner of the couch.

Betty indicated the gallery of pictures. "I noticed you looking at them earlier. There's a wealth of history there."

"Not to mention an old mystery," Chester added.

My writer's interest perked up. "Oh?"

Betty jumped in. "Oh yes! The handsome guide, the missing woman, the fatal canoe accident…."

"Hold on." I took out my notepad and pen. "When was this?"

"Before the war," Chester said. "Betty and I were here for our…let's see…our twenty-third anniversary."

"Our twenty-fourth, dear. 1938." Betty sighed. "It really put a damper on our celebration."

"It did." He looked over at the other women. "You three girls were here that year too, weren't you?"

"Thelma and I were," Suzie said. She indicated the quiet woman in the couch corner. "Laura wasn't."

"And *this* year," Betty said, "we're here for our thirty-ninth anniversary."

Time to get back on track. "So this missing woman and the guide…?"

"Frank Laidlaw," Betty said. "Chester, go get that picture of him…you know the one?"

"Sure thing, sweetie."

"The most experienced, most skilled and most popular guide in the area," Betty said, knitting and talking in perfect time. "A living legend."

"Until he wasn't," Thelma murmured.

"He was awful popular with the lady guests," Chester said, returning with one of the pictures I'd seen earlier. The good-looking guy in outdoor gear.

"I can believe that," I said. "What happened to him? Accident? Drowned? Murdered?"

"Just the first two," Thelma said.

"That pretty lady artist hired him for an outing," Chester said. "She wanted to do some watercolors along the far shore."

"She was in your party, wasn't she, Thelma?" Betty asked. "You were here from Ohio?"

"New Jersey. No, she wasn't exactly *with* us."

"Thelma and Laura and I usually go camping in the wilds together," Suzie said. "But that year, as a treat, we arranged for a week at Misty Pines. We'd heard how nice it was. Then Laura had to drop out at the last minute. So we advertised for someone else to join us, to save the cost of her share."

Laura, in her corner, nodded.

"Cornelia Gardiner." Thelma's voice held disdain.

"When we met up with her at the train station in Toronto, she wasn't at all what we expected," Suzie said. "She didn't know a j-stroke from a cross bow rudder, and she couldn't even swim. She didn't want to wear a life jacket. Not that I blame her…those bulky kapok things we used to wear."

Chester's look went hazy. "I remember she was pretty as a picture in her summer dress and big sun hat. All those curls. Very feminine, I thought. Not at all like, um…." He stopped, perhaps wisely.

"Blonde from a bottle," Betty said, "and a cheap permanent wave. Batting her big blue eyes at all the men." She glanced at her husband.

"Did she, dear?" Chester was a study in innocence.

At this point, Peggy appeared and put a coffee tray on the low table. As everyone helped themselves, she perched on the sturdy log arm of the couch.

"You're not talking about that old Frank Laidlaw business, are you?"

I could see why she'd rather we didn't, but I ploughed on. "So, what exactly happened, Peggy?"

Peggy looked reluctantly reminiscent, then she conceded.

"It was a sunny, calm morning. They set off just after breakfast in Frank's little 14-foot day-tripper canoe."

"I thought she couldn't paddle," I said.

"Oh, she couldn't." Suzie said. "Her idea of canoeing was to sit in the bow, backwards, and let the stern paddler do all the work."

"Very ladylike," Chester said.

"They headed west," Peggy went on. "Down towards the next lake, Selkirk, among the cluster of islands near the opposite shore. I guess the plan was to stop off here and there. She could stay and paint while he went off fishing. He liked to go in and fish among all those islands and inlets."

"So what happened?" I repeated.

"They didn't return by mid afternoon. Worries didn't really set in until four o'clock. There was no sign of them, and so some of the old hands and guests began a search. Chester, you went with them, didn't you?"

"Sure did. We didn't find anything." He looked troubled at the memory. "We finally had to stop for the night."

"Early the next morning, someone at the lodge on North Wendigo found a paddle midway across the lake. The search party headed out that way...." She paused.

"What did they find?"

"There's a stretch of rapids from Selkirk into North Wendigo," Peggy said. "Even expert paddlers have to portage it. They found the canoe—what was left of it—smashed up on the rocks at the foot of the rapids, on the far shore. It's all crown land over there. No hint of civilization. That's when we got the police involved.

"Over the next few days, they found some of Frank's fishing gear, bits of Miss Gardiner's painting supplies. Both life jackets. One of Miss Gardiner's shoes. Her hat."

"What about the bodies?" I asked.

"Frank's body washed up downstream six days later. Not a pretty sight, I heard."

"And Miss Gardiner?"

"Her body was never found."

A respectful silence hovered for a few moments.

"What about this Frank Laidlaw?" I finally said. "What was he like?"

"The best guide in the area, bar none," Chester said. "He knew these woods like—"

"Yes, I gathered. But as a person? You all knew him—or knew of him. Decent guy? Heroic?"

"Actually," Thelma said, "people said he was a real shit."

Several heads turned towards her. "Oh dear," Betty said.

"Oh, he *was*," Suzie said. "We all heard the stories about him. Couldn't keep it zipped. Good looking, rugged, masculine. He used it to charm any girl he could get his hands on. The local girls working as waitresses, some of the women guests. Especially if their husbands spent all day out in the wilds, doing all that manly stuff they do, leaving their wives to knit or play bridge."

Betty looked up from her work with a frown.

"Aw, he was no worse than the next guy," Chester said.

The women, even Betty, sent him a look of disgust. I kept it neutral, since I had a story to write, and this was getting more intriguing by the minute. How much could I include?

Betty, focusing on her knitting, said, "Oh well, I suppose we *did* hear things about him. How he didn't always take 'no' for an answer? You're right, Suzie. No pretty girl was safe from him. Why, I remember even—" She broke off. "Sorry, dropped a stitch."

Peggy picked up the tale. "Oh, you mean that girl, the previous summer? She simply fell head over ears in love with him. Seventeen. Here with her parents—older couple. Strait-laced, religious types. She was their adored only child."

"Yes, that's the one…" Betty murmured, concentrating on her work.

"So Frank Laidlaw and the daughter…?" I asked.

"We heard he ruined her," Suzie said. "Seduced her in the woods."

"Well, you know, it takes two to tango…." Chester said.

Peggy leveled him a look that could fillet a lake trout. "Not when one of them is 34 and a man like Frank, and the other a complete innocent half his age."

Chester cleared his throat and murmured something about "the same old story."

"We heard all about it later, when the parents learned she was pregnant. That's when she told them about Frank. But he claimed he hadn't done more than flirt with her. Must have been some other guy."

"What happened after that?" I asked.

Peggy looked grim. "She left school, outcast from society, from her church—lovely Christians that they claimed to be."

Thelma frowned. "As you said, Mr. Daniels, the same old story. And it will keep being the same old story until men finally take responsibility for their own actions."

"Did she have the baby?" I asked.

Everyone suddenly appeared interested in their empty coffee cups.

"She died." Peggy's blunt words shut it down. She started gathering up the coffee things.

* * *

After breakfast the next morning I tracked down Peggy, having a coffee and cigarette in the deserted dining room.

"Interesting story we heard last night," I said, joining her uninvited.

"Which one, in particular?" Peggy drew on her smoke. "Laidlaw the Lech? Cornelia the Dainty, Doomed Painter? Or The Tragic Tale of the Innocent Daughter. Her name was Esmé, by the way. Esmé Plunkett."

"Well, they're all part of the same story, aren't they?"

"Are they? I suppose so."

"So…. Back street abortion?"

Peggy nodded."Nowhere to turn. She somehow found someone to 'help' her. The parents had no idea until the police showed up at their door."

I spent a few moments picturing it. Yeah, the same old story.

"Who else got mowed down in his path?"

Peggy raised an eyebrow.

"For a moment Betty Daniels was starting on a different tale," I said. "Then she stopped short, though I don't believe she ever dropped a stitch in her life. That's when you brought up the wronged ewe lamb."

Peggy gave me a hard look, along with a grunt of acquiescence.

"Oh, I suppose Betty or Chester or any other old-timer could spill it. But listen, if I tell you, none of this is going to find its way into your article."

I swore to keep mum. I couldn't use it in my story—more's the pity—but I was still curious.

"As you heard, Frank Laidlaw was the star guide here, and not unattractive to the ladies. I mean, he could be charming. Some women were more than ready to fall for him."

"And others…?"

"Well, if he set his sights on a pretty—and vulnerable—girl, she was susceptible to his flattering interest in her."

"Your father didn't try to rein him in?"

"He was Dad's golden boy. The most popular guide around. And like Chester Daniels, Dad wasn't going to blame Frank when he could blame the woman."

She paused, as if deciding how to go on. Finally…

"Nancy has always been a bit of a fool when it comes to men."

I nodded. I'd met Doug.

She read my mind. "Yeah. Her first husband was no prize either. He died in the war."

"So, uh, Nancy and Frank…?"

"Yup. It was early in the season, before the arrival of the Plunketts. The guests were mostly fishing parties, without their wives. I guess that's when Frank realized Nancy, at 16, was pretty, impressionable, *and* heir to half the lodge. But I found out—I'm two years older. I told her to have nothing to do with him. She didn't listen to me at first.

"Then something happened—she wouldn't tell me exactly what. So I wrote to Aunt Isabelle in The Soo and got her to invite Nancy to visit her for the summer, and then stay on for her final year of high school. No, she wasn't pregnant, in spite of the cliché."

"So she was spared a tragedy like Esmé's."

Peggy nodded. "I tried to convince Dad Frank was up to no good, but he wasn't having any of it. And Nancy had begged me not to tell. But I kept my eye on him."

"Even when the Plunketts accused him of messing with their daughter?"

"Like I said, Frank denied it all. Said it was some other guy. Some hotel guest. And Dad was happy to believe him."

"And the parents?"

"They were devastated, completely broken."

"So… there was nothing to be done?"

"Well, nothing *I* could do, except protect my little sister." Peggy drew on her cigarette. "The following summer, Providence, in the form of Miss Cornelia Gardiner, intervened. It's terrible what happened to her, but…"

She blew a perfect smoke ring.

"I'm not sorry he's dead."

* * *

I should be working. Interviewing, finding out old stories—more innocuous ones. I was out on the deck again, gazing down at the busy dock. Energetic swimmers of both sexes, laughing and shouting and diving into the water, still chilly in August. A pair of fishermen returning from their morning expedition with impressive catches.

Three young women in shorts and plaid shirts, the tails tied in a knot around the waist, were setting off in a canoe. They were clearly capable of telling a j-stroke from a cross bow rudder. Except for the outfits, they could be Thelma and her gang from 15 years ago.

Fifteen years ago… Where had I seen a vintage version of these girls? It might be interesting to have a pair of pictures for the article: women adventurers—then and now.

I recalled some of the other framed photos in the lounge. The shot of three young women, two in canoeing gear and one in… what was it? A pretty flowered dress, holding a big sun hat.

The picture was gone from the wall.

Peggy had mentioned photo albums in the dining room. If it was missing from there too.…

I soon found the album I wanted. And the picture, above a neat caption in white ink on the black page. "The girls from New Jersey." Snapped by Peggy's mom with her Kodak.

Thelma and Suzie and the ladylike woman they'd never seen before.

I focused on the doomed Miss Cornelia Gardiner, with (according to Betty) dyed blonde, chemically induced curls. It was interesting, or perhaps morbid, to look at the face of a woman who would be dead within days.

Or…would she?

I flipped back through the pages.

* * *

The three women were sitting on a secluded rustic bench near the shore, looking out to the lake and the far side.

"Hello, ladies." They all turned at once.

"Oh hi, Jessica," Suzie said. "Still working on your article?" The others smiled polite greetings.

"Something like that." I pulled out the picture to show them. "I found this in the lodge's collection of photo albums." I didn't mention the missing framed copy. "It's the three of you?"

They all took a look.

"Not quite," Suzie said. "That's Thelma and me, all right, but the other one is Cornelia."

"The one who drowned." Thelma's tone was unequivocal.

"Oh, right. Whose body was never found."

They exchanged impassive glances.

"Just what are you getting at?" Thelma asked.

"Well, I'm thinking about how *I* might deal with vermin like Frank Laidlaw."

"You mean how a menace to society in general—and innocent young women in particular—could be removed from the world?"

I nodded thoughtfully. "Did she ever give you the impression she'd arranged to come here with a purpose…other than painting wildflowers?"

Suzie looked intrigued. "You mean, did she somehow know about Frank the Pond Scum, and decide to deal with him? She shows up, bats her eyelashes at him, then hires him for a paddle in the wilderness."

Thelma picked up the theme. "Then she swamps the canoe, hoping Frank will drown and she'll somehow survive?"

"Not quite," I said. "If it were me, I'd suggest we go ashore in some secluded spot, for a little, well, light romance? Then, when Frank's busy— maybe pulling the canoe onto the shore—I'd just pick up a handy rock and bash his skull in."

Laura said nothing. She stared across the water to the endless wilderness.

"It wouldn't have to kill him," I went on. "Just knock him out, and let his body fall into the canoe. Add a few of my own things, such as my shoes and hat, and then push it off directly towards those treacherous rapids. There's a straight fast run there to build up speed before it would all smash into the rocks and break apart."

"Leaving her stranded in the wilds, helpless," Thelma pointed out.

"Oh, the helpless-little-me persona would be just a pretense. She might actually be an expert outdoorswoman. It would all be planned in advance. She could have a cache of outdoor gear and survival equipment. A canoe. Some getaway route worked out. It might take days to reach a place to connect to the outside, but if she were actually an experienced swimmer and paddler and camper, I'll bet she could manage it."

"It's an idea," Thelma said. "But far-fetched."

"And remember," Suzie said, "she had no plans to come here until the last minute, when Laura had to drop out."

"So the story goes…." I said.

They were all quiet again for a few moments. Laura's face was still a blank. Hell, I was accusing her of conspiracy and murder, and she wasn't even twitching an eyebrow.

"It's a great plot, Jessica. In fact…" Suzie looked around at her friends, "it sounds like something we might have thought of ourselves, if we'd had to."

"But as it turned out, no one had to do anything." Thelma shrugged. "Fate stepped in and took a hand."

I'd heard that already. "Or Providence."

At some invisible signal, they seemed to have heard enough. They got up and collected their things from the bench.

Before they headed up the wooded path to the lodge, Thelma said, "Don't forget what he was, Jessica. A monster.

Suzie chimed in. "He'd been having his way with young women and girls around here for years, but I think most of them were afraid to say anything. Afraid of being called liars."

"Or sluts," Thelma added. "Look at Chester Daniels' attitude."

"I know," I said. "Even Peggy's sister wouldn't say anything."

"You heard about that? So you know Esmé wasn't the first girl he took advantage of."

"But she *was* the last." Laura's first words closed the subject.

The three women turned and vanished into the woods.

I stood there for a few seconds, feeling foolish and wondering what next. If anything.

Then I heard someone running back. Laura.

"Forgot my sunglasses," she murmured in a spate of loquaciousness. She snatched them up and put them on, then turned to leave.

"Wait, Laura."

She waited.

"I found some other photos, from the year before Frank died." I showed her a picture from 1937. It had been captioned, "The Plunketts from Chicago." Fiftyish man and woman, in plain, sensible clothes. Standing in front of them, an adorable girl in her teens, with short dark curls and big eyes, exuding innocence.

"Esmé and her parents," I said.

"Poor kid."

I showed her another picture from the same page. "Esmé and her cousin, according to the label." Two girls standing in front of the Misty Pines sign. The cousin was a few years older, with straight dark hair.

"So?"

"Funny… Peggy never mentioned there was a cousin with them." I looked at the picture of Cornelia again. "You know, except for the curly blonde hair, they could almost be the same woman."

I didn't say, *and so could you.*

"Laura…?" Thelma called from the woods above.

She gave me a shrug and a smile and ran back up the path.

* * *

I suppose I should have gone to the police with my vague and unsubstantiated suspicions. But yes, the man was a menace to women and girls. Was it a crime if three women had made sure Esmé *was* his final victim? Or was it justice?

* * *

My article was well received and led to more assignments from *Outdoor Leisure.* The following June, I dropped by their New York office to discuss some future articles with the features editor.

"Oh, by the way," she said as I was leaving, "that piece you did last year on that lodge in Canada…?"

"Yes…?" Should I be uneasy?

"I contacted them for some follow-up information. Did you know the manager, Doug Chrysler, died last fall. Pity. He seemed a nice guy."

Died. "Uh, it wasn't a canoeing accident, was it?"

She looked at me funny. "How'd you know? Actually, a power boat accident. Water-skiing."

I kept my mind blank until I reached the street.

Three women, I wondered. Or four?

* * *

Susan Daly writes short crime fiction as her way of crusading for social justice. Her stories have appeared in a surprising number of anthologies, and "A Death at the Parsonage" won the Arthur Ellis Award for best short story from the Crime Writers of Canada. She lives in Toronto and hangs out with Sisters in Crime, Crime Writers of Canada and other known criminal types. She can be tracked down at www.susandaly.com

The Road to Limerick

By Chris Dreith

Ireland

If someone asked what our worst moment was during the Active Senior Society's Irish Super Tour, we would all have had a different answer.

Thalia, as a retired attorney, would of course say it was when the Garda arrested us, but that was all sorted out within a day or two and the constabulary was nothing but polite when we pointed out their mistakes.

Polly, a former journalist, was upset when the American Consulate strongly suggested she not use some of the candid videos she took for her blog, Polly's Perils. However, after discussing the consequences with Thalia, Polly gave in, although I noticed she hadn't deleted the videos on her camera.

Sweet Calliope quietly said the worst moment was when she slid down the ravine and landed on the dead body. But she would, wouldn't she? The ravine was wet and slippery. The body was naked and hairy.

As for me, I don't feel there were any bad moments, just a few small honest mistakes. Anyone could have made them.

Let me explain.

Our trip started out wonderfully. LeRoy had stashed my luggage in the trunk of the Sterling Hotel's limo and opened the back door for me. Such a gentleman. My dear friends were already inside, each with a martini, our drink of choice.

The four of us met in the Sterling Hotel's historic Tea Room every Wednesday at noon for more than forty-five years. LeRoy had always been our loyal and steadfast waiter. He handed me my own glass and refilled the others, before climbing into the limo drivers' seat and heading toward the Sacramento International Airport.

It might seem a bit early for martinis to some, but we toasted our 5:30 a.m. flight to Ireland and turned to acknowledge LeRoy, who had somehow already rolled up the glass separating the luxurious seating area from the driver. It was LeRoy we had to thank for this adventure. He had mysteriously won this three-week, all-expenses-paid trip for four to Ireland and generous man that he is, gifted it to us.

We, of course, politely declined. We usually spent several hours in the Tea Room, receiving his rapt attention, and knew it was the highlight of his week. He kept our drink glasses filled, brought us our meals quickly, and wiped the table and floor if we became slightly animated. What would he do each Wednesday for three weeks without us? But he seemed extremely excited about the idea, so we eventually accepted.

As we took the airport exit off Interstate 5, I reached into my market bag for our tickets and pulled out a head of lettuce instead. An honest mistake. Anyone could have made it. I visit the Midtown Farmers Market weekly and use the handy market bags for everything, including packing for a trip to Ireland. After a quick look through the bag, we concluded that our tickets were probably in a different market bag, still sitting on my kitchen counter. Polly was sitting closest to the driver's side so she tapped on the glass behind LeRoy's head, sloshing some of her martini over the Chico's Travelers No-Iron blouse we had all agreed would be best for her.

LeRoy rolled the glass down a few inches, listened to our dilemma, and immediately slammed the limo into a sharp U-turn. We were thrown to one side of the back seat, spilling most of what was left of our martinis. But luckily, I had noticed where LeRoy had stored the extra cocktail shaker in the narrow bar near the door, so we were able to settle back into our individual seats with refilled glasses.

LeRoy skidded to a stop in the No Parking space in front of my building, grabbed my keys and the market bag holding lettuce and bounded up the stairs. We were amazed at how fast he could run for a man of his age and cheered when he reappeared, tossing us another market bag, this time with our tickets instead of lettuce. He jumped into the driver's seat and sped back toward the airport. We held on to each other and hardly spilled a drop.

We waved goodbye to LeRoy when he dropped us at the United departure door and once again when he circled back to hand Polly the camera she had left in the back seat. He seemed so happy, dear brave soul, but we were sure he was already missing us.

* * *

It wasn't until we were comfortably seated on the plane that Thalia asked why we were flying to Dublin instead of the Shannon airport where we were to meet our tour guide. I explained that although 'Shannon' is a lovely name, I felt that 'Aerfort Bhaile Atha Cliath' sounded much more Irish and would give us the whole Irish experience, so I had changed all of our tickets to the Dublin Airport instead. It's a small country, after all. I was sure that the tour guide could find us.

"Clio! The Shannon Airport has an Irish name too, I'm sure," Thalia said a bit louder than expected. "What were you thinking, girl?"

Polly was waving down the stewardess to order drinks while Calliope patted Thalia's shoulder. Since she retired from the law, we found that Thalia's patience was sometimes shorter than necessary. We all knew it occasionally took teamwork to calm her, but after four small bottles of Irish whiskey were delivered to our fold-down trays, and we toasted with a hearty "Slainte", Thalia was back to her normal, take-charge self.

"As soon as we land, I will call the tour company. I'm sure they can arrange a car for us," Thalia stated. She flashed her stern attorney-look at me, but I pretended not to notice.

"Oh," Calliope's breathy whisper always caused us to lean forward to hear her better. "If we are in Dublin, do you think we would have time to stop by Trinity College and see the Book of Kells?" Her large, puppy eyes shining.

Polly snorted into her refilled whiskey, sloshing some down her generous front. "I thought you would be tired of looking at old books," she said, popping a biscuit from the breakfast tray into her mouth, crumbs covering the paper napkin tucked into the neckline of her No-Iron top.

"But this is an illuminated manuscript from the medieval period." Calliope had retired from the California State Library system where she had worked for over forty years. She was obsessed with books, order, and consistent schedules.

Polly mumbled something with her mouth full of chips from her $4 tiny cardboard tube of Pringles. None of us understood what she said, but Calliope had already given up.

Thalia pulled the United in-flight magazine, *Hemispheres*, from the seat-back pocket. "What about Bog Bodies?" she asked. "I've always wanted to see those, and they are on display at the National Museum of Ireland in Dublin."

Calliope shuddered, covering her eyes with her hands, but Polly and I both sat forward to see the article about the ancient human remains found preserved in the peat regions of central Ireland.

"Not a smart place to drop a body if you want it to disappear." Thalia, always thinking of how a jury might see things.

"Mmmph." Polly nodded her head. She pulled the magazine across her plate to get a closer look at the pictures, dragging it through her catsup-covered scrambled eggs. I handed her another napkin to wipe up the mess, but a streaky red smear was as good as Polly was going to be able to get it.

"Looks a bit like the preserved flesh, doesn't it?" I said. Polly and I compared the stain to the photograph.

A small squeak came from Calliope.

Because of time, we decided to skip the Natural Museum of Ireland. I noticed the color coming back into Calliope's face.

* * *

Thalia made her phone call to the tour company as soon as we landed in Dublin. Limerick was the city where our tour was to start and apparently the Shannon Airport was closest. Who knew? It was an honest mistake. I thought Limerick was just a rhyme. 'There once was a young lady from Limerick, who danced like a …', well, you know. Anyway, it turns out that Limerick is on the other side of the country from Dublin, but the tour company said they would send someone to Dublin's airport to pick us up. Or at least that's what Thalia heard them say. But she admitted that the Irish accent was a bit strong, and it seemed there was raucous music in the background.

We gathered our luggage, struggled through Customs and onto the sidewalk.

"Well, will you look at that!" exclaimed Polly, pointing to a bright yellow van waiting at the curb, doors wide open and the motor running.

"Would that be for us?" Calliope was cautiously looking for a driver.

"It says ASSIST on the side," Polly pointed out, tossing her bags into the back. "Active Seniors Society's Irish Super Tours. That's us."

"Did the tour company say they had a driver for us or are we supposed to drive to Limerick?" I asked Thalia, who was already loading her luggage into the van.

"I couldn't tell," she admitted. After trying to get cell service again, Thalia let us know her phone was dead. Since the rest of us had not brought ours, she said, "This van is here now so we shouldn't waste any more time."

"But who's going to drive?" Calliope can sometimes look like she will burst into tears, but she never does. Just threatens. "They drive on the other side of the road here. It would be too scary to try."

We discussed the benefits of driving in the U.S. versus Ireland and concluded that since Polly had the least experience driving at home (Polly likes Uber), she would be the one who would be able to pick up driving on the left side of the road easier than the rest of us, who were more used to driving on the right. It seemed like a good idea at the time. We piled in and off we went.

None of us had had much sleep on the plane, so the first stop, not counting running into the curb and over some red raised strips in the road, was for coffee. Thalia spotted a large sign for Carroll's Irish Gifts and Coffee, and we were pleased to note the vast parking lot that Polly was able to maneuver.

Four women loose in a large souvenir and coffee shop might take longer than you would expect but we all eventually emerged with treasures and caffeine. Since I had retired from forty years as the merchandising vice-president at Nordstroms, I knew what to purchase, went immediately to the Aran wool and selected three beautiful long scarves. Calliope, ever organized, bought a large road map of Ireland and was anointed our Navigator. Thalia found a Donegal Tweed jacket and a Claddagh ring. Polly loaded a shopping bag full of cheese and brown bread, as well as picking up an extra-large kelly-green cape with The Mighty Electricians printed on the back. The pleasant lady who helped us explained The Mighty Electricians were the local hurling team and were on their way to their first winning season. We congratulated her on the team, although none of us knew what hurling was.

Calliope took her navigation responsibilities seriously, pointing the way out of the parking lot, screaming only once when Polly turned into the wrong lane. As the road became narrower, Polly drove faster. Green fields of fluffy sheep whipped by, then stone walls flashed close to our windows. Tree limbs slashed at the van. Someone, I think it might have been me, yelled at Polly to slow down. She turned her head to yell back when we heard scraping and screeching on the left side of the van. It took several feet to slow down enough to pull over and stop. Three of us were gasping for breath. Polly looked around and said, "Did any of you hear that?"

We all got out of the van to check. Thalia noticed it first. The side-view mirror on the left must have hit something and was ripped off. A track of scars ran the length of the van from the gaping hole to the rear bumper. The mirror was nowhere to be seen.

"I would have thought the Irish would build better cars than this,"

Polly said, pulling wires from where the side-view mirror had once been attached.

"It's a Chevy, Polly," Thalia said.

"Oh, well." Polly tried to come up with an excuse but gave up. "We probably need that mirror thing, right?"

"Why don't you stay with the van, Polly," I suggested. "We will walk back along the road to find it."

Calliope, Thalia and I began the search. The lane was quiet now. No other cars, thankfully, so Thalia walked down the middle, Calliope and I along each side of the road. We had gone at least the length of a football field, or maybe a hurling field if we knew how long those were, when Calliope cried, "I see something." We rushed over to her and sure enough, a glint of metal was at the bottom of a deep grassy ravine.

Rock, paper, scissors determined Calliope would be the one to climb down the steep bank to retrieve the mirror. Thalia and I stood by the roadside and watched her carefully step into the tall grass and immediately slip onto her back and slide all the way down. Flattened, wet foliage showed her pathway to the bottom.

"Did you slide down on purpose?" Thalia called but Calliope wasn't calling back. She had jumped up as soon as she landed at the bottom of the ravine with her arms flapping at her sides. We watched as she turned toward us. Her mouth was wide open. Her arms continued to flap.

"Calliope! What's wrong?" I called.

"M-m-m-man," her voice cracked. "D-d-d-dead!" she yelled with force this time.

"What?" Thalia wanted to be sure what we were hearing.

"And he's NAKED!" Calliope screamed, jumping up and down, splashing around the bottom of the wash, flapping her arms even more. The tears came then.

"Oh, crap," Thalia muttered.

* * *

"I'm sure I would have noticed a naked man on the road," Polly said, looking down at Calliope still splashing around in the ravine.

We had motioned for Polly to back the van up to the side of the road where we found the broken mirror. And the naked, dead man. Thalia's first thought was that Polly had hit the man, killing him, and his body was thrown down the ravine.

"We need to get the body up here," I suggested.

"If my cellphone was charged, I'd call the authorities to do it," Thalia was in her lawyer element. "We can't disturb a crime scene."

The three of us discussed crime scene protocol in the US versus what Ireland might have. Since none of us wanted to climb down to check it out and Calliope had undoubtedly disturbed any possible evidence, we decided to have Polly film everything from the side of the road.

"That should do it," I said. Thalia looked doubtful.

Polly pulled out her video camera and called Calliope to look up and wave, but she only continued to jump about and flap her arms.

"How big is he?" Thalia yelled down. "Can you carry him up here?"

That stopped Calliope in her tracks.

"No, I can't carry him up there," she stated. I heard something that sounded like sarcasm, but that's not Calliope's style so I must have been wrong. An honest mistake, given the situation.

After more deliberation, we decided we needed a rope to attach to the body and drag him up the embankment. None of us had packed a rope. Thalia looked at me and said, "Your new scarves could work."

I tried to come up with another solution but failed. My beautiful Aran scarves were tied together to make a long rope that could reach from the side of the road, down to Calliope and the body. Several moments of moaning and gagging later, Calliope had managed to tie a tight knot around one of the body's ankles. She grabbed the side-view mirror and scrambled up the side of the bank, using the scarf rope while the rest of us held on to the other end. And then we all pulled and pulled.

I will excuse you from reading the details of hauling a rather large, hairy, naked man up the steep embankment by his ankle but if you are interested,

Polly got most of it on video for her blog.

"He doesn't look like you hit him with the van." Thalia leaned over the sprawled body to look at him closely. "Beside the fact that he is dead, he looks pretty good."

Polly and I agreed and continued the inspection, while Calliope turned her back, breathing deeply, making small mewing sounds.

"Why are his hands and feet so black?" I pointed.

"He's muddy, but that black doesn't look like mud." Polly got close-ups of the bottoms of the man's feet and the palms of his hands.

"Interesting." Thalia stood back up. "We should get him into the van. Can't leave him out here in the elements." Raindrops had begun to splatter, causing the mud to run down his hairy body in rivulets.

Although Calliope needed a bit of convincing to help, all four of us propped, pulled and pushed the large man into the back of the van. Once in, we determined he was too big to fit along the center aisle, so sat him on the floor, facing out the back window. Thalia's idea to tie his shoulders to the arm rests on either side with my scarves secured him from tipping over.

Wet, exhausted and smelling a bit like compost, we stood outside the van and gazed through the back window at the dead man who seemed to gaze back at us.

"He hardly looks dead," Polly said.

"Quite good looking, actually," I agreed.

"His long red hair and full beard are rather attractive," Thalia noted.

"He is dead," Calliope whispered. "And naked."

Polly climbed into the van, rustled through her bag, pulled out the kelly-green, extra-large Mighty Electricians cape she had just bought and draped it around our dead friend's broad shoulders. Our Polly is so giving.

"I would like to clean up," Calliope said, holding up her shaky hands. We all agreed that cleaning up would be nice. We loaded back into the van and were once more on our way to Limerick.

＊＊＊

Calliope saw a Circle K Petrol Station and pointed to the large parking lot. Polly took aim and was able to stop before hitting a row of trees on the opposite side. The van's interior odor was beginning to become overwhelming, so we rolled down the windows before finding the ladies room where we took turns washing in the single sink.

Polly wanted to check out the snacks inside the convenience store. Thalia went in to ask where the closest police department was. Calliope didn't want to get back in the van yet so followed the other two into the building.

I was enjoying the refreshing walk across the parking area when I noticed two young men on a scooter looking into the back window of the van. They both looked like they had seen a ghost. I wanted to let them know the handsome red-headed man was simply dead and couldn't hurt them, but they rushed away, almost crashing the scooter before I could catch them. Their kelly-green shirts seemed to blend into the surrounding trees and bushes. Something seemed familiar to me about the two boys, but I was probably mistaken.

Once back on the road, Thalia reported that the closest police department was behind us and suggested we continue forward toward Limerick so as not to miss our tour. We were sure to find another police department, she assured us. That seemed reasonable to me, but Calliope was anxious to move the body out of the van.

"What if we can't find a police department soon?" Calliope whined. "We can't take him on the tour with us."

Trust our Calliope to point out reasonable issues. Our hotel room was for four, after all. We all agreed we couldn't possibly move him into our room but where could we safely put him until we could notify the authorities?

"There's always a bog," Polly suggested.

After a short discussion, we agreed that dropping our dead passenger in a peat bog would preserve him enough to allow the constabulary to retrieve him without too much problem. Calliope immediately went to her map to find the nearest peat field.

The scenery was delightful, green rolling hills, a rock wall on our right and on our left, a long freight train rattling beside us. Polly and Thalia, both waving to the conductor, cheered when they received a loud toot for their efforts.

Calliope still had her head in the map when I noticed a motor-scooter advancing on our right side. Two riders in kelly-green shirts were waving long wooden sticks and seemed to be yelling at us. I opened my window to hear better and saw several more green-clad scooter riders behind us, all waving wooden sticks. The Irish folk are so friendly. I waved back.

Calliope suddenly cried, "Turn here!" pointing left. Polly whipped the van onto a dirt road, bouncing across the train tracks and cutting in front of the fast moving train. Another long toot from the conductor seemed louder this time. We blasted down the dirt road with rows of brown bricks of sod lining the edges.

"I think those are the peat briquettes," Calliope said. "We are in the peatlands now. These wet, mossy areas are one of Earth's most important carbon sinks, storing more carbon than all of the trees in the world's forests!" Sweet Calliope was in her happiest place when she could educate us.

"We should look for a nice hole to drop our friend in," I said. Polly slowed the van and we all searched out the windows for the perfect spot.

We soon came upon a deep trench, not far from the side of the road. Polly was able to stop the van and we all hopped out to investigate. It was ideal for our purpose, so we set to work pulling our dead buddy out of the back of the van and dragging him into the trench. Polly hung the kelly-green cape from an upright shovel that had been left nearby. The cape rippled like a flag and would be a good marker for the authorities to find our friend when we notified them.

"I probably wouldn't be wearing it anyway," Polly admitted.

Thalia wrote 'R.I.P. Pete' in the moss next to the trench. Polly filmed us as we all said our goodbyes to the body we had named in honor of his temporary resting place.

* * *

Back on the road to Limerick, we were surprisingly quiet. Thalia cleared her throat, I sniffed, and Calliope started to tear up.

"Perhaps a quick stop at an Irish pub for a wee dram to honor Pete is called for," Polly's voice cracked.

We happily agreed and soon found a tall red building in the pleasantly named village of Birdhill. A Guinness sign painted on the side of The Coopers Pub welcomed us from the gravel parking lot. Our moods lifted as soon as we walked in and were served tall glasses of the ebony nectar. The moods continued to lift with every raise of additional glasses. After a while, all the occupants of the little pub were sharing Irish toasts to Pete. We were having a grand old time until a tall, uniformed policeman appeared in the doorway and the room went silent.

"Ahh! There you are." Thalia tried to stand and welcome the Garda, but didn't quite make it. We helped her up from the floor and back into her chair.

I have to admit, the policeman was impressive; tall, strong, handsome, as he strode toward our table, but I might have been wrong. When I blinked again, he had morphed into a much shorter and wider woman. Honest mistake given the amount of Guinness consumed.

"Would that happen to be the vehicle you'd be driving, out there in the car park?" she asked as she leaned over us.

We all nodded, but quickly realized moving our heads only made things blurrier.

"We've been looking for you," Thalia explained.

"We've been looking for you lot too," the officer said. "We've been able to follow the GPS tracker in that vehicle since you left Dublin. Come along now, loves."

Suddenly we were being helped out of our seats by a group of uniformed officers and shuttled outside. The rest of the pub-goers stood and applauded, giving us salutes as we walked by. These Irish. They are such welcoming people.

The parking area was more crowded than when we had arrived. At least six yellow and blue painted cars with blue flashing lights surrounded our vehicle.

Beyond the police cars sat three yellow vans, similar to ours except the printing on the sides said, 'ASSIST MEDICAL TRANSFERS'. Comparing those with our van, I could barely make out the same signage but ours was scraped where the mirror had been ripped off. Glancing at Polly who was squinting at the sign, I realized we might have made a small honest mistake when we assumed the van at the airport was for us. Their drivers, dressed in white medical coats, were standing in a group. They didn't look happy.

The largest congregation of folks were all wearing kelly-green, waving long wooden sticks, and yelling in unison. I couldn't quite understand what they were saying but they had the same Mighty Electricians logo printed on their shirts. It was probably some sort of hurling cheer, but I might have been mistaken.

A bright blue tour bus turned into the drive. On its side, large letters proclaimed ACTIVE SENIORS SOCIETY'S IRISH SUPER TOUR. When the driver came to a stop, a large leprechaun in a snug green jacket and tights hopped out and ran toward us. The police stopped him, and an exuberant conversation ensued. The leprechaun turned out to be not a leprechaun at all, but our tour guide. An honest mistake at first glance. I ask you, who wears clothes like that?

Thalia was spouting legalese. Polly was filming everything until an officer was able to wrestle her camera away. Calliope was meekly climbing into the nearest police car, and I was trying to explain the honest mistakes they were making. The Gardai ignored all our efforts and directed us into their waiting cars.

* * *

It was Wednesday and we were sitting at our regular table in the Sterling Hotel Tea Room. We had asked LeRoy to sit with us since we noticed he had seemed out-of-sorts when we surprised him with our early return. His blank stare was starting to worry us, but Polly had helped herself at the bar and returned with a martini for him. We were sure that would help with the shock.

"So, we would have stayed a bit longer if the U.S. Ambassador hadn't suggested it would be best if we went home," Thalia was trying to explain to him. "It's not like we weren't having a wonderful time and we still want to thank you for your generous gift of this vacation."

We all nodded, holding our martini glasses high to toast him. A small tear slid down his cheek and we understood how much we must mean to him.

"We were so surprised to hear that Pete had been the Mighty Electrician's head coach." I leaned toward LeRoy, sure that he was interested even though he didn't seem to respond.

"As it turned out, he had fixed a game, making them lose their first championship," Calliope whispered. "And we thought he was so nice," shaking her head.

"Honest mistake," I explained. "How would we know if he was nice? He was already dead when we met him."

"Turns out when someone gets electrocuted in the locker room shower, the shock can run through the body from the source of the electricity," Thalia patiently explained.

"Apparently the team found out about Pete cheating and wired the shower handle. Besides killing him, it burned his hands and feet, turning them black," Polly said. "Want to see the pictures?"

LeRoy made a small moan.

Polly was pulling out her camera, but Thalia placed a hand on her shoulder and shook her head. "Maybe not now, dear," she said. Polly slipped the camera back in its case and picked up her martini glass instead.

"What is surprising is it turns out most of the Mighty Electricians were in on this vigilante justice. The whole team wanted him dead," I said.

"It was so 'Orient Express'," Calliope whispered, her eyes wide. We all took a sip. Even LeRoy.

"Once the Garda saw Polly's videos and heard where and how we found the body, they were able to solve the rest of the crime," Thalia proudly stated. "It's good that we were there to help them."

We all nodded.

"How fortunate that this wonderful trip you won included insurance to cover the medical transfer van repairs," I said. "That could have been extremely expensive."

We smiled at LeRoy, holding up our empty martini glasses. He slowly stood up, walked stiffly to the bar and returned to fill us up.

We assured him we wouldn't leave him alone again. He suddenly left the room. I think I saw tears in his eyes, but I might have been mistaken.

* * *

Chris Dreith got hooked on writing mysteries while creating plays for her local Carnegie Library's fundraiser, Mystery in the Library. While running her design/remodel business, she wrote several short stories, including "Old Soles" in the Bouchercon 2020 anthology and "Unknown Male and Parts of Two Others" in *Cemetery Plots*, the Capitol Crimes anthology. Recently retired, she is happily adding more quirky short stories to her arsenal and working on her first thriller novel.

Grave Expectations

By Marni Graff

Oxford, England

The young woman sat alone in Brown's Café inside Oxford's Covered Market, tuning out the morning bustle of the indoor space of over sixty shops. The tea in front of her had grown cold as she concealed a mini thumb drive in her palm. She risked a furtive look at the other patrons and didn't recognize anyone, but knew she was being watched and felt in danger. Her heart raced. She needed to stash this, to secrete away her evidence until she could bring it to the police's attention. She couldn't risk leaving the market with it.

She had every expectation once she went to the police with this concrete proof, the whole thing would blow wide open, but she regretted hurting her mother.

The woman left and walked through the scrum of people past the bakery with its colorful cakes and fondant figures, then down another avenue of shops, searching for a hiding place. She moved quickly, clutching the drive in her hand. She'd reached the coffee shop when she was thumped in the back. The punch made her stagger against the wall as she inhaled the rich scent of freshly roasted beans.

The tiny hat shop across the avenue caught her eye. She coughed; a sharp pain between her shoulder blades made her lurch over to the shop.

* * *

Nora Tierney strode up St. Giles past the Martyr's Memorial in the heart of Oxford and continued to the Covered Market, happy she'd worn her quilted vest over her thick jumper. With her toddler son at his Cornish grandparents, she waited for edits on her latest children's book, and with no current assignment from the magazine she wrote for, Nora felt a distinct freedom from responsibility. She had every expectation today would be a terrific day.

First stop was The Hat Box for the one she'd chosen for the christening of her fiancé's goddaughter. Nora entered the market, in existence since the 1770s, and headed for Avenue 3 and the robin's egg blue painted shop. She was captivated by the colorful profusion of women's hats and fascinators crammed alongside men's flat caps and fedoras stacked upon each other, hanging from hooks and pegs. Nora found the owner sewing tartan ribbons on a hat.

"Morning, Gillian. Here for my hat."

"All done, Nora. That velvet flower looks grand." Gillian removed the cover of a red hat box filled with glossy tissue; the felt cloche Nora had chosen nestled inside.

"This is the same camel shade as my coat, and the teal flower matches my dress." She lifted the bell-shaped hat out of the box.

"Very chic. Try pulling your hair in a bun."

Nora twisted her auburn hair into a scrunchie and sought the mirror buried between rows of hats. The teal flower brought out the green in her eyes. "Gillian, it's lovely."

The shop door opened to admit a young woman with silky blond hair and pale skin wearing a dark coat. Her startling blue eyes glanced around and settled on Nora's hat box.

"Can I help you?" Gillian asked, as the woman wobbled in and grabbed the counter's edge.

Nora placed her hat back in the box as the woman's face lost more color. She touched Nora's hand and looked at her beseechingly. "Find the truth," she whispered, and slid to the floor, unconscious.

"Call 999!" Nora knelt down to turn the woman on her side in the recovery position and found a weak pulse.

Then Nora saw her hand was bloodied.

* * *

The young woman, identified from the license in her handbag as 23-year-old Alice Fenton, was taken away in critical condition, leaving the cordoned off shop and lane outside littered with detritus from the medic's efforts. The first officer on the scene recognized Nora and called Detective Declan Barnes. Declan perused the iPad with their statements, and told them Alice Fenton's mother was en route to the hospital. "Miss Fenton was only here for two minutes, correct?"

Gillian nodded. "If that."

"The EMT said she'd been stabbed, Declan." Nora explained to her fiancé how Alice had stumbled into the shop, and what the young woman had whispered before she collapsed.

"'Find the truth'?" he clarified.

Nora nodded. "The look in her eyes was pure terror." It had filled Nora with a dread she still felt.

His phone rang, and Declan stepped outside the shop. When he returned his face was sorrowful. "Alice Fenton has died."

"That poor woman, Declan," Nora said. Gillian's face mirrored her dismay.

"You'll have to close for the rest of today, Gillian, although there won't be much for the forensics guys," Declan said.

Gillian rose. "I can't get home fast enough." She handed Nora her hat box, then left her key with the officer to lock up as Nora and Declan filed out.

"I can drop you home, Nora," Declan said. "I have to speak to her parents."

Nora checked her phone. So much had happened, yet it was only after noon. "Can't I come with you, Declan? I was the last person to see her daughter. Mrs. Fenton might want to meet me." She saw him hesitate. While unusual to bring a civilian, she'd helped Declan with his cases before. Nora's presence might encourage Alice's mother to talk.

"Fenton was Alice's father," Declan said. "She's married to Hugh Sayers, the crime writer."

"Hugh Sayers? I interviewed him last year."

"I thought the name was familiar. Didn't you say he was full of himself?"

"Absolutely. He changed his name to 'Sayers' hoping people would assume he was related to Dorothy Sayers and think he wrote great books."

"I gather you don't agree."

Nora grimaced. "The two books I read were…competent, but under-whelming. He kept trying to impress me." She put on her most winning smile. "Can I tag along, please?"

* * *

Nora stood beside Declan while he knocked on the glossy green door of an imposing three-story house made of the same golden stone as Oxford's colleges, set in the affluent suburb of Summertown. At least reporters hadn't descended—yet.

"You're here for emotional support," Declan reminded her, as the door opened and a fair-haired man wearing a pin-striped suit emerged and turned to a taller man standing behind him.

"I'll call you tomorrow." He swept past in a cloud of spicy aftershave to a silver Audi parked in the drive.

"Thanks, Guy." Hugh Sayers recognized Nora and his lip curled. "Nora Tierney. I hope you're not here as a journalist."

Declan flashed his warrant card and introduced himself. "Nora was with Alice when she collapsed. She thought your wife would want to meet her."

"How thoughtful. Then do come in." He opened the door wider to let them pass into a sitting room where Sarah Fenton Sayers rested on a green damask couch, crumpling a sodden handkerchief in her hands. Heavy oil paintings, high ceilings, and decorative moldings picked out in cream paint gave the room a feel of grandeur. Sarah had the same silky blonde hair and bright blue eyes as her daughter.

"Darling, Nora was with Malice in the market and has come with the detective on her case."

"Malice?" Nora blurted out.

"My nickname for Alice, being a crime writer," he simpered.

"Hugh, please." Sarah's swollen and red-rimmed eyes met Nora's sympathetic smile. "You're very kind. Please sit down." She patted the seat next to her.

Nora sat next to Sarah. What kind of father, even a stepfather, bestowed a name like "Malice" on his daughter?

Hugh hovered in the doorway. "Tea? Or a spot of sherry?"

Nora thought he sounded like a bad Golden Age character and turned her attention to the bereaved mother. "I'm truly sorry for your loss."

"I was shocked when the hospital called. We drove straight over but Alice was gone when we arrived. I told her how much I loved her and would miss her." The woman started to weep, and Nora clasped her hand.

"Tea perhaps, then." Hugh turned on his heel and disappeared as Sarah composed herself.

"Sorry. It's all so new."

"No need to apologize, Mrs. Sayer," Declan said. "If you feel up to it, though, a few questions might help us."

She sniffled. "I want to help."

"Was anyone threatening or stalking Alice?"

Sarah shook her head. "Not that I know."

"Your daughter lived here?"

"Yes, after art school she moved into the third floor. She did graphic design, business cards and logos. Alice kept her own schedule, but it was nice having her around. Flat prices are so dear, and we have all of these rooms to rattle around in..."

Her voice trailed off and Sarah looked into the distance. Nora could picture her having to learn to stop listening for sounds of her daughter.

"Does anyone else live here?" Declan continued.

"No. We have a daily housekeeper, but she's visiting her sister this week. Hugh's assistant, Guy Bellows, is here often but has his own flat."

Declan noted both people's contact details. "What about a boyfriend?"

Sarah looked down. "She'd been seeing Gary Pritchard, but Alice broke it off as he wanted a commitment she wasn't ready for—although she recently told me she regretted it. I hoped they'd reconnect." She picked up her phone from the coffee table and gave Declan Pritchard's phone number.

"Can I ask where you and Mr. Sayers were this morning?"

Sarah didn't notice the significance of the question. "We were here, Hugh writing, while I worked on a charity dinner for the RSPCA until lunch. Soon after, the police called me to the John Radcliffe."

Nora caught Declan's eye. He gave a discreet nod. "Sarah, Alice's last words before she collapsed were 'find the truth.' Any idea what she meant?"

Sarah frowned and considered the question as Hugh reappeared, pushing a drinks trolley with a silver tea service. "Here we are, a spot of anything you'd like. What can I get you?"

"We're fine, Mr. Sayers." Declan redirected his attention to Sarah. "Mrs. Sayers? Mean anything to you?"

"Does *what* mean anything?" Hugh interjected tersely.

Nora decided Hugh was clearly used to being the center of attention and unhappy at being dismissed.

Sarah twisted her wedding ring. Finally, she said, "Nothing comes to mind."

"What are you going on about?" Hugh poured a sherry and handed it to his wife. "Try this, dear."

Sarah took a miniscule sip and put the small etched glass down. "Alice did seem...distracted recently."

Nora saw Sarah's eyes dart a glance at Hugh, who poured himself a large whiskey. She raised an eyebrow at Declan and pushed a curl off her face, discreetly pointing in Hugh's direction.

Declan stood. "Mr. Sayers, mind giving me a tour of Alice's rooms? This is quite the house."

Hugh hesitated; the pull of showing off the house made him acquiesce. "Certainly. It's Georgian, you know, quite the find."

Once they left, Nora patted Sarah's hand. "You had a reaction to that, Sarah."

The woman's sigh was heavy. "Alice seemed jittery these past few days. I said 'distracted,' but it was more as if she had a momentous decision to make." She lifted her hands and let them fall into her lap. "I'm explaining it badly." She met Nora's eyes. "Hugh and I both noticed it. This morning as she left I tried to pin her down, but she said she didn't want to involve me."

"You don't have any idea what upset her?"

"No, I wish I had. I'll never forget her face—she looked terrified."

* * *

In their living room, Nora and Declan sipped wine in front of the fireplace, where Typo the beagle slept on his back, legs splayed in the warmth, and Nora's thoughts turned to Alice Fenton.

"I wish I knew what Alice meant by 'find the truth.' She seemed so frightened." Nora had told Declan what Sarah said about Alice's mood.

"We're scouring CCTV from the Covered Market. The team is checking into her former boyfriend and Hugh's assistant too. We spoke by phone to the housekeeper. Her sister confirmed they hadn't left Brighton all week, so she's in the clear. I'll know more tomorrow about Guy Bellows and Gary Pritchard's alibis."

"I had no idea my hat would lead to this."

"You never showed it to me."

Nora arched an eyebrow. "I don't show you everything."

"Go on, let's see this hat with the flower the color of your dress." Nora's surprised look made him laugh. "I do listen when you talk."

She brought the red hat box from the stairs where she'd dumped it when she returned home, and modeled the hat. "Comments?"

"Charming. Perfect color too."

Nora swatted him playfully as she removed the hat and started to place it back when something twinkled in the nest of tissue. She put the hat aside and waded through the tissue to see what caught the light. "Declan, look." She pushed the folds aside and found the source: a mini flash drive. "I bet Alice dropped this in here on purpose." Nora described how Alice had lurched against the counter and peered into the box.

"Don't touch it. I'll get an evidence bag." He returned with his briefcase and drew on gloves. "I'll log it in first thing."

"But we need to see what's on it," Nora protested. "It must be important for Alice to have left it."

Declan hesitated. "By rights I should log it into evidence now instead of leaving it overnight."

"By rights, you wouldn't have known about it if I hadn't found it." Nora set her chin. "Look, it might be password protected and won't open, anyway. You're the boss—use your initiative."

"I hope I don't regret this." He opened his work laptop and plugged the drive in.

Nora hung over his arm while several photos and one video file appeared.

Declan clicked on a photo of a manuscript title page with DEATH IN THE COTSWOLDS crossed out; written above it in pencil was THE CAMBRIDGE MURDER. The author's name was heavily scored out.

The next several photos were subsequent pages of the manuscript. Next to the page numbers was the header: *Cotswolds/SCB.*

"Do we think the famous crime writer has been buying his stories?"

"Play the video, Declan." Nora hunched closer as Declan started the video. Nora flinched at the sight of Alice's face looking back at her.

"This is Alice Fenton on Monday, October 14th. Today I came into my stepfather's office to borrow printer paper and saw the manuscript he's working on appears to belong to someone else. I'm documenting my actions and the depth of his deceit." The camera panned the office, taking in the large ornate desk and several framed photos of Hugh Sayers with celebrities, before it narrowed its focus to the contents of a console table along one wall. "I've been through his file drawers and there's nothing but business-related things like contracts and expenses." She knelt down in front of the table and opened the doors. Two locked file boxes took up the entire lower shelf.

Nora could hear Alice's ragged breathing. "Where would Hugh hide the key?" The camera tracked the room and stopped at a shelf with photos of Hugh Sayers at book events. In its center was an American award, a ceramic teapot. "Of course." Alice's hand lifted the lid; a small key lay inside.

She struggled to use one hand to open a file box. Nora heard her groan of dismay at the stack of manuscripts inside. "My poor mother, married to this charlatan." Alice lifted out the top page, whose title had been crossed out and renamed. A Post-it note read: "*Same terms—G.*"

A noise must have startled Alice, for she thrust the paper back and relocked the box with trembling hands, the camera going crazy and videoing the floor, ceiling, walls, as Alice moved swiftly. "Someone's home." The video ended abruptly.

Nora said, "I'm gobsmacked."

Declan agreed. "This gives Sayers motive. Tomorrow I'll pull him in for questioning."

* * *

Alice Fenton's fearful look had kept Nora awake, coupled with how awful Sarah would feel when she learned of her husband's betrayal. Who had fed Hugh his manuscripts?

Once Declan left for work, she Googled addresses, always surprised how much detail the internet provided. She piled Typo into her car and drove north to park near Gary Pritchard's flat in Jericho. As she leashed the dog and grabbed her backpack, Nora realized he lived in the area seen in the first filmed Morse episode, "The Dead of Jericho." Could Gary's duplicity have been what made Alice break up with him? But where would he obtain manuscripts?

Nora walked Typo on the towpath, Typo sniffing delightedly, while she watched the canal-facing flat door over a garage, hoping the bicycle out front meant Gary was home. A gaily painted canal boat chugged past on her third trek when the flat door opened and a young man emerged.

As he fussed with the lock, Nora called out before he could ride away. "Mr. Pritchard? Gary?"

The young man's haunted look told her Declan's team had been to see him yesterday to confirm his whereabouts at the time of Alice's death. A woman with a puppy straining at the leash seemed unthreatening enough. He answered her, albeit stiffly. "Yes. What do you want?"

Typo jumped up to be petted. The man absently rubbed the dog's ears.

"Typo, down. Sorry, he loves people." She pulled the puppy away. "I'm Nora Tierney and I wanted to extend my condolences about Alice. I was with her yesterday before she died." He frowned and she quickly added, "Her mother spoke highly of you when I saw her yesterday."

"Sarah? We got on well. She knew I genuinely cared for Alice." His eyes filled and he looked away.

"Care to walk along the towpath? I'd love to learn more about Alice." At this rate Typo would sleep all afternoon.

He hesitated, then leaned the bike against the wall and relocked it. "All right."

As they walked, Nora explained her brief meeting with Alice, leaving out the flash drive. "I'm sorry I didn't get to know her." She explained she was a feature writer for *People and Places* magazine. "Sarah said Alice was a graphic designer. Maybe I could write an article about her promise, cut off early." Nora stopped at a bench, took a collapsible bowl and water bottle from her backpack, and poured Typo a drink.

While the dog lapped, Gary talked about Alice. His face glowed. "...And she had such an artistic eye. We'd talked about starting a marketing firm together." He looked down. "I pushed her to get engaged and she backed off. Then this week she became caught up in this weird idea..."

He seemed genuinely bereft at Alice's death. Nora trusted her instincts and crossed him off her suspect list. "Something to do with her stepfather?" Nora knew she was leading her witness but needed his information.

Gary looked at her in surprise.

"I've met Hugh Sayers before." Nora explained her interview and impressions.

"Alice worried he'd married Sarah because Alice's father left her well off. She hated that he called her 'Malice,' too, and thought it amusing."

"Smarmy," Nora agreed. "Do you think she was afraid of him?"

"At first I thought she disliked him because he didn't measure up to her dead dad. But then the other day she called me, very upset, said Hugh was a cheat and she could prove he hadn't written his recent books." Gary's eyes blazed. "He's involved in Alice's death in some way, I know it."

* * *

Nora dropped Typo off for a well-earned rest, and met Declan for lunch at The Old Tom pub on St. Aldate's, near his station. After they'd ordered the pub's specialty Thai food, she asked him about progress in Alice's case.

He lowered his voice. "We've found her on CCTV leaving Brown's, can follow her to the coffee shop where she stops suddenly, then crosses to the hat shop. The crowd around her shows a man wearing a hoodie right behind her, not tall enough to be Hugh Sayers, who by the way, lawyered up immediately when we brought him in, despite his alibi. He's cooling his heels in a cell while we keep searching."

"He wouldn't like his reputation or his income string compromised if he knew Alice had found out what he was doing."

"We're comparing the local CCTV with known criminals too. The question is if whoever sold the manuscripts is the same one who stabbed Alice. What have you found out?"

Nora opened her eyes wide in feigned innocence. "Who says I found anything out?"

"I do. I know your tendency to investigate my cases. Spill."

Nora related her feeling Gary had nothing to do with Alice's death. "He's not fond of Hugh, and he doesn't have an outlet to find the manuscripts. And Alice trusted him enough to tell him earlier this week about Hugh's plagiarism, but I didn't say she had photographs."

"His background check shows he's solvent, doing a paid internship for a public relations firm while finishing his graduate degree."

"I liked him."

"Then I'll surely cross him off my suspect list." When he smiled, the corners of his eyes crinkled.

With the housekeeper in Brighton, and Gary deleted, Nora was at a loss. "What about Guy Bellows, Hugh's assistant?"

"Been working for Hugh a while. I'm waiting on his background check before I see him."

* * *

But Nora didn't want to wait for a background check. She walked over Folly Bridge to Waterman's Reach on the Isis, and entered the car park for the red brick flats, where a sign on the building indicated one of the flats was for sale. The posh riverfront flat was in one of the most exclusive areas in Oxford, and she recognized Guy's silver Audi.

As a journalist, Nora had doorstepped interview subjects many times. She rang the buzzer to the penthouse; an intercom asked who wanted in.

"It's Nora Tierney. You were leaving when I visited the Sayers yesterday so we weren't introduced. I was with Alice after she was stabbed." The buzzer sounded. When the lift opened on the top floor, Guy Bellows stood in his doorway.

"To what do I owe this pleasure, Miss Tierney?" He'd taken a page from Hugh Sayers' formal speech.

"Nora, please. I'm hoping my editor at *People and Places* will allow me to write a memorial article on Alice, the daughter of the famous crime writer gone too soon, and need background."

"All publicity is good, right?" He motioned her to enter the flat, whose large main room had tall river view windows. "Not that Hugh would capitalize on Alice's death."

"But hard to pass up an opportunity, right?" Nora hoped she'd kept out the snarky tone she felt as she tried for conspiratorial. "Great view."

Partially-filled cartons sat in front of a bookcase. Guy was packing up.

Nora's phone pinged as she scrutinized the green river where sunlight sparkled on the water. The flat was furnished with lustrous black leather couches; glass and chrome tables added a cool masculine air. She glanced at her phone, tapped a brief reply, and pocketed it quickly. "Babysitter."

"You have children?"

"A toddler son." He didn't need her details, especially after Declan's text: *Bellows worked at publisher in Acquisitions before Sayers; don't go there.* She hoped her succinct reply hit home: *Too late.*

Guy leaned on the sleek granite-topped island, and pointed to a leather stool. "Get you anything?"

"Water, thanks." Nora's mind raced. If Guy had worked in publishing, he'd had access to slush piles of manuscripts he could have kept, then sold on to Hugh to rework. Few dismissed authors would distinguish their work if modified enough and if they read Hugh's books. It was a gamble but the percentages were on Hugh's side for fresh storylines. But why would Guy kill Alice?

"Think your editor will go for this article?" Guy gave her filtered water and poured himself a glass of white wine. Nora noticed the high-end range looked as if it had never been used to cook a meal.

A wooden knife block on the counter next to it had one empty slot.

Her stomach churned. Had Guy killed Alice to keep her quiet, or had Hugh orchestrated it? Where to start with her questions without cluing Guy in to her thoughts? "It's exactly the type of article they thrive on," she answered. "How well did you know Alice?"

Guy looked at her sharply. "I need background so I don't disturb Sarah," she explained, and opened the Notes app on her phone after surreptitiously turning on the record button. "How long since you left publishing to work for Hugh Sayers?"

"About four years now." He took a swig from his glass. "You were with Alice when she collapsed?"

"By happenstance. She came into the hat shop where I was talking with the owner. She'd already been stabbed and fainted. We called 999 but there wasn't much we could do."

Guy looked relieved. "Sad she didn't get a chance to talk to you, I mean, about what happened to her."

"Yes." Nora sipped her water and wondered if Declan was on his way or if she should leave. "Look, I imagine this is painful for you. I can come back when it's more convenient." She glanced out the window to the carpark but couldn't see any squad cars. *Where was Declan?*

"Not at all. Hugh is busy with Sarah today so I'm not needed there." He met her eyes with a piercing look. "Why don't you tell me why you're really here, Nora Tierney?"

Nora's heart raced. "For an article on Alice Fenton." She hoped she could keep a blush from suffusing her face.

"And yet you know I worked in publishing, when neither Hugh nor I have ever mentioned that in any publicity."

Oops. She shrugged. "You'd be surprised what you can learn on Google. How do you think I found this address?"

Guy narrowed his eyes while he examined her closely. "It wouldn't do to lie to me, Nora."

She bristled. This man was at least a fraudster, and possibly a killer. "Are you threatening me?"

"Why would I do that?" He took a deep swallow of wine.

Nora estimated the distance between Guy and the knife block, and hers to the flat door. He could grab a knife before she could get to the door, but could he reach her? She stalled, blustered with righteous indignation. "It sure sounded like a threat."

He laughed, a false, hollow sound. "You Americans. So touchy."

Fury swelled over Nora. She pictured Alice's pale face, her eyes beseeching Nora to reveal the truth. She thought of Sarah, mourning her daughter. Her phone pinged again. Declan: *keep going.* He must be in earshot. She erased the text and shoved her phone back in her pocket.

"Babysitter again?" Guy mocked her.

"Anxious to see her boyfriend. You know teens."

Guy stood up straight. "Perhaps you'd better go then."

No, for Alice's sake she needed to get him to say it. "I will, after you tell me how long you've been selling Hugh manuscripts to rewrite."

Her statement fell like a boulder into the room. Nora held her breath as Guy's eyes widened. Then he did the last thing she would have thought. He threw his head back and laughed.

"You think you have it all figured out, don't you?" He shook his head. "If only you knew the reality."

"Go ahead, tell me about this great plan of yours."

"But that's where you have it all wrong. This plan was all down to Hugh, who'd dried up and had no new ideas." He shrugged. "The man's a cretin, but he pays well."

"How did you know Alice had photos?"

"Hugh saw her leaving his office, and knew she'd figured it out when she started avoiding him and became hostile. Stupid man left the current manuscript out."

Nora eyed the knife block. Knowing Declan was in earshot gave her courage. "I suppose you'll claim killing her was Hugh's idea too."

"He worried she'd go to the police, and his reputation would never recover. My bonus for that has me on my way to the Algarve to an early retirement." Guy walked the few paces to the stove. "There's only one thing standing between me and my departure, and that's *you!*"

Guy grabbed a knife and lunged for Nora, who ran for the door as it slammed open. Declan and three uniformed officers swarmed in. "Drop it, Bellows!"Declan yelled, and drew Nora behind him out of harm's way. Two of the officers grabbed Guy's arms and put him in handcuffs, while a third retrieved the knife. "Read him his rights and get him out of here."

Nora gulped and fought back tears as she tried to control her rapid breathing. "Did you hear him? He killed Alice for a bonus to take early retirement."

"At Hugh's instruction. We heard it all."

"And I have it recorded." She held up the phone.

Declan took it from her and dictated: "This is DI Declan Barnes ending this recording made in the penthouse of Waterman's Reach at"—he consulted a clock on the wall—"2:45 PM on first November." He threw an arm over Nora's shoulder. "You were very brave but don't do it again. Let's get you home. Thanks to you I have a lot of paperwork and a special interview waiting for me with Hugh Sayers."

Alice's expectations of revealing Hugh's deceit would finally be revealed to his other victims. Yes, a writer's life was difficult with the pressure to develop new ideas. But never worth someone's life. "Not home, Declan. I want to be with Sarah."

* * *

Marni Graff is the award-winning author of The Nora Tierney English Mysteries and The Trudy Genova Manhattan Mysteries. Her stories are in several anthologies, including the Anthony Award-winning Malice Domestic's *Murder Most Edible*. She is Managing Editor of Bridle Path Press, a crime book reviewer, and blogs for Miss Demeanors. Graff is a member of Sisters in Crime, Mavens of Mayhem SinC, Triangle SinC, Mystery People UK, and the International Association of Crime Writers. She lives in eastern NC with her husband and two Aussiedoodles.

White Elephants

By Peter W. J. Hayes

Hong Kong and Singapore

"I wait for you here. After, we go airport again. Okay?"

"Okay. An hour at most." Levon Grace thanked the elderly limousine driver, maneuvered his oversized metal briefcase across the back seat and stepped into the apartment tower's courtyard.

Humidity coated his skin. Far below the driveway's low safety wall, Hong Kong's office towers and shopping malls crowded the bright blue of Victoria Bay. Beyond, Kowloon wavered peacefully in the heat. Levon took a slow breath, excitement and fear mingling in his stomach, and started for the building's entrance.

The guard at the front desk straightened when Levon asked for Eddie Lau. He confirmed Levon's appointment with a brisk phone call and led him to a private elevator. As Levon whooshed upward, he hefted the briefcase. Inside was an oil painting worth two million dollars. He was headed to a penthouse worth twenty times that.

"Eddie Lau won't try anything funny," Carter Quince, Levon's CIA handler, had said with a grin when Levon collected the painting in New York. "Not in his own house."

Levon disliked it when Carter grinned, because it meant Carter was glossing over something. In this case, he suspected it was MSS, China's

Ministry of State Security.

"The job's simple," Carter had continued. "Beijing appointed a whole slate of new government officials after they broke up the pro-democracy protests. Eddie has a journalist friend—Jeffrey Kwok—who supported the protestors. You trade the painting for the dirt Kwok dug up on the new officeholders. We can use it in next month's trade talks."

MSS wouldn't want that to happen, Levon knew, but the odds felt manageable. The exchange was secret, and if MSS did know about it, they would wait until after the trade. If that happened, Carter had given Levon a scram number to call.

The elevator doors opened into a lobby thirty floors above the courtyard.

A muscled, middle-aged Chinese man in a tailored suit raised his chin in a hello. "We meet again." His eyes twinkled.

Levon fought down the surprise at seeing him. "The casino in Macau."

"A convenient place."

Of course it was. Levon didn't know the bodyguard's name, yet, four times, he'd handed this man a black roller-bag containing one million dollars. Four times he'd watched the man hand the case to the casino's cash exchange teller.

And just like that, the money became the casino's perfectly legal gambling revenue.

Levon knew Eddie Lau owned the casino, most likely from behind a thicket of shell companies. He guessed Eddie's Guangdong manufacturing center and fleet of cargo ships were managed the same way.

The bodyguard led Levon into a living room that ran the width of the building. Two separate groupings of low, modern furniture offered a heady view of Victoria Bay and Kowloon through floor-to-ceiling windows. The green and white Star Ferry—no larger than a tac-head—chugged away from its Hong Kong Central berth.

Three Chinese men waited at the far end of the room, an empty easel nearby.

Levon recognized Eddie Lau from his photos. Tall and thin with smooth cheeks and prominent eyes, his slacks and shirt were tailor-made to match the color of his gray pompadour.

Levon also knew the man to Eddie's right. He wore blue jeans and a white cotton shirt so tight the buttons barely contained his chest. His eyes were close-set, his arms thick enough to wrestle down a rhinoceros.

That was Horace Bang, the hatchet to Eddie's whetstone.

To Eddie's left stood a short man with square black-framed glasses and unkempt hair. He wore an ill-fitting brown suit with sagging side pockets, his plum-colored tie askew.

"I appreciate you coming all this way." Eddie's accent was British public-school, the grip of his handshake just as affected and disinterested.

"Part of my job. I'm pleased to meet you." Levon waited for an introduction to the other men, but Eddie was silent. Levon motioned at the windows. "Gorgeous view."

Eddie didn't turn to look. "You've had a long flight. Can I get you something?" Eddie's tone suggested he didn't mean it, and didn't care if Levon knew.

"Thanks for the offer, but I'm fine."

"Good. Down to business." Eddie's eyes gleamed greedily.

Levon hefted the briefcase and held it out to him. "With the compliments of Walter Euston of New York's Euston Gallery."

Eddie accepted the briefcase and placed it on a coffee-table cleared of everything but an open laptop. Eddie checked his phone for the codes Walter had emailed him, spun the combination dials on the briefcase and popped the latches. From the pocket in the lid he removed a thick envelope of provenance documents and handed it to the man with the sagging pockets. He unwrapped the painting and placed it on the easel.

The sight of the painting caught in Levon's chest, the same way it had when he first saw it in Walter Euston's gallery. An oil painting of small boats dwarfed by thunderous waves and clouds, illuminated by an explosion of setting sun.

"Is that a Turner?" Levon had asked Walter, unable to keep the awe out of his voice.

"It is."

Levon remembered how Walter almost vibrated in that moment. Walter's words followed in a rush. "Late career, you can see it in how he added color to the shadows and wanted you to know how he *felt* about that sunset. Groundbreaking, at the time."

Levon had seen Turners in museums, of course, but never intimately, this close. Even now, in Eddie Lau's eyrie, the painting loosened him inside. In a good way.

As the brown-suited man studied the provenance documents, Bang yawned and glanced at his fingernails.

In case MSS appeared, Levon thought he should make noises that fit the cover the Homesteaders at the CIA had given him. He turned to Eddie. "It's quite something, isn't it?" It was his best impression of an employee from Walter Euston's gallery, although he knew it would fool no one.

"Not my usual taste, I like modern. Although I do prize my jade collection." Eddie nodded at a glass display cabinet crammed with small pieces of carved jade. It too faced the vista of Hong Kong harbor.

The man in the brown suit said something to Eddie in Mandarin. Eddie gestured to the painting. The man folded the papers back into the envelope, stepped to the easel and bent close to the canvas. With a quick movement he removed his glasses and put a loupe to one eye.

Eddie waved at the man. "This is Lu Yulong. He's an expert in Chinese and British art. He studied in London. He will authenticate the work." He nodded at the third man, suppressing a smile. "And this, of course, is Jeffrey Kwok."

Levon was stunned by the lie. No, this was Horace Bang. Levon had seen Bang in countless photographs of Eddie Lau, always off to one side, watching the people around Eddie or staring down the lens of the camera taking the photograph.

Then again, Levon realized, he'd never seen a photo of the democracy activist Jeffrey Kwok. Had anyone? And Carter hadn't said anything about the painting being authenticated.

His mind racing, Levon felt like one of the painting's tiny, weather-tossed ships.

Levon concentrated on Yulong and his loupe, steadying his heart rate. The introduction didn't make sense. Eddie had to know Levon would do his research and recognize Bang on sight.

Yulong scrounged in one of his baggy suitcoat pockets and exchanged the loupe for a digital camera. He shot several photographs of the painting's ocean and sky. He connected the camera to the laptop and clicked through several computer screens. A red image appeared.

"Infrared," Eddie said. "Until we can run the proper tests."

Yulong studied the red photographs and looked up, smiling. He spoke rapidly to Eddie in Mandarin and turned to Levon. "Authentic," he said in English. "Very beautiful." Levon could tell he meant it.

Eddie clapped his hands. "Good." He turned to Levon. "Well, I know you are in a hurry to return. I won't delay you."

Levon's heartbeat spiked again, afraid of being dismissed without Jeffrey Kwok's information.

Eddie tapped his forehead theatrically. "Oh, where are my manners?" He crossed to the jade display and removed a small statue. Returned to Levon. "Please. Take this and give it to Mr. Euston as a token of my appreciation. I truly value his help in acquiring the painting."

Levon stared at the carved, baseball-sized figurine of an elephant, the lines elegant and spare. The unique white jade glowed in his hands. "This is very kind of you," Levon said.

Eddie returned a knowing smile.

Yulong said something sharply in Mandarin to Eddie, who pivoted slowly and looked at Yulong in disgust. Yulong flushed, reset his glasses on his nose and slammed the laptop closed. The bodyguard Levon knew from the casino offered a wooden box with a padded velvet interior. Levon placed the jade inside and closed the lid.

Eddie offered Levon the metal briefcase. "Are you headed to the airport?"

"I am." Levon saw Yulong glance at the wooden box. Levon turned to Bang, deciding to play along. "It's good to meet you, Mr. Kwok."

Bang glanced at Eddie, a knowing grin on his lips. "Isn't it, though?"

"Goodbye, Mr. Grace," Eddie said quickly, ignoring Bang. He and Levon shook hands. At the elevator, as an argument erupted between Yulong and Eddie in the distance, the blocky bodyguard leaned past Levon, pushed the call button, and said softly, "Careful, now."

* * *

Levon stepped into the courtyard outside the apartment building, the box with the jade cradled in one arm, briefcase dangling from the other. His black Mercedes limousine slid forward. A heavyset man Levon had never seen got out from behind the wheel.

"You aren't my driver," Levon said quickly, noting how the man's eyes fixed on the wooden box.

"Ah. Mr. Chan called away. Personal request from client." He met Levon's gaze. "I am your driver now. I am Choi. We go to airport?"

Every instinct Levon possessed vibrated. He didn't like the driver's neck tattoo or how his bulk strained his jacket seams. Behind them, the automatic entrance doors shushed open. Levon turned to see Yulong hurrying toward him.

"Mr. Grace," Yulong called in English. He smiled deferentially. "Excuse me. I believe Mr. Lau said you are going to the airport? Perhaps I could ride with you? Beg a ride, as you say? I also have an airplane to catch."

Levon organized his thoughts. "My driver changed. Can you ask him what happened?"

Yulong glanced at Choi. "Certainly." He launched into Cantonese and listened to Choi's reply.

"Okay." Yulong turned to Levon. "He says a wealthy client called and asked for your driver personally. Choi is his replacement. And he says I can accompany you."

Levon didn't hesitate. Choi's explanation to Yulong was consistent, and he'd seen no recognition between Choi and Yulong. But Levon wouldn't disobey his instincts. He looked at Yulong. "Please apologize to him. I'll find another ride."

Yulong spoke rapidly to Choi. Levon returned to the lobby, Yulong trailing him, and asked the guard to call a taxi. Outside, Choi clambered into the driver's side of the limousine and drove away.

Five minutes later, Levon and Yulong slid into the back seat of a boxy red cab. Levon directed the driver to the airport.

Half-way down the hill toward the bay, Levon turned to Yulong. "That disagreement between you and Mr. Lau at the end of our meeting. Did it involve the painting?"

Yulong shrugged. "No. The painting is beautiful. Truly. For my doctoral examination, I had to authenticate a Turner, a Van Gogh and a Goya. A real Van Gogh." He let out a breath of pleasure. "The Goya was counterfeit and I caught that. Your Turner is real, and exquisite."

Oddly, Levon felt he had dodged a punch. "And was that really Jeffrey Kwok?"

"Ah. That surprised me. I was never introduced, but I thought he was Mr. Bang. A long-time associate of Mr. Lau."

As Levon pondered this information, he glanced ahead and saw the road blocked by a construction sign. "What's that?" he asked, quickly.

Yulong said something to the driver, who gave a languid, and lengthy, reply.

"Road work," translated Yulong. As the driver steered into a side road, Yulong added, "He says he'll take us through Admiralty, the central shopping area. A bit more traffic, but only a few minutes delay."

They trundled through a pair of green lights, stopping for a red light a block later. Levon looked to his right, across two lanes of traffic, at a plaza fronting an office building and the Star Ferry entrance.

A black Mercedes glided to a stop in the lane between their taxi and the curb. Levon saw the windows were down and his heart skipped. No one's windows were down in this heat. He scanned the occupants. The driver was a thin man wearing a jaunty cap. Sitting in the rear seat nearest him, looking right at him, was Choi. Levon turned to Yulong. "Get out."

"What?" Yulong looked confused. Ahead, the traffic light turned green.

"Stop!" Levon called to the driver, and reached for his wallet. To Yulong he snapped, "It's a trap. Get out now. Your side."

"It's the middle of the road."

"Now!" Levon dropped a handful of Hong Kong dollars on the front seat.

"I don't understand."

Levon reached across Yulong, popped the door and pushed Yulong hard toward the opening. "Run for the ferry."

The cars leading the oncoming traffic squealed to a stop, horns blaring, as Yulong staggered into the road in front of them.

With a loud crunch the taxi bucked and shuddered into the opposite lane of traffic. Tires squealed. Levon's driver wailed in fear. Levon glanced at the limousine and saw the skinny driver hanging onto his steering wheel with both hands, his eyes wide and manic, directing the limousine into the left front wheel of the taxi. Smoke from his limousine's spinning tires washed over the windows.

Levon started for Yulong's open door, dragging the briefcase, the jade box tight to his side. The front of the taxi shuddered another six inches into oncoming traffic. Levon stumbled into the road.

As he straightened, Levon checked Yulong was running and looked to his right. A wide, beefy man circled the back of the taxi, a knife in his right hand. Levon hopped forward and swung the briefcase at his head. Too slowly, the man raised a protective arm. The metal case deflected off his forearm and raked his face. He grunted and staggered. Levon swung again, overhand. The briefcase crunched on top of the man's head, locks popping open. The man sank to his knees.

Levon swung a third time, the briefcase opening and the foam inserts spinning away. He connected with the man's left ear. The man toppled to the road with a groan.

Levon looked over the car roofs and locked eyes with Choi. Like Levon, Choi had needed to slide over the back seat to exit. Levon stepped to the rear corner of the taxi, hesitated to get the timing right, and slid the mangled briefcase over the road to the spot where Choi would round the back of the limousine. He pivoted and sprinted toward the Star Ferry entrance, the jade box clutched to his stomach, dodging cars like a running back.

At the ferry entrance, he stutter-stepped long enough to look back and see Choi clambering up from the ground, the briefcase tangled in his feet.

Levon caught Yulong only a few feet inside the ferry entrance. "Faster," he hissed, and passed him.

Levon knew the ferry approach was a series of lengthy passageways that ended in ticket machines and a boarding area. He also knew that boarding the ferry was like running into a dead-end alley.

Glancing back, he saw Yulong's pale face, but no Choi. Ahead, a newsstand stood to one side of the hall, and beyond it, an emergency exit. Levon sprinted forward and slammed the exit's door bar. A bone-shuddering alarm sounded. Levon darted through the doorway. Yulong followed, stopping to push the door closed. The alarm fell silent.

Levon hopped down a short staircase to the office plaza and slowed to a jog, watching for Choi.

"This takes us back to them," gasped Yulong.

"They can't stick around." Levon glanced at Yulong. "Not after hitting the taxi. They'll take the hurt guy and leave. Choi will either take the ferry, or if he heard the alarm, double back."

Levon spotted a side door to the neighboring office building and led Yulong inside. They emerged in the building's lobby and Levon slowed to a walk, Yulong panting beside him. Levon threaded among office workers to the front doors and scanned the office plaza and road. Their taxi was stalled in oncoming traffic, a police officer approaching. The limousine and injured man were gone.

Levon was sure Choi lurked nearby.

He spotted the mouth of a narrow alley on the opposite side of the road.

"Come on." Levon grabbed Yulong's arm and fast-walked him along the backside of a row of head-high potted plants. He plunged into a crowd crossing the street and dragged Yulong into the mouth of the alley. From cover, he checked back and spotted Choi at the ferry entrance, head swiveling from side to side, searching for them.

Levon led Yulong into a nearby store jammed with tourist t-shirts, hats, mugs and harbor paintings. He exchanged his sport coat for a navy-blue windbreaker, transferring his belongings to the new jacket. He told Yulong to do the same. He paid and stepped back into the alley, sporting a new baseball cap and sunglasses.

Yulong joined him, still wearing his brown suit.

Levon decided it didn't matter. He was sure MSS would be waiting for him at the airport, and he needed a new plan. He hefted the box holding the jade and started for the far end of the alley, where a cluster of dumpsters created a funnel to the next street.

"We need to split up. They're looking for two men," Levon called over his shoulder.

"No. We stay together. Wait."

Levon stopped and turned to argue, only to stare into the barrel of a small revolver. Yulong's eyes were wild behind his glasses.

"The jade." Hoarse, Yulong shifted closer. "Give it to me and you can go."

Levon knew Yulong was standing too close. It was a mistake. "No."

Yulong's eyes widened. "That jade will never leave my country! Give it to me."

"No."

Yulong thrust the gun at Levon's face. Levon dodged right, dropped the jade box and clamped both hands over the revolver. He wrenched it from Yulong's hands and drove the bottom of his right fist and the gun butt into Yulong's forehead.

Yulong collapsed between two dumpsters, his glasses in his lap. Blood welled from a cut on his forehead.

It was too easy. Levon stared at Yulong. "What kind of training did MSS give you? You never hold a gun that close to someone."

Yulong blinked in confusion. Grasped about for his glasses.

"Give me your phone."

Yulong looked up. "What?"

"Give me your phone."

Yulong searched his baggy jacket pockets and held it out. Levon took it gingerly, retreated a step, held the buttons and turned it off. Slid it into his pocket.

Yulong found a handkerchief and dabbed at his forehead. He finally managed to slide on his glasses.

"Why did you say I was MSS?" He sounded betrayed.

"What else could you be? Unless your real name is Clouseau?"

Yulong blinked, not understanding the reference. He straightened against the wall. "I am not MSS. I am Lu Yulong, Deputy to the Minister of Culture. I protect China's antiquities." He pointed at the box on the ground. "I cannot let that leave the country. Do you understand its importance? Ming dynasty, at least 600 years old, one of the best examples of ancient carving. Rare white jade." His voice rose higher in frustration. "And this rich Eddie Lau throws it away like scorched rice? To someone in another country? I cannot let that happen." He sobbed in a breath, eyes beseeching.

Levon lowered the pistol. "Do Deputy Ministers of Culture usually carry guns?"

"Sometimes. In case I run into men like Choi. Did you see the dragon tattoo on his neck? He's a criminal. A Triad."

Levon knew that MSS and the Triads sometimes worked together. So Choi was a contractor, just like him.

Levon picked up the box. "I'm sorry, but this goes with me."

Yulong adjusted his glasses. "And you do not work for an art gallery. I know this now."

Levon smiled at him. "But I do believe in art." He turned and hurried out of the alley. Sinking into the crowd, he dialed the scram number Carter had given him.

✳ ✳ ✳

The hotel room in Singapore's Little India neighborhood was the type Carter loved. Inexpensive, with exits into two different streets and an alley. Carter sat in the room's only armchair, the box containing the white jade elephant on his lap.

Levon pointed at it. "I was kind of expecting a flash drive, or maybe a note."

"MI6 gave Eddie invisible ink with taggants in it. There was a web address written on the bottom. A spectrometer read it."

"That took two days?"

"Yes."

"And now it's clean?"

"Again, yes. And the web site taken down. But you need to explain why you want it back. You said you have something to trade?"

Levon gathered his thoughts. "Do you know who that scram number connected me to?"

Carter shrugged. "The Brits set it up, but I can guess. Without a car or the airport, only a boat gets you off the island. Eddie Lau runs a shipping company. Two plus two…"

"Yeah. I got picked up by one of Eddie's guys. Not Bang, but the bodyguard I always met in the casino. Turns out he's a good guy. His name is Ip. He brought me here on a cargo ship. We talked a lot."

"Yes?"

"Plus, I had a few days to think. I don't think you're going to like that."

"Why not?"

"Because you wouldn't have asked me to walk into Eddie Lau's home carrying a two-million-dollar Turner."

Carter's mouth tightened.

"I'll start at the beginning." Levon tried to get comfortable on his desk chair, without luck. "Eddie Lau, okay, his father made his money in real estate. Sent Eddie to Oxford, right?"

"That's on his Wikipedia page."

"Wikipedia doesn't mention the Brits recruited Eddie out of Oxford. That was the nineteen-eighties. Eddie was what the Brits call an occasional, not a full-blown asset, just someone who helps them sometimes. It worked for both of them. Eddie got political leverage among the Brits running Hong Kong, and MI6 got access to Hong Kong's wealthiest Chinese families. And in our business, it's all about access."

Carter shrugged. "Nothing new so far."

"Then it's 1997, the lease runs out, and England returns Hong Kong to China."

"Again, not worth a white jade elephant."

"Not long after, the democracy protests ramp up."

Carter started to speak and Levon held up his hand. "Let me finish. England and America supported the pro-democracy protestors. We like China distracted and struggling with internal problems. Makes it less likely they'll cause trouble elsewhere in the world. And what happens? Eddie Lau mentions to the Brits that he has a journalist friend, Jeffrey Kwok, who's in tight with the protestors and needs money to produce a pro-democracy newspaper. Close enough?"

Carter hesitated, but nodded.

"So I end up in Macau handing Ip roller-bags of cash to fund Kwok. And I bet I wasn't the only one. I'm guessing the Brits did it too."

Carter's eyes tightened to match his lips. "Yes. They matched your deliveries. But Kwok was successful enough the Chinese wanted to arrest him. That's why Eddie Lau offered to broker this deal. We got Kwok's information, Kwok got the Turner and citizenship in Canada, and China pulled a thorn from its foot. Everybody wins."

"Exactly. But two questions. First, how good is Kwok's information?"

Carter blinked. "It's okay. The teaser was very good, but what we got in the exchange for the painting not so much. Still, it'll be helpful with our trade talks." He grinned broadly.

There's that grin, Levon thought. "And has anyone met Kwok?"

Carter was silent for several seconds. "We haven't, I'm sure the Brits have."

"Maybe, but I bet Kwok never showed for his trip to Vancouver, and the Brits are wondering why."

Carter frowned. "They did say something about that."

"Well, here's the fun part. When I was with Eddie Lau, he introduced Bang to me as Jeffrey Kwok."

"He can't be, we know Bang."

"Exactly. It was some kind of inside joke between Eddie and Bang. It took me awhile to figure it out." Levon took a breath. "When the pro-democracy protests started, Eddie needed to protect his businesses. Since he didn't know who would win, I think he played both sides. He sweet-talked Beijing, while secretly using us and the Brits to fund the pro-democracy activist Jeffrey Kwok. That way, Eddie was loved by both Beijing and the pro-democracy activists. But, Beijing got fed up with the protestors and stamped down hard. Hong Kong's pro-democracy leaders ended up in jail or exile. But no one can find Kwok. Do you know why?"

Carter was silent.

Levon smiled. "Because Kwok never existed. Eddie and Bang invented him."

Levon watched Carter's eyes widen. "Inventing Kwok was clever, really. But with the crack-down, Eddie had a new problem." Levon waited for Carter to absorb his words. "Beijing would know Eddie was close to Kwok. They aren't stupid. I bet they pressured Eddie to produce Kwok. Eddie's solution? He offered to broker a deal that exiles Kwok to Vancouver. Like you said, everyone wins. Then, to really smooth things over, Eddie figures he'd better butter up the new governor of Hong Kong. Ip explained that part to me. According to Ip, the new governor—the one hand-picked by Beijing to run the island—collects British art."

Carter closed his eyes and slowly shook his head as if he didn't want to hear more.

Levon pushed on. "I bet the Turner painting went straight to the new governor as Eddie's apology for dabbling with the pro-democracy Jeffrey Kwok. Just a friendly demonstration of Eddie's loyalty to China. And our four million dollars? Well, some paid to create fake articles for Kwok's website, some went to Beijing's new hand-picked officials to smooth things over, the rest into Eddie's pocket. That's why Eddie gave us a scram number. If MSS caught me, I might tell MSS just enough for them to work out Eddie's scam. Eddie needed Ip to babysit me all the way to Singapore. If MSS showed up along the way, I'm sure Ip's orders were to put a bullet in my head and drop me overboard."

Carter opened his eyes. "Damn," he said finally. "It holds together."

Levon smiled. "No kidding. And the Brits will be pissed. The Turner is their cultural heritage and Eddie their asset. And even worse, Eddie spit in our collective eye." Levon pointed at the box holding the white jade elephant. "You know the symbolism of a white elephant, right? The old Thai kings gave real white elephants to people in their court who were out of favor and no longer needed. That was Eddie's message to us."

Carter sighed. "The Brits need to know all this."

"Yes, and when you tell them, also mention this…" Levon paused. He knew the repercussions of his next words. The chain of events they would unleash. He took a breath. "Like I said, I got to know Ip pretty well. He started out with the British police force in Hong Kong. He has a grandchild coming and wants to retire, but he's worried about whether he has enough money. He also wants out of Hong Kong."

"And he's Eddie's bodyguard?"

"When Bang isn't around, Ip has the keys to the castle. Yes."

Carter was silent for a moment. "You're right, it's all about access." He held out the box. "Okay. You get to keep the jade."

* * *

Six months later, Levon spotted a headline in the *South China Morning Post*. Eddie Lau found dead in a Bangkok luxury hotel following a weekend tryst with Miss Universe, Malaysia. An overdose. But it was the last detail in the article that stuck with him. The heroin that killed Eddie sold under the street brand White Elephant.

So. Never spit in the eye of the British.

The same newspaper had more fun two weeks later, when they reported how a car bomb in Kowloon killed one Horace Bang. Horace's surname made for a very humorous headline.

After reading about Horace, Levon did an internet search for an address and placed the wooden box holding the jade inside another box filled with foam peanuts. He added Yulong's phone and an unsigned note that said only, "I also believe art deserves a home."

He addressed the package to Yulong Wu, Deputy to the Minister of Culture, Shanghai, China.

A few days afterwards, a courier delivered an envelope. Inside was a postcard showing the skyline of Vancouver. It contained no postmark, stamp or return address. Written on the back in small, neat printing, was the note, "I have retired and moved my family from Hong Kong. I will not forget our trip to Singapore. So here I live, just another white elephant. Best, Ip."

Levon guessed the postcard was passed from MI6 to Carter. He tapped it against his thumbnail, smiled, and said aloud, "Actually, being a white elephant can be a good thing, my friend. A very good thing."

* * *

Peter W. J. Hayes is the author of the Silver Falchion-nominated Vic Lenoski mystery series, and is a Derringer and Al Blanchard Award-nominated author of short stories. His short work has appeared in various publications, including the *Best American Mystery Stories of 2023, Black Cat Mystery Magazine, Mystery Magazine, Crimeucoppia, Pulp Modern,* and various anthologies, including three Malice Domestic collections and *The Best New England Crime Stories.* He can be found at www.peterwjhayes.com.

Sweet Revenge Hotline

By Deborah Lacy

Tecate, Mexico

"Sweet Revenge Hotline," she said into her phone. "Tell me who did you wrong, and I'll help you get even."

The caller didn't respond immediately, but she'd learned in the three months since they'd started the hotline that sometimes people chickened out.

This caller paused longer than most and she was about to hang up when he spoke, "Hey, Blue Eyes. You didn't get very far."

Her body tensed. She'd recognize his deep voice anywhere.

"You can't hide from me forever," he said. "I'll always find you."

She hung up and blocked the number so fast she almost dropped the phone. She'd been so careful covering her tracks. None of her friends or relatives knew they were in Mexico.

"Loma!" she yelled, "Loma!" Her beautiful golden shepherd dog came running. She buried her face in the dog's soft, soft fur.

The Sweet Revenge partners had taken every precaution to protect themselves—moving the operation over the border to Tecate, burner cells, the umbrella corporation, fake names—to keep their real identities separate from the company. She petted Loma.

Miguel was busy on another call across the living room of the villa. "The exploding glitter package is sold out for the month, and seriously, it's a touch overdone. May I suggest one of our foul-tasting sweet packages? The Liver Filled Cupcakes are on special this week. They'll never know what's under that sugary frosting until they take a bite. Grossness guaranteed. I know because I personally tested it on my ex-boyfriend. The photos are all over Tik Tok. Just search the phrase, 'Liver Puss.'"

Setting up the Sweet Revenge business was a dream in the making, built on the premise that if living well is the best revenge, then why not live well by helping other people get even.

Sara, Miguel, and Angela met in a divorce group and formed an unlikely bond. The three of them were successful at their first revenge prank when they hired a guy in a motorboat to dump horse manure into Miguel's ex-husband's yacht. The adrenaline rush was exhilarating, and a great friendship was born, despite their age differences.

Testing their new revenge prank packages on their former husbands was better than therapy, or even alcohol.

Angela had suggested they move the business just over the Mexican border to Tecate a few weeks ago. Angela cited tax benefits as her number one reason, but it was clear to all of them that the border provided distance from angry prank victims and from evil husband number one: Ricky.

Her ex-husband had beaten her, threatened to kill Loma, and had a nasty habit of setting things that didn't belong to him on fire. She kicked herself daily for falling in love with him in the first place and agreeing to a quicky wedding during a wild weekend in Puerto Rico.

Miguel was on another call. "This sounds like an ideal situation for our exploding soup gift. Not only does the target get soup dripping everywhere within a four-foot radius of the package, but we also put another company name on the return address and if they call to complain, they'll hear medicine ads for things like hemorrhoids, jock itch, and toe fungus played repeatedly on an endless loop."

She walked straight to the big wooden front door and locked it.

Caffeine. That would help her think.

The big Mexican tiled kitchen was her favorite part of the rental house.

The large glass windows faced majestic Mount Kuchumaa. Their neighbor said the word Kachumaa meant exalted high place and it was sacred to the Kumeyaay Indians. People went on vision quests there and looked for guidance. She hoped the mountain could protect her and give her guidance now.

She turned on the espresso machine, poured in the water and the milk, and let it warm up.

Maybe Ricky was just bluffing, and he didn't know where they were. Or maybe they should move just in case. Maybe they could go farther into Mexico to Cancun or the Yucatan. Or even drive all the way to Belize. She heard Ambergris Caye was lovely and cheap. She didn't think her sweet senior doggie Loma could make an airplane trip, so Europe and Asia were out.

Still, she'd rather stay in Tecate. The weather mirrored Southern California, the fresh tortillas were amazing, the people she'd met were friendly, and the colorful décor energized her.

The neighbor's dog started barking. Sara moved quickly to lock the sliding glass door to the back yard. It took a moment for her to figure out how to work the lock.

Running their business out of other people's homes by the week instead of leasing office space was a brilliant idea. These kinds of rentals were so much cheaper in Mexico, and since they didn't have to buy office furniture, commit to a lease, or buy property insurance, they saved a bundle. And sometime this week, if online orders kept growing, they would sell their five hundred thousandth revenge package.

The overhead was low, and the profit was high. Next month, if all went according to plan, they could hire college students to take these stupid phone calls for beer money.

Maybe she'd even buy her own houseboat with her share of the profits; then she and Loma could move from marina to marina in Baja to keep away from her ex. She imagined herself in a cozy bed as the waves gently rocked her to sleep.

Miguel joined her in the kitchen while she was getting her beloved espresso from their precious machine. It was one of the few things the Sweet Revenge team took with them from house to house. The delicious scent of coffee filled the kitchen. She was trying to decide if she should confess to him that Ricky called when she saw that worried look on Miguel's handsome face.

"Down it," he said pointing to her freshly made espresso. "We've got problems."

She took a sip and braced herself. And then she remembered that Miguel didn't know what her true problems were.

"There's $300,000 extra dollars in our bank account."

"What?" She put down the coffee. "An extra $300,000? It's got to be a mistake."

"You didn't do anything crazy, did you?"

"Like what? Rob a bank?"

Her phone started ringing. His phone started ringing.

"Like selling part of the business without telling us."

"We agreed no investors. Sink or swim. I've stuck to our agreement. I don't even know anyone who has $300,000."

"Angela knows plenty of people with that kind of money," Miguel said. "Where is she anyway? She always says she's going to take care of everything, mostly while she's doing nothing."

"I'm going to call the bank and tell them the 300K isn't ours and find out who made the deposit."

"Don't do that, let's keep the money and see what happens."

She rolled her eyes. "We have enough trouble. I'm calling the bank now." She trudged back to her laptop on the massive dining room table. She thought about what she would say to the bank. She wasn't even sure which department to call.

Her line rang. She froze. She couldn't talk to Ricky again. She didn't have the energy.

Already on another call, Miguel waved at her, pointing his finger frantically at her ringing cell phone.

She inhaled deeply and picked up. "Sweet Revenge Hotline…" she said, ready to hang up immediately if necessary.

"Hello? My husband is having an affair with my son's soccer coach." The voice was female. "His MALE soccer coach. I let him come back home after the yoga instructor for my son's sake, but now I'm done. That man will sleep with anything. My son doesn't ever want to play soccer again."

"Do you have a divorce attorney?"

"Um, not yet. Do I need one to buy a prank?"

"Of course not, but it might be best to talk to one first if divorce is your ultimate goal, especially if there are children involved. Our pranks are harmless, but in situations like yours, our legal revenge services are more satisfying and long term."

"I don't have a divorce attorney."

"Then I suggest that I transfer you to our legal revenge department. Gwen will take very good care of you, I promise. After that, she will transfer you back to us for the prank."

Then she transferred angry wife number four of the day to Gwen; smart phones made these things so easy. Gwen was a saint. Half divorce attorney, half gal pal, she represented Sara in her divorce from Ricky and helped her find his hidden money.

Now she was helping Gwen sign new clients at the rate of three or four a day. Of course, the partners at Sweet Revenge Hotline got a cut of every divorce case they referred, and the tally was mounting. A divorce referral was worth twenty times the profit of a prank. Angry husbands and angrier wives were the Hamburger Helper of Sweet Revenge.

With that referral, she had earned another break, and she needed one before she called the bank. Ricky had to be involved somehow, but she couldn't figure out the angle. Miguel was deep in a call, but Angela was still nowhere to be seen. The poolside stereo blasted heavy metal music, which was odd, because none of them were fans.

There were moments when she thought maybe they should have only had two partners, but she and Miguel agreed to make Angela a partner if she willed her part of the business to them.

The quirky, 74-year-old lady didn't work hard, but she was a lot of fun.

Sweet Revenge had been her idea, as had the legal referrals and farming out the dirty work so none of them got any manure—literal or figurative—on their hands. Sadly, Angela often forgot her brilliant ideas almost as soon as she had them, and Miguel and Sara did the real work, making sure Angela ate well, took her meds, and got to her doctor appointments. But if you asked Angela, she'd say that she was teaching them a lifetime of wisdom. She told great stories about her first husband who ran a Mexican cartel out of Tijuana, her second husband the movie executive, and her third who was the automotive king of Escondido. She never talked about the fourth husband and Sara never asked.

She put her phone down on the coffee table and walked outside to see if Angela was in the back. Often Angela could be found swimming in the infinity pool with the view of the mountain. But not today. She wasn't on any of the blue chaise lounges either. Sara walked over to the stereo to turn the music down. She froze when she saw a strange man in the hot tub.

The no man rule was absolute. Today's boyfriend could be tomorrow's enemy. And yet, there was clearly a man in the hot tub who was handsome enough to belong in a swimsuit ad.

"Get out," she said. "This is private property."

The man didn't move.

"I asked you to get out. I mean it. MIGUEL! MIGUEL!"

Her partner came running out of the house, with Loma following close behind him. He tripped on his flip flops and landed face down on the cement. "My nose. My nose. I'm bleeding." Sara ran over to Miguel and helped him up onto a lounge chair. His nose bled onto his hot pink shirt. Loma stood protectively between the stranger and Sara. Sara grabbed the dog's collar to make sure the dog didn't attack.

"This morning I put $300,000 into the Sweet Revenge the bank account. Over there," he said pointing to a folder on a chair, "you'll find papers transferring the business to me. Once you sign those papers and hand them to me, you'll get Angela."

"What are you taking about?" Miguel said. "Where is Angela?"

"I need to put the dog back in the house," Sara said, grabbing Miguel's arm. "We'll be right back."

"Angela's dead, if you call the police."

Sara and Miguel went inside with Loma and shut the door behind them. Sara wet some paper towels and washed the blood from Miguel's face.

"How did he find out about the business? How did he find the rental house?" Miguel asked.

"Have you seen Angela's tote bag? It has her medication in it. She had it with her this morning."

"You mean this?" Miguel held up a canvas bag that said 'We love Abuela' with photos of Paul, Max, and Josephina, her three grandchildren, at Halloween. He reached in and pulled out a plastic bag full of pill bottles.

"Even if they don't hurt her, she could have a heart attack."

"I could have a heart attack after the day we've had."

"Really, Miguel? That isn't helpful. Why aren't you worried? Is that your latest boyfriend out there trying to steal the company?"

"Me? You think I did this? I've made more money in the past three months than I've made in the past ten years. And I've gotten revenge on everyone who ever looked at me sideways. Sweet Revenge is the most fun I've ever had in my life. And I wouldn't want to do it by myself."

He leaned over and hugged her. His huge frame dwarfed hers.

"We need to get Angela back. She needs her meds."

"This has got to be a joke," Miguel said. "Don't you see? Someone is pulling a revenge prank on us."

"I've been thinking about what Gwen said about all the people who could sue us because of the pranks. Maybe we got into this thing too quickly. Maybe this is our way out. Let's ask for a half a million dollars and Angela in exchange for the whole company."

"I want to keep the company," Miguel said.

"At least we'd be completely out, and we wouldn't have to worry about anyone coming after us or working with a blackmailing kidnapper every day."

"We should stall until we figure this out," Miguel said. "Angela is always saying she does the hard work, but it seems like we always have to do the hard work and now I don't know what to do."

"We sell him the company and save our friend. What else can we do? Besides, I have another idea for a business. It's an alibi service. Want to miss a day of work? We get you a doctor note. Tell your wife you were on a business trip to Boston when you were in Cabo with your mistress, we go to Boston with your credit card."

"How do you know we wouldn't be helping criminals create an alibi?"

"We'll check out the risks before we start. We'll use our $300K to start fresh."

"I still think this is a joke."

"Do you have a better idea?"

He shook his head no.

They went back outside. The man still sat in the hot tub.

"We have a counter proposal," Sara said. "We want half a million dollars for the entire company and Angela. And we need proof that she's safe and the money in the bank before we sign anything."

The man looked at his phone. "Three hundred thousand," he said. "That's my final offer." He pressed another button and held up a photo of a grey-haired elderly woman with a blindfold over her eyes and tied to a chair. "Do you want her or not?"

"Where's the contract?"

He pointed to the papers on the chaise lounge next to him. "I need both of you to sign using your real names, please. As you can see, Angela's signature has already been added."

Sara picked up the paperwork.

"Don't you dare sign a thing," Angela said. "Put those papers down."

"Angela? You're free!" Sara said moving towards her to give her a big hug.

"Stay right where you are," Angela said. "Of course, I'm free. This num-nut couldn't kidnap a watermelon at a picnic. I let him take the picture, signed the paperwork, and escaped after he left. Now we need some music."

Angela walked over to the stereo being careful to step over the extension cord. "I can't seem to figure out how to work this thing. I find music so calming."

"You press the button at the bottom," Miguel said. "I have it all set up."

"We don't need music," Sara said.

"Sara," Angela said, "why don't you go into the house while I'm dealing with this? Miguel will stay with me."

"Gladly." Sara turned towards the house and started walking.

"I can't ever figure these things out," Angela said. "Luckily this is a nice long extension cord. Now which button do I press?"

Sara heard a loud zapping noise before she got to the door. She turned around to see the electric stereo was in the water with Carlos. She screamed.

"Shhh, Sara," Angela said calmly. "It was instantaneous. Carlos is now in a better place."

"I'm calling for help," Miguel said, dialing his cell phone.

"Oh, I already called. A few minutes ago. To let them know that I was kidnapped and that we needed paramedicos. My cousin works with the federales here. Help is already on the way." She leaned over carefully and looked at the man. "That's one problem solved. One more problem to go."

"How is that a problem solved?"

Angela smiled.

Sirens blared in the distance, getting louder and louder.

"Who are you?" Miguel asked Angela.

"I'm the one who takes care of the hard stuff. Although Carlos here was my problem. My stepson from my first marriage. Always trying to muscle in on my business. Steal my money. And in my old age. I'm almost sorry to see him go, but I couldn't allow him to take over. And I'm not as sharp as I was."

There was a loud knock at the door.

"Now, Sara dear, go answer it. We'll see who got here first, federales or paramedicos. Let me do the talking. And don't worry about a thing. Tengo esto manejado. I have this handled."

Sara walked to the door, still stunned by what had happened. The paramedics arrived first, followed shortly by the police. The paramedics quickly confirmed that Carlos was dead.

Sara curled up on the couch, her arms around her knees as Angela talked. It was all too much. She could barely listen.

"He hit me over the head," Angela said weakly. "My stepson. He took a photo of me to get ransom money from my business partners. I escaped. " She sobbed as she told them the story, one policewoman stopping her at one point to try to calm her down.

The paramedics shone lights in Angela's eyes and listened to her heart. The cops looked at the photos of her on Carlos' phone. She told them about the $300,000 in the bank account and showed them the paperwork that he had wanted them to sign. "The speaker fell into the hot tub in the struggle. He's dead. Dead," Angela sobbed.

The policewoman put her arms around Angela to comfort her. Sara's phone rang, she moved away from it on the couch.

"We've been getting evil calls," Angela told the policewoman. She said everything in Spanish, then repeated it in English. "Sara's ex. He abused her. There's a restraining order in the States. His name is Richard Williams. He's a contract lawyer."

Sara was sure she had never told Angela her ex's name, much less that she had a restraining order against him.

"Can you answer the phone for me and put it on speaker?" said the policewoman. She punched a button on her phone to record.

"It might not be him," she said but did what she was asked.

"Hey, blue eyes." It was Ricky's voice.

"Hey."

The policewoman mouthed, "Keep him taking."

The other officer went into the other room with his radio.

"What do you want, Ricky?"

"Can you guess why I took your stupid dog into the shelter? Because I knew you'd change your contact information in her microchip. That's how I found you, your little friends, and your stupid little business. And now I own you, again."

Sara looked up. "What are you taking about? What business?"

"Sweet Revenge Hotline. Don't play dumb. Carlos and I came up with this little scheme together. By now you've signed the paperwork and you work for me. If I decide to let you live. And your stupid dog. As if you could ever get revenge on me."

The policewoman kept waving her hands at Sara. She knew she had to keep him talking, but she didn't know what else to say.

Then they all heard a dial tone. He had hung up.

The policeman came out of the other room, "Nosotras sabemos donde esta."

Angela gave Sara a big hug and whispered in her ear, "They know where he is. See, I told you that I do the hard work."

"But just because the Mexico police know where he is, doesn't mean they can get him in the States."

"Oh, he's here. Here in Tecate."

* * *

The federales arrested Ricky later that day for conspiracy to kidnap, fraud, and coercion. His lawyer failed to get him extradited to the United States before the trial or after. He was dealt a ten-year sentence, but he was shanked to death by another inmate over a donut in the sixth month of his Mexican prison term.

Carlos' death was ruled accidental.

Sara often marveled at the amazing luck she had that somehow Carlos had dragged Ricky into this scheme.

* * *

Luckily for Sara, Angela knew that in the real world you must make your own luck. She also knew that to pull off his plan, which she discovered early in its development, Carlos would need a crooked contract lawyer who would want a cut. She was only too happy to send him in Ricky's direction.

Her cousin made sure Carlos' death was officially ruled accidental.

The Sweet Revenge Hotline became a large and successful business which still runs today. If you call the number, you may still get Angela, Miguel, or Sara answering the phone with their signature greeting,

"Sweet Revenge Hotline. Tell me who's done you wrong, and I'll help you get even."

* * *

Deborah Lacy's short stories have appeared in *Alfred Hitchcock's Mystery Magazine*, the Anthony Award-winning Bouchercon anthology *Blood on the Bayou,* and many other magazines and anthologies. Her non-fiction byline has appeared in *Investor's Business Daily, MacMillan Publishing's Criminal Element*, and 24-Life. She has twice served on the committee for Bouchercon, the world's largest mystery convention, and once for Left Coast Crime. You can find her at deborahlacy.com

Dragos & Son

By Alan Orloff

Montreal, Canada

Rick Radovich stepped into the cavernous showroom. A dozen bookcases of different sizes and styles lined one wall. The opposite wall featured six fireplaces, some basic, some with ornately carved mantels. In the back corner, a spiral staircase with brass railings dead-ended at the ceiling, seemingly a stairway to nowhere.

Rick had never been in a place like this before, but he supposed this was exactly the type of showroom he should have expected from a company called Dragos & Son Secret Passageways, Inc.

Out of nowhere, a man materialized at Rick's side. *"Bonjour.* Hi. May I help you?"

Since he'd arrived in Montreal a few weeks ago, Rick had been pegged as an English-speaking American ninety percent of the time. Just as well, his high school French wasn't very *bien.* "Yes, please."

"I'm Goran Dragos, the 'Son' in Dragos & Son. Please call me Goran. And how may I be of service?" He spoke with a slight accent, but more Eastern European than French.

Goran was trim and tiny, dressed in a perfectly tailored three-piece suit, sporting a fresh haircut. Rick supposed his compactness was a definite boon for working at a place like this, where squeezing into tight spots was a job requirement. "Well, I suppose I'm here about secret passageways."

Goran reared his head back and laughed, as if Rick had cracked the best joke he'd heard in a month. "You've come to the right place."

A few people milled about. Rick lowered his head as he lowered his voice. "Is there someplace private we can talk?"

"*Certainement!* Please, this way."

Rick followed Goran to one of the faux fireplaces along the wall. Goran grabbed a candlestick on the mantle and pulled it toward him. The fireplace façade swung inward. "Watch your step."

They stepped into the hidden chamber, and Goran shifted into full sales mode. "As we go along, allow me to highlight a few items. This fireplace features our WhisperQuiet line of ball bearings, which employ Teflon coatings to minimize friction and noise." He pointed to a bookcase on their right. "This way."

Goran reached around the side of the shelving unit, tugged a lever, and the entire bookcase spun on its axis to reveal another secret entrance. "As I'm sure you've noticed, our EasyGlide sliders allow each revolving unit— be it a bookcase, grandfather clock, or sideboard—to operate easily and noiselessly. Let's squeeze through here, shall we?" Goran slipped behind the bookcase, with Rick on his heels.

A short walk down a dim corridor and Rick found himself at a dead end, staring at his reflection in a full-length mirror.

"Now what?" Goran shrugged theatrically, then tapped a spot on the bottom of the mirror with the toe of his shoe. The mirror dropped into a slot in the floor with barely a *whoosh*. "SilentSprings, at your service, a mainstay for our line of dropaway mirrors, sliding wall panels, and trap doors. Every piece of hardware is designed for both reliability *and* stealth."

"Follow me." Goran forged ahead and after negotiating several more fake-outs, false fronts, and retractable panels, they entered a small room where a table held a rack of slick product brochures.

"Have a seat," Goran said.

Rick sat. "Very impressive."

"I'm proud to say our company is the undisputed world leader—for the past fifty years—in designing, manufacturing, and installing secret passageways and hidden rooms." Goran paused his sales spiel to suck in a quick breath. "Now, is there something specific you came in for today?"

"Yes, there is. My father recently had a stroke, and he lives in this old house, and, well, there's always been rumors of hidden passageways and secret rooms and all that. I have no firsthand knowledge of them—my parents got divorced when I was two, and I went to live with my mother in Chicago. But there's no one to take care of him now, and..." Rick held out his palms. "Anyway, my father isn't very communicative and when I asked him about the rumors, all he could do was mumble, '*Something something call Dragos.*' It took me a while before I figured out he meant for me to call your company."

"I'm glad you did," Goran said.

"I guess what I'd like to know is if there *are* actually any secret passageways in the house. I've spent hours looking, but I don't really understand what I'm looking *for*, if you know what I mean. I figure you would be much better at this sort of thing than I would."

"Very true. There isn't a mechanism my staff hasn't seen or a contraption we haven't dealt with." His face brightened. "In fact, I'd be happy to investigate myself. Although I run the North America division, I'm always looking for a chance to get out in the field. I love a *bon mystere.*"

* * *

"Can I get you something to drink? Some tea?" Rick tucked the wool blanket under his father's chin.

Lech Radovich shook his head and a thin trail of drool dripped from his mouth onto the blanket. Rick could only imagine how difficult it must be for his father—his proud, strong, overbearing father—to accept his fate of being stuck in a wheelchair unable to say more than a few words. Unable to write. Unable to feed himself. Unable to go to the bathroom on his own. Unable to do just about anything.

He was once a mover-and-shaker in the business world, amassing a small fortune, able to buy anything he desired.

And now, a stroke. The great equalizer.

Rick sat in a leather club chair next to his father. Even though there must have been twenty rooms in the decaying mansion, his father always seemed to end up in the dark den. "I went to that Dragos place. They're coming by today to see what they can find."

His father tried to say something, but Rick didn't have the foggiest idea what. "You really think there's something valuable hidden there?"

Another nod, this time more forceful.

"But you can't remember what? Or where?" Rick had been through this before, and each time his father had insisted there were hidden treasures but that he didn't remember what they were or how to access them. Rick kept trying, hoping for that one moment of lucidity where the truth would emerge. A futile effort, it seemed.

Two more nods, then his father closed his eyes. A moment later, the gentle snoring began.

At half past nine, Goran Dragos arrived at the Radovich mansion, and Rick welcomed him into the grand foyer. Goran wheeled in several pieces of electronic equipment. "The latest in ground radar and echo location and a few other goodies that would impress even a NASA scientist. I'll poke around a bit and take some laser measurements of the entire structure, making sure things add up. Don't mind me, just go about your regular business." Goran raised an eyebrow. "I assume that I have free rein throughout the house?"

"Of course. My father is in the den, so don't be alarmed if you hear someone snoring."

"Your father! I would so love to meet him. I'll admit that I googled you after you left the other day, and I found that your father is from the same region as my family, back in the old country. You don't meet too many people who hail from Argonia and wind up here."

"Argonia?"

"Yes, a tiny region of what used to be Yugoslavia. It has changed hands—and names—many times in the past eighty years. My father still runs the company's worldwide operations from the same office he's been using for the past sixty-two years."

"I'd be happy to introduce you. But I should warn you, he's not very responsive."

Rick and Goran found Lech in his usual spot—in his wheelchair in the den, with the blanket pulled up to his chin. A Toronto Blue Jays baseball cap rested on his head.

"Lech." Rick had always called his father by his first name, a way to keep him at a distance, he supposed. He touched his father's shoulder to get his attention. "This is Goran Dragos. From that company you wanted me to call. He's here to look for the secret rooms."

"It's a pleasure to meet you, sir."

When Lech saw Goran, his eyes went wide, and he tried to speak, but no sound came out. One of Lech's hands appeared from under the blanket, and he pointed a crooked finger at Goran. Then he tried to speak again, and this time, there was an audible sound. "Funar."

"Funar?" Rick said. "What's that?"

"Funar is not a what. It is a who," Goran said. "Funar is my father's name. Uncommon here, but popular in Argonia. At least it was eighty years ago."

"But how—"

Lech said, "Funar," again, hoarse and gravelly, but this time with more conviction.

"I think he believes I am my father. I've been told I resemble him when he was my age."

"But how is that possible?" Rick asked.

"Perhaps our fathers knew each other in the old country."

Rick glanced back at his father, but Lech's eyes had closed, and it was back to dreamland.

Goran said, "I shall have to ask my father if he knows your father. What a coincidence that would be!"

* * *

Two hours later, Rick and Goran were alone in the den, ready to discuss the results of his preliminary investigation.

"I think you will be very interested in what I have discovered." Goran rose and went to one of the den's bookcases. He pointed to a book on the second shelf. *"Treasure Island*, by Robert Louis Stevenson. One of my favorites as a boy." Goran grabbed the book and pulled the top of the volume toward him. The bookcase revolved, creating an opening.

"Shall we?" Without waiting for an answer, Goran slipped behind the bookcase. Rick quickly followed. They didn't emerge in a passageway, but in a chamber, about as big as a bathroom. The floor was concrete. The walls were plain drywall. A single wooden chair stood in one corner.

That was it.

That was it? A secret room with a single, uncomfortable-looking chair? Rick's heart sank. Where were all the rumored riches? Jewels, a vault full of gold coins, stacks of cash?

"I can tell by your expression that you are disappointed," Goran said.

"A little, I guess."

A smile grew on Goran's face. "Well, don't be."

"I don't follow."

There was a single light switch on the wall, and Goran flipped it up. A portion of one wall slid aside, revealing a spiral staircase, headed down. He gestured to Rick. "Shall we descend?"

Rick's pulse quickened. "Absolutely."

Down they went. The spiral staircase wasn't long, and they alit at the end of a hallway. After the first step, a series of wall sconces switched on, shedding light along the entire passage.

"Motion-activated," Goran said.

Goran ran his fingers along the wall as he strode down the hall. He stopped at one of the sconces, then he yanked it back. A wall panel creaked open revealing a dark space within. Overhead lights flickered on. A hidden room beckoned.

Goran swept his arm toward the opening. "After you, Rick."

Rick stepped into the room. While the hallway and the upstairs chamber had been empty, this room was *full*. Paintings, sculptures, jewelry, and other types of valuables were everywhere—on the floor, on the walls, on tables and pedestals and shelves.

Rick gasped, and behind him, Goran gasped too.

"Well, this is certainly a surprise, *non?*" asked Goran.

"Unbelievable." Rick's nerves were jangling. Everywhere he looked, treasure. "I should probably complete an inventory before we start moving things."

"Yes, of course. I'll leave you to it. But there is something I need to tell you."

"What?"

"My measurements indicate that there is more."

"More what?"

"More hidden passageways and rooms, approximately one thousand square feet worth. Remarkable, really. Quebec is full of castles, many patterned on those in Europe, but we don't usually see secret annexes this large in North America."

"Where is it all, then?"

"That cinder block wall at the end of the hall? Seems your father built it to seal off the remainder of the complex. I don't know exactly what's behind it, but there's only one way to find out." He tilted his head at Rick. "You do wish to proceed with the project, *oui?*"

"Sure." Rick was certainly intrigued, although he couldn't imagine what more could be hidden.

"Perfect. My team and I will return in the morning."

* * *

After Goran had left, Rick plopped down on the floor of the treasure chamber with his laptop. He'd heard the rumors—for years at family events—but he'd never really believed them. Just figured they were part of the mystique surrounding his eccentric father. Of course, finding the treasure trove just sparked a thousand questions. Where had they come from? And why were such valuable and beautiful items hidden away in what was essentially a subterranean tomb?

Rick dove in and began to catalogue all the valuables, taking photos and conducting web searches. He was able to identify the majority of the items, usually by their pictures. Most were listed as "purchased at auction by anonymous bidder." Obviously, his father.

Lech had been amassing this impressive collection for decades without anyone knowing about it.

Rick continued his inventory. A few pieces of gold jewelry—rings featuring a wolf's head—were grouped together, and after going down several internet rabbit holes, he was able to identify them as part of a larger grouping, The Argonian Collection, whose two main pieces were gold statues of a wolf and a wild boar. There was no valuation indicated; the listing simply referred to them as priceless. The entire collection had been stolen from a Parisian art gallery in the eighties, in a high-profile heist, and the pieces had never been recovered.

It was ludicrous to think his father had been involved in the theft, but had he purchased the stolen goods knowingly from the thief?

There was a lot about his father he didn't know.

Rick kept a running tally of ballpark price estimates, and based on what he'd learned, it wouldn't be crazy to think that everything together was worth upwards of ten million dollars.

When his father passed away, all of it would be his.

What the hell would he do with it?

***

By the time day dawned, Rick had examined all the valuables and packed them away. Sweaty and physically exhausted, he managed to grab a few hours of sleep before Goran and his crew arrived. Armed with demolition tools, they got to work knocking down the cinder block wall. Rick stayed upstairs, out of their way, but the incessant pounding and jack-hammering and *whirrr* of power saws were inescapable, no matter where in the house you tried to hide.

His father, however, remained semi-comatose, unperturbed.

At noon, Goran reported to Rick. "After we gained access by knocking down the wall, we discovered many passageways and hidden rooms, but—unfortunately—we have not found anything else of value. We are not quite finished, but do not get your hopes up."

Rick wasn't really disappointed. "That's okay. We've already found plenty."

"Indeed," Goran said. "By the way, your father used devices manufactured by our company, but for some unknown reason, this installation doesn't appear in our records."

"And that's unusual?"

Goran shrugged. "My father ran the North American office when it was first established about fifty years ago. He may recall the reason."

"When you ask him about that, please remember to ask if he knows my father," Rick said.

"You can ask him yourself. I'm picking him up from the airport today and bringing him directly here."

* * *

Later that afternoon, Goran returned from the airport with the elder Dragos. "Rick, this is my father, Funar. He flew in specifically to speak with your father and to inspect this installation."

"It's a pleasure," Rick said. Goran and Funar seemed to have come off the same assembly line. Small, compact, a sense of confidence. Of course, Funar had a few more miles on the chassis, and he spoke with a pronounced accent, one Rick couldn't remember ever hearing.

"The pleasure is mine." Funar bowed his head slightly. "I remember this home. Such character."

"You've been here?" Rick asked.

"My company installed all the secret passageways and hidden rooms," Funar said. "This was my first job in this country. I have returned to see how it has held up over the years."

"But how…?"

"I knew your father a long time ago, back in Argonia. We were from the same village and became close friends. He settled here first, and I followed a few years later, to start up operations." Funar cleared his throat. "I am terribly sorry to hear of your father's condition. I would very much like to speak with him."

"He's not always alert."

"Let us try." Funar bowed slightly again. "If that is okay."

* * *

Lech Radovich was in his usual spot in the den, slumped in his wheelchair, covered by a blanket, eyes closed, mouth slightly open. A faint whistling noise accompanied every breath.

"Lech, wake up." Rick jostled his father's shoulder.

Nothing.

Rick shook a little harder. "You've got company. From Argonia. Funar Dragos."

His father grunted, then his eyes fluttered open. It took a moment, but when he saw Funar, his entire face came alive. He worked his lips, trying to say something, but nothing intelligible came out.

"I think he remembers you," Rick said.

Lech sat up a little straighter and brought his hands out from underneath the blanket. He strained to speak, emitting gurgling sounds.

Funar stepped closer. "I am sorry you are in such an unfortunate situation, my old friend."

Lech's face got redder. More sputtering and flying spittle.

"I shall get straight to the point, Lech," Funar said. "I know that you think we are, how do you say, *squared away*, but that is not the case. You owe me…" Funar glanced at Rick, then concentrated again on Lech. "You know what you owe me. And if it is here, I shall find it and take it as mine. It is only fair."

127

Funar inched even closer, got right in Lech's face, and spoke rapidly, insistently, in a different language, full of harsh consonants and clipped syllables.

Whatever he was saying wound Lech up, because he responded by gesturing wildly with his hands and gurgling, still trying to speak. Unfortunately, it was all sounds and saliva.

"Stop it." Rick pushed between his father and Funar. Some friends. Maybe his father had been saying *DON'T call Dragos* the other day. "You've agitated him."

Funar stepped back and smoothed the front of his suit jacket. He switched back to English. "Forgive me. My manner was unacceptable. But my message was clear. Your father owes me something. I did not come all this way to go home empty-handed. Mark my words."

"What is it?"

"I am not at liberty to say." Funar's face was as cold as steel in a snowbank. "But it belongs to me."

* * *

Later, Rick met Goran in the driveway. He'd just finished packing up all his team's gear into his van. "Done?"

Goran nodded. "Essentially."

"What does that mean?"

Goran shifted from foot to foot. "Well, according to our volume calculations, we have discovered virtually all of the secret space."

"Virtually?"

"Yes. A very small percentage of the calculated area has not been accounted for."

Rick liked all his Ts crossed and Is dotted. "And this discrepancy is okay with you?"

He swallowed. "Ordinarily, we would double-check our work and figure it out."

"So why aren't you doing that now?" Rick's irritation grew. When he paid for a job—especially when the price was borderline exorbitant—he expected it to be done properly.

"Most likely, it is simply a mistake on our part. Besides, I have the feeling that it would be best if we left the premises—all of us. In fact, I sent the techs—and my father—home hours ago. Your father seemed quite upset earlier. Regrettably, my father can have that effect on people. He is very, uh, direct. On behalf of the company, I apologize for his behavior."

"You could complete the job without him."

Goran offered a rueful smile. "My father would not stand for that, and he is the company president. Your father and my father are similar, so you may know what I mean. If they wish something, it is very, very difficult to say or do otherwise. It took me quite a lot of convincing to get him to leave." He sighed. "Rick, I am sure it is nothing important. A rounding error, perhaps."

Rick hated loose ends, but he figured Goran had done the right thing. "Before you go, do you have any idea what your father thinks my father owes him? He was pretty angry. I thought they were friends."

"Who knows?" Goran's expression soured. "Probably a cheap watch worth fifty dollars. You know how stubborn old goats can be. It is a shame, but sometimes friendships go bad. I believe it best if both parties go their separate ways and never meet again. Your father deserves to live his last days in peace."

* * *

The thing about stubborn old goats was their predictability. And even though Rick had just met Funar Dragos, he felt he knew the man intimately. Just a carbon copy of his own father. Rick's mother had been telling him stories about Lech for decades, and Rick had been paying attention, even when he pretended he couldn't care less.

Rick had known Funar Dragos was up to something, the old man's rage-filled tirade playing in Rick's head. *Mark my words.* So after Goran and the others left, Rick did some investigating. First, in the house itself, where he'd noticed that the back door was unlocked, and the alarm system had been disabled. Then, he'd gone down into the labyrinth of secret passageways but couldn't find the "missing" area. Was it really a rounding error? Or something more?

All of which led him to his current stakeout in the den.

Now, approaching four a.m., he heard noises before he saw movement.

He'd been awake this whole time. Watching. Waiting. For a stubborn—and angry—old goat on the prowl.

Across the den, Rick finally spotted the dim glare of a headlamp, bobbing as the figure made its way toward him. When the interloper was five feet away, Rick cleared his throat loudly. The beam of light shone his way.

"Lech! What are you doing awake?" Funar's accent seemed more pronounced in the middle of the night, in the dark.

Rick slumped in his father's wheelchair, a blanket covering his entire torso. He wore his father's baseball cap, too, and his chin rested on his chest. Only the corner of one eye was visible to Funar. Rick simply grunted.

"The ravages of a stroke are terrible," Funar said. "And for it to have rendered you speechless! If I took delight in these sorts of things, I'd be delighted now."

Rick resisted the urge to pop out of the wheelchair and slug Funar in his smug face.

"As promised, I am here to claim what is mine. What *you* promised me all those years ago. And there's nothing you can do to prevent me. How does that feel, being completely and utterly powerless? It is how I have felt all these years, knowing you have what belonged to me and there was nothing I could do about it."

Rick grunted again.

"It is only fitting, what with your impending demise. Why should the spoils of our brilliant theft die with you? I know you were ashamed of what we did, once you learned the truth, but you also were naïve. Only two people in the world know about the hidden chamber you insisted I build for you, and only one person can access it now. Me. Soon, the collection will be whole again. And in my sole possession."

Rick pretended to be agitated for a moment, then grunted again as Funar activated the revolving bookcase and disappeared through the secret passageway.

As soon as he'd disappeared, Rick tossed aside the blanket and ditched the cap. Off he went after Funar, slipping as quietly as possible into the hidden chamber. He paused, listening for Funar's footfalls on the spiral staircase. When they'd stopped, Rick tiptoed down, after him.

He stopped at the bottom of the staircase and peeked around the corner, down the long corridor. Funar was at the end, past where the cinder block wall had been. Rick watched him take a screwdriver from his pocket and pry open a small panel in the wall, about shoulder height. Then he reached in and flipped some kind of switch.

A portion of the wall *whooshed* aside. Funar dropped his screwdriver and entered the hidden room.

Rick dashed down the passageway, whipping around the corner of the chamber Funar had just entered. Funar whirled about, clutching an object.

The golden Wolf of Argonia statue.

"I knew you were up to something devious," Rick said. "By the way, that doesn't belong to you."

"It doesn't belong to you, either." Funar's knuckles turned white as he gripped the statue.

"Hand it over, Funar."

Funar's eyes shot past Rick, searching for an escape route, but Rick blocked the small chamber's only entrance.

"You think you are so smart, but you do not fully understand." Funar spat out the words. "Your father and I, we engineered one of the biggest art heists in history to get this. It belonged to us in the first place!"

"You're saying that the statue belonged to *you*?" Rick asked.

"To our *people*. The Argonians. The golden Wolf of Argonia is part of our heritage, stolen from our people and put in a French museum, along with its mate, the Wild Boar. We protested to the officials involved, but our voices were not heard." Funar displayed an expression of disgust worthy of a Broadway actor.

Rick's bullshit meter spiked. "Is that the story you told my father to get him to help you with the heist?"

A flash of surprise sparked on the old man's weathered face, then it was gone. "It is the truth. Your father and I could not let that heinous theft stand. An affront to our country. So we wormed our way through some long-forgotten catacombs beneath the museum to pull the heist. I'll be damned if I'll die without returning it to Argonia, where it rightly belongs."

"And you'll do what with it, put it in an Argonian museum? Surely that's where a national treasure belongs. I suppose the statue of the wild boar is there too."

One of Funar's eyebrows twitched. "Impossible. The owners of the French museum would come after it, claim it as stolen property belonging to them. No, I would keep it in my possession. Keep it safe." He pulled the statue close to his chest.

"Very noble of you," Rick said. "But I don't think so."

Something shifted behind Funar's façade. "Step aside, Rick. No one has to know of this. The rest of the treasure is yours. Your father would have wanted me to have this."

"I don't think so. That was me in Lech's wheelchair just now, under the blanket and ball cap, and your taunting revealed your true desire. You're not taking the wolf." Rick sprang forward and grabbed the statue from Funar. Then he shoved him to the floor and darted out of the small chamber. He hit the switch on the wall and the door closed. Rick picked up Funar's screwdriver and jammed it into the electronic controls until the switch shorted out with a puff of smoke, effectively sealing Funar inside.

Rick ascended the spiral staircase, ignoring Funar's calls for help. Back in the den, he sank into a club chair to figure out his next moves, but it was difficult to think straight with Funar screaming to be let free, audible even from a floor below.

Luckily, Funar ran out of steam in about thirty minutes.

Rick mapped out his plan. Once his father died, he'd sell all the legally purchased valuables and start a charitable foundation. Something in the arts, most likely.

He'd move into the mansion and restore it to its former glory. Upkeep had never been his father's strong suit.

The last decision was the most difficult. What about the exquisite golden wolf? Had Lech sealed it up to prevent Funar from getting it? Had his father thought it better to keep it from everybody, rather than let Funar have it? Was Lech so ashamed of what he did?

Rick would never know what his father's true motivations had been; all he could do was plow ahead and try to make things right. He would return the wolf—and the rings from the Argonian collection—anonymously to the Paris museum where they belonged. He knew Funar would be infuriated— white hot, in fact—seeing the statue back on public display, instead of in his trophy case.

A fitting punishment. But would that be enough? Should he tell the museum where the golden wild boar statue resided? Rick would have to think about that, but he doubted he'd rat on the old goat, afraid that when cornered Funar would implicate Lech in the heist too.

As much as he despised Funar, Rick was not a murderer; he knew he would let Funar go eventually.

Maybe in the morning?

Rick headed upstairs to get some much-needed sleep.

Or maybe the day after?

* * *

Alan Orloff has published eleven novels and fifty short stories. His work has won an Anthony, an Agatha, a Derringer, and two Thriller Awards. He's also been a finalist for the Shamus Award and has had a story selected for *The Best American Mystery Stories* anthology. Alan's latest suspense novel is *Sanctuary Motel*, from Level Best Books. He lives and writes in South Florida, where the examples of hijinks are endless.

www.alanorloff.com

Death at Dunarven: A Jane Bennet Mystery

By Annie R McEwen

Hertfordshire, England, 1811

Had Jane known there'd be murder for tea, she would've arranged to be elsewhere engaged on that day. Everyone invited would have done the same, especially the victim.

She'd spent the previous week sitting by her mother's couch—it was always something with Mother, vapors, flutterings, sinkings of the heart—and returned to Netherfield just in time to wave goodbye to her husband as he set off for business in London. The house seemed very empty after Charles departed. Not for the first time, she wished Pemberley were closer or she closer to Pemberley. Her sister Elizabeth was a peerless companion and Jane missed her sorely.

After a few days of moping, the invitation to tea at Dunarven arrived like sun on a drear day. She would go, of course. Tea at the manor home of the Marquess and Lady Carmody was always pleasant, sometimes even interesting.

She hadn't the slightest flicker of doom as she dressed. Humming 'Gathering Peascods,' she dropped a sprigged muslin gown over her head and buttoned a pelisse against the slight chill of late summer. Along the grassy, familiar path from Netherfield, her worst fear was of having to endure the vicar's prattle about theology.

As it turned out, the vicar was nowhere in sight at Dunarven when she reached there. Jane gave her bonnet and pelisse to a footman and smothered an urge to look pleased. Not that a pleased look wouldn't have company. Three other guests were loudly committing the same social sin when she entered the drawing room.

"We shall take our pleasure without benefit of clergy." Sir Anthony Gillette, loud as usual, and hinting at something indecorous. The skittering laugh that followed belonged to Lady Marjorie Ennis. The dowager viscountess simpered and smiled at everything Sir Anthony said, encouragement he could use less of.

Constance Guindere Carmody, Marchioness of Dunarven and a friend to both Charles and her, rushed forward, hands outstretched. "Here is lovely Jane, just come over the fields with roses in her cheeks and—" Lady Carmody dropped her eyes, as did Jane, to the wet slippers soaking into the Tabriz carpet, "—damp on her shoes. Come, dear, sit by the fire and remove that exquisitely useless footwear before it is stained beyond repair."

Jane protested futilely, a sparrow twittering at an eagle. Installing herself on a hassock by the hearth, she did as she was ordered and untied her soft kid slippers. As though magically summoned, the footman who'd taken her bonnet in the foyer appeared with a white towel. Deftly swaddling the slippers like an unwanted infant, he whisked them out of the room to some place where shoes are rendered more presentable. Jane tucked her feet under the hem of her gown and strove to look unperturbed.

"We were speaking of the Reverend Mr. Harbuckle, and where he could have gone so precipitously." Lady Marjorie's voice fluted and whispered by turns, concern and curiosity curdling like milk and cider in a syllabub. "I think it most uncivil, to say he will come to tea and then not arrive."

"Nor send a note of regrets," added Lady Carmody. "Most unusual. I've asked Ferris, my gamekeeper, to make a circuit of the grounds in case our guest is loitering somewhere with his pipe and a theological treatise." With a vexed sigh, the marchioness gazed out the long windows into the garden.

Perhaps she thought the vicar was hiding among the roses.

Lady Carmody turned suddenly to Jane. "What say *you* about our absent vicar, lovely Jane?"

She did so wish Lady Carmody would stop calling her 'lovely Jane.' There were many young women more handsome than she. Even now, incorrigible blonde ringlets escaped her hair dressing, and she was painfully aware of the freckles marching across her nose and cheeks.

She forced her feet a few more inches under the hem of her gown. "The vicar is, I believe, in the vicinity of sixty years. Perhaps…" Delicacy demanded a tactful pause, but the stares of her companions rode roughshod over it. "Perhaps Mr. Harbuckle suffers from an indisposition?"

"Nonsense!" If Sir Anthony's bellow didn't rattle the windows it was only because they were generously sealed with putty. "The man's as hale as I am at five and forty. Though he lacks, of course, the physique with which I have been blessed by a lifetime of vigorous sport." Sir Anthony thrust out his chest and placed his fists on his hips like a pugilist assessing an opponent. Lady Marjorie rewarded the effort with a deep blush. In a woman well over forty, the color incited alarm over the state of her circulation.

Lady Carmody put an oar in. "He was well at service on Sunday, or so I presumed since his homily on The Usurpations of Reason demanded both stamina and wind."

"A suggestive title, that," Sir Anthony barked like a happy wolfhound. "Perhaps the vicar's own reason has been usurped."

"*Our* vicar? Oh, really, Anthony. By what cause?"

Sir Anthony's ruddy face creased in a leer. "The usual. *Cherchez la femme.*"

Lady Carmody laughed, hearty and genuine. "Anthony, you dear ass, even you cannot believe our vicar would—why, at his age and station!" Silence followed, each of them conjuring and then trying to banish a mental picture of the hoary cleric in some wanton's embrace.

A ruckus in the hall broke the silence. Muddled voices preceded a rap at the drawing room door, followed instantly by George, the first footman. George's face was white as his powdered wig. He stood just inside the door, mouth working soundlessly.

"Well?" snapped Lady Carmody. "Has Ferris found Mr. Harbuckle?"

The footman's reply emerged low and tremulous. "Ye-es, Your Ladyship. But the Reverend—he—I—"

With visible effort, Lady Carmody spoke levelly. "Where. Is. The vicar?"

George's eyes widened in his ashen face. "Mr. Harbuckle is in the folly."

"In the—?" If the footman had told her the vicar was seated on the Stone of Scone, the marchioness couldn't have shown more amazement. Jane was likewise at a loss. The folly? The vicar was Nature's sworn enemy. He abhorred anything that might soil his pristine linen or expose him to spider webs and damp. She visualized Dunarven's folly a half mile from the house. A vaguely Gothic architectural mishap, open on three sides to cold, rain, and windblown leaves.

The marchioness huffed. "Perhaps he's taken up meditation, like one of those Eastern mystics. Tell him to join us in the house. We shan't hold tea forever."

George's mouth opened and closed twice before he stammered, "Th-that will not be p-possible, your ladyship. Ferris has c-conveyed a most distressing—there are circumstances—if Her Ladyship would care to—" The footman waved toward the lawns and Lady Carmody clucked once, loudly, like a bothered hen.

"As usual, I must take things in hand. Do not trouble yourselves," she said to her guests and then, to the footman, "Lead on, George!" He scurried out of the room, bowing, and his mistress followed.

Nothing promotes flight so well as an order to stay put. Lady Marjorie and Sir Anthony made for the door, scuffling genteelly for precedence at the threshold. Jane, with her damp feet, was thankfully forgotten. She had no interest in vicar hunting.

She stretched her feet toward the fire and wriggled her toes. Some minutes, perhaps a quarter hour, passed quietly, and wisps of steam began to rise from her stockings.

Peace never lasts, whether in war or Hertfordshire. Through the open drawing room door, she watched the house servants commence an odd parade, sprinting to and fro in the hall. There was a general air of panic. First the second footman—Henry, she thought his name was—jogged toward the front door. Then the butler strode purposefully in the same direction, only to wheel around and stride back into the house, muttering loudly enough to be heard in the drawing room. Next the housekeeper went past, bleating like a worried ewe and waving a large handkerchief. On her heels scurried two chattering housemaids who peered into the drawing room, saw Jane, and halted in their tracks. They dropped a curtsey in unison, like automata, then fled back toward the lower reaches of the house.

Clearly something more extraordinary than a wayward vicar was afoot. Jane no sooner thought it than George streaked across the hall from the front door like a liveried greyhound. She jumped to her feet.

"George!" Her shout brought him to such an abrupt halt he skidded on the waxed parquet floor. He held his wig in his hand, his stubbly shorn head looking incongruous atop the rich uniform of his station. While his face had lost the pallor of a quarter hour earlier, he now bore a livid spot of red on each cheek.

"Madam," he choked out, struggling to install his wig as he entered the drawing room. It sat ludicrously awry on his head like a floured hedgehog.

"Where are you going, George?"

"I—her ladyship asked me to send a boy to the village and, from thence, a man to Meryton."

"Meryton? Whatever for?"

"For the Justice of the Peace, madam."

Jane's mind raced. "There has been some untoward event."

The footman nodded, miserably. "Yes, madam. As untoward as may be."

"I am not given to fainting, George. What happened?"

George gulped mightily, as though swallowing a plum pit. "The vicar, madam. A grievous accident. It's quite horrible, madam, but he is—he is—"

"Are you trying to say dead, George?"

The footman nodded, more miserably than before.

"How?"

The footman's cheeks went redder, then blanched again.

"*George.*" Her tone was as good as a jab with a hatpin.

"Stabbed in the heart," the footman blurted, "with a kitchen knife."

Hence the Justice of the Peace, Sir Robert Witherspoon. Jane's mind was galloping like a steeplechaser. *What would my sister do?* Lizzy was the quick one in crises. But Lizzy was at Pemberley and Jane was here.

Even in extremity, it was unmannerly to order someone else's servants about. Ignoring that, Jane spoke firmly to George. "Fetch the boy and put him to his errand. Calm yourself. You've had a terrible shock and there's no great hurry at this juncture. Mr. Harbuckle is unlikely to decamp and Sir Robert is two hours away if he's a minute. Is that the housekeeper I see sniffling behind you?" George's head whipped over his shoulder, dislodging his wig even more.

"Yes, madam. Mrs. Philpot, that is."

"Good." She gestured to the housekeeper, a thin woman of middle years who moved timidly into the room, twisting a handkerchief. "Mrs. Philpot, please stop strangling that nice square of linen and come forward. George, what are you waiting for?" The footman bowed sketchily and bolted from the room. "Mrs. Philpot. Take me to the servants' hall, please, if that is where the greatest number are at this hour."

"Yes, madam, they'll be there, most of 'em. Cook had just laid on our tea and we've not had so much as a bite nor a sip."

Jane's stomach was sympathetic; she'd had no lunch. "Show me to the servants' hall, then, please."

She added nothing about discovering how the vicar ended up in the folly with one of Cook's knives in him.

* * *

In the servants' hall, the staff rose with a general scraping of chairs along the long wooden dining table when they spotted her over Mrs. Philpot's shoulder. Rigidly polite, everyone pretended not to see Jane's stockinged feet. Their faces were grave and their plates empty, despite the smells of stewing tea and mutton.

"Please pardon my intrusion upon your tea. An extraordinary event has occurred. We must respond with extraordinary measures." Jane looked along the table at servants young and old, fresh and weathered, scullery and house maids, footmen, grooms, gardeners, cooks, the butler standing stiffly at the head and an empty place at the foot where Mrs. Philpot would be were she not at Jane's side.

"Might you tell me, is anyone not present who should be?"

Only a few heartbeats passed before a very young housemaid spoke. "Yes, madam. It's Hazel. She's been gone since afore I woke, madam."

At the head of the table, the butler—Simpkins, she recalled—bridled. "Perhaps if the young person had spoken of this sooner—"

Jane held up her hand and addressed Simpkins. "Is Hazel a housemaid?"

"A *lower* housemaid, madam. Taken on this past winter and not long in service, though her character was acceptable. From Yorkshire, I believe."

"Lancashire," piped the maid who'd spoken before, "like me."

The remark earned her another sharp look from Simpkins. *It's violent death, Simpkins. Perhaps custom can be put aside for a few hours?*

"The young person's name is Alice," the butler said sourly to Jane.

"Alice." The girl colored as Jane's eyes, along with everyone else's, fixed on her. "Are you Hazel's friend?"

"We share th' attic room, madam. Have done these past eight months."

Jane looked up and down the table but no one else volunteered anything helpful. "Simpkins, I'd like Alice to show me the room she shared with Hazel."

Simpkins' response was a bow, followed by a brusque jerk of his chin in Alice's direction. The maid alternately flushed and blanched as she came around the table. Together, she and Jane made for the back stairs.

Some minutes and a number of narrow and steep staircases later, she and Alice all but pulled themselves hand over hand up the narrowest and steepest of them all. At the top was a dormer room.

The room was so small the door had to be pushed shut from the inside to allow the two of them to stand within. The back of the door held wire hooks for clothes. Two hooks held plain cotton nightdresses. A third held a white apron and matching cap. Hazel, wherever she was, wasn't in uniform.

There was a battered oak commode with a wash basin and pitcher atop it, and a very tiny window. Two narrow beds sat a few feet apart. One bed—Alice's, she guessed since the maid stood by it—was neatly made. On the other, the thin coverlet and worn sheet were pulled down nearly to the foot, and the pillow retained a hollow where Hazel's head had rested last night.

"Didn't you notice when you woke," Jane asked, "that your friend's cap and apron were hanging on the door?"

"No, madam, not at first. When door is full open, them hooks lay against wall. There be only one other attic room in this wing, and it be empty just now. Bein' warm up here, Hazel and me keep door open. For air, y'see."

She saw. A garret like this would be an ice cave in winter and a sweltering mouse hole in summer. The single window was dirty and nailed shut.

Which also explained the odor. Jane's nose had wrinkled the second she entered. Going to the commode, she opened its lower cabinet and found, as expected, a chamber pot. A very full one. The contents gave off a singular tang.

Time to press Alice for details. "Your friend was gone from the room when you woke." The girl nodded, looking more hunted than sad. "Missing, as well, at breakfast." Alice nodded again, her eyes filling. "Yet you said nothing to Simpkins or Mrs. Philpot."

"No, madam. I didn't think overmuch, at first, about it. She hadn't sat to breakfast in some weeks, y'see. Mind, she were never one to eat much in the mornin', Hazel, on'y a bit of toast and tea. But for a month or more she's left off even that. When I asked, she said she weren't hungry." Alice sniffed, used a corner of her apron to wipe her nose, and then looked embarrassed. "I thought she were frettin' about her figure, madam. Her dress 'ad got that snug, of late, she couldn't do it up at the waist. She were coverin' the gap with her apron strings."

Jane looked hard at the maid but couldn't see deceit or evasion in the weepy eyes. Pushed much harder, she'd probably burst into tears and be no use at all. She was very young, fourteen years or a bit less. A country lass so fresh she knew no better. And she'd think no ill of her friend, possibly the only one she had in a great house full of servants, all strangers.

"Alice, had your friend spoken of leaving Dunarven, of taking employment elsewhere? Or returning to Lancashire?"

Alice bit her lower lip. At length, she answered cautiously, as if afraid to say too much or too little. "I never heard aught of her goin' home, madam. Nor that she was hopin' for other employment. If she did want another position, she'd not have left without a character."

Alice's logic was unassailable. Without a reference, her friend's prospects were few at best.

The maid chewed her lip again, then very hesitantly offered, "She did say, well, mentioned, like, that she might be done with service altogether."

They both became quite still at that, considering how a country girl could make her way without money, well-placed friends or relations, or marriage. Jane's mind circled the last possibility, though it seemed remote.

"Had Hazel a suitor, Alice?"

The girl chewed her lip so vigorously Jane feared she might draw blood. At length she blew air through her lips and said, "I can't see how, madam. We had just the half day free, an' we spent it together. Exceptin' that an' church, we was never off the estate. Where would she meet a sweetheart? An' who might it be?"

"Dunarven is vast, with many workers. The gamekeeper Mr. Ferris—one of his lads, perhaps? Or an under-gardener? A groom, a stable hand…"

"No, madam, I can't see it. If it be one o' the men servants, Mr. Simpkins would know straightaway, him bein' that sharp. Mr. Ferris, even more, an' none of the lads is missin'. No, madam, I can't see it at all."

Was she truly that naive? Or was she hiding the knowledge that Hazel had sloped off with a man, any man. "Never mind, Alice. We'll go back to the kitchen now, shall we?"

* * *

In the servants' hall, the table was empty, a scullery maid scouring it with a brush. Alice made a quick curtsey and turned to go, but Jane stopped her.

"Alice, one more question, if you don't mind." The girl turned back with wide eyes. "You and Hazel are both from Lancashire, you said. Are you from the same place in the county?"

"No, madam. I'm from Whalley and Hazel's from Barrowford."

"Barrowford. Is it a large place, do you know?"

"Not over large, madam. Hazel's father, though, he's right well known, as he owns th' one smithy. Hazel was that proud of him and he'd taught her somethin' of the work, he havin' no son and his wife long dead. Were she a boy, Hazel always said, she'd have never gone into service. She'd have stayed to home, working along with her Da'."

"A smithy in Barrowford. A handy thing to know if I were in Lancashire and my horse—lost a shoe. The family name?"

"Wheelcock, madam."

"Thank you, Alice."

The girl curtsied again and hurried away. Jane drew a deep breath, letting it out slowly. She padded her way silently up the stairs, went through the green baize door, and crossed the hall to the drawing room.

Her slippers, dried and brushed, were neatly placed in front of the fireside hassock. She barely got her feet into them when a rout burst into the room. The Ladies Carmody and Marjorie and Sir Anthony, all talking at once. Several servants trotted behind them bearing the tardy but most welcome tea.

Pandemonium ensued. Lady Marjorie screamed at intervals like a parrot, Sir Anthony bellowed about the state of lawlessness in England, and Lady Carmody called for "More tea, George! More cakes!" Despite the turmoil, the others were ghoulishly pleased to tell her about the vicar's death. She forebore to say she'd learned the whole story from George while they were still gawking at the corpse.

Happily, no one asked her to respond, only to sit by the fire and look lovely. She did, enjoying her warm toes and an even warmer cup of China tea. Servants came and went, laden with trays and dishes. The windows gradually fogged from food, drink, and gabble.

After a time, Lady Carmody addressed her directly. "Dear, lovely Jane, it's most distressing that such horridness should mar your visit. Such a shocking thing and the darkest mystery, as well! Our vicar, *poor* Reverend Mr. Harbuckle, as neat a man and as fine a cleric as you'd find in the breadth of England, murdered just as though a London footpad had sent him to his end."

Sir Anthony jabbed the air with a scone. "Wallet gone, mark you, and a cracking gold watch and chain I have many times noted on the vicar's waistcoat. Worth five guineas any day, I should think."

"We are none of us safe!" Lady Marjorie clutched the fine garnet necklace at her throat as though expecting *banditti* to rise any moment from the teapot.

"I believe we're in no danger." Jane calmly placed her teacup on the nearest table. "The person who sent the vicar to Judgement is by now some distance away and concerned not with death but life."

"Oh, Jane, angelic child." Lady Carmody spoke as though addressing a five-year-old. "You cannot take in this villainous event, can you?"

"Villainous? Perhaps. Certainly sad. But we all heard Sir Anthony reveal the tragic core of the event earlier."

The squire managed to display both confusion and pride. "We did? That is—did I?"

"*Cherchez la femme.*"

Confusion won out in Sir Anthony's face. "Yes, but I wasn't—see here, are you truly suggesting that a woman could have done such a deed? That a woman could have driven that, that *tool* so deeply into a man's chest as to rupture his heart?"

"Not every woman, perhaps. But a strong young woman, one brought up from childhood to help her father at his forge, a young woman inflamed and made powerful with rage, a young woman, moreover, who has been used and discarded along with the child she bears…" In the shocked silence, Lady Carmody filled Jane's teacup out of habit. "*That* woman could send her seducer to Perdition with a sewing needle. Luckily for her, she had a cook's knife to hand."

"Who is this avenging female, Jane?" Lady Carmody asked, "and how in the name of Heaven do you know these sordid facts, if indeed facts they are?"

"As to the second point, I simply asked a few questions of the servants and made some surmises from their answers. As to the first, she is one of your maids, Lady Carmody. A Lancashire lass of just fourteen years, Hazel Wheelcock by name. She has fled and by now is well on the road to—London, probably. From there she'll go abroad, I imagine."

Lady Carmody's cup and saucer landed on the table with a sharp rattle. "She must be found, she must be apprehended! When Sir Robert arrives, you shall relate all this to him, Jane, every word! He will send men into all the countryside hereabout. They will find the girl and take her in charge!"

"Ah, yes, that's one way to handle it. Justice should be served." A general susurration of approval rose. and Sir Anthony gave a vigorous "Hear, hear!" Jane waited ten seconds. Then she shrugged slightly and spoke.

"The affair will, of course, be very noised about. The capture of the girl, the trial, her piteous and very visible condition, her youth, her country innocence. Her frail form a-tremble in the dock, the iron chains on her wrists, her sobs and those of her blameless father... A widower, I believe, and the girl his only offspring, his sole joy and comfort for years. And how interested the public will be to learn of the intimate attention the late Reverend paid to a girl hardly more than a child."

She shook her head sadly. "Pity poor Dunarven, its master and mistress. However unknowing of the vicar's true nature, and however undeserving of guilt, they may be smeared by..." In the profound quiet that followed, Jane took another sip of tea and sighed. Deeply.

"Fleet Street hounds are a hard lot," she began anew. "Wolves who hunger for the meat of notoriety. They will—as they invariably do—scent the scandal and come howling down upon the locals. With them will come, I fear, the broadsheet writers, the gossips low and high from every lane and every manor, from the whole county. From the *ton*."

"Heaven preserve us!" Lady Carmody gasped, pressing her plump hand to her bosom.

"It'll be unavoidable, I'm afraid. Some—no worthy person, I'm sure, but the countryside is lamentably well-stocked with unworthy ones—will even suggest that since the business transpired here at Dunarven and the late vicar was a particular friend of the household… Well, as I say, no *right*-minded person would think anyone here was involved, but—"

The marchioness shot to her feet. "Harbuckle was a libertine, a rake! I never trusted him!"

"True, I'm sure. But *some* will observe that the affair took place under this very roof. Er, the folly roof. That being the case, *some* persons might infer that the household knew—"

"Nothing, we knew nothing! A serpent in our midst, that's what Harbuckle was! An ungrateful, odious, deceptive, low-born, ill-favored mountebank!"

Placidly, Jane smoothed her skirt while she thought about taking a second slice of seed cake and Lady Carmody simmered like a teakettle. "Exactly so," Jane finally breathed out, reaching for the cake, "and that being the case, why should the noble name of Dunarven be sullied by such a wretch?"

The marchioness sat heavily. She blotted her brow with a napkin. "*Newspapers.*" She hissed the words with the same venom she'd say *harlots* or *actors*. "To think Harbuckle was among us for more than a year, drinking our tea, eating our scones, boring us with his sermons. All the while debauching a young woman while we *never* suspected—"

"No fault of yours, Lady Carmody." Sir Anthony drew himself up, ready to defend the manor from an invasion of hacks and gazetteers. "Deceived us all, the blagger."

"And a man's foes shall they be of his own household." Everyone gawped at Lady Marjorie, the last person they'd have expected to spout Scripture. "To think he placed his hand on mine, the last time he was in this very room." She withdrew a fan from her reticule and flapped it vigorously.

Casually, as though noting the hour or the weather, Jane said, "There are always vagrants about at this time of year."

"The very thing!" Sir Anthony sang out. "Sleeping rough in every hedgerow and field, worrying the servants at the back door."

Lady Carmody took the next verse. "Cook told me she chased a pair of them out of the kitchen garden last week! Nasty, thieving things."

"After the plate, I should think," rumbled Sir Anthony darkly, "and whatever else they might lay their hands on."

Lady Carmody recovered her martial spirit. "I shall tell Sir Robert about them, I certainly shall! To think they were on the grounds all this time, waiting, marking their chance—"

There was a reprise of *appalling!* and *despicable rogues!* Jane applied herself to a third slice of cake.

An hour later, the sun was low but still gave enough light for her homeward walk across the fields. After the close and clamorous drawing room, it was pure delight to breathe country air and feel grasses swiping at her hem. She buttoned her pelisse against the cool of the waning day, then swung her reticule by her side and pondered what she had done. Was it right? Was it just? Was it the letter of the law? Perhaps not the last, but she'd seen the law do things neither right nor just in following its letter.

She might not tell Charles about the afternoon's adventure. She might not even tell Lizzy. Everyone agreed that Lizzy possessed the family's quickest wit and sharpest mind. Thus it had always been and Jane had no wish to see that change. She was only an accidental investigator, after all. Chances were excellent she'd never investigate anything again.

She'd wait a decent interval and then find a way to bring Alice, the young maid she'd put in the wretched position of betraying her friend, to her own employ. Never good form to pinch a servant, but the girl would never again be happy at Dunarven. And Jane needed a lady's maid. Charles had offered to ask his sisters, Miss Caroline Bingley and Mrs. Louisa Hurst, to find someone, but Jane declined. She tried daily, sometimes with success, to increase her affection for those proud relations, but she'd rather find her own maid.

By the time Alice was in place, there'd be much for her to do. Jane wasn't entirely sure she was increasing but another week or two would tell. She spared a thought for Hazel Wheelcock's bleak future. Abandoned, alone, disgraced, with child—was that not punishment enough? If Hazel and her infant survived the birth, would her child's face not remind her every day of the violence to which shame and betrayal had driven her?

Coming over the last rise before Netherfield, Jane reminded herself that she was blessed. Home, husband, family, health, means—all hers. Cresting the hill, she saw a fox peering at her from the edge of the copse and spoke to it. "I shall have no more adventures!"

Down the hill she went toward home.

***

A career historian, **Annie R McEwen** has lived in six countries and under every roof from a canvas tent to a Georgian Era manor house. Annie's books are published by Harbor Lane Books (US), Bloodhound Books (UK), and The Wild Rose Press. When she's not in her 1920s bungalow in Florida, Annie lives, writes, and explores castles in Wales. Find Annie at:
www.anniermcewen.com
https://facebook.com/Quillist/
https://www.instagram.com/anniermcewen
YouTube: @anniermcewen

The Voynich Manuscript

By Bev Vincent

Zürich, Switzerland

When the stranger bursts into his hotel room, Rick is lying in bed reading a paperback novel he bought at JFK while waiting for his connecting flight to Zürich. Before Rick has time to react, the man lunges. The book absorbs the tip of a hunting knife aimed at his heart. When his attacker withdraws the weapon, presumably to stab again, the book goes with it.

Fueled by adrenaline, Rick takes advantage of the man's momentary confusion to leap from bed. He grabs the first thing he sees: a desk lamp with a marble base. Sparks fly from the socket when he yanks the cord from the wall. With his first swing, he knocks the knife—and book—from the man's hand. Without hesitation, he strikes again, making solid contact with the man's temple, dropping his assailant to his knees. As the man attempts to regain his footing, Rick delivers a coup de grace to the back of the head. The man collapses. Blood seeps into the carpet around him.

Adrenaline coursing through his body, Rick drops the lamp and sits heavily on the bed, attempting to regain his composure. After a few deep breaths, he kneels next to the fallen man, checking for a pulse. He can't find one.

With a trembling hand, he picks up the phone. He should call the police, but he doesn't know the Swiss equivalent of 911. Besides, his limited German isn't up to that sort of conversation. Instead, he punches the button for the front desk.

The manager appears a few minutes later, wringing his hands and expressing dismay over the situation. He is apologetic, but Rick can tell the man is suspicious of his story. Rick can't blame him. There's a dead man on the floor of his hotel room, after all.

After the manager retreats to phone the police, Rick perches on the edge of the mattress again to allow a wave of nausea to pass. A few minutes later, he hears klaxons approaching. Soon, the small room is filled with men and women barking at each other in Schweizerdeutsch. The officers examine the body and ask Rick questions, but their English isn't much better than his German. The broken door frame supports his assertion that he didn't invite his attacker into the room, but that doesn't negate the fact that he killed the man.

The officers allow him to get dressed. They retrieve his passport from the hotel safe and take him by car to the Criminal Investigation Division on Zeughausstrasse. His story only takes a minute or two to tell, but he has to repeat it several times—through a translator, to people who don't appear to believe him—then answer the same questions over and over. Finally, the chief detective takes over the interrogation, showing him a piece of paper containing his name and room number, found in the dead man's pocket. He asks Rick how—not if—he knew his attacker. Then he asks what the man said after he entered the room.

"He didn't enter. He broke in. And he didn't say anything," Rick tells him. "He came at me with a knife. If it wasn't for my book, it would be me who's dead." The last time he saw the paperback, it was on the floor with the knife still protruding from it, labeled with a small fluorescent yellow cone bearing the number 4.

The detective fans out several pictures of the corpse, eyes closed, mouth slack, blood visible behind his left ear. "I don't know him," Rick says. The detective shrugs when Rick asks the man's name. Either the police haven't identified him yet or they don't wish to share that information.

He tells the detective he obtained a Master's degree from the University of Zürich five years ago and he's in town attending a retirement symposium for his mentor, Paul Muller. He's supposed to deliver the keynote lecture at the university later that morning.

"The subject of your talk?"

"My translation of *The Voynich Manuscript*. It's a medieval book people have been puzzling over for over a century." He walks them through his movements since he arrived in Zürich. When he mentions the Australian woman who sat next to him at the fondue dinner at Adler's the previous evening, the chief detective sits up straight.

"Her name's Clare," Rick says. "She's a postdoc at the University of Berne. Her supervisor's a friend of Professor Muller's."

"You knew her before?"

"No. I don't even know her last name."

"After dinner? What then?"

"We window-shopped along Bahnhofstrasse and sat on a bench on the quay at the edge of the Zürichsee. She wanted to watch the swans swimming in the moonlight."

It was, in fact, a memorable evening. Rick enjoyed Clare's company and, when he escorted her to her hotel around midnight, he'd hoped to be invited in—a detail he doesn't share with the detective. However, she merely smiled and said she looked forward to his lecture before disappearing inside. Rick wonders how she'll react when the police show up at her hotel to confirm his story.

"After that," he says, "I walked back to my hotel. I couldn't get to sleep, so I read. Jetlag." The translator's rendering of the last word has several syllables.

"Perhaps a jealous boyfriend?" the detective suggests.

Rick hasn't considered that possibility. All he can do is shrug.

After signing a formal statement, he is escorted to the CID building's exit. His passport has been impounded pending further investigation and he is forbidden from leaving the canton. He catches a tram to Limmatplatz and another to the Irchel stop near his hotel. During the ride, he tries to process everything that happened over the past several hours. When he remembers the sound of the lamp striking the man's head, queasiness overtakes him again.

His room is still being processed by the KTA, the Swiss forensics division. The day manager informs him that every other room is occupied. Without a passport, getting new accommodations won't be easy, and he has no luggage.

It's still early, a little past seven. With nowhere else to go, he takes the footpath up the hill to the university. At the top he surveys the cityscape to the south, punctuated by church spires, the gleaming lake and the distant Alps. This was his favorite view when he used to live here. In the early morning sun, the snowcapped mountains seem to levitate above the horizon, a meteorological condition called "föhn" the Swiss blame for headaches, depression, argumentativeness and suicides. In some cantons, föhn could be used as a mitigating circumstance for committing a crime. He keeps that in mind in case he's arrested.

He turns away from the panorama and trudges along the path to the lecture hall. In the lobby, he sees Clare, sprawled in an armchair reading the symposium program, sunlight highlighting her honey blonde hair. She's a few years younger than Rick, with pale blue eyes he'd found enchanting the night before. When she sees him approaching, a smile brightens her face. "Looks like you had a rough night. Did you go on a pub crawl after you left me?"

"Rough—I'll say." He summons a smile. "Have you had breakfast?"

"Yup, but I wouldn't mind another cup of coffee." She glances at a wall clock. "We have loads of time."

They cross the street to a fast-food restaurant. He orders a breakfast sandwich and two coffees. Clare grabs the cardboard cups and heads for the condiment stand. "Black?" she asks. "Or mit milch?"

"Right the first time." He grins. "Thanks."

When his sandwich is ready, he carries his tray to the upstairs dining area, where Clare is already seated. The chrome décor casts a surreal aura over the bright room, a phenomenon Rick attributes to his lack of sleep.

Sitting across from Clare, he takes a sip of the robust coffee, already feeling his head starting to clear. "I thought the police might have been to see you by now." She gives him a perplexed look. "Someone tried to stab me at the hotel last night. My room's a crime scene."

Clare's eyes widen as he tells the rest of the story. "I woke up early this morning, so I went for a walk," she says. "I haven't been back to my hotel since. What was this guy after?"

Rick shrugs. "I don't know. And the police won't tell me who he is—if they know."

"That's incredible," she says, reaching across the table to rest her hand on his. "You could have been…wow. To think, I almost asked you—last night—you know, but…" She looks down, her face burning red.

Rick finishes her thought. "But we just met."

"Exactly!" She doesn't move her hand, and stares straight into Rick's eyes.

While he debates raising the jealous boyfriend theory, he notices a thin man in a dark blue suit at a nearby table. He's staring at the *Neue Zurcher Zeitung* without seeming to read it. A leather document portfolio sits on the table beside his coffee cup.

Rick tells himself he's being paranoid. The man isn't watching him. "We should probably get back," he says, although he'd prefer spending the rest of the day enjoying Clare's company. "Can't be late for my presentation."

She nods and drains her coffee cup. Rick carries their trash to the recycle bins, taking time to figure out the complicated sorting system. If he simply throws everything away, he will be rewarded with disapproving looks, clucking tongues and shaking heads.

Joining Clare at the top of the staircase, he suppresses the urge to take her by the arm. Slow and easy, he tells himself.

"Entschuldigen, bitte," someone says from behind.

Rick turns.

"Der Mann sagte mir, das ist dein." An elderly woman is holding a portfolio that looks like the one from the stranger's table.

"What man? Wer?"

The woman gestures toward the table where the thin man was sitting, but it is empty except for his abandoned newspaper. She shrugs. "Er ist weg."

"Danke schön," he tells the woman.

Clare runs her finger over the LV embossed on the golden brass lock closure. "This is Louis Vuitton," she says. "It's worth about two grand."

"A case of mistaken identity, I guess. I'll turn it in to one of the cashiers."

"No nametag," Clare says. "Maybe we should look inside for ID."

Rick rests the case on the banister. "It's probably locked," he says, but the tab pops open with an audible click when he pushes the button. The smell of expensive leather envelops him when he lifts the flap. Inside he finds a manila folder with his name written in marker on the tab. He and Clare exchange glances. She holds the case while he flips through the file.

The top document is a copy of the symposium program with the title of his lecture highlighted. "Cracking the Mystery of *The Voynich Manuscript*" by Professor Richard Wright, Yale University. Beneath are drafts of articles he's preparing for the *Journal of Cryptography* and the *Journal of Medieval and Early Modern Studies*. The only other copies in existence are on his office computer in New Haven and on the flash drive that also contains his presentation. He pats his pocket to confirm it's still there. The file folder also contains his CV, a printout of his academic web page, numerous photos of him leaving from and returning home taken during the past two weeks, according to their timestamps, and copies of e-mail correspondence with colleagues about his breakthrough.

"This is too weird," Clare says. "We need to tell someone."

But who? Rick wonders. The local police won't appreciate the invasion of privacy the file represents. All they would do is ask more questions, and he's had enough of that for one day. He takes the portfolio from Clare, shoves the folder inside and fastens the latch, struggling to catch his breath. Someone is stalking him. The man who broke into his room wasn't a jealous lover and he wasn't working alone. Whoever is behind this has been outside his home, in his office, and has rifled through his papers and his computer—and they aren't done with him yet.

"Maybe Paul Muller will know what to do," he says.

As they descend the stairs, Rick keeps the case clenched under his left arm. Clare surprises him by taking his right hand in hers. Their fingers interlace. He squeezes her hand and smiles as they retrace their path to the university.

They find Rick's mentor outside the auditorium. Paul Muller is sixty-five and sports a full head of snowy white hair. He is short and stocky, with a bulbous nose holding up dark-rimmed glasses that do little to obscure his bushy eyebrows. "You had some excitement last night, I hear," Muller says in a thick Swiss accent after they shake hands.

Rick laughs. In Switzerland, everyone knows everyone else's business. He remembers how invasive it seemed when he lived here, being scolded by a neighbor for doing his laundry on Sunday mornings, reporting to the Kreisbüro when he changed apartments and having to carry his alien identification card everywhere he went. "A little," he says.

"Do you need help straightening things out with the police?"

"Maybe," Rick says. "They still have my passport."

"Ja, that is normal," Muller says. Rick rolls his eyes at Clare. The Swiss accept without question anything they consider normal. "They will return it in due course," Muller continues. "Things like this do not happen here so often. Already it is on the news. We should talk, though." He looks at Clare. "Do you mind if I borrow him for a few minutes?"

"I'll meet up with you in the auditorium," Rick tells her. He follows Muller to a quiet corner. "Someone is following me," he says. "I think it has to do with *The Voynich Manuscript*."

"I believe you are right. This morning the department chair received a call threatening violent reprisals if you were allowed to speak."

"What?"

"We received similar warnings after we announced that you would be presenting your work here."

"Why didn't you tell me?"

"We thought it was nothing, really. The Planet Voynich Society. Kooks. But perhaps now they are dangerous kooks."

During his research into the manuscript's history, Rick encountered the PVS, conspiracy theorists who touted the book's elfin script and enigmatic sketches as evidence of fifteenth century alien visitations.

"If your research exposes the cult leaders as charlatans, they stand to lose much. I regret to tell you this, Rick, but the university regents have decided to cancel your lecture. They are not willing to take the chance that anyone will be harmed."

Rick is about to protest, but stops when he realizes nothing he says will change the mind of cautious Swiss administrators. He keeps his hands from clenching through sheer force of will. Muller isn't the person he should be angry with. The problem is, he doesn't know where to direct his frustration.

"You understand, I'm sure," Muller says. "The organizers will make the announcement momentarily. You will be able to relax for the rest of the day. Over Zürigschnätzlet, rösti and some good wine this evening, we will laugh about this."

Rick suppresses a sigh and forces a smile. After they shake hands again, he heads toward the amphitheater in search of Clare. As he pushes his way through the crowded foyer, someone snatches the Vuitton portfolio from under his arm. When he turns, he sees the man from the restaurant heading for the exit. Rick contemplates giving chase, but the man might be crazy or dangerous—or both. If he talks to the police later—and he has no doubt he will—he'll decide whether to report this incident. At least he has Clare to back up his story about the case and its contents.

"Ist hier frei?" he asks Clare when he finds her in the amphitheater, recalling a phrase he often used when traveling by train as a student. He tries to smile to hide his disappointment and consternation, but she frowns at him.

"What's up? Did you give Professor Muller the portfolio?"

"It's not that," he says. He is about to explain when one of the event organizers takes the stage to announce that, due to circumstances beyond their control, Professor Wright's lecture has been canceled.

Clare grabs his hand. "Because of what happened?" she whispers.

"Yeah. That and the fact that they received death threats."

"That sucks," she says, squeezing his hand. "Seriously."

"Thanks. I've been looking forward to presenting my findings here. Muller encouraged my sideline work on the manuscript, even though he probably thought my chances of success were slim." Rick shrugs. "It was to be my way of paying tribute to him." Now people were probably speculating that Muller had scrutinized his interpretation and found it lacking. Eventually the truth would come out—that he'd unraveled a mystery that confounded code breakers and historians for decades—but not today.

A woman behind them makes a shushing sound. Rick and Clare exchange knowing grins. Clare leans over and whispers into his ear. "Let's blow this popsicle stand. We can go to Jelmoli and gorge ourselves on cervelats and Mövenpick ice cream."

He follows her as she squeezes past other attendees. Their departure after the surprise announcement is bound to set tongues wagging, but so what?

When they reach the lobby, he says, "I must look like a mess. I've been up all night, I'm wearing the same clothes I had on yesterday, and I haven't had a shower in two days."

"If the police still have your room sealed, where are you staying?"

"I'll find a place later, I guess. Somehow"

She chews on her lower lip. "You can pick up some things at Jelmoli and shower at my hotel."

"Lead on," he says.

On the way down the hill, Clare takes his hand again and urges him to run when they see a tram approaching, panting and laughing like teenagers. The tram is crowded, so they end up standing, bumping against each other when the train lurches around a corner. Clare doesn't seem to mind. Rick certainly doesn't. She drapes her arm around his waist to steady herself. He feels almost human again.

After visiting the huge department store, where Rick buys a change of clothes and some toiletries, they head to Clare's hotel. His nerves tingle while he showers, acutely aware of her presence on the other side of the flimsy door. After he's done, Clare says he can leave his discarded clothes in her room. Rick doesn't say anything but is thrilled by the promise of a return visit.

They walk back to Uraniastrasse. At a kiosk outside Jelmoli, he buys two fat, pink cervelat sausages with thick slices of crusty bread and packets of brown mustard, and a couple of bottles of water. They find an empty park bench facing the crowded sidewalk and busy street. Before Rick has a chance to take a bite, someone sits beside him. "I assume you looked inside the case, Professor Wright?" the man in the dark suit says.

Rick can't identify the man's accent. "Who the hell are you?" he asks. Clare has her hand on his arm and is leaning against him. He can both hear and feel her breathing. His eyes dart back and forth in search of an escape route.

"If you publish your results, you will come to great harm," the man says. "We've been watching you for years. No one thought you would succeed, until we learned of the symposium. Agree to abandon your research and we will leave you alone. You must stop this foolish pursuit if you value your life." The man gives Clare a meaningful look. "And the lives of others."

Clare tugs at Rick's arm. He looks up. Two men are approaching. From the determined looks on their faces, Rick suspects Clare is right to be concerned about them. They need to make tracks—and fast.

He swivels and shoves the man off the bench onto the ground, then pelts him with his water bottle. Then he and Clare jump up and push through the crowd. Rick considers running into the department store, which has several floors where they could hide, but they might end up cornered. Even if store security came to their assistance, he can't expect them to fend off dangerous attackers.

He grabs Clare's hand and drags her around a corner. He regrets involving her in this crazy situation. Although he is their target, his adversaries might try to use her against him. He glances over his shoulder and sees the thin man in pursuit, but not his two cohorts.

"This way," Clare says, almost pulling him off his feet as she veers left.

With no time to discuss strategy, he follows without question. The side street isn't as busy, allowing them to pick up speed. Hand in hand, they emerge on Löwenstrasse. Wires crisscross the sky above them. When he sees the statue of railway magnate Alfred Escher and the red and white *SBB CFF FFS* sign ahead, he realizes where Clare is taking him.

The central train station.

One of their pursuers emerges from a side street with a cell phone in his hand. He's probably communicating with his colleagues, meaning to box them in, Rick realizes. He spots a blue and white tram approaching from the west. When it stops, it will obstruct the view of anyone behind it for several seconds. He yanks Clare across the tracks. The driver clangs his bell and waves a hand at them through the front window.

They elbow their way through the crowds in front of the high arched entrance into the hauptbahnhof. Angry voices chastise them. "Keep going," Rick says, pulling Clare toward the far exit. If they can get out the other side without being seen, their pursuers will waste valuable time checking the departure area to see if they're boarding a train.

Once outside, Rick notices a set of escalators that descend to the shopping arcade under the station. He remembers a novel set in the 1970s where a girl being chased by government agents takes her story to *Rolling Stone*. It gives him an idea. "This way," he says, leading her to the wide central staircase between the escalators.

"What are you doing?" Clare yells as they take the stairs two at a time.

People turn to look—the Swiss do not yell. Rick puts a finger to his lips, hoping to get out of sight before their pursuers emerge from the station. "Back here," he says when they reach the bottom, guiding her past a chocolate shop and a camera store to a shop that sells computers and telephones. He goes straight to a display of laptops and confirms they're connected to WiFi.

Rick pulls his memory stick from his pocket and inserts it into a USB port. He launches a web browser and navigates to the *CNN* page where people can submit pictures and video of breaking news. His fingers fly over the keys as he types a brief message to accompany his files. Then he grabs the mouse and uses the upload tool to select the documents from his drive, including his presentation.

A stocky teenager with bleached blond hair and a ring piercing his upper lip, wearing a blue shirt that identifies him as an employee, approaches to find out what Rick is doing. He says something in a thick Swiss accent that Rick can't process.

"Rick," Clare yells. When he turns to see what she wants, his heart drops. The man in the dark suit has her by the arm. His hand is in his jacket pocket, where an awkward bulge leaves Rick with no doubt that he has a gun.

"Move away from computer," the man says. "Or she dies."

Other shoppers turn to see what is happening. The kid with the pierced lip pauses.

"Move away, I said." The man pulls out his gun and fires into the ceiling. Screams erupt in the small shop. Some people head for the exit while others duck behind counters. Rick takes advantage of the pandemonium to click the mouse, accepting the site's terms and conditions. His hand is trembling, so it takes two tries. He has never been more afraid in his life. If he doesn't do something, he and Clare will be killed. "One more click and everything goes to *CNN*. Let her go. She's not involved in this."

The man stares at Rick for several seconds, then pushes Clare aside. She falls to the floor and cries out. "Give me the drive and no one gets hurt," the man says. His gun is now pointed at Rick.

Rick knows the man won't let him live. Even without his papers and files, he'll be able to recreate his work now that he knows the truth about *The Voynich Manuscript*. "The police will be here any minute," Rick says.

The man glances over his shoulder. "Give me the drive or I'll shoot."

Rick's index finger refuses to obey his command for a full second. Then it depresses the left mouse button. The resulting click is almost as loud as the gunshot that follows a moment later. Rick flinches, then realizes he hasn't been hit. Neither has the computer—the progress bar shows that five of the ten documents have been uploaded and the rest are in the queue. There's a tiny hole in the wall an inch above the monitor.

He looks up to see Clare struggling with the man, holding his arm in the air so the gun is pointed at the ceiling. Several bystanders leap to her assistance and bring the man down. His gun clatters to the floor. Two men stand over it but do not touch it. By the time the first police officer arrives, the man has been subdued.

"There are two others," Rick tells the officer, and provides their descriptions. "They sent a man to kill me at my hotel last night. They're probably armed." The officer speaks into a radio on his shoulder, then handcuffs the shooter.

Clare is standing alone, away from the crowd. Rick goes to her and takes her in his arms. "Are you all right? You saved my life." She clings to him, and he returns the embrace. Then he leads her to the computer and puts a finger in the hole in the wall. His files have finished uploading. This isn't how he planned to publish his results, but it will have to do.

"You attract trouble," a man says. Rick recognizes the detective who interviewed him earlier.

"I never thought medieval literature would be so harrowing." Rick says, struggling to catch his breath.

"We have some questions, as you might expect. For you too, fraulein. This way, please."

The young man with the pierced lip emerges from the front counter. Rick doesn't understand what he's saying.

"He's asking if you'd like to buy the computer you've been using," the detective says.

Clare laughs. "Typically Swiss. Always business first."

"Nein, danke," Rick says.

Rick takes Clare's arm. As they walk toward the escalators with the detective, his cell phone vibrates in his pocket. The caller ID says "CNN Atlanta." After a brief conversation with a network producer, he turns to Clare and asks, "Wanna meet Anderson Cooper?"

* * *

Bev Vincent is the author of several books, including *The Road to the Dark Tower* and *Stephen King: A Complete Exploration of His Work, Life and Influences.* He co-edited the anthology *Flight or Fright* with King and has published over 120 stories, with appearances in *Ellery Queen's, Alfred Hitchcock's,* and *Black Cat Mystery Magazines.* He has been published in twenty languages and nominated for the Stoker (twice), Edgar, Ignotus, and ITW Thriller Awards. To learn more, visit bevvincent.com

A Warm Moscow October

By Nina Mansfield

Moscow, Russia

It was 1995 and Moscow was dripping with capitalists. And not just the ones with Amerikanski dollars in their pockets.

There were the babushkas in the metro stations hawking fish in one hand, and *Playboys* in the other. There were the grizzled kiosk men who sold canned vodka, and the home-brewed stuff I'd been warned against. And there were the well-dressed women who strutted down Tverskaya Street, willing to step into your car if you flashed enough cash.

And of course, there were all those clean-shaven, wrinkle-free young men, barely out of business school, ready to make Mother Russia great again.

Cigarettes were cheap and the ruble unpredictable.

But this story doesn't start in Moscow.

I was young and stupid then, and Moscow was still one of those places I'd only dreamed about. It was like some forbidden city, stuck far behind a wall for much of my childhood. I'd graduated *cum laude* with a Russian Lit major from Yale, and had moved to New York. I was waiting tables and pretending to be a writer. I wanted to write like Tolstoy. Instead, I was on my feet all day, forcing smiles at ass-grabbing customers so I could pay my rent. I took on extra shifts so I could make a dent in my student loans. I had no time to write.

I thought I knew who I was and what I wanted out of life, but that was a lie. If you'd asked me then, I would have said I was looking for romance. I'd read enough thick Russian novels to know better, yet I still believed it was possible to find love that wasn't abysmally tragic. I wanted to find my very own Pierre. I wanted Vronsky to walk into the ball before I settled down with the wrong man.

My mother had always told me it was just as easy to fall in love with a rich man as it was a poor man. Why my mother didn't think that maybe I was capable of making my own money, I couldn't quite say. In any case, I had no interest in the rich boys at Yale, reeking of overconfidence and the stench of Daddy's money. Most of the guys I'd met since college bored me, and the ones who didn't were on a track to nowhere. Maybe it's because I fancied myself a storyteller, a free spirit, but I had a penchant for attracting the unhinged. There was Gary, the gray-eyed actor who was always asking to borrow money. There was Josh, the photographer who took lousy headshots and snorted too much coke. There was Viktor, the petty criminal who claimed to work for the Russian mob, with whom I fell stupidly in love. And when I fell in love, I'd do anything for a guy.

And then I met Misha. I couldn't tell if he was already rich, or just planned to be. We met at a too crowded party on the Lower East Side where I didn't know a soul. Something about him made me hold my breath. He had blue eyes I wanted to swim in, and a look that said he wasn't afraid of anything. I wouldn't let myself fall for him. No, I'd already fallen in love one too many times. But then we got to talking Tolstoy. He'd actually read *War and Peace* in Russian, which he spoke fluently.

"Anyone ever tell you that you look like Anna Karenina?" he asked.

No. No-one ever had, but I had recently radically altered my look.

"I mean before she jumped in front of the train," he clarified.

It was the worst pick up line I'd ever heard, but it worked.

Two weeks into our affair, he told me he was leaving for Moscow. He had some business dealings there. I knew he liked long showers, cornflakes in the morning, and his steak rare. I also thoroughly knew his comings and goings, since I had made myself very comfortable in his bedroom most mornings and nights. But it had never occurred to me to ask him what exactly he did for a living.

"What kind of business?" Did I even want to know?

He rattled off something about the emerging Russian stock trade.

"I've always wanted to go to Moscow," I said, half-heartedly hinting he should take me.

"Like Masha, Olga and Irina, all pining to go to Moscow. They never do go, do they?" he said.

But I wasn't some tragic Russian heroine, as much as Misha wanted to cast me in the role.

I pulled him back into bed. "Take me." Suddenly, it seemed like the perfect thing to do.

"You aren't serious. I'll be back in a few weeks."

"I don't want to wait a few weeks," I said.

"Wait for what?" he asked, like I was planning something. Then he kissed me gently on the forehead. "It wouldn't be a good idea."

"Planning a hostile takeover?" I asked.

He smirked. "Maybe."

"Do they even have a word for that in Russian?"

"They will soon enough."

"How long will you be gone?"

"I don't really know," he said. "I'll be busy all day."

"And all night?" I slid my hand up his thigh.

"Would you really go to Moscow with a man you barely know?" he asked.

I told him I would, if he'd go to Moscow with a woman he barely knew. Misha knew less about me than I knew about him.

It took me two more days to convince him. "You aren't going to give me a choice are you," he finally relented.

I thought about a paper I'd written about Dostoyevsky and free will. He said he knew a guy who could expedite my visa application. I told him I had a friend at the Russian Consulate.

One week later, we were sharing a room at the Hotel National on

Tverskaya. Red Square was just a short stroll way. We could see the Kremlin from our window.

My first doubts about the wisdom of traveling to Moscow crept in as we were unpacking. I'd stuffed comfortable shoes and assorted lingerie into an old Samsonite, a confused blend of tourist and mistress, trying to play some part I wasn't entirely suited to. Misha had a garment bag filled with crisp suits. I lounged on the brocaded red bedspread, still glassy eyed from the overnight flight and drifting off. Half asleep, I watched him hang clothing in the closet. Then I gazed with bewilderment as he slid his hand along the top shelf of the closet, as if looking for something he knew would be there. I grew alert as his arm tensed. He'd found something.

He pulled down a compact, metallic object.

"Is that what I think it is?" I asked.

Misha turned. "I thought you were napping."

I continued to look at the gun in his hand. For a very brief moment, I thought he might turn it on me.

"Doing business in Moscow is dangerous," he said.

"But a gun? Did someone leave it here for you?"

"I didn't think it would clear customs. One of my business partners has a connection at the hotel," he said, as if needing a gun was par for the course.

Perhaps my mouth hung open. Perhaps my body froze. I can't say for sure how I reacted. Things were more dangerous than I expected. He sat down on the bed and took me by the hand. "Look, just a few years ago they put men like me in prison here."

"Men like you?"

"Entrepreneurs. Now, they like to kill off the competition."

"Do you really think someone will try to kill you?" I laughed nervously.

"Don't worry. This isn't a play. Chekhov's gun doesn't need to go off."

We made love with the red curtains drawn and the Kremlin in view. A thought passed through my mind. Something about getting screwed by capitalism. Too exhausted from our travels and sex, we ordered meat pies and champagne from room service.

The next day, I slept in. When I woke, Misha was gone. He left me a map of the metro system, a thick roll of rubles and a note. "I'll be back tonight. I've locked our passports in the safe. Leave the room key with the front desk if you go out. Don't take cabs, they aren't safe. Metro and trolly are fine. You're a smart girl, you'll figure it out."

There was something I needed to figure out, and it wasn't the Moscow Metro system. I first checked the closet. Then his drawers. I searched the inside of his garment bag. Of course he kept his suitcase locked. And I didn't have the key to the safe. He might have left the gun behind, or he might have taken it with him. I wasn't sure which I preferred.

I switched on the television while I tried to come up with a plan for the day. There were Spanish telenovelas dubbed into Russian on one channel. News on another. The delivery of the anchor man was clipped and mechanical, almost without inflection, and very difficult for me—despite studying the language in college—to comprehend. There was something about a hijacking. Something else about the state of the Russian economy. I wondered how sanitized the news was, how scrubbed of content. Would they report the murder of an American business man? Would that make the news here?

That day, I walked through Red Square. I stood in line to see Lenin's embalmed corpse. I strolled through GUM, Moscow's premier department store. There were moments when I got lost in the sights. I wished I had a disposable camera, but I hadn't brought one along. I was enthralled to be in a country that I'd read so much about. But even the sight of St. Basil's couldn't make me forget. Misha had a gun.

Maybe I should have stuck to dating penniless actors.

That night, Misha took me to dinner at a Mexican restaurant on Tverskaya. The salsa tasted like ketchup but the margaritas were good. We debated Raskolnykov's state of mind in *Crime and Punishment*, the student who is consumed by remorse after murdering his landlady.

"Not everyone would be so guilt-ridden," said Misha. "It's possible to commit the crime without the punishment."

"And you?" I asked. "Could you kill someone without feeling guilty?"

"It depends on who and why," he said.

"Yes," I agreed, and for some reason, hoped that this was true.

Misha ordered another round of margaritas. He kept looking over his shoulder, as if expecting someone to enter. He eyed the assorted characters who sat at the bar. A group of students slowly sipping beers. A tall guy with an unnaturally blonde woman. And a man with a rumpled suit, thinning unwashed hair, and an ashtray full of cigarettes. The man's face looked like it had been molded out of mashed potatoes. Misha stared at the man a little too long.

"What kind of business dealings are you involved in, exactly?" I asked.

"We're buying up shares in a successful steel factory. The workers don't want to sell."

"So it's Communism vs. Capitalism?' I asked.

"Not that simple. The Russian mob is involved. So it's really capitalism vs. capitalism. The workers just don't know it."

"So will people lose their jobs, their livelihoods, if the deal goes through?" I asked. Misha shrugged. "Does that bother you?"

"It's the way of the world. There are winners, and there are losers."

"And that makes it okay?"

"Look, I'm not going to be the one firing them," he said.

"So, it's okay if you don't pull the trigger?"

"I suppose that's one way to look at it."

"But why the gun?" I asked.

He told me about a couple of businessmen who'd been shot down in a night club the week before while attempting to broker a similar deal.

"And if someone came in here right now, and pulled a gun on you, what would you do?"

"Strike first, if I could." Misha opened his jacket slightly. He was armed and ready to kill.

The next day, when Misha was out, I took the metro to Gorky Park. It was a warm Moscow October, and I only needed a light jacket. The park was much bigger than I had ever imagined, and I wandered for hours. I couldn't help but think about the novel of the same name, but I wasn't looking for bodies, I was looking for clarity. How much was I willing to risk for love? And what kind of woman was I if I could so easily fall in love with a man who could…what? No one had been killed yet. Maybe no one would be.

I swung by a kiosk on my way home, and asked the toothless man who worked there for his strongest home brew.

That night, Misha insisted we stay in.

"Our deal is getting very close to closing, so perhaps I'm just being extra cautious. But I'm fairly certain someone is following me," he said. He described a chain-smoking man. "He has a unique face. All pudgy and white. Like…"

"Like mashed potatoes," I offered.

We stayed in the next few nights. I still played the tourist during the day, even though Misha asked me not to. I explored the streets around Tverskaya. Walked up to the Pushkin monument. Admired the architecture, the alleyways. Misha would come back to the hotel each night and lock the door.

But we couldn't stay in the hotel forever. Chekhov's *The Seagull* was playing in rep at the Moscow Art Theatre, and I convinced Misha we should go.

"No one's going to attempt an assassination in a crowded theater," I said.

Misha wasn't so sure. "Um…Lincoln," he said.

"You're not Lincoln. Besides, they would need to know that you'd be there. They would need to know where you're sitting. I got the tickets this afternoon. You'll be safe."

I'd read *The Seagull* many times, but I'd never seen it performed. Poor misguided Nina, the actress who didn't know what to do with her hands, falling in love with the wrong guy. I knew how she felt—playing a role I wasn't entirely suited for.

Our seats were in a private box. "I'd feel safer down there," Misha said, motioning to the seats below.

"I thought this would be more romantic," I said, taking his hand in mine. The two of us looked down at the theater where Stanislavsky got his start.

The production was sparser than I'd imagined, or maybe it just appeared that way on the large Moscow Art Theatre stage. Chekov's gun was introduced in Act I. Misha gave me a knowing glance. We both knew it would go off before the end of the play.

I spotted the mashed potato faced man during intermission. He was at the bar sipping champagne. He gave me a little nod. I pretended not to notice.

"Should we get something to drink?" Misha asked, wrapping his arms around me.

"I'm not thirsty," I said. "I think we should get back to our seats."

I'm fairly certain that most of the audience knew the exact moment in Act IV when the shot would ring out. And still, they gasped.

I turned to see Misha's reaction. But he just twitched and slumped forward ever so slightly. I supposed if I'd looked closer, I would have noticed the blood trickling down from the back of his head.

I stopped breathing for a moment. When my lungs started working again, I almost choked on my own breath. I looked behind me, but the mashed potato faced man—if that's who'd shot Misha—was already gone. I supposed he'd timed his shot with the one on stage. But he'd used a silencer. A small caliber gun. This was all speculation. What did I know about such things? I had studied literature.

I had to get out of there. We might have been sitting in a private box, but surely someone would notice Misha's slumped figure. In any case, I needed to escape before the show ended, before the police were called. As the audience rose to their feet for a standing ovation, I raced down the stairs, out the door, and into the Moscow evening. Cool air had replaced the warm.

I headed onto Tverskaya. The street was crowded. Cars honked at expensively dressed women. Men flashed cash at them. "Funny, they don't look like prostitutes," I thought.

Back at the hotel, I retrieved my passport from the safe. I'd made sure to get the key from Misha earlier that night. It wasn't my real passport, of course. I'd been traveling under an assumed name. My bag was already packed. I wiped down the room, even wiped down the key. I thought about taking a swig of the homemade vodka I'd bought the other day, but no. I needed a clear head.

A car was waiting for me on Mokhovaya Street. A man who didn't look at me when he spoke drove me to an apartment where I could shower and change my clothes. Then he drove me to the airport, where I boarded a flight to London. There, I checked into a hotel near the airport. I dyed my black hair back to its original blonde. Misha was right—with it black, I did look like Anna Karenina. I flew back to New York under my real name.

Viktor, the petty criminal I'd fallen in love with—the one who did in fact work for the Russian mob—was waiting for me at the airport.

"You did well," he said.

"Did it make the news?"

"Not over there. But yes, over here. They're looking for a mysterious dark-haired woman."

"I guess he shouldn't have traveled abroad with a woman he'd just met."

Viktor had set up everything. He'd arranged for me to meet Misha at that party on the Lower East Side. At first, he just wanted me to keep tabs on him.

"Watch him night and day if you can," Viktor had said. "Have an affair with him if you must." Viktor didn't say why, just that his associates wanted to keep a very close eye on Misha. I reported all of his comings and goings back to Viktor.

The trip to Russia—that had been a spur of the moment improvisation. Viktor didn't like the idea at first, but then I guess he spoke to whoever it was that gave him his orders. They decided they could use a woman like me over there. They secured a passport for me, a visa. I had no friend at the Russian Consulate, like I'd told Misha. Then they put me in touch with their people in Moscow.

I told myself they were just keeping tabs on him.

I told myself I was doing it for love and not money.

Misha's gun told me he knew the risks of his business dealings. I was the one who was in denial. But in the end, he was right. His gun never did go off.

When they gave me the theater tickets, I knew what they were planning. But I wouldn't be the one pulling the trigger, so in some warped universe, I wasn't to blame.

From what I could figure out, the deal with the Russian steel factory never went through. The workers kept their factory, at least for a while. The company was bought by a Russian investor a few years later. Many of the factory workers were laid off.

In some other story, I might have fallen in love with Misha. But I'd fallen in love with Viktor first. It never occurred to me that a man willing to have his girlfriend sleep with another man in order to have him killed perhaps wasn't as invested in the relationship. As I said, I was young and stupid.

Two weeks after I returned to New York, Viktor was stabbed to death. The police suspected a lover. Apparently, I wasn't the only one. That's how I discovered Viktor had been unfaithful. I was questioned but had a solid alibi—working a double shift that day.

I suspected that Viktor was a loose thread that needed to be cut. Maybe I was a loose thread too.

I spent a night sipping that horrid homemade vodka I'd brought back. The next day, I took what was left of the 50K I'd earned in cash from the Moscow job and got myself out of the city. Moved somewhere where I didn't have to sell my soul to make ends meet. Somewhere where I could read thick Russian novels, and maybe write one of my own.

A story with a lot of romance.

A story in which people would do anything for love.

***

Nina Mansfield is the author of the YA mystery *Swimming Alone* (Fire & Ice YA). Her short mystery fiction has appeared in *Ellery Queen's Mystery Magazine* and *Alfred Hitchcock's Mystery Magazine*. She is also a produced and published playwright. Nina is a member of The Dramatists Guild, SCBWI, The Mystery Writers of America, and International Thriller Writers. She is a co-President of the NY/Tri-State Chapter of Sisters in Crime.

A Farmhouse in Provence

By Merrilee Robson

Provence, France

1974

I can't believe I'm in Provence! From watching projected paintings in the darkened auditorium with my Fine Arts class to the real thing.

That view, with the red roofs of the village sloping down to the sea, is exactly like a Cézanne.

Complete chance. Because David, a boy who lived next door when we were kids, just happened to be at the youth hostel in Bruges when I got there.

Now

"You are the nephew?"

The doctor spoke in English. Luc turned away from the hospital's reception counter and answered in French. "Yes, I'm here to see my uncle."

"You may see him for a minute. The nurses tell me he is agitated. They hope having family near may calm him." The doctor gave Luc a look that blamed him for not arriving sooner, as if arranging time away from work, booking a plane ticket, taking a transatlantic flight and then a second flight from Paris was something Luc could have done faster.

"How is he?"

"It is too early to tell. It would be better if he would rest more. He says only one word and repeats it regularly. The nurse thought he was saying 'Nell.' I thought perhaps a wife or daughter but the neighbor who called the ambulance says he's never seen a woman there."

The fatigue from his overnight flight washed over Luc. "A neighbor found him?"

"Yes. It was lucky for my patient. The neighbor was passing by just as your uncle collapsed. We had difficulty tracking down family, but I gather your mother's name is Élise, so perhaps your uncle is trying to say her name."

"Maybe. My mother is sorry she is not able to come but she is in the hospital herself. I will help if I can."

The glaring light in the intensive care unit brought tears to his dry eyes, which seemed fitting, but completely false. If the room had contained more than one man hooked up to an array of machines, he wouldn't have known which one was his uncle.

He stood nervously beside the bed. "*Oncle* Pierre?"

The man opened his eyes. "Nell…"

"Are you saying El? Are you asking for Élise? I'm her son. She's in the hospital too, having a hip replacement, but she sends her love."

The man reached out his arm, and Luc took the hand of the uncle he had never met.

"Nell…"

"Yes, I'm Élise's son," Luc repeated, "She…"

His uncle tried to pull the oxygen mask away from his face. "Nell…"

"My mother should be home in a few days. You have no need to worry. She can't travel right now but maybe…"

The lines on the monitor screen jumped alarmingly. The nurse hurried to adjust the mask over her patient's face. He gripped Luc's hand with unexpected strength. "No," he said. "Nell. Find."

The monitor beeped frantically, and the nurse did something to the IV drip.

"He should rest now," she said. "You can come again tomorrow."

Luc turned to leave, the jet lag suddenly making his legs so heavy he could barely move.

"Monsieur!" The ICU nurse caught up with him, handing him a small bundle. "His things. It is better if the family keeps them."

Luc thanked her and glanced inside the plastic bag, seeing dusty denim jeans, a shirt that smelled of sweat, a few crumpled euros, and a large metal key.

Hopefully one problem solved.

1974

I didn't really know David when we were kids. He's three years older than me and he was more my brother's friend. But I was sure glad to see him when I walked into the hostel.

I was alone after Amy decided she didn't like Europe and wanted to go home. She didn't *hate* England, although she thought the B&B we stayed in was too cold.

But at least she could speak English there. In Belgium, she wouldn't even try to understand what people were saying. I was getting by in English or high school French, and I know she'd taken the same French classes as me.

I guess she missed home, even though we'd planned to spend the whole summer over here.

If she hadn't left, I wouldn't have been so thrilled to see David. I wouldn't have ended up drinking too much beer and making out with him beside the canal. And I wouldn't have agreed to meet him later when he invited me to come with him to the south of France, asking if I didn't long to swim in the Mediterranean.

And I did, but I also wanted to see more of Belgium, and I couldn't miss Paris. He said he would write to me at the *poste restante* in Paris so we could meet up later.

It seemed like fate.

Now

Probably his tiredness made the place seem worse than it was.

The stone farmhouse couldn't have looked like this when his mother had been growing up. Unwashed dishes filled the sink, empty wine bottles were piled in one corner, and dirty, tangled sheets covered a single bed in one room. The other rooms were crammed with accounting ledgers, old photo albums, mismatched housewares, and pieces of broken farm machinery, all covered in dust.

His phone buzzed with a text from his mother. "How is your uncle? Have you seen him?"

It seemed she couldn't wait for a reply. His phone rang before he could even start to answer.

His mother was speaking quickly in French, which she tended to do when she was upset. "Have you seen him? And have you been able to care for the animals?"

"Yes, *Maman*, I've seen *Oncle* Pierre but only for a minute, I will go again tomorrow."

"And the farm? Is everything all right?"

The smeared window showed a farm that had been neglected for more than the three days his uncle had been in the hospital. The grapevines needed water. A ruin with gaping holes in the roof might once have housed the goats his mother remembered. The chicken coop was in better shape but there was no sign of poultry. Half the drystone wall was crumbling, and the house shutters had lost most of their green paint. The rutted area in front of the house was littered with sharp rocks, broken branches and garbage, making him worry about the tires on his rental car.

Luc didn't want to tell his mother. "The farm is okay. *Maman*, did your brother call you El or Nell? That seems to be what he is saying."

It was so long before his mother replied that Luc worried the call had dropped. Then he heard her sigh.

"No, he called me Lise, if he shortened my name at all. He must mean someone else. And I was hoping, after all these years…"

Luc could tell his mother was crying. "Don't worry. I'm sure I will find out more when I visit the hospital tomorrow and then I will call you. Now, how are *you* feeling. Are you starting physiotherapy?"

After ending his call, Luc stripped the grubby sheets from the bed and dumped them in the ancient washing machine. He thought about checking into a hotel, as he had planned before his mother had begged him to look after the farmhouse. But he was too tired to go anywhere. He found some folded bedding in a cupboard and shook it out by the kitchen door.

The sliver of the Mediterranean he could see in the distance glowed almost turquoise, making him wish he was here on vacation.

Luc plucked a few sprigs of lavender from the garden to tuck under his pillow, as his mother used to do. The scent might help him sleep and he hoped it would mask any mustiness in the bedding. He quickly made up the bed and collapsed into it, asleep almost as soon as he pulled the sheets over himself.

He was wide awake by midnight, when his jet-lagged body realized it was still daylight back home. He looked around the cluttered bedroom, remembering where he was.

He felt nervous, worrying about his mother, although she seemed to have come through her surgery well. Worrying about his uncle, hooked up to all those machines.

He wondered what he would need to do to make the house fit for his uncle to come home to. And what if he couldn't return, what then?

Luc decided he might as well tidy the place while he was awake. He washed the dirty dishes, found a broom to clean the floor, and used a dishcloth to dust the whole place.

He noticed some pictures scattered on top of a box of old accounting ledgers. One photo was clearly his mother as a girl, standing in front of a house that looked much better than it did now. Another was probably the grandparents he had never met.

A photo, folded in half, slipped from between the pages of one ledger as he shifted it.

It showed a young woman in a flowered dress swirling almost to her bare feet. Her hair was parted in the center and fell to her waist in light brown waves with streaks the color of the sunflowers in the field behind her.

Luc felt, for a moment, as if her beatific smile, that look of joy and love, was for him. But, of course it was for the photographer.

He knew before he flipped the picture over what he would find there, the name written in pencil on the back. Nell.

1974

David seemed so glad to see me.

I hadn't even thought about staying with him. I knew there was a youth hostel nearby, and a *pension* that didn't cost too much. I planned to stay for a day or two, spend time at the beach, maybe take a day trip with David. There's supposed to be a Chagall mural in a little chapel not too far away. But David seemed to take it for granted I would stay with him.

He greeted me with a sloppy kiss, shoving his tongue down my throat in a way that almost made me gag. I regretted the kisses we shared in Bruges. David seemed to think it meant something more than that we'd both had too much to drink. Today, I was sober, and his mouth tasted sour, like cheap wine.

The room he's staying in is a simple place, two beds made of flat wooden slats, with David's sleeping bag tossed on one. There's a sink in one corner, and a cupboard with a hot plate on top. A lightbulb hanging from the low ceiling is the only source of light, except the sunlight pouring through the open door. The only window has no glass, but a thin curtain seems to keep out some of the dust and flies.

"It's quite comfortable," David said. "The stone walls keep the place cool, even in the heat of the day. And look at the view!"

It is amazing. The olive trees and vines slope down the hill from the humble little shed, to the small village, with the blue of the sea in the distance.

The sun was setting but the air was still warm. A breeze rustled through the trees, carrying a faint scent of the Mediterranean.

The golden light seemed tinged with the color of the sunflowers planted in nearby fields, set beside lavender turning the hillsides blue.

David explained how he'd persuaded the owner to let him sleep in the shed, in exchange for doing casual work around the farm.

"This place used to be where they kept the goats, can you believe it? Goats with this view! They fixed it up for the people that work here for the harvest. But I bet we won't need to hire anyone else, with the three of us here."

I couldn't bring myself to remind him that I would be back in college by harvest time.

Now

Luc woke with the lights still on but the daylight pouring through the window where a broken shutter hung loose on its hinge. He didn't even remember crawling back into bed, but he was sure his dreams had been filled with his uncle's anguished voice calling for the smiling woman in the picture.

The same nurse greeted him when he arrived at the hospital.

"He had a good night. He seems relieved to have family by his side." She gave him a smile that almost rivalled the young woman in the picture and led him in to see his uncle.

The man in the hospital bed did look better, his skin less grey, looking more like a person than a corpse. Luc smiled at his uncle.

"I hear you had a good rest, *Oncle* Pierre. My mother...your sister...will be glad to hear that. Maybe you can talk on the phone soon. Not now..." Luc glanced at the time on his phone. "It's the middle of the night at home right now but perhaps..."

"Nell."

Luc smiled. "Well, I don't know who she is but she's certainly a beauty. Look what I found." He held out the folded picture to his uncle.

Oncle Pierre opened his eyes wide, seeming to shrink in his hospital bed.

"Nell," he groaned, breathing heavily. "Find."

The nurse hurried over to check the monitors.

"Can you tell me who she is, uncle? Her last name?"

"Find Nell." There was a long pause, the monitor screens showing leaping signals. "Rest."

"Okay, *Oncle*. I'll let you rest." The nurse was making shooing motions to him as she checked on his uncle.

"Nell rest," the man in the bed whispered, then added one more word. "Book."

1974

"You'll love it here," David said. "It's so real—living off the land, growing your own food. It's way better than those touristy places. I get up with the sun and I sleep so well at night."

We were in the kitchen garden—David called it the *potager*—set between the shed and the farmhouse. The astringent smell of lavender and herbs mingled with the perfume of the roses climbing the walls of the farmhouse.

"Perhaps your friend might not appreciate the outdoor privy and the cold water," said a voice behind me. "That might be a bit too real."

A figure moved from the shade of the house into the golden light of the garden.

He isn't quite as tall as David, but he makes David look like a gangly puppy, all shaggy hair and rough edges.

His hair is golden in the sunshine, his eyes the deep blue of the lavender.

And his body! I haven't made it to Florence yet but the muscles his open shirt revealed are just like the ones I hope to see on the statue of Michelangelo's David. Only his are not white marble but tanned flesh.

"Hi, Pierre, I'm glad you're back. I was hoping I could help with that wall you're building, if you can show me how," David says. "Oh, this is Nell."

David threw his arm around me. I wanted to rip it off. Instead, I took a step forward, away from him, and smiled at Pierre.

"I knew David back home," I said. "He's a friend of my older brother. He asked me to look him up when I got to Provence."

I wanted to place distance between David and me. Because I might not believe in love at first sight. But lust at first sight seems entirely possible.

Now

The farmhouse house looked better when Luc returned from the hospital. His midnight cleaning spree had been worth it.

He looked around him. *Oncle* Pierre's voice had been faint, hard to hear, but he had said something about books. He walked into the room where the ledgers were stored, where he had found the photo. It was a small room, the flaking paint a pale yellow, with a view past the crumbling outbuildings to the village.

Luc checked each of the ledgers carefully but didn't find any more photos. The records went back decades, some filled with neat writing that must have been his grandfather's. A newer one had equally neat writing, listing purchases of farm supplies, sales of grapes to the co-op. Smaller income from olives and eggs. The farm had done well in the past.

And then the ledgers stopped. He looked through the other boxes, but they seemed mostly to contain broken cups with handles that would never be glued back on, bent forks and threadbare bedding. The few photo albums seemed older, with black and white pictures of people he didn't recognize. His grandparents, perhaps, maybe even his great-grandparents, judging from the clothing. The infants might have been his mother and uncle, but they were so young they could have been any baby.

There was a bookshelf beside the bed where he'd slept. Luc glanced at the titles. The books looked ordinary enough, mostly paperback thrillers, a surprising number in English, but a few older hardcovers. Had some of them belonged to Nell? Would he find more pictures stuffed between the pages.

He pulled a leather-bound volume off the shelf. The book looked old, but he didn't think it was valuable, and there was nothing hidden in its tattered pages.

He pushed it back on the shelf, but something stopped it from sliding into place. Pulling out the book and the one beside it, Luc saw a slim volume stuck behind the other books. His own bookshelves were stuffed full, and it was easy enough for a book placed on top of the other books to slide down behind them.

But *Oncle* Pierre had been talking about a book with some urgency. Was this book hidden?

It was a lined notebook with a cardboard cover in a lavender paisley print. The writing that filled the page was written in a large, looping script with curlicue flourishes and Is dotted with circles or daisies. The ink was a purple that almost matched the cover. The first pages were an excited account of arriving in Provence, followed by more of the purple writing, all of it in English.

1974

"I think you would be more comfortable in the house," Pierre said. "There is a proper bathroom, and you can use my sister's old room." David was bristling, pulling himself up from his usual slouch to make himself look bigger. Pierre looked at him and quickly added, "I could bunk in here with David to give you more privacy. Although my sister did have a lock put on her door after I decided to use her paint set to draw pictures on the henhouse." He flashed his smile again, revealing a dimple in one cheek. "I don't think she ever forgave her little brother."

I thought hot water and a proper bed would be much more comfortable. But I didn't want to put Pierre out of his own house. David seemed to think the lock on the bedroom door would keep me safe. Which it might have, if I intended to lock it.

Now

The journal lay on the blanket where he had dropped it when he fell asleep. He wondered when he would adjust to the time difference.

His body was stiff and sore from his nap in the unfamiliar bed, and he felt the need to move. The walk to the village square was pleasant, with the afternoon sunshine still warm but cooling from the heat of midday.

The road had switchbacks leading down the steep hill, making the village seem farther away, but a footpath led straight downhill through the fields. The neighboring farm was very different from his uncle's, the vines green, with small bunches of grapes plumping up. There seemed to be a drip irrigation system stretching below the vines. Did his uncle have something like that? And was he supposed to do something with it? His vines certainly looked unhealthy. Maybe his mother would know what to do.

The village looked a little more working class than some of the touristy places closer to the sea. But it was pretty enough, with narrow streets of stone houses following the curve of the hillside, pink geraniums spilling out of window boxes.

And best of all, the green tables and chairs outside a small café in the square. Luc sank into one of the chairs and asked the efficient waiter for a glass of the local rosé and then, realizing he was hungry, a slice of quiche.

The quiche seemed like the most delicious thing he had ever eaten, with a warm, custardy filling and none of the rubbery texture of some quiches. It blended the sweetness of onion with cheese and salty bits of ham. The slightly bitter greens at the side were the perfect complement. Luc tried not to wolf it down. When it was gone, he ordered a second glass of wine and settled back with the journal he had brought with him.

1974

If I'm going to stay at the farm, the least I can do is cook a meal. David coaxed Pierre away, asking to be shown how to build the drystone wall, but they left some eggs from the henhouse. I picked herbs from the kitchen garden and gathered lettuce leaves. I was overwhelmed by the smell of the tomatoes growing in the sunny spot against the farmhouse wall. Tomatoes from the store at home never smelled like this.

The orange yolks gave a lovely warm color to the eggs I whisked for the *omelettes au fins herbes*.

When everything was almost ready, I walked out to where the guys were looking at the drystone wall. Pierre snapped a picture of me by the field, saying he would send me a copy.

The air was warm, and the bees were still buzzing around the garden as we sat down at the wooden table outside the kitchen door.

We stayed there as the moon rose and the bees were replaced by fireflies.

Pierre opened a bottle of wine, and then another one as we sat talking and laughing.

David complimented me on the food but, though he drank the wine as quickly as we did, he complained about it. "You should think about opening a boutique winery, instead of just selling to the co-op. I'm sure I could learn about winemaking and wouldn't it be great..."

That's when Pierre told him he planned to sell the farm.

"I stayed here while my father was alive, but I don't want to farm for the rest of my life, like he did. I want to study art." Pierre smiled at me, and the dimple flashed in his cheek again. "Perhaps in the States."

"But it's a great life," David said. "Everyone wants to live like this. How can you give it up?"

Now

"Excuse me." A voice interrupted Luc's reading. "Are you Pierre's nephew? The waiter said you came down the path leading from the house, and he thought you might be him."

Luc looked up at a man with a golden tan and sun-bleached hair, dressed in red cotton pants and a boat-neck tee.

"Ah, yes, I am. Are you the neighbor who found him? I gather you may have saved his life."

The man shrugged. "It was just chance. I was walking back from the village when I saw him fall. I didn't do much more than call for help. How is he?"

"The doctor says it is too soon to tell, but he looked a little better today." Luc studied the man. He had clearly spent time outdoors, but his hands didn't look like a farmer's hands.

"Are those your fields I passed as I came here? I noticed the vines looked in better shape than my uncle's and there was an irrigation system. I wondered if you..."

The man threw his head back and laughed, displaying very white teeth.

"No, I'm your neighbor on the other side, past the vines and the olive trees. And it's just a holiday house. I'm a dentist from Paris. I can advise you on which pool service to use but you'll have to ask old René, on the other side, for advice on your grapes. He came here just after my father bought our land and he seems to know what he's doing. I think he would like to buy some of your family's land, but I gather there are complications."

"I'm sorry, I haven't had much contact with my uncle. There was a bit of a rift when my mother left home. I don't know anything about his land."

The man looked puzzled. "Your uncle is not a good farmer, as you can see. My father said he tried but failed and had to sell land to pay his debts. *Papa* wanted a bigger place, but I gather the house and the remaining land belong to his sister, your mother, *non.*"

"No. My grandfather was very angry when she left for art school. He thought she should stay and run the house after her own mother had died. And then, of course, she met my father at the school, married him and moved to Canada with him, so she was cut out of the will."

The man frowned. "But that is impossible."

"My mother was very upset. She tried to maintain contact with her father, but he was a stubborn old man. Her brother used to write to her but that stopped after a while too."

"No, you don't understand. Under French law, the land is protected for the children. That's why you see properties that are just long strips, where the land was divided between the offspring. Your mother might have been able to relinquish her share, but she should not have been disinherited. Did she not know?"

1974

Pierre sighed. "David, you've only been here a few weeks. You don't know how much work it is at harvest, how boring it is in the winter. My father tried to leave it all to me, but he couldn't legally do that. Half of it belongs to my sister and I haven't had a chance to tell her about this offer, but I plan to sell."

"Maybe I can buy it?" David says. "It can't be much."

"I've heard from people in Paris who want to build a vacation home. They are offering a good price."

David stormed off back to his shed. And Pierre looked like he planned to follow him, to explain. But I stood up to clear the table and Pierre gathered the other things and followed me into the kitchen.

And when he kissed me, it wasn't at all like necking with David in Bruges. And when I went to my room, I was not alone.

I think David might have seen Pierre leaving my room this morning. But he simply asked Pierre to come and look at the drystone wall.

I heard them talking outside, Pierre patiently explaining how David should place the stones. And David's voice getting louder and louder. And then silence.

I need to see what's going on.

Now

Luc called his mother as he climbed the hill back to the farmhouse.

"*Maman,* I was wondering, when did you last hear from your brother?"

I could hear her sigh. "Well, I used to write to him all the time after I left home. We were so close when we were children, you know, even though I was older."

"Even when he used your paints to draw pictures on the hen house?"

"Did he tell you that? He must be feeling better if he's telling stories. I suppose he stopped just after you were born. My father had died just around that time. I couldn't make it back for the funeral and I knew Pierre was struggling a bit with the farm."

She sighed. "You know, I always felt a bit guilty for leaving. I think Pierre might have liked to paint too, but my father thought art was a waste of time. Poor Pierre, he was such a sweet little boy, with his blond hair and those big blue eyes. I was very angry about my paints, but you couldn't stay mad at him when he grinned, and you saw that dimple."

And then Luc remembered Nell's romantic description of the blue eyes the color of the lavender fields.

The dark brown eyes of the man in the hospital bed. And the abrupt end of the journal.

After searching his phone for combinations with the name Nell and other hints from the diary—Bruges, Paris, Amy—he found an article mentioning the cold case of a student named Nell Wilton, who had disappeared on a European summer trip, with a tearful account from her roommate Amy, veering between wishing she had stayed with her friend and fears that, if she had, she might have suffered a similar fate.

There was more, of course. A photo of the missing woman. A sloppy signature on the sale of the land, bearing no resemblance to the neat hand in the ledgers. Uncomfortable talks with lawyers and with the bank where the money from the land sale had been deposited and slowly spent over the years.

And the drystone wall, half of it strong and still standing. And the other half falling down, as if it had been built by a different person entirely.

And of course, the two skulls, both of them cracked, as if by one of the stones they were buried under.

Luc was always certain that the brown-eyed man in the hospital bed had died at the exact moment he had dug up those two white skulls.

* * *

Merrilee Robson has published over two dozen short stories in *Ellery Queen's Mystery Magazine, Alfred Hitchcock's Mystery Magazine, the People's Friend, Mystery Magazine*, and other magazines and anthologies. Her traditional mystery, *Murder is Uncooperative*, is set in a non-profit housing co-op. She lives in Vancouver and spends a lot of time with at least one cat on her lap. https://merrileerobson.ca/

Swan Song

By donalee Moulton

Iqaluit, Nunavut, Canada

The call came in at 1:24 p.m. I heard Ahnah answer, "Iqaluit Constabulary," but my attention was focused on the Keurig coffee maker I had brought with me from Humboldt, Saskatchewan. This was only the third day the city's new police force was officially up and running, and the plan was to slowly take over full responsibility from the RCMP. Good coffee would be critical.

As my dark roast continued to drip into a new blue-and-white IC coffee mug, I heard Ahnah's soft voice in the background, but it was the silence that compelled me to turn around.

"Everything okay?" I asked our exec assistant.

"No," she said. "There's a dead body at the Tundra Inn and Suites. It appears to be murder."

Before she could finish, I was reaching for my coat and yelling for the two constables in training, Kallik Redfern and Willie Appaqaq, to follow me. Our office was only five minutes from the hotel (although in Iqaluit, I was learning, you're really only five minutes from anywhere). By the time we arrived, there was a crowd of people. That crowd included David Picco, the government's elected representative for Rankin Inlet and the driving force behind the establishment of the Iqaluit Constabulary, a first for the twenty-year-old territory.

"I was across the street at the legislature," he said. "What's going on?"

"I don't know," I admitted, "but it's not good."

People moved back to let us through, a consideration I was also learning is second nature to Iqalummiut. The hotel manager was waiting for us in the lobby. "Doug Brumal," I said by way of introduction. "I'm the new police chief."

"This is awful, just awful," said the manager, a small, round man who in his distress had forgotten to give us his name. I nodded at Kallik, who moved quietly to the front desk. He would get the names and contact information for everyone in the hotel at the time of the incident.

By now, the unnamed manager was leading us down a long hallway past the dining room and lounge to a series of meeting rooms. The first door on our left was the only one closed. When I opened it, I saw round tables with linen tablecloths positioned throughout the room. Two coffee urns and one teapot were resting on a tilted table. (Floors here often shift because of the ice and permafrost.) There were muffins, fresh fruit, and a cheese plate on the table. A large screen faced a projector, which held centre stage in the room.

Except, of course, for the dead woman on the floor. She was reed thin, about 5'8", silver-grey hair that may have been dyed. She was wearing a black skirt, checkered jacket, and white blouse. Well, now the blouse was white and red. Blood red.

Willie moved forward and started taking pictures. I returned to the hallway and shut the door behind me. The manager was nowhere in sight, but a young, brunette woman was waiting for me. "I'm Elsa Nattaq, assistant manager," she said. "I found the body."

"Is there somewhere quiet we can talk?" I asked. Kallik had joined me, and we followed the assistant manager into an adjacent meeting room. As I was dropping my big butt (at 6'6" most of me is big) into a boardroom chair, I looked up to see Ahnah Friesen standing in the doorway.

"I thought you might want me to take notes," she said, settling into the chair on my left.

Elsa Nattaq didn't wait for our questions. We learned the dead woman was Eira Winter, owner of HR Exemplary, a training firm out of Calgary. Winter was a regular visitor to the hotel, a contractor from the south who flew into Iqaluit several times a year.

"I'll ask Carol Logan to drop by this afternoon to speak with us," Ahnah said as the assistant manager stopped to take a breath. "She's the training coordinator for the GN."

I had learned enough to know GN stood for Government of Nunavut. Apparently, I had not learned quite how sharp our admin support was.

The assistant manager assured us she had not touched anything in the room, including the body, and had locked the door after she backed out of the room. "Do you know who was on room duty over lunch?" Ahnah asked.

I didn't even try to mask my surprise.

"Meeting rooms are cleared over lunch to make way for the afternoon break," Ahnah said, looking me in the eyes. "I used to work here."

"But the room wasn't cleared," I noted, seeing where Ahnah was going. I also noted, to myself, that Ahnah had been in the murder room.

I thanked Nattaq for her help and told her we might have more questions. She agreed to let us use the boardroom for the afternoon. Then the three of us joined Willie in room 101. Another woman was also there. I recognized Kari Frost, the chief coroner.

Frost, a Southerner, was all business. "Dead as a nit," she said. "Stabbed, repeatedly, with what appears to be a steak knife." I looked over at Willie, who was holding up an evidence bag with a small, bloody, serrated knife.

"I'll know cause of death for certain once I do the autopsy. Likely hit a vital organ or two. Nasty business," Frost said, grabbing her crime scene bag and heading out.

I looked at my team, already knee deep in murder. This wasn't what any of us had expected. Were we ready? As if she could read my mind, Ahnah said, "We're all good. I've set up an interview with Carol Logan for 3:30, and Paul Saila is coming in at 4."

"Who the hell is Paul Saila?" I asked.

"The busboy sent to tidy up the training room," said Ahnah. Seeing my confusion at her apparent psychic ability, she added, "Elsa texted me." Almost as an afterthought, she said, "I also ordered some coffee, juice, and muffins for us in the boardroom. It might be a long day."

Promptly at 3:30 Carol Logan, a big-boned brunette with a warm smile, breezed in. After expressing her distress and her belief that she wouldn't be much help, Logan went on to give us much-needed background on our victim. An HR specialist, Winter had been conducting training sessions in Nunavut for four years. The sixty-three-year-old was mid-way through a lucrative contract with an option to renew for another three years. That contract called on Winter's company to certify GN employees in human resources and payroll services.

"How important is that certification?" I asked.

"Without it, employees cannot continue in their jobs," Logan said simply.

Skilled labour is an ongoing issue for the GN, I knew. The Government of Nunavut had committed to creating a public service that is representative of the population it serves, and qualified Inuit applicants are given priority for all job competitions. It was the word "qualified," however, that posed significant problems. Indeed, it was the reason I was sitting in the police chief's chair.

"How many people fail?" I asked.

"In the last few years, not many. In fact, none," Logan said. "But that may have been about to change. Eira and her partner, Crystal Pele, divide the curriculum. They don't usually come together. You should talk to Crystal." I could see Ahnah reaching for her phone.

"Did you like Eira Winter?" I asked.

"She's very good at her job, and she has helped us advance our HR skills significantly," Logan said. She didn't meet my eyes.

Within seconds of Logan leaving the boardroom, a lanky young man in his late twenties was ushered in. I held out my hand and thanked Paul Saila for coming. He looked at the floor and mumbled something. I wasn't sure if this was respect for an older person, shyness, or something else altogether.

"You know why you're here?" I asked.

Saila nodded.

"I need you to tell me," I said without rancour.

"It's about the dead woman."

"What about her?" I asked.

"I was doing her classroom."

"What exactly were you doing, Paul?"

"I bring the food in and take it out," he answered.

"Did you speak with Ms. Winter or see her over the lunch hour?"

Paul continued to look at the floor. "No," he said. I didn't know if he was telling me the truth.

"Did you like her?" I asked.

Saila shifted in his seat. "Didn't know her."

Crystal Pele was more talkative. The trainer showed up a few minutes after Saila left. (Ahnah's work, I presumed.) She entered checking her watch, hand outstretched. "I can't believe this. Who would want to hurt Eira?"

"We're hoping you can help us with that," I answered. "Why was she here on this trip?"

Pele appeared confused. "It's her job."

"I understand the two of you didn't usually come together."

The Calgary trainer nodded. "Yes. It's more productive for one of us to travel, where possible. But these are the final exams for the group, and we both felt we should be here."

"Why?" I pushed.

"It's about quality control and due diligence," Pele said, sitting a little taller and a little more stiffly. The educator's hat was on, but before she could explain quality control and due diligence to me, I interjected.

"I understand you oversaw exams individually in the past."

The stiffness remained. "We review each class and determine the schedule accordingly," Pele said. "In this case, we felt it would be beneficial for us both to be here."

"Why?" I persisted.

You could see Crystal Pele deflate. "There is a participant who is struggling. She may not pass. Eira thought we should both be here to break any bad news."

"Do you agree with that decision?" I asked.

"What decision?" Pele countered.

"To remove an employee from their job."

I watched Pele's jaw for a reaction. It clenched ever so slightly. "We work with every person to help them reach the best possible outcome. Some people just don't make the grade. Literally." Before I could speak, Pele continued. I'm not sure whom she was trying to convince. "It's best for everyone. If an employee can't grasp the HR essentials, it makes them feel inadequate, and it makes the government less effective and efficient."

I switched lanes. "When did you last see Ms. Winter?"

"We had dinner together last night at the hotel."

"You didn't see her today?" I asked.

"No, we decided only one of us would be needed in the classroom to oversee the exam itself. Eira drew the short straw. I slept in and ate breakfast in my room."

"Did you like Ms. Winter?" I asked. I could see the surprise on Pele's face. I didn't know if it was the switch in questioning or the question itself.

"She was my colleague. My partner," Pele said. She sounded a little breathless. Defensive, perhaps. Or nervous.

"Not what I asked," I said. I could feel my team looking at me with a similar expression to Pele's. I made a mental note to discuss questioning strategy with them when we debriefed.

Pele sat up straighter. "Of course I liked Eira. She was a dedicated, skilled professional who put her heart into everything she did."

"So you liked her." It was a question and a statement. And it got me a glare. "Did other people like Eira Winter?" I asked, veering slightly.

I could feel Pele relax—and hesitate. "Eira was a perfectionist, and she could be impatient. People may not have appreciated those qualities."

Now it was my turn to check my watch. I thanked Pele for coming and walked her out. Three sets of eyes were staring at me when I turned back to the boardroom. "What do you want us to do now?" Willie asked.

"Go home," I said. "Enjoy your dinner. Watch some TV. Let's meet tomorrow at 7:30 for a debrief and strategy session. We may have more information by then."

"I'll bring bannock," Kallik said.

* * *

My government-provided apartment reminded me I was not home as soon as I pulled in front. Permafrost prevents buildings in Iqaluit being built from the ground up. I was on the first floor, a short walk up a small flight of steps with a clear view of the "stilts" on which the building sat. This was not familiar territory.

Before I had a chance to think about food, my phone rang. It was David Picco. "Have you eaten?" he asked before the word "hello" was fully out of my mouth.

"No," I said.

"Do you want some company? I have char."

"Come right over," I said. I meant it. I really liked and respected David. He was gently and skillfully introducing me to Nunavut, the culture, and the role I would play in life here in Iqaluit. I also really liked Arctic char, a rich, delicate taste somewhere between trout and salmon.

David let me enjoy dinner—we pan fried char with a splash of lemon, boiled potatoes, and zapped some frozen peas. (In a community where a head of lettuce routinely costs $6.99, frozen vegetables are more common than fresh.)

Over coffee and a plate of packaged cookies (brought from Humboldt), we got to the unspoken matter at hand. "Doug, do you have a handle on this?" David asked without any preamble.

"It's been all of six hours," I pointed out.

"Would you like to call in the RCMP for assistance?"

"I'd like to meet with my team tomorrow, review the forensics, and continue interviews," I said. "If I feel we need RCMP support, I will ask

195

for it."

"This is the first test of the new force. Everyone is watching," David said, reminding me of the pressure we were under to succeed. And quickly. "There are opponents, as you know, people who strongly objected to establishing our own constabulary."

"We're untested, and we need to find our footing," I acknowledged, "but the team is trained, I'm experienced, and we're following protocol. Give us a chance to breathe here."

"It's not me you have to worry about," David said.

***

I arrived at the office at 7 a.m. The team was already there, and the bannock, a deep-fried bread, was warm. I brought molasses, a tradition passed down from my Newfoundland grandmother. Willie, Kallik, and Ahnah thought this was sacrilege but agreed to give it a try. Willie tossed his in the garbage when he thought I wasn't looking, and Ahnah wrapped hers neatly in a paper towel, also when she thought I wasn't looking. Kallik ate everything on his plate and reached for more bannock—and molasses.

After small talk and big bites, we got down to business. We reviewed what forensics we had, the most important being the knife. "Not a typical murder weapon," I pointed out. "It's too small to be guaranteed effective, if murder was what our killer had in mind."

"So do you think this was a crime of passion?" Kallik asked. He'd clearly been reading mystery novels.

"It would appear to be spur of the moment," I agreed. "Perhaps grabbing a weapon close to hand."

Ahnah looked at the ground and shuffled her feet. "It's a steak knife from the dining room," she said.

I nodded.

"Steak is only served on Tuesdays," she noted.

I immediately understood the implication. "So, either someone took this knife from the dining room on Tuesday, the night before the murder, or someone with access to the kitchen grabbed it yesterday. Either way, it looks premeditated."

Now, it was Ahnah's turn to nod.

"So why would someone want Eira Winter dead?" I asked, more to myself than the group.

"She doesn't sound like a nice lady," Willie said. We all agreed, but we all wondered if that was enough for someone to want her dead.

In my experience, it wasn't.

* * *

Lumi Nakasuk showed up for her interview fifteen minutes after our debrief. I wasn't aware we'd booked an interview, but I wasn't surprised when Ahnah told me Carol Logan had emailed the info last night about Nakasuk, an HR and payroll clerk with the Executive and Intergovernmental Affairs department. And the failing participant in Winter's certificate program. I also wasn't surprised when Ahnah joined us in the interview room.

Nakasuk, a plump, 5'3" woman in her early twenties, would be unlikely to take Winter down in a fist fight, but if she caught the trainer off guard, she'd have no trouble driving a steak knife into human flesh.

The young woman was clearly nervous, but then she had reason to be, even if innocent. There are two options for interrogation: tough cop, gentle cop. If the Iqaluit Constabulary was to be accepted in the community, we had to earn its respect. I opted for gentle cop.

"Thank you for coming in," I said. Nakasuk looked up from the floor for a second.

"I didn't do anything wrong."

"I'm sure you didn't," I responded, "but we understand you were having problems in Ms. Winter's program."

"No reason to kill her," Nakasuk countered quietly. So perhaps all the women in Nunavut would be one step ahead of me.

"Can you tell us where you were yesterday from noon to 1 p.m.?"

Nakasuk stared at me, then the floor. "We have Ms. Winter's calendar.

It says she had an appointment with you yesterday over the lunch hour," I said, lying through my teeth. Gently.

"I went to meet her, but she was busy," Nakasuk said softly. I couldn't tell if she was lying.

"Doing what?" I pushed.

"She's not a nice lady," Nakasuk said suddenly and a little loudly. And here it is, the moment when the suspect lets go, says to hell with reticence and caution. "She's mean. She yells. She thinks she's better than everyone."

I waited. Nakasuk hesitated, but the gate was open. There was no going back. "I showed up yesterday, but she was yelling at someone. Really yelling. It was awful. I got the hell out of there."

"Who was she yelling at?" I asked. This was why Nakasuk was holding back—the information she didn't want us to have. But she was in too deep now.

"Paul Saila," Nakasuk said. "She told him she couldn't wait to leave Nunavut, to get away from all this crap, and no little pissant like him was going to stand in her way. She called him a thief. Said he was taking the food from the classroom for himself."

Now she looked at me, defiant. "So, what if he was."

* * *

Once Nakasuk left, we gathered to review what we now knew and the implications of that new knowledge. Nakasuk was still a suspect, but she had moved way down the list. There was no duplicity in her. The story about Saila and Winter rang true.

"Is theft an issue at the hotel?" I asked Ahnah.

I could feel her tension. "The hotel has to throw leftovers out. So sometimes employees take home the fruit, muffins, and cheese."

Without pause, she added, "The Southerners do the same. They take the food to their rooms and eat it for breakfast or supper." I could understand why. Chicken fingers here could cost $20 and a clubhouse even more.

"So maybe Saila was taking food home and Winter objected," I said, ignoring Ahnah's tone and the bait. "Are a few muffins and cheese bites worth killing for?"

"They are if you're hungry enough," Ahnah said.

* * *

I decided to walk home, about ten minutes. I had been warned about the winter temperatures in Iqaluit, sometimes as low as -50º C. At that temperature, the hair in your nose and the cilia in your lungs can freeze. But this was October. The first snowfall had lightly blanketed the city of roughly 8,000. The air was crisp and dry. Without many of the daytime lights from offices and other buildings, it was dusky. Stars draped the sky. Few people were outside, and the city felt like it was my own. I breathed deeply.

The feeling of contentment lasted throughout the evening. I heated up caribou stew, compliments of Kallik's wife. (I really liked her. Couldn't wait to meet her.) I put Elvis on the stereo and put my feet up on the sofa. This was not laziness, but ritual. It's my way of thinking through things. As "Suspicious Minds" played, I reached the obvious conclusion. I simply didn't know enough to think anything through.

I got up and grabbed my parka, rammed my feet into my Bugaboots, and headed for my Ford F150. There wasn't going to be any more Elvis for me tonight. I'd be settling in with Eira Winter's laptop and the thousands of emails and files she had stored in hundreds of folders. Such a night.

* * *

The first drips of coffee were winding their way from pod to cup when Ahnah walked into the office. "You're early," I said. It wasn't even 7 a.m.

"Couldn't sleep," she responded. "And I figured you'd want to speak with Paul Saila first thing this morning."

She was right. I did want to speak with Saila. I also wanted to speak with Crystal Pele. I needed to learn more about the victim to understand why someone would want her dead.

Saila proved to be elusive. He didn't show up for work at the hotel, and he wasn't at home when Willie and Kallik went to look. They continued the search starting with his mother's house. Meanwhile, Pele arrived, simultaneously uneasy and annoyed. Both are common reactions to police requests for an interview.

"I told you everything I know," she said before I could ask a question.

"Yes," I agreed. "Thank you."

That left her a little confused. Point one for the Iqaluit Constabulary. "I want to learn more about Ms. Winter. I was hoping you could help."

"How?" Pele asked. Her tone was not warm.

"We're getting the distinct impression your colleague was not a nice woman."

"So what?" Pele said. You could almost see her body resign itself to the inevitable.

I didn't have time for petulance or reticence. "Ms. Pele, we can do this one of two ways. Your choice. Good cop or bad cop." I saw Ahnah smile into her Dell laptop.

"What do you want to know?" Pele asked. The annoyance was gone.

"Tell me why someone would want to kill Eira Winter."

"She's mean, she's heartless, she's inflexible, she's arrogant… Do you want me to continue?" Pele asked. She stared at the floor.

"Please," I said. My tone was not warm, either.

"Look, Eira was not an easy woman. She prided herself on being rigorous, but that left little room for openness or flexibility. Eira defined fairness as treating everybody the same."

"Isn't that a good thing?" I asked.

"It could be, but with Eira it meant no exceptions, ever. For example, she didn't tolerate lateness. Arrive after class started and you weren't allowed in the room. It didn't matter if someone had been up all night with a critically ill baby or the minister of health had called them in for a meeting. No exceptions."

I could see how that would rankle. "How did she treat you?"

"The same as everybody," Pele said. "But I have worked with Eira for more than five years now. I know how to avoid the outbursts, the cold shoulder, and the retribution. I also know what to expect when I've crossed one of her lines. We found a balance that worked for us."

"What happens now?" I asked.

"Happens with what?" She seemed confused.

"With your work in Nunavut?"

"The contract continues," she said. "This course is winding up; the next one will start in another month. If I need help, I'll subcontract work just like Eira did with me."

"I know this is a long shot," I said, "but do you have any idea who might have killed Ms. Winter?"

Pele looked me in the eye. She didn't hesitate. "Anyone who ever met her."

*** ***

I grabbed a sandwich for lunch at The Snack. When I got back to the station, Willie and Kallik nodded toward the interview room. Paul Saila was waiting for us. Truculent and terrified. "I didn't kill that woman," he said. Defensive and defiant.

"I didn't say you did," I answered. "Want a coffee? Muffin? Piece of fruit?"

"Piss off," Saila said, and deservedly so, but now I had him off balance.

"So you got yelled at," I said.

"No big deal," Saila said, trying to appear nonchalant.

"Not what we heard."

"Okay, so the bitch tore one off me. Big deal."

"It is if you lose your job," I said.

"Then they'd have to fire everyone," Saila snapped. "And I'd have another job five minutes later." I looked at Ahnah. She nodded yes.

"Tell me what happened," I said.

"I was cleaning up the room and taking some of the leftovers when that woman walked in. She screamed at me. Called me a thief. Called me a low life. Nothing I haven't been called before. Said I wasn't going to ruin her reputation."

"And then…" I prodded.

"I got out of there fast. She was alive and foaming at the mouth when I left. Calling me nasty names. Screaming something about me trying to ruin something for her and not letting her go in peace."

Saila was almost out the door when he turned.

"Don't know if it matters," he said, "but she was really upset about some bird that was singing." He grinned at Willie. "Qugjuk."

I looked at Willie in bewilderment. He shrugged. "It's nothing. Guy's an idiot. He's spent so much time down south he doesn't even know his own language anymore."

* * *

I told the team I was making a Timmy's run, which they understood but found a little strange. We have coffee in the station. I returned with hot chocolate and doughnuts. That enhanced the understanding significantly. A few minutes later, Carol Logan walked in. She grabbed a Boston cream and said, "I understand you wanted to see me."

I looked at Ahnah. "About the contract," Ahnah said. Apparently we have the most fascinating floors.

Carol followed me to my office. "I brought a copy with me." She handed me a fairly thick wad of paper. "But it may be easier if I walk you through it."

The Government of Nunavut had a four-year contract with HR Exemplary, Winter's company. The contract was worth at least $250,000 a year, and was automatically renewable for another three years. There were standard clauses for indemnity, termination, and confidentiality. If something happened to Winter mid-contract, it would be fulfilled by Crystal Pele.

"There's nothing sinister in that," Logan said as if sensing where I was going. "Same clause as in the previous contract, and Winter lived through that."

* * *

The remainder of the caribou stew was settling nicely in my stomach and Elvis was mid-way through "Don't be Cruel" when I sat upright. I needed to get my hands on three things: Eira Winter's contract, her laptop, and an Inuit dictionary. The first two were at the station; the other was on the Internet.

I texted the team. Thirty minutes later, everyone was sitting in my small living room. Willie had made a Timmy's run.

"Let's go through what we know so far," I said. "We're close." I could feel the pride. I could also feel the surprise.

Willie and Kallik thought Paul Saila the most likely suspect for obvious reasons. I thought the murderer was Crystal Pele. Ahnah agreed, but she was uncertain of the motive.

"Pele stood to lose a very lucrative contract," I pointed out.

Ahnah frowned. "But she wasn't losing the contract."

"Yes," I said. "She was."

"How do you know?" Willie asked.

"Paul Saila told us."

Now everyone looked at me in bewilderment. "What's a qugjuk?" I asked.

"It's a big white bird," Willie said, still puzzled.

"Yellow around the eyes," Kallik added.

"It's a swan," I said. "That's the bird that was singing for Eira Winter." Three pairs of eyes looked at me blankly.

The phrase "swan song" may have mystified the team, but the termination clause in the contract was crystal clear. If Eira Winter chose to terminate the contract, Crystal Pele was out of a job. And nestled in her laptop under a file called, aptly, "Swan Song," was Winter's letter bringing her contract with the GN to an official end.

* * *

Crystal Pele was arrested at the Tundra Inn before she finished her Caesar salad. It took less than an hour for her to confess. Actually, it was more of a declaration than a confession. Winter was retiring, closing her company's doors, and Pele was out. This final trip to Iqaluit was Winter's swan song. Pele wanted to make sure it wasn't hers.

* * *

Ahnah beat me in to work the next morning. Coffee was on, and there were fruit, cheese, and muffin trays, compliments of the Tundra Inn and Suites.

"You know you don't have to come in early every morning," I said with a smile.

"I have a question," Ahnah said without a single glance at the floor. "Pele has money, a job, a career. She likely has a house, a car, a vacation every year. So why kill Winter?"

"She was hungry," I explained.

"She had plenty of food," Ahnah said.

"Not that kind of hunger."

I'm not sure Ahnah understood, but she would, especially when she became the first female constable of the Iqaluit Constabulary. But that was a path yet taken.

Ahnah turned to go to her desk but stopped after a few steps. "I forgot to tell you. Carol Logan texted. All the participants in the current course passed their exam."

* * *

donalee Moulton's first mystery book, *Hung out to Die,* was published in 2023. A historical mystery, *Conflagration!,* was published earlier this year. donalee's short story "Swan Song" was one of 21 selected for publication in *Cold Canadian Crime* and was shortlisted for an Award of Excellence. Other short stories have appeared in *Black Cat Weekly, After Dinner Conversation,* and *The Antigonish Review,* among others. donalee lives in Halifax, Nova Scotia.

Murder in the Wine Cellar

By Aimee Kluck

Paris, France

The Incident

As told by Pierre Benoit, Maître d', Chez Hugo, Paris

The front door of Chez Hugo swung open and in strode the restaurant critic from *Le Monde* and his latest red-hot flame. Etienne Pompeux tossed his raincoat, demanded his usual table, and called for the Maître d'.

Pierre Benoit appeared at his side. "So good to see you, Monsieur." He forced a spurious smile reserved for serving difficult customers. "And your lovely companion." The newest redhead buxom, clad in a short, shiny shift. "Follow me." Pierre guided the pudgy gastronome past the narrowly spaced tables. Pompeux, surprisingly spry and agile for his size, wove between the seats to the round table in the corner by the green velvet wall.

"Two martinis, very dry and dirty." Pompeux pinched his date's cheek. "And after that, Maître d'," he patted her leg, "Rosalie would like a bottle of the Domaine Matray Saint Amour 2020."

"Mais oui." Pierre quickly backed away. He summoned the sommelier. "Jean Paul, go to the cellar. Our imperious friend ordered to impress. Rosalie must be playing hard ball." They hid their laughs and went their

way. Pierre alerted the chef and waiters that the critic was present and to be on their best. They always were, but the critic searched for any dissatisfaction.

Pierre remained occupied seating guests and offering thanks as they left satisfied. The waiter approached him. "Jean Paul has not returned with the wine, and we are about to serve Monsieur Pompeux's table."

"The last thing we need tonight is a glitch." Pierre clasped his hands. "Send Annette down to check on him."

Pierre hustled to the critic's table. "Monsieur. My forgiveness for the delay in the wine." Perspiration glistened on Pompeux's chubby, ruddy face. His breath blew out hard and fast. "Are you feeling all right, *mon ami?*"

"The temperature in here is not suitable for dining." The critic fanned himself with the napkin.

Pierre had not noticed the heat. "Till the wine arrives, could I bring you—"

A scream shot out. A high-pitched, ear piercing shriek.

Diners directed their attention to the entrance of the wine cellar. Pierre rushed forward, waving his arms. "Everyone stay calm." He flew down the stairs where Annette stood stock still, hands covering her mouth, glaring in fright at the lifeless body of Jean Paul sprawled on the floor. Pierre pulled her back and handed her off to the waiter. He returned his attention to his sommelier. A rope wrapped around his neck; head twisted sideways; one eye bulged wide open. Pierre crouched and felt Jean Paul's neck for a pulse. None. Bent his head to listen for breath. None.

Pierre crumbled, pressure magnifying in his chest, head throbbing. "*Mon Dieu.* Poor Jean Paul." His shoulders shook with rage. "What happened here?"

The Investigation

As told by Inspector Jacqueline Dupen, Préfecture de Police, Paris

Inspector Dupen examined the dead man: Jean Paul Rimes. White, twenty-nine years old, one-point-seven meters, sixty-eight kilos. Gripped hands clutching a rope at his neck, expression of horror planted on his face. Surrounded by broken bottles and a widening crimson pool of red wine. Every homicide, a waste of a life. Since she joined the force, following in her father's footsteps, she vowed to dedicate her career to the victims. She worked for them.

"Where had the weapon come from?" On an oblong oak table, Dupen spotted ropes used in packing, and compared them to the one around the sommelier's neck. The same. A crime of opportunity. Perhaps not premeditated.

The maître d', Benoit, through gasps and sobs, recounted the sequence of events, then showed her the two entrances to the basement, one for staff that led to the restaurant and one to the outside for deliveries. Dupen had never seen a wine cellar before and was impressed by the narrow rows of bottles tilted on racks and huge refrigerators filled with light colored bottles, nestled in the cobblestone underground storage with golden lights. Almost magical, except for the odor of spilt wine, mold, and death. And the corpse.

"What about the victim's relationship with his colleagues? And family?"

Benoit swiped his nose with a soggy lavender cravat. "Everyone adored Jean Paul. He made people laugh." He sniffled. "Well, not his wife. She's divorcing him. Foolish woman." He clucked and shook his head.

Dupen made a note. She examined a broken case and shattered glass covering the floor. "Was this case smashed before?"

"*Non. Mon Dieu*. The Domaine de la Romanée-Conti." Blanched, Benoit staggered as if he might faint.

"Have a seat." She led him to a worn wooden chair. "What exactly is the Domaine…?" The name of the wine eluded her.

Benoit shot her an incredulous gasp. "Only the most elegant, the most expensive, the most exclusive wine in the world." Conspiratorially, he whispered, "It's valued at one hundred and forty-five thousand euros."

Dupen nearly choked. "For one bottle of wine?" She usually spent under six euros on her drink. "Who would steal it?"

Benoit shook his fists. "Jules Roussillon."

Dupen eyed her partner, Maurice Maigrit. Not again. That snorting-pig sound he made when his sinuses clogged. The damp mold set him off, no doubt, but if she had to listen to that on top of Benoit's passionate sniveling, she might just…

She straightened her shoulders. "Tell us more about Roussillon."

"His restaurant, Le Milieu," Benoit lifted his nose and grunted, "is in competition against ours for the top wine list in Paris. *WE* have the '34 Romanée." He mewled. "Had. Now it's gone, we might not best his mediocre restaurant." Pierre's nostrils flared; his eyes bulged. "Roussillon's the one who benefits from robbing us."

"This is the only bottle of its kind?"

"No one else claims to have it."

"How did you get it?"

"A benevolent benefactor willed it to us when she departed this daily life and strife." Benoit placed his hands together in a prayer. "Chez Hugo was her favorite place to eat in all of Paris and she wished that we win the contest."

Dupen reflected on the consequence of the theft. "But could the thief display the bottle or enter it in a competition if he stole it? Why poach it now, before the contest?"

Pierre brayed. "In order that we wouldn't have possession. We were certain to win."

So much excitement over a bottle of wine.

Dupen considered another angle. "Has any employee been let go recently? Someone unhappy with his departure, who needed money?"

Benoit wrung his cravat in a knot. "I was forced to dismiss the dishwasher, Marcel Corbin. He didn't show for work for three days. When he returned and I fired him, he called me a tyrant and threw a croissant at me."

Not exactly a vicious killer. "We'll check him out." She wrote his contact information in her pad, noting he resided on the tougher, poorer side of the city, chockfull of ruffians and wastrels.

Benoit cringed. "I'm afraid you'll find he has a criminal history." He held up his hand. "You'll say I shouldn't have hired him, but he's my cousin's husband's neighbor's son."

Silly man. She nodded. "You tried to help." If burglary was listed on the dishwasher's rap sheet, Corbin would rise to suspect number one.

Benoit's expression turned somber and sullen. "It's a covetous, depraved person who did this, Inspector. If you find the bottle of wine, you find the killer."

Dupen agreed. She intended to nab the villain and rid the world of one more maleficent miscreant.

Dupen and Maigrit headed out.

"We have suspects." Dupen would have preferred a witness but alas, the unfortunate Jean Paul died alone. "We must inform the sommelier's wife." The hardest part of her job, but the most important to handle well.

Dupen passed the table where a young cadet interviewed a quarrelsome, corpulent man and a racy redhead. The woman, flashy in her sparkling outfit and fluffy fur, gazed at Dupen, dressed in dowdy twill slacks, a cheap wool jacket and worn, crepe-soled shoes. Dupen stared at the stunner. Who dresses like that for dinner? And how?

* * *

Thirty minutes later, Dupen and Maigrit knocked on the Rimes' front door. An angular-faced woman, the tip of her nose squared off like a surgeon's disastrous deed, answered. Dupen hovered with hat in hand. "Madame, I'm afraid we have bad news. May we come in?"

Dupen's gaze wandered the hall, where two packed suitcases rested. In the sparsely furnished living room, Madame Rimes gestured for them to sit on a designer sofa that appeared barely sat upon. Dupen delivered the heartfelt report, keeping her voice steady with a touch of sympathy. A stillness lingered while the wife processed the news without the usual surprise or grief.

"Madame Rimes, do you know of anyone who would want to kill Jean Paul?"

Her rouge lips twitched in a bittersweet smile. "No one. He never offended. He was carefree. A bit too nonchalant for me. That's why we're divorcing. We are very different."

Interesting that she would offer this tidbit of information about the divorce, but then people loved to justify their lives. Dupen spied two plane tickets on the table. "Are you traveling, Madame?"

Rimes started. "*Oui,* to the Riviera for a few days. To clear my mind."

Dupen squinted to see the name on the second ticket. "With Monsieur R. Vachon? Who is he?"

Rimes blushed. "My *advocat.* He's assisting me through this difficult divorce." She wiped the corner of her tearless eye with a tissue.

Exactly what kind of assistance would her lawyer offer her on the romantic Riviera, Dupen wondered. "Where were you last night?"

"Here, packing and preparing for my journey."

"Can anyone verify that?"

"*C'est dommage, non.*"

Dupen had no idea how a divorce changed people. She'd never been married, never found a man who didn't want to tell her what to do, how to act, where to work. Easier to live on her own. But she expected a sorrowful spouse, even one amid a divorce, would show a little emotion. Madame Rimes acted unfazed, almost annoyed to be interrupted from her trip preparations.

* * *

The inspectors returned to their drab, dingy headquarters and spoke to the eager team internet wizard assigned to uncover the suspects' deepest secrets.

"A background check on the sommelier's wife, Veronica Rimes. No record."

"How about their finances?"

"Not much there. Two medium salaries, barely enough to cover their bills. Significant credit card debt. There is a life insurance policy. Wife's the beneficiary. Except there's a divorce clause. If the couple legally separate, the policy holder can pass the payout to another beneficiary. Jean Paul chose his sister."

"The widow doesn't draw the disbursement if she's divorced." Dupen pondered that information. "She requires money to manage her new state of affairs. But is that worth killing her husband?" Unless she really didn't like him. Dupen shuddered at the thought. "Madame Rimes has motive and no alibi. Add her to our list of suspects."

"Inspector." A junior officer with huge hair and a flirtatious smile handed her a report. "Monsieur Roussillon is out of town as of this morning. He returned to his vineyard in the Loire Valley."

"This morning, hmm? The Loire is about two hours by car. Maigrit, we'd best get going."

* * *

Dupen and Maigrit drove through the Loire Valley, past acres of grape vineyards and castles nestled in the hills, through tiny ancient towns with meandering lanes, surrounded by farmlands where cows grazed. Dupen relished the view as Maigrit sped down a winding dirt driveway to a field of vines on poles and wires, springtime grape buds suspended from glorious green leaves. Maigrit parked the car and the two inspectors headed to a stone building, into a tasting room, a long wooden bar with bottles of wine, ready to serve. Dupen couldn't tell one wine from another, except red versus white, and never drank the fancy kind. The idea of various blends, contrasting tastes, good French wine bewildered her.

Dupen flashed her identification. "We'd like to speak to Monsieur Roussillon." The server hurried away. Hurried back.

"I'll take you to him."

Out in sunshine, across the yard to a rustic barn where, inside the cavernous building, lay rows of oak barrels. A rich, earthy scent filled the dry, cool air. Dupen strained to listen in on a mumbled conversation in the distance, coming from the direction they were heading. The server led them toward a worktable where two men deep in conversation lorded over a pile of papers. The server yelled ahead. "Monsieur Roussillon, we're here."

Roussillon, a stern, serious man with deep set eyes, one blue, one hazel, greying hair and close-cropped beard, his pale rose shirt tucked neatly in pressed jeans, held out his hand. "Inspectors." Dupen shook the connoisseur's firm, gripping hand. Strong enough to tighten a rope around the sommelier's neck.

She turned to the other man who had backed away in the shadows. "And you, monsieur, your name, *si vous plait?*"

The swarthy man, dressed in worker's clothes, his face burrowed with the wrinkles of a life spent outdoors, farmer's hand covered in dirt, hacked a raspy smoker's cough. "Archambeau."

"He is my *vigneron.* The finest winemaker in all of France." Roussillon glared at the man, a look that seemed to silence and dismiss him.

"We are investigating the death of Monsieur Rimes, sommelier at Chez Hugo and the disappearance of a bottle of…" Dupen checked her notes, "the 1934 Domaine de la Romanée-Conti."

Roussillon scoffed. "Naturally, you think I am guilty, since I am the competition, correct?"

"Not making assumptions, Monsieur, just following leads." Dupen smiled the restrained grin she saved for uncooperative witnesses. And probable criminals. "Where were you last night?"

"In Paris, at my restaurant. Staff can attest to that." He smirked, an impertinent gesture that irked her. Raised him higher on her list of suspects and guaranteed she'd scrutinize every statement he made.

She tapped her pad with her pen. "Staff names, *si vous plait.*" He rattled off a list faster than she could write, unsure whether she would be able to interpret her scribble later.

In a haughty voice, Roussillon spoke as if to reprimand her. "Mademoiselle Inspector. If I had any intention to steal that most desirable paragon of wine, I would not be so mindless to interfere during the dining hours, when witnesses abound." He waved a dismissive hand. "And I would never kill a sommelier, a member of our esteemed community of wine virtuosos. *Non*, my fair lady, you can eliminate me from your line up."

His fair lady. Ha. The muscles in her jaw tightened. "May we look around your winery? I'm curious to inspect your collection." To discover the missing bottle.

Roussillon grumbled. "I'll have the server take you on a tour."

"Your personal collection, Monsieur, not the public tour."

His face contorted with displeasure. "Then you'll have to meet me in Paris, and I don't plan to return till tomorrow. Bring a warrant."

Barely enough time to obtain a search warrant, but sufficient time for Roussillon to hide what he preferred to keep secret.

* * *

With their car doors locked, Dupen and Maigrit drove to le Banlieues Rouges district, once famous as the French communist seat of power, now known for its impoverished residents and dilapidated dwellings. At the address given to them by Benoit, they passed through a red entryway and climbed four flights of stairs to apartment 4D. Loud, metal music emanated from inside, muffling their hard knocks and calls. Finally, the door swung open and a woman with tangled hair dressed in torn jeans and an oversized dirty sweatshirt stared back from dilated eyes. The stench of smoke and stinky socks seeped out.

"Police. We're looking for Marcel Corbin."

Behind the woman, others leapt from their seats and scattered. The woman wheezed and coughed. "He ain't here."

"Where can we find him?"

"Do I look like his secretary?" The thin-boned waif planted her hands on hips. "Marcel's been gone since yesterday. He don't say where he goes or when he comes back."

Dupen sighed. Another warrant request. Though she doubted the valuable bottle of wine would be hidden in a dump like this. But never underestimate the treachery of thieves. And Dupen was nothing if not

214

thorough.

* * *

Driving back to headquarters, along the Seine, Maigrit battled the throng of cars as if fighting for the crown. Dupen gripped the armrest as he swerved between the maddening traffic.

"Three suspects: the wife who stands to gain financially, the competitor who stands to win the coveted prize, or his hired lacky, and the angry, destitute dishwasher."

Maigrit blasted his horn. "The wife isn't strong enough to strangle a man."

"People overcome with passion can demonstrate an uncanny surge of power." Dupen had witnessed her own remarkable strength, given her petite frame and height, when needed during emergencies.

"Despite my unfavorable opinion of Roussillon, he made a valid point about the timing of the robbery-homicide. He had no motive to kill the sommelier."

Maigrit sped through a red light at an intersection near the Eiffel Tower. "Unless Rimes got in his way, and the wine connoisseur had no choice."

She pressed her imaginary brakes to the floor. "His associate, Archambeau, could have done the deed." A suspicious character with shifty eyes and monotone answers. She wouldn't dismiss the snobby Roussillon as the killer either.

She peeked out of one eye as Maigrit cut off another driver. "The dishwasher stands out as having motive, knowledge of the wine cellar and possible opportunity. We need to find him."

"That's our man." Maigrit slammed the car to a halt.

Dupen would not rush to judgment. She needed evidence, verified alibis, and witness statements. Then, she would solve the crime. But first, she must get out of this car alive.

* * *

On Tuesday, Dupen and Maigrit sipped café au lait and nibbled on éclairs among the hum of voices and the clatter of cups on saucers at the Café du Mort.

Dupen wiped the corners of her mouth. "Let's review the new information. First the wife. It's been confirmed: Madame is having an affair with her *advocat*. That's the reason for the divorce." She pinched her lips. Didn't approve of adulterers. Her brother-in-law had deserted her sister and two children for a tart. Shameless and selfish, all of them.

Maigrit bit his pastry, cream oozing out the end. "As for the connoisseur, staff reported seeing him early in the evening, but as usual, he disappeared to his office, and no one saw him between twenty-thirty and twenty-one-thirty." He wiggled his bushy eyebrows.

"Time of the murder." She made a satisfactory note in her pad. "Sadly, since the judge didn't approve the warrants for his vineyard, home or restaurant for lack of just cause, we have no proof if the wine is in his possession."

Maigrit licked chocolate off his fingers. "The dishwasher served time for burglary. And now he's disappeared. We have an APB blasted and Border Control is alerted."

Whoever did this, Dupen would not permit the perpetrator to get away with it. But without hard evidence, she was stuck. She needed a fresh approach.

"Let's revisit the scene of the crime."

* * *

At Chez Hugo, Dupen and Maigrit huddled alongside the mournful maître d' where the crimes took place in the gloomy basement. Dupen searched for one clue that would solve the case, one she might have missed when she first surveyed the place.

"According to witness statements, no one saw any unusual person descend to the wine cellar from the restaurant entrance. Our murdering thief must have arrived from the street."

Benoit muttered. "The door is always locked. But Jean Paul was known to slip outside for a smoke when he got a chance." He wailed. "What if he got accosted in the street and forced to the cellar?" He fluttered his hands. "It's too much to imagine."

Dupen proceeded to the back door, opened it, gazed in the unlit alley, found a pile of cigarette butts, checked the lock. Plenty of places to hide, but nothing out of order. How would the assailant know when Jean Paul took his break? Did he wait around for the opportunity? Or did he watch from inside?

"Who was dining here that night who may have an interest in this particular bottle of wine?"

Benoit fanned himself with a mother-of-pearl fan. "*Voyons…* Truffaut, Chastain, Lavigne, and Pompeux. They all have extensive wine collections."

"Were any of them acting odd that night?"

"As usual, Truffaut commanded everyone's attention. Chastain caused a scene weeping like a silent movie star over her latest lost love. Lavigne kept busy signing autographs. Pompeux, disagreeable and demanding…" Benoit paused. "Now that I think of it, the man looked awful, ruddy, perspiring and heaving like a consumptive. I feared he was having a heart attack."

The reaction one might have if he'd just killed a man. "Would Pompeux have had enough time to leave the restaurant, go to the back door and attack Jean Paul?"

Benoit sat in quiet contemplation. "We were busy that evening, even at that hour. He had asked for a special wine we only keep in the cellar, so I sent Jean Paul in search of it." He gasped. "You don't think Pompeux could have done this despicable deed?"

"We must investigate every possibility. Where did he sit? And where are the exits?"

They returned to the dining room. Benoit pointed to the corner table by the green velvet wall. "One can leave through the front door or the kitchen."

Maigrit checked his notes. "No one from the kitchen reported seeing anyone out of the ordinary, and you would have noticed if he left through the front door."

"Not necessarily. I could have been seating guests."

Dupen sat where Pompeux had eaten. "Time me, Maigrit." She excused herself from her imaginary date, shuffled through the restaurant, casually but with a quickness in her step. Exited the front door, ran around the alley to the back door, confronted her invisible mark, pretended to push him down the stairs to the cellar. The coroner estimated it took six minutes to kill a man the size of Jean Paul by strangulation. Dupen counted the minutes on her watch. Imitated breaking the wine case and retrieving the priceless bottle. Ran back outside to a nearby car, imitated opening and closing the trunk, straightened her clothes and returned with calm assurance to the seat.

"Seventeen minutes, twelve seconds."

"Would you have noticed if he had been gone that amount of time?"

"*Avec regret*, not that evening. We had three large parties arrive after the theatre closed."

Dupen pondered the possibility. Her phone rang. "*Oui?*"

"Inspector, Officer Peloquin. The dishwasher, Marcel Corbin, has a solid alibi for the time of the homicide. He was locked up in jail, sleeping off a doozy of a drunk. And Archambeau, he sang in the choir at his church that night."

Dupen blanched and reminded herself to hold judgement based on appearances.

"*Merci.*" She relayed the news to Maigrit. "The wife unlikely, the dishwasher unavailable, the connoisseur improbable, the *vigneron* engaged. Perhaps the critic is our prime suspect." She turned to Benoit. "How can we discover if he has possession of the wine?"

Benoit flushed. "That rogue most likely hoards it in his home to covet it privately."

Another warrant, which with Pompeux's connections, may be denied. "How can I get in his house? Pose as a plumber or cable repair person?"

"He hosts a reception at his residence after the awards ceremony, this Saturday night. You might attend and look around then."

"How can we get invited to the reception?"

Benoit lit up. "Madame Comtesse DuBarry will not be attending. She had to leave suddenly for Cannes and sent her regrets. You could use her invitation."

Dupen chortled. "A Comtesse? Me?"

Benoit eyed her from head to foot and grimaced. "A considerable transformation will be essential."

* * *

On Saturday night, Jacqueline sat in the dressing room of Brigitte Royale, a highly respected esthetician, while she teased and styled limp hair into a French twist, and applied foundation, blusher, and eye make-up to make Jacqueline appear as a genteel woman of means. Dupen squeezed in an off-the-shoulder black satin tea-length cocktail dress that cost almost her annual salary. The fashionable attire purchased by the police department came with the directive it must not be soiled and must be returned immediately after the undercover event.

"And, lucky lady, you get to wear a pair of Jimmy Choo's," Brigitte croaked in her husky voice. She held up impossibly high black stilettos.

"I'll break my ankles in those. Don't you have flats?"

"Dahling, La Comtesse never wears flats."

Jacqueline practiced walking in them until she could mostly balance if she took small, slow steps. She swirled in front of the mirror. Remodeled from a frog to *La Grande Dame*. She felt ridiculous.

* * *

Dupen arrived at the critic's party fashionably late in a room lit with warm glowing lights, melodies drifting from a classical quartet, filled with festive guests. Beautiful women dressed in elegant gowns and dashing men in tuxes acted as if they belonged here and made Jacqueline anxious as a first date. Teetering in her heels, she mingled and scanned the crowd for

Pompeux. At the far end of the ballroom, the host entertained a gathering, the redhead attached to his elbow glittering in her golden gown. Tonight, Dupen appreciated the effort it took to look like that and decided she could never keep it up.

She ducked down a corridor, hunting for the wine collection. Benoit had told her where to look, having seen most of the treasure at Pompeux's previous post-awards party. She descended a flight of stairs, and at the end of the hall, opened a door to an inky, chilly room. Dim blue beams lit shelves crowded with wine bottles. With so many, how would she ever locate one single selection?

It appeared as a beacon: a single bottle displayed in a beveled glass case, under a halogen light, encircled by red security lasers. The Domaine de la Romanée-Conti. The sight of it made her gasp, not from the beauty or the value, but because she'd found her killer.

Doors smacked open and in barged two burly bouncers in black, accompanied by two domineering Dobermanns, claws clicking on the polished parquet. "Don't move."

Dupen raised her arms. "Police. Let me get my badge."

The men surrounded her, pointing pistols, one at her head and one at her chest. Her breathing quickened; her pulse raced. "In my purse." One ruffian rummaged through her crystalline clutch and retrieved her ID. They lowered their guns. "This room is off limit to guests. You triggered the alarm when you entered."

"I need to speak to Monsieur Pompeux. Bring him here to me, please." The tough guy left while the other kept a watchful eye, with two dogs guarding. She phoned Maigrit. "Come in now for backup."

Pompeux and Maigrit accompanied by two officers entered the wine exhibit room at the same time from opposite directions.

"What is the nature of this intrusion?" Even in the subdued ambiance, Dupen could see the critic's nervous irritation wracked across his face.

"Monsieur Pompeux, you are under arrest for the murder of Jean Paul Rimes and for the theft of the Domaine de la Romanée-Conti."

"You are wrong! This is my own bottle."

"Open the case, *si vous plait*," Dupen demanded.

The guard took the key from Pompeux and unlocked the cabinet. Dupen carefully removed the bottle and twisted it around to the back. "You see this mark, the cursive capital H? The insignia of Chez Hugo. Placed there by Monsieur Benoit upon receipt of the bottle to verify ownership. How do you explain that?"

Pompeux huffed. "I want my lawyer."

"The murder of the young man over a bottle of wine, Monsieur, is most reprehensible. The bright light of Jean Paul Rimes' life snuffed out too soon." She glared at him. "You are a disgrace and should be ashamed."

Pompeux's lip curled in a smirk. And then, his chin quivered. He flinched as the officers cuffed him and led him away.

Dupen beamed with delight. Another scofflaw captured.

"Excellent, Inspector Dupen. Case solved." Maigrit patted her on the bare skin of her back, then withdrew his hand in awkward haste.

Dupen removed her Jimmy Choo's. "If he won't confess, I'll make him wear these torture devices for an hour." Flat-footed, she and Maigrit returned to the ballroom.

A waiter approached them, balancing a silver tray with two glasses. "Our specialty this evening: La Grande Dame Rosé, Veuve Clicquot's rarest champagne from elusive Pinot Noir grapes."

They graciously accepted the offer. Maigrit toasted her. "La Grande Dame for La Grande Dame."

Dupen took a sip of the pink gold liquid, and an exquisite taste of peaches and pralines aroused her senses. "Ah, I'm starting to understand all the fuss. But not at all worth killing for."

She raised her glass. "Wine, theft, and murder: never a virtuous blend. But champagne and a case solved: that I can celebrate."

* * *

Aimee Kluck has a short story published in *Shotgun Honey* and a poem in *Punk Noir*. She has completed a murder mystery novel that takes place in

the cocaine-crazed 1980s. She is a member of MWA, SinC, WFWA &
SMFS. Formerly from New England and S.F., she lives in Santa Barbara,
California.

Tent City

By Rob McCartney

Toronto, Canada

You'd never catch me sleeping in a homeless shelter, especially during a pandemic. All those dirty people spreading germs. Not to mention if I took off my army boots, they'd be gone by morning. And hell, don't get me started on the bedbugs; those nasty little buggers leave scars.

Scars like you get from war.

When I returned from Afghanistan in 2014, I spent several years living on the streets of downtown Toronto. I didn't get a pension and couldn't hold down a job. Bad memories pierced my soul like the scattered shards of a detonated grenade.

At first, I did a lot of drugs, but I kicked that habit thanks to a peer support group my former army sergeant ran. I still drank like a fish to drown out the foul nightmares of Kandahar.

Eventually, an old army buddy, Wally, spotted me panhandling on Yonge Street, one of Toronto's main arteries. He'd gone to university after returning to Canada, found a good job and got married. I guess he felt sorry for me because he let me couch-surf at his apartment in the Annex, a residential part of Toronto. The deal was no getting drunk. Besides my big feet hanging over the end of the couch, it was all good.

Then the COVID-19 bug landed with a sting.

Wally got worried that I'd bring the virus into his home and get his wife and their kid sick or dead. I had to kiss my cozy couch good-bye and headed back outside the wire, as they say in the army. I was terrified of being homeless again. Luckily, a teenage runaway asked if I'd take his mangy light-brown Rottweiler because he couldn't afford to feed it. I jumped at the prospect of a guard dog. I named that mutt Jacko because when he flashes his crooked grin, he looks like a jack-o-lantern.

That winter, me and Jacko slept on subway grates to catch the rising hot air. Eventually, we moved under the Gardiner Expressway, the elevated highway that runs along the south end of the city. Our shelter was a big cardboard box. The cars zipping overhead scared the bejesus out of Jacko, though.

One day in early May, I bumped into this drunk who street folk called Toothless Terry. He started gumming away about homeless people living in tents at Trinity Bellwoods Park on the west side of town. "They'll be hell-bent before they go to a shelter with this COVID spreading," he said, pulling down his soiled mask to take a pull from a Smirnoff bottle.

I decided to check it out. I rolled up my sleeping bag and stuffed it in my backpack. Jacko and I set out walking along Queen Street, with its mix of kitschy and quaint shops, restaurants, and fast-food joints. After about an hour, we reached the park. Tourists with cameras lined a fence surrounding a small orchard of cherry trees that had blossomed in a sea of light pink fluff dancing in the breeze. Corny as it sounds, those blossoms boosted my spirits and gave me a bit of hope—something I was short on.

We reached a tall, white stone gateway with wrought-iron doors leading into the park. Beyond the gate, I saw a sprawl of tents knitted loosely together like a dirty, unraveling quilt. Some tents had lawn chairs out front shaded by rusty patio umbrellas. A few tents looked like they belonged to hoarders, with broken tables, grocery carts, and plastic bags filled with clothes piled up outside them. Makeshift laundry lines ran between some of the tents. Pasty-faced folks in tattered clothes milled about aimlessly or sat smoking at wooden picnic tables.

Nobody wore protective masks. That made me edgy, and I was about to split when a blonde with matted hair sprang out of a tent and skipped barefoot toward me. She wasn't wearing a mask, and I pinched my own mask tight around the bridge of my nose. From a distance she looked like a hottie, but up close her face was weathered, probably from a drug habit, I figured. She was about the same age as me but looked older.

She was either brave or crazy because she went straight up to Jacko without fear and playfully scratched his head with her face up to his nose.

"Hello, poochie poo," she said like she was talking to a baby. Her raspy voice suggested she smoked two packs a day. My so-called guard dog wagged his stubby tail and his pink tongue rolled out of his mouth in a happy pant.

"I'm Carolyn," the blonde smiled, revealing darkened, yellowed teeth.

"Jimmy," I replied.

"Ain't you a big, strapping lad," she said. "Pull down that damn mask and let's see your face."

Reluctantly, I unhooked one of the strings of my mask.

"Oh, tall, dark *and* handsome," she said. "You here to pitch a tent?"

"I got no tent, and I can't afford one from Canadian Tire," I said sheepishly.

She tugged at my hand. "C'mon," she said. "Let's talk to Bennie. He's like the mayor here. Maybe he can set you up."

Carolyn asked if she could walk Jacko. I was skittish about that, but we didn't have far to go, and that stupid dog was smitten with her. I handed her the leash and she wrapped it around her thin, freckled wrist.

We approached a big green tent, the kind they use in army camps. Out front, a middle-aged guy was rolling around hot dog wieners on a propane barbecue using a long, rusty fork with a wooden handle. He had a long salt-and-pepper beard like the guys in ZZ Top. He wore a green Adidas track suit with white stripes down the sides and beat-up Birkenstocks. His mask hung below his chin, and a cigarette dangled from his lips.

"Got a live one, Bennie," Carolyn said. Bennie glanced up briefly then turned his eyes back to the flaming grill.

"Name," he said with a sigh, as if I was interrupting something important.

"Jimmy. Jimmy Holmes. Look, I don't mean to intrude…"

Bennie raised his plastic-framed sunglasses and inspected my army jacket.

"Military, eh?"

"Afghanistan, Kandahar," I replied.

Bennie's eyes met mine squarely. "You ever kill anyone, soldier boy?"

"Can't say for sure, but I imagine so," I said. "Saw combat but firefights can get messy. Sometimes, you just close your eyes and pull the trigger."

Bennie checked out Jacko, leaning against Carolyn's leg.

"His bark is worse than his bite," I said.

Bennie plucked a wiener off the barbecue with his fork and flicked it to Jacko, who gobbled it up and whimpered for more with sappy eyes.

Just then Carolyn chimed in. "Bennie, we must have a spare tent, eh?"

Bennie eyeballed me up and down, then pointed his fork at me.

"Here's the deal, soldier boy," he said. "This place is filled with junkies, drunks, dealers, and thieves. Some of 'em are nuts. There's also good folk, people like me who lost their jobs due to this pandemic. Tell me, Jimmy, which are you?"

I stared at my feet. "I've got PTSD, and I drink too much."

Bennie smiled. "Honesty. I like that. A big guy like you could come in handy around here.

"A few rules," he said. "No stealing from other tents. No bothering people walking through the park. No fighting unless I say so. And if you get sick, you go to Toronto Western Hospital on Dundas Street and get checked out in the emergency department. We don't want any outbreaks."

Bennie reached into a plastic Wonder Bread bag and fished out a hot dog bun. "Here," he said, chucking it at me. "Welcome to our tent city."

After we each ate some hot dogs, Bennie walked me nearby to this cozy little blue, dome-shaped tent. It turned out that this junkie known as Scary Harry had gone AWOL and abandoned the tent several weeks earlier.

"Tent's yours if you want it," Bennie said. "But you gotta clean it." He unzipped the flap and handed me a garbage bag. The tent smelled like piss.

I tossed Harry's musty sleeping bag outside and gathered up clothes he'd strewn about. Everything stunk to high Heaven.

Home, sweet home, I thought, as I spread out my sleeping bag.

* * *

Us tent folk often got dirty looks from people who were walking through the park. Our tents backed onto a residential street called Crawford Street. The neighbors complained among themselves and sometimes publicly that we were an eyesore and intimidating. I had to admit, they had a right to bitch. Garbage cans in the park overflowed with trash and used syringes could be found lying around in the grass. Some campers even pooped in the residents' yards instead of making the walk to nearby port-a-potties. It wasn't uncommon for some tent dwellers to be drunk, stoned or both, and a nuisance to regular folks just out for a walk. There wasn't much else they could do during the pandemic, and I saw a lot of uneasy faces.

Bennie had managed a strip joint before the virus shut it down. He dealt with lots of drunken frat boys and dirty old men who didn't treat the girls respectfully. That's why he was such a stickler for rules. We often patrolled the encampment together. He was like the boss, and I was the muscle.

One day, this junkie named Darryl tossed an empty heroin syringe onto the grass after shooting up between his toes. A little girl picked it up and her mom went ape-shit crazy. Bennie had some sharp words for him. I shot Darryl the stink eye.

But even Bennie found himself in the crosshairs occasionally, like the time this old fancy dan dressed in yellow slacks and a plaid button-down shirt marched up ranting about Bennie stealing his barbecue propane tank.

I wasn't sure if Bennie had stolen it, but I wedged myself between them and backed the old-timer down. He retreated, tripping over a tent peg. "You no-good degenerates! Get out of the damn park!" he hollered before getting up and storming off.

This one tent guy, Tom, spent his days higher than a kite painting graffiti on the park's concrete walking path. Let's just say he didn't have much talent and made an awful mess. His paint cans, stacked up along the path, were an eyesore. And so was he: he was scrawny, never wore a shirt, and his soiled blue jeans hung low, exposing the crack of his ass when he bent over to make his brush strokes.

"He's a tweaker with a nasty temper," Carolyn warned me one day when we were walking Jacko. "Before you got here, Bennie told Tom to clean up his paint cans and it ended in fisticuffs. Bennie won that round, but Tom has had it in for him ever since."

Then there was Scary Harry, whose tent I'd taken over. I met him for the first time when he returned to the park one day to find his tent occupied.

"That was *my* tent, you have no right, you son of a bitch," he growled at Bennie. Harry was short but stocky like an ox, and he had menacing brown eyes. I placed him somewhere in his twenties. Despite the warm weather, Harry wore a puffy winter ski jacket with white cotton stuffing poking out of several rips and tears. I took note of the metal steel toes in his well-worn work boots. One kick from those could shatter a shin. The guy was a plastic explosive ready to go off.

Bennie was tongue-tied and I could tell he was scared. He tried to back away, but Harry kept pursuing him. Harry cocked back an arm and made a fist. I wasn't sure if he was tripping out on something or not, but I grabbed his wrist as he swung. Harry took one look at my size, shook his wrist free and stepped back.

"You got to get other guys to fight your battles, eh, Bennie," Harry screamed. "You'll get yours, you pussy, just you wait!" With that, he stumbled off toward Queen Street.

* * *

Carolyn and I often walked Jacko around the park. I found myself taking a shine to her. We were both screw-ups.

Trinity Bellwoods was a tapestry of trees and Carolyn could name them all. "That's a White Ash," she'd say, or "That one's an English Oak."

"How do you know so much about trees?" I asked.

"I used to be an elementary school teacher," she said.

"So, how'd you end up here, strung out on meth?"

Carolyn sighed and flopped down on a green bench, patting the space beside her. Turns out in another life she'd married a lawyer with a mean streak.

"He'd work long hours, come home drunk, and accuse me of cheating on him. One night, he grabbed my elbow, flung me across the kitchen and broke my arm. I ended up in the hospital. I said I fell down the stairs. I don't think the doctor believed me."

"Did you call the cops?"

"I was too afraid of what Fred might do to me," she said. "I went to a women's shelter."

Carolyn shook her head in shame. "I was down in the dumps, you know? This woman I met at the shelter talked me into doing some meth to cheer me up. I got hooked and lost my job."

Jacko licked her hand, and I awkwardly put my arm around her shoulder.

"What about you, Jimmy?" she asked.

"Oh, I dunno…"

"C'mon now, Jimmy, let's have it."

I felt funny wearing my emotions on my sleeve but spilled my guts anyway.

"I grew up on a dairy farm in Southwestern Ontario. My folks were hardcore Bible thumpers, but I never believed in all that hocus-pocus. My father wasn't what you'd call the warm and fuzzy type, and he couldn't figure out why I wasn't more like my two younger brothers. I guess you could say I was the black sheep of the family.

"My parents reckoned I'd take over one day, but I hated every minute of farm work. When I graduated high school, I volunteered for the army. I couldn't get off the farm fast enough. When my dad found out I'd signed up, he lost it. 'God didn't put you on this Earth to kill people,' he said. 'If you go off to war, don't ever step foot back on this farm. I didn't raise no murderers.' He even got the priest to try to talk me out of it. He made me feel guilty as hell, but I knew what I wanted, so I left."

I stopped talking and Carolyn rubbed my back. Then a cop on a bicycle approached us. I figured we were going to catch shit for something, but he just jumped off his bike, hitched up his shorts and adjusted his navy blue COVID mask.

"How's it going, Carolyn? Who's your buddy?"

"Howdy, Officer Rick," Carolyn chirped. "This here's Jimmy, and this is Jacko. Don't worry, Jacko's a pussycat."

We weren't supposed to touch each other during the pandemic to avoid spreading germs, but Officer Rick shook my hand. "I've heard about you, Jimmy," he said. "Bennie says you've really helped keep the peace around here."

"Just trying to make your job easier, sir."

After that, I saw lots of Officer Rick on his daily patrols. We became pretty good buds. I'd tell him what was going on in camp and share soldier stories about Afghanistan. He'd tell me about how he caught bad guys.

"You know, Jimmy, with your skills and background, you might make a good cop," he said one day. It was nice to have someone take an interest in me.

I stayed in that tent city all winter. Sure, it got cold, but my tent was better than being in a shelter or on a subway grate. During the days, I'd sit cross-legged on the sidewalk with Jacko under a Queen Street ATM machine hoping folks withdrawing money would take pity on me. But hardly anyone was using cash during the pandemic, and handouts were rare. Still, Jacko and I often made enough to buy McNuggets and beers. Jacko loved McNuggets. Anyway, I was glad when spring rolled around, and those cherry trees blossomed again.

***

I'm creeping up on a cinder block schoolhouse surrounded by marijuana crops in Kandahar Province. Taliban insurgents are inside, and we've been ordered to attack. We're about a football field away when we're ambushed. I'm on the ground shaking, gritting my teeth, and holding my helmet tight to my head as bullets zing by me. I try not to scream; I don't want to give away my location. I can't see the enemy.

I wake up sweating with a bright white light shining down upon me.

"Jimmy, get up!" Carolyn was shrieking. "It's Bennie! Come quick!"

Disoriented, I squinted into her flashlight. I wiggled out of my sleeping bag and crawled out of my tent. Carolyn pulled me by the hand to Bennie's tent and handed me her flashlight. Bennie's tent flap was unzipped. Inside, he lay on his back, motionless, his eyes wide open. A chunk of orange plastic stained with blood stuck out of his chest. It looked like the handle of a screwdriver. I thought I might puke, but I'd seen and smelled much worse. A can of beer called *Bad Man's Brew* lay beside him.

"I saw someone leaving his tent a while ago," Carolyn whispered. "It was too dark to see who, but I thought it was unlike Bennie to have a visitor this late. I went in to see if he was okay and found him like this." She began to cry.

Me and Carolyn got hauled down to the police station. We were put in separate interview rooms. This fat detective with an ugly tie peppered me with questions. I couldn't help him much because I'd slept through the killing. I told him what I saw in Bennie's tent. He said they would take fingerprints from the murder weapon, and an officer took my prints to rule me out as a suspect.

I don't know if it was because Bennie had given me a home or because we'd become good buds, but I felt an overwhelming urge to find out who'd stuck him.

I was sitting at a picnic table stewing about it the next evening when Carolyn came by with Rosie, another tent city dweller. They planted themselves across from me, and Rosie pulled out a baggie stuffed with clumps of marijuana.

Rosie was a super-sized gal, and her stubby little fingers expertly pinched a chunk of weed from the baggie and sprinkled it onto a rolling paper. She twisted up a tight joint, lit it, and took three quick puffs before handing it to Carolyn. I'd normally jump on Carolyn for doing drugs, but I let it slide. She'd had a rough go convincing the cops she didn't have anything to do with Bennie's murder.

Rosie took another drag and exhaled a plume of smoke. "Cops don't know who offed Bennie," she said with a cough. "They would have arrested someone by now."

I sure had my suspicions. "Tom had an axe to grind with Bennie," I said. "And Scary Harry threatened him. Both those guys are crazier than shit-house rats."

"Word is Scary Harry is hanging out in Coronation Park down by the waterfront," Rosie said.

I left the women there and was headed back to my tent when Officer Rick rode up.

"My condolences about Bennie," he said. He meant it, I could tell.

"You guys figure out who did it?" I asked.

"We lifted fingerprints from the screwdriver, but didn't get any hits in the system," he said. "But you and Carolyn are in the clear."

I guess Officer Rick could tell from my angry expression that I didn't intend to sit on the sidelines.

"Jimmy, I hope you're not planning on doing anything stupid," he said. "You leave this up to us. No point in you backing a rabid dog into a corner."

But I'd already made up my mind. I wasn't going to wait for the cops to find Bennie's killer.

* * *

Tom had more opportunity to kill Bennie than Scary Harry because he still lived in our tent city. I found him painting *RIP Bennie* on the path in big letters.

"Wow, I didn't know you cared," I said.

He'd clearly caught my sarcasm and bolted upright.

"Everybody knows you had no love for Bennie," I continued. "I don't think what you're writing is sincere. More like you're trying to make it look like you gave a shit about Bennie and didn't kill him."

Tom's green eyes filled with fire. He aimed his dripping paint brush at me like a handgun. Paint specks splayed onto my mask and forehead. "Now you listen to me, you big son of a bitch," he said. "Bennie was an asshole, but I didn't kill him. He shouldn't have gone out like that."

I stared him straight in the eyes. "Where were you when it happened, Tom?"

His face grew red. I could tell he was aiming to take a swing at me, but Jacko growled.

"You wouldn't sic that dog on me, would you, Jimmy?" he said, his voice rising an octave.

"Depends on whether you tell me where you were when Bennie was murdered."

Tom rested his brush on top of a paint can and wiped his hands with a rag he'd stuffed in his belt loop.

"If you really gotta know, I was tweaked out on meth. I passed out pissing in the bushes. Jenna and Bob dragged me back to my tent and put me on my side so I wouldn't choke on my puke if I tossed my cookies."

A guy who interrogated Taliban fighters in Kandahar told me liars always look down and off to the side, avoiding eye contact. Tom looked me square in the eyes. I believed him, but I had to check out his alibi with Bob and Jenna, a nice couple I'd spent many evenings drinking with outside their tidy little tent. I found them in their listing lawn chairs sipping beer and asked them flat out about Tom.

"He couldn't have stabbed Bennie," Bob said. "We found the crazy bastard with his zipper undone and his pants halfway off."

Jenna nodded in agreement. "I watched him all night. I wanted to take him to the hospital, but he was dead weight."

Hearing that, I felt sorry for Tom. Addiction is a terrible thing. I took a rain cheque on a beer and headed back to my tent.

Time to find Scary Harry.

* * *

Coronation Park was a 15-minute walk south of Trinity Bellwoods. Jacko and I set out the next morning as soon as the sun rose. I could see the CN Tower off in the distance, its needle-shaped top piercing the fluffy clouds like a syringe into flesh. We passed the Princes' Gates which led to "The Ex," the annual Canadian National Exhibition grounds. We crossed Lakeshore Boulevard and arrived at the park.

I sat down in a red Muskoka chair by the shoreline and waited for Scary Harry, my head on a swivel. About an hour passed with no sign of him.

I really had to pee. I'm not one of those homeless people who goes anywhere, so I found some shrubs at the edge of the park. I waded in a few feet and unzipped my pants.

"Hey, what the hell! You're pissing all over me!" I recognized the voice. Scary Harry had made a little nest in the bushes. His eyes widened when he recognized me, and he made a run for it. One of his work boots slipped off, and Jacko chomped on his sock, tripping him up.

"Why'd you kill Bennie?" I yelled.

"I couldn't have," he said. "I was in the drunk tank. Just ask the cops, man!"

I had been so sure Harry was my man. I felt like I was back to square one. I whistled for Jacko to follow me, and we walked away.

* * *

When I ran into Officer Rick in the park that afternoon, I asked him if Scary Harry was a suspect.

"He was, Jimmy, but between you, me, and the fencepost, the bum was in jail when Bennie was killed," he said. "Don't tell anyone I told you that."

Harry was officially off the hook. And all my leads had dried up.

I had failed Bennie and felt low. Jacko was flat on his stomach in the tent looking as forlorn as I felt with his head between his paws. It was around dinner time, and I had no money, so I swallowed my pride and set out to go dumpster diving. It was recycling night on Crawford Street.

At first, it was slim pickings. I plucked a few money-back cans and bottles from the big blue plastic bins residents put out at the feet of their driveways. But nothing near enough to buy McNuggets or beer.

I was about to work the other side of the street when I spotted the mother lode—a bin so full that its lid wouldn't close. There must have been 40 beer cans stuffed in a bag inside.

The cans were all the same brand: *Bad Man's Brew.*

It was dark and I crept up the driveway to the side of the house. I ducked into the walkway between the house and its neighbor's home and quietly put down my bag of beer cans. I crawled across the backyard to a wooden shed. The lights inside the house were off, so I turned on my flashlight and shone it in a small window on the side of the shed. Inside, tools filled the shed, all neatly organized and hanging on shiny hooks in corkboard walls. The tools all had orange handles. One section was all screwdrivers.

The odd thing was that a space where a screwdriver should have been was empty.

** * **

The next morning, I borrowed Rosie's cell phone to call the police. I explained about the beer cans and the missing screwdriver, and that fat detective showed up shortly afterward to take away my beer cans.

At twilight, three cop cars rolled up to that house on Crawford Street. No sirens. One of the cars was an unmarked sedan. Neighbors stood on their porches watching as the detective and two cops walked up to the porch and knocked on the front door. Who should appear at the door but that fancy dan who'd confronted Bennie about stealing his propane tank. He poked his nose through a crack in the doorway, and one of the cops shoved the door open wider. They exchanged words. The man stepped hesitantly out on the porch. The cops spun him around, then slapped handcuffs on him. A man holding a camera with a big lens stood on the sidewalk, snapping photos the whole time.

The next morning, Carolyn came by my tent waving a copy of *The Toronto Sun.* A headline splashed across the front page read, *"Park Killer Nabbed!"*

A full-page photo showed Lester Gerald O'Keefe, 67, being stuffed into the back of a police cruiser. The actual story was on page 3. The reporter quoted several neighbors who said they were shocked and dumbfounded by the arrest. Lester had seemed like such a nice man.

Funny, that reporter never bothered to ask any of us tent folk how we felt about it.

* * *

Jacko sat obediently waiting for me to tell him it was okay to eat the McNugget that I had balanced on the tip of his wet nose. Officer Rick showed up and broke Jacko's concentration. So much for that McNugget.

"You did it, Jimmy," Officer Rick said. "That guy's fingerprints match those on the beer can found in Bennie's tent and on the beer cans you gave us. They were also on the screwdriver used to kill Bennie. We've got him dead to rights."

None of that had been in the newspaper, and I felt privileged that Officer Rick was sharing that information with me.

"Jimmy, this old guy wasn't even on our radar until you dug up the evidence," Officer Rick said. "We all had tunnel vision and assumed Bennie's killer was someone living in the park."

I shrugged and shuffled my feet. "Didn't we all?"

* * *

About three weeks after Bennie's death, cops, security guards, and city officials descended on our tent city like locusts on a farmer's field. We were given a few hours to gather our stuff and leave. I wasn't surprised. We'd all been issued trespassing notices earlier.

By early afternoon, blue metal fences went up. Police in riot gear and on horseback were everywhere. They clashed with protesters who supported us and linked arms to form circles around our tents. Several people got nabbed by the cops.

I wanted to keep my nose clean, so I packed up my backpack. Carolyn put her clothes into a wobbly-wheeled suitcase. As we were leaving the park, a city official approached us and offered to put us up in a hotel. Carolyn and I jumped at it.

Officer Rick and a group of bicycle cops were stationed nearby. "Here comes the guy who solved the O'Keefe case," he said, pointing at me. I turned three shades of red.

"We're moving to a hotel," Carolyn said.

"Great!" Officer Rick handed me a business card. "Let's talk about getting you enrolled in a college police foundations program. I think you'd make a fine cop."

"Do you think Jacko could become a police dog?" I joked.

Officer Rick smiled. "He might have to lay off the McNuggets."

* * *

Rob McCartney's interest in crime fiction stems from his days as a reporter covering the police beat at *The Sun Times* daily newspaper in Owen Sound, Ontario, Canada. Rob has studied novel, screenplay, TV, and comedy writing through various workshops at George Brown College, Raindance Canada, and The Second City. He lives in Toronto and is working on his first novel.

Stranger on the Train

By Kate Lansing

Hungary and Slovenia

We were six hours into what was supposed to be a four-hour trip from Budapest, Hungary to Ljubljana, Slovenia. Don't get me wrong, the scenery was epic. Gentle mountains covered in lush greenery and a wide river running alongside the tracks. The problem was, I had to pee like nobody's business but couldn't because a) I didn't want to miss my stop and be stranded alone in a foreign country and b) leaving my belongings fresh for the picking was asking for trouble. More than I already was.

Knees bouncing, I'd eyed the upcoming station with a mixture of hope and desperation. But from the sign, it appeared we were still somehow, inexplicably, in Croatia. *How were we still in Croatia?!*

A new feeling settled in: panic.

What if the extended family I was meeting at the station in Ljubljana assumed my tardiness meant I wasn't coming? What if no one would be there to pick me up? Proving once again how little thought I'd put into this trip.

A station official in uniform—military uniform, which threw me the first time but I've since grown accustomed to—entered my compartment and stamped my passport. Again. Before this excursion, I'd been eager to get even one measly stamp to prove I'd been somewhere. Seen a different corner of the world. Done *something.* Now it was littered with stamps from the borders this train had woven in and out of like my grandmother's embroidery.

I slumped back in my seat and tried to ignore my screaming bladder.

That was when the boy entered my compartment, which, until this point, I'd had to myself.

His voice was rich and melodic when he spoke, in a language I could only vaguely discern as French. That was one of the things I loved most about Europe, the prevalence of languages, all so close together. What I didn't love was how little I spoke of any of them.

"Parlez-vous anglais?" I replied sheepishly.

"Is this seat taken?" he asked with only a slight accent.

"No," I said, waving toward the seat across from me with the sophistication of a distressed chicken. "Help yourself."

He set his backpack on the ground and slouched into the seat while I opened my book and covertly studied him. His hair was dark and styled in spikes with gel, his capris pants and polo shirt showed off tanned skin, and his tennis shoes had tiny alligators on them. His army-green backpack was worn and had a label that identified him as Henry.

He cut a glance at me and I started, dropping my eyes to the page, heat flushing at the nape of my neck.

"The Brothers Karamazov," Henry said with a nod.

I lifted the book from my lap, using my finger to mark my spot. "Yes."

"Who is your favorite character?"

"Alexei," I answered and then clarified, "Well, Alexei Karamazov." Because I swore, everyone in this book was named Alexei.

Henry narrowed his eyes, giving me the distinct impression I'd disappointed him. "Alexei is too perfect. I like Ivan."

"He's so tortured, though."

Henry just smiled at me with his cool-gray eyes. "Life reflects art."

I didn't know if it was the obscure Russian literature, the foreign setting, or the attention from this boy, but that moment was imbued with importance. The lines between reality and fantasy grew fuzzy; surreal. What else was surreal was how badly I needed to pee. I mean, could a bladder literally explode?

Hedging my bets, I asked, "Would you mind watching my things for a minute?"

Henry raised his eyebrows and bobbed his head, which I interpreted as a yes.

I darted out of my seat and to the restroom on the other side of the compartment door as fast as my flip flops could carry me. Was I insane to leave my possessions alone with a boy who found the unlawful Ivan compelling? Possibly. But nothing about this trip was sane, anyway.

When I returned, I was relieved to find my suitcase and messenger bag intact and Henry slouched in the same position.

I slid into my seat and retrieved my book.

"You know," Henry started, "You need to be careful who you trust."

A chill swept over me at his words. "Don't I know it," I said, and meant it. More than he could ever comprehend.

* * *

My great aunt was waiting for me at the station. Turned out she had access to this thing called the internet and had been tracking my journey online.

I recognized Ula from her Facebook profile picture, but noted she was taller in real life. I also noted that we had the same eyes. Hazel flecked with gold and slightly narrowed at the corners.

"Thanks for meeting me," I said, extending my hand.

A handshake may seem like a strangely formal greeting for family, but we'd never met in person. My grandmother came to the United States when she was eighteen years old, leaving behind her entire family. While she and my mom had visited a couple times, I'd never been. It broke my heart to be here without them now, the lone stateside representative.

"Lana, thank you for coming all this way," Ula answered in perfect English, ignoring my hand and pulling me in for a hug.

Ula drove me to her house where I met her husband, a jolly man named Vito who was already prepping what appeared to be a feast. "Tonight, we celebrate," he said. "Everyone is coming over before we go to the exhibit."

"That sounds amazing," I answered, looking toward Ula.

A storm of emotions descended over her and the first Slovenian phrase I'd heard Ula speak slipped from her mouth, the intonation making me suspect she was swearing. Up one side and down the other.

I knew the exhibit was a point of contention for Ula—and the rest of the family, for that matter. It would be the last time an original manuscript by the famed poet France Prešeren would be on display for the public before being boxed up and given as a wedding gift to the daughter of a wealthy foreigner who'd supposedly written a blank check to acquire it. Never mind the poem was about unrequited love. Never mind it was a national treasure. Never mind that Prešeren's descendants weren't consulted.

Still grumbling, Ula led me to a room upstairs. There was a cozy twin bed, armoire, and gauzy curtains around a window that opened to an apricot tree laden with ripe fruit. All told, I could have stayed here far longer than a weekend.

"Get settled and then we'll go into town."

She left me and I took a minute to let reality sink in. I was here. I was doing this.

Nerves rattled through my body and my confidence wavered. What would my grandmother say if she knew what I was about to do? What about my mother? Maybe it was a blessing they'd never find out, even if they were the reason I was here.

I stifled my insecurities and busied myself unpacking and freshening up. Then I went in search of Ula.

Downtown Ljubjana was a burst of color and activity. Stone pedestrian bridges zigzagged over the river where tour boats and paddleboarders floated by and willow trees dipped their branches into the water. Buildings in a rainbow of pastels were every bit as colorful as the tents over the farmers' market, artisans peddling fresh-caught fish and produce galore. And don't even get me started on the gelato.

Oh, the gelato.

I'd never tasted anything so creamy and vibrant as the scoop of strawberry Ula practically forced upon me. We licked our melting cones as we walked, weaving our way through the bustle to Prešeren Square.

That was when I saw Henry.

He was dressed in old-timey clothes, slacks and a linen shirt complete with a top hat and cloak. He was in the middle of a performance, but paused mid-sentence when he saw me, honing in on me in a way that made my stomach flutter.

"This was always my favorite part," Ula whispered beside me.

We watched, hypnotized, as Henry recited each verse of the Wreath of Sonnets, acting out this piece of our heritage in the place it all started. This was where France Prešeren first professed his love for Julija Primic, but he was a lowly poet and deemed unworthy. While Prešeren eventually moved on—securing the blood line that lives in my veins—he never forgot Julija and wrote about her the rest of his life.

A crowd had gathered around us by the time Henry came to a close with a flourished bow. When he looked up, his eyes locked on mine and his eyebrows ticked upward in question.

I nodded and clapped along with everyone else, although for me there was more behind the appreciative gesture. An acknowledgement and an answer.

* * *

Dinner was a raucous affair. Relatives were introduced with such alacrity my head spun with faces and names. The homemade brandy my great uncle thrust upon me didn't help. One sip was enough to get me buzzed. Or maybe that was the atmosphere.

The feast Vito had spent the afternoon making was sprawled across a long picnic table beneath a pergola in their backyard. Roasted fish doused with herbed butter, citrusy salad with grapefruit, radishes, and frisée, some sort of salty potato dumpling, and apricot tarts with jam made from the fruit of their tree. There were also cracklings and a special dessert called *potica* supplied by family members keen to share recipes that had been handed down from generation to generation.

It was like a dream and I savored every bite. Every second.

Chatter and laughter floated around me, a mixture of Slovenian and English.

"Show her the family tree," Ula's daughter, Natasa, suggested. She'd been at my side most of the evening, helpfully translating and pointing out the different foods on my loaded plate.

"Super," Ula said, rolling the 'r'.

Ula went inside and emerged a minute later with what appeared to be a large poster. Finding a clean spot on the table, she carefully unrolled it. The paper was thick and so long she could only show portions of it at a time. Carefully penciled names were connected by lines that stretched in every direction.

I eventually found my name and traced along the branch with my finger, marveling as it connected my mother to my grandmother and then all the way back to France Prešeren—and beyond. It was like coming face to face with a piece of myself I never knew existed.

"Your grandmother would be so proud to see you here," a great-great aunt said as she patted my cheek.

Losing my grandma and my mom so close together had been tough (understatement of the century). There was a part of me that worried I'd never feel whole again, that I'd never escape the sorrow and grief. But this helped. And I hoped what was coming next would too.

I smiled and blinked back tears, resolve solidifying in my gut.

"Enough talk," Ula interjected. "It's time."

I fortified myself with one last sip of brandy. Then I followed my family toward the door.

* * *

The castle sat at the top of a hill overlooking Ljubljana. To the north, the Alps rose in an impressive crescendo and to the south, gentle slopes separated Slovenia from Italy. No matter where you looked, there was a breathtaking view.

The stone walls of the castle used to house royalty, but now proved to be a popular tourist destination and venue. Chairs were being assembled for a wedding reception in the courtyard, dinner service was in full swing in the restaurant in the main hall, and up a winding staircase, through security and a metal detector, in what used to be the archer's tower, was our event.

It was already packed when we got there and our group fell in line, no one the wiser that descendants of Prešeren himself were, as they say, in the house.

My lips twitched into a smile. The crowd would play in my favor.

The event was formal and I was grateful for the taffeta dress and heels I'd donned. They would help me blend in. Guards were stationed at each of the entrances and outside the restrooms in the back, with intimidating stances and earpieces, and I counted six video surveillance cameras placed strategically on the ceiling.

Servers in black slacks, collared white shirts, and thin ties circulated the room with trays of hors d'oeuvres and drinks. I wasn't even surprised when I saw Henry, holding a tray of champagne on his open palm.

He caught my eye over the shoulder of a lady fanning herself and I subtly winked at him.

"You need to see this while you can," Ula said, leading me by the elbow to a display case in the center of the room.

There, beneath the glass, were pieces of yellowed parchment with looping cursive sloped to the right. The original handwritten pages of the Wreath of Sonnets.

"It's incredible," I said, somewhat breathless.

Ula sniffed. I knew this was difficult for her, had been since she first learned the manuscript would be moved. The last time she'd called my mom, I'd shamelessly eavesdropped on their conversation from the other room. Gotta love speaker phone.

"It belongs in Slovenia," Ula had argued. "It belongs to the people."

"What you mean is it should belong to you," my mom had answered patiently, exhaustion tugging at the edges of her voice.

"Not just for me, for everyone." Emotion welled in Ula's voice. "It's a point of pride."

"I wish there was something we could do." By then, my mom was living on wishes and prayers, the cancer having spread to other organs. She'd only had days left at that point. In the end, she died exactly one month after my grandmother.

I shook the sad memories from my mind, bringing my fingers to the elegant knot atop my head and the bobby pin lodged there, nearly splintered in half. The bobby pin fell to the floor and I covertly covered it with the toe of my shoe and swiped it to the edge of the display case. Then I turned my back on the manuscript.

"What else do they have here?" I asked as I plucked a flute of champagne from—wouldn't you know it—Henry's tray.

Ula sought comfort from Vito, which was for the better, while I strayed to the far corner of the room where a less popular case held a golden appliqué from the Bronze Age, discovered on the shores of Lake Bled.

History was important. If we paid attention, it instructed, gave insights into the future as well as the past.

I set my glass on the corner of the display case and, leaning in for a closer look at the treasure, knocked it over with my elbow. Champagne dribbled over the surface in a stream of translucent bubbles and the glass cascaded to the floor and shattered. An alarm blared and lights flashed, the screeching so intense it rattled my bones and seared my temples. I pressed my palms over my ears to muffle the noise.

Guards surrounded me in seconds. All of them, by a quick count.

"I'm so sorry," I said over the racket, not having to try to add extra embarrassment to my tone. "I'm such a klutz."

Around us, the alarm continued to blare and chaos ensued. Confusion and panic proliferated, gaining momentum as it circulated through the frenzied attendees.

"That's okay, miss," one of the guards answered in English. The others inspected the case while another barked something into his ear piece. "The displays are waterproof, but they are not tables."

"Right," I said with a tense smile. A quick glance told me Henry was still lingering near the Wreath of Sonnets manuscript, the masses distracted around him.

While the security system would be down for approximately three minutes to reset, the guards could see perfectly fine.

"Will this piece be moved too?" I half shouted-half asked, keeping their attention on me and the ornate appliqué. It worked better than I could have hoped, the alarm falling silent as my voice resounded through the space.

The guard appraised me with newfound interest as suspicion darkened his eyes. "This will remain here."

"Is there a problem?" Natasa asked, sidling up to my side with Ula hot on her heels.

"No problem," I lied.

I felt the guard watching me as I retreated, like an aggravating itch between my shoulder blades. *Two minutes.*

I could still walk away, abandon this foolhardy plan. My mother's words flitted through my mind and compelled me onward: *I wish there was something we could do.* This was bigger than me.

"Is that a Kralja?" I asked, pointing at a random painting and hurrying toward it. After shaking off Natasa and Ula—if things turned south, I didn't want them implicated—I looped back around the room, squeezing through the horde until I was at Henry's side, a maneuver that cost me precious seconds.

"What's the holdup?" I hissed out of the corner of my mouth.

"The lock isn't budging," Henry said, agitated. Even in the wake of the pandemonium and with his uniform and tray providing coverage, people would notice him soon.

"Let me try."

He cocked an eyebrow at me. "Really?"

"Yes," I said. "Now move."

He passed me the bobby pin, now split into two pieces, and took position behind me.

My heart lodged itself in my throat as I reached for the lock. There was no turning back now. With one of the pieces, I applied tension at the bottom of the keyhole, and, with the other, I maneuvered it in the lock to slowly lift each of the pins to mimic the teeth of a key.

Lock picking is about balance, about moving forward, but not so quickly as to cause the entire mechanism to seize. A bit like life, really.

My fingers were swift and adept and I felt the pins of the lock slowly—too slowly—level above the shear line, just like the YouTube tutorials said they would. Just like I'd practiced alone in my bedroom before leaving for this trip.

Sweat beaded on my forehead and my fingers shook. With one final, subtle push, the resistance disappeared and the lock clicked open.

"Excuse me," a stern voice said over my shoulder and I jumped, dropping the bobby pin pieces. I turned to find the guard who'd been watching me.

I swallowed, not sure how much he'd seen, nor what he was about to say. I soothed my features into a calm mask and lifted my chin to him.

"Do not get so close to the case," he ordered. "You don't want to trigger the alarm again."

My mouth was bone dry as I responded, "Absolutely not."

I shot Henry a meaningful look as I rejoined my family at an arched window overlooking the courtyard with downtown Ljubljana glittering in the background.

"Isn't it spectacular?" Ula asked. Stars twinkled overhead in constellations that were foreign to me, but the pale moon was the same.

Over my shoulder, I caught sight of Henry leaving through the service exit. "It sure is."

The first shouts arose, alerting attendees—and guards—to an empty display case. The Wreath of Sonnets was missing.

* * *

The first time I talked to Henry, pronounced *on-ree*, was on a secure Skype line the night I booked my airfare and train tickets.

I'd gotten his name from the boyfriend of my college roommate. A friend of a friend of a friend who was a part of a global organization that preserved cultural artifacts. At all costs.

Had grief and loneliness warped my moral code? Perhaps. But it would be worth it if the Prešeren manuscript ended up in the right hands. If what remained of my family was given some solace.

Henry was in the same compartment as the one we'd agreed to meet in on the way to Ljubljana, recognizing each other by the book I was reading: *The Brothers Karamazov.*

Every encounter had been carefully planned and executed. From our first conversation to the final nod of approval in Prešeren Square to playing our parts at the exhibit. Everything led to this moment.

"What a coincidence," I said as I took my seat.

His eyes twinkled. "Funny how that happens sometimes."

I waved at Ula and Natasa out the train window. We'd parted with a promise to stay in touch. They had no idea just how soon they'd be hearing from me.

Henry and I waited until the train began to move before risking further conversation. I ticked seconds off in my head, keenly aware of Henry sitting across from me with his legs extended, as if he didn't have a care in the world. I picked up my book and pretended to read, not nearly as successful as Henry at my attempt at nonchalance.

The train rumbled to life and began moving. My heart skittered in my chest as a station official checked our tickets. As soon as she was farther along the hallway, Henry sifted through his backpack for a paper-wrapped package.

"I believe this belongs to you."

It weighed almost nothing and I was struck by how something so priceless could feel so inconsequential. "This is it?"

"Yes," he said, a dimple forming at the corner of his mouth.

I couldn't believe he did this regularly, like some sort of scholarly Robin

Hood.

"You weren't bad," he said. "Good improvising."

"Thanks," I answered. "I think."

"HARPS could use someone like you." HARPS, an acronym for the Historic Artifact and Recovery Preservation Society, which made what they did sound more legit than it really was.

I kept my face impassive, although inwardly, I beamed. "I'll keep that I mind."

I stood and made my way to the compartment door. My stop was next and it was paramount that I not miss it; the last thing I wanted was to be searched crossing the border.

"Is your favorite brother really Alexei?" Henry asked.

"Looks can be deceiving," I replied with a wink.

I disembarked and went directly to the post office where I wrote a note to Ula:

> *A stranger on the train gave this to me. I think you'll know what to do with it. Love, Lana.*

I posted the package and waited for the next train. Henry wasn't on it, of course, but somehow I knew that wouldn't be the last time our paths crossed.

* * *

Kate Lansing is the author of the award-winning Colorado Wine Mystery Series. She lives in Broomfield, Colorado, with her husband, daughter, and two mischievous kitties.

Thin Air

By Katherine Ramsland

County Galway, Ireland

I stood near the stairs that once had sparked images of mystical gyres. Thoor Ballylee, this four-story Roman keep, has endured for centuries in Ireland's County Galway. I'd been lucky to get in. Rain like this often closed the place. Even now, the thunderous Streamstown River rammed the bottom of its seven-foot-thick walls. Only Driscol McKeer, a Thoor Conservancy volunteer, manned the Interpretative Centre. He was pleased I'd braved the weather to visit.

"Will ye have tea?" he asked.

I accepted, but I wasn't exactly a tourist. I was tracking my father. This tower was a crucial spot for my pursuit.

Dad didn't kill himself, as some believe, distraught over a lost love. He'd merely erased his presence—known in my circles as pseudocide. I'm a behavioral investigative analyst. I know when something's staged. I'd found breadcrumbs by way of flickers on Dad's AI decoder app.

He'd developed this app himself. He'd heard about the 'large language' tools that had scraped every word and image from the Web into one vast pool. The intent was to generate personalized responses to prompts based on predictions. Dad had mimicked the effort on a smaller scale, for a different purpose. He'd amassed every manifestation he could find of

AW—automatic writing—to compile alleged communications from the dead. Using these messages, he'd created an AI app, which he called AWAI, as in 'away.' Given his current status, the name likely amused him. But his app isn't for ghosts. It's for *portals*—the fabled 'thin air' that supposedly facilitates otherworldly contact. Many cultures have myths about these liminal thresholds. Dad wants to figure out if they're actually spots where people have disappeared. I think he faked his death to test them in private.

But he'd trained me well. I could follow air dimples, a.k.a., ghostprints. They act like the images in augmented reality games like *Pokémon Go*, only they're not cartoons, they're ripples. Once I saw one, I knew how to spot them. Unfortunately, I have no game plan with pre-arranged locations. I must deduce where these portals might be, so I let the lore guide me. This tower's a beacon. Thanks to William Butler Yeats, it was once an AW magnet, inspiring some 4,000 pages of communication.

I told none of this to Driscol McKeer. I let the thin young man with an Irish accent I couldn't place show off his training. Pronouncing Yeats as Yeets, he stood to attention as he began his spiel.

"The poet and Nobel Laureate William Butler Yeats purchased Thoor Ballylee in 1916 from Lady Augusta Gregory. T'was called Islandmore Castle, but Yeats renamed it to connect it with its Irish heritage. Tat's grand! Tere were no plumbin' er heat, but Yeats fixed da place an' brought his wife 'n' children here ta endure eight rrrainy summers." He gestured toward the fogged window. "Like dis. Yeats tought da place'd inspire his wroitin'." Driscol pointed out exhibits around the shop, recommended some books, and offered a basic tour. I accepted.

"Pay attention," he said, as we entered the first-floor living area. "Watch everyting, down, aroun', above, an' under. Dere are tings to see you won' expect."

I hoped so. "Like what?"

"Well, like da *meurtrière*, da murder hole. When we take da stairs, look up. It's a large openin' overrhead. If the enemy breached da place, da soldiers at da top will be pourrin' boilin' water an' hot ash tru it ta brreak dee advance."

"Fascinating. This place is haunted, right?"

Driscol chuckled. "So Yeats believed. A soldier might pass as ye ascend da stairs. Sure, jus' let 'im squeeze by. An' caretakers haff tales, they do."

I raised an eyebrow. "Do you?"

He glanced away. "Nuh-tin' like dat."

I watched for spots that might register on the app. I'd tested it at Glencar Waterfall, a reputed thin place in the County Leitrim two hours north. Yeats had written a poem about a child vanishing there, abducted by fairies to garnish their lair. The AWAI app had shown a density dip in the air. Still, I knew Dad would seek out a place with a definite record of AW psychography. Like this "thoor."

Automatic writing has a long history, with documents primarily from the nineteenth century when spiritualists posed as 'transmitters' or 'scriptors.' Typically, they'd hold a pencil (or some similar instrument) to paper, enter a trance-state, and let a 'force' take over their hand to generate a communication. Some scriptors have allegedly produced quite a lot. Brazilian medium Chico Xavier, with only a simple education, claimed to have penned more than 400 volumes of AW in a wide range of styles.

The science for this talent is lacking, but I found a study that involved ten psychographers. As the subjects performed exercises of both automatic and normal writing, researchers scanned their brainwaves. The highly experienced scriptors—and *only* them—showed diminished brainwave activity during AW sessions. The researchers concluded that these subjects were not 'merely' relaxed. Something else was happening. They never said what.

Dad's notes indicate that these conduits for contact offer portals through which people slip when they inexplicably disappear. He'd crafted his app to detect these 'soft spots,' using special prompts for the most puzzling incidents—the cluster vanishments.

One such mystery spot is on Ireland's eastern coast, south of Dublin, called the Vanishing Triangle. Six women went missing there between 1993 and 1998. Two had gone to the post office, another to the doctor, another for a walk. Still another disappeared from her bedroom. No bodies turned up. Rumors blamed a serial killer, but Dad thinks it's a threshold. The Celtic world, in particular, has many tales about people seeming to evaporate. But Dad had a personal reason for probing these portals. One of his research colleagues might have gone through one—a lover for whom he left my mother. According to his notes, just before his 'suicide,' he'd been on a trek with her to a thin place. She'd gone around a corner and *whoosh!* That was the last he'd seen of her.

"Shall we go up?" Driscol gestured toward the circular stone staircase. I noticed the sign: *Mind Your Head. Low Ceilings.*

"Yes, please."

"Hope ye don' moind close quarters."

Driscol entered the narrow area first. I had to take a breath before I followed. He pointed out the iron railing. "Sorry, grrrab this." I stepped carefully up the surprisingly high steps. Unable to climb and also watch the app, I slid my phone into a back pocket. The place did have a damp sense of being haunted.

"Da staircase links rrrooms on each floor," Driscol said. "At top are battlements and a lovely view." He glanced back. "Not today, not wit' da rain."

We entered Yeats' sitting room. It featured a large fireplace and a small writing desk that faced a green-framed double casement window. A simple pen-and-ink pot sat ready for action. Here, Yates had listened to the river and conducted the music for his most lyrical poems.

"Please sign da guestbook," Driscol said. "Add a po-em, if ye feel inclined."

I looked through the recent notes before I chose a blank spot. Without much thought, I scribbled, *I'm at the brink, Closer than you think, A. Hunter.*

I stood back and looked at it. Where'd *that* come from?

Driscol leaned in. His eyes widened. "Include where yur from, if ye don' moind." I did so. He read it. "North Carolina! Dat's grand."

"Yes," I said. "Ever meet anyone else from there?" *Like my father, Lang Hunter?*

He hesitated. "Could be." His left eye twitched and his warm manner dispersed. "Let me show ye one more room, sure, and den ye kin wander on yur own. Oi should go back down in case someone comes."

That seemed unlikely, but it was fine with me. I needed to use the app in private.

Yeats had embraced this abode as an ideal place to syphon the dead. He'd once said, "The mystical life is the center of all that I do and all that I think and all that I write." He'd even participated in the Ghost Club, a paranormal research group.

I followed Driscol up another confining flight of stairs, through a bedroom, and up again. On the next floor, we entered a large room with massive arched windows and an imposing slate-trimmed hearth. Straw stuck out where a bird had made a nest in a nook high up. The murder hole started here.

"As ye can see, t'was a co-eld place to live," Driscol said, "especially durin' da winterr. T'was mostly a summer retreat." He gestured around him. "Dey called dis da Strrrangers Room. We tink dey used it as a guest room. Hence, da name."

I smiled and nodded. He didn't know. But I did. The 'strangers' weren't guests. They were the *Others*, the ones whom the Yeatses had invited to fill the room with an ethereal force. In fact, suicidal poet Sylvia Plath had 'felt' a profound connection here to the late Yeats. To strange ones, it seems, the Strangers are friends, perhaps providing a seductive gust of transformative air.

"If ye'll excuse me, sorry," Driscol said. His body leaned toward the door, as if he were in a hurry to leave.

"Of course," I said. "I'll be down soon."

Driscol departed. He flung me a look that made me feel like a bug for which he must find a swatter. Was it something I said? Whatever. I was alone.

I stood in the middle of the large space and marveled that Yeats had convinced his wife, George Hyde-Lees, a.k.a., Georgie, to reside here. The stone floors and walls looked decidedly cold and hard. But then again, she'd set herself up.

Reportedly, the astute twenty-five-year-old knew she had a rival, Maud

Gonne, whom Yeats, 52, had begged in vain to marry him. He'd also proposed to Maud's daughter, Iseult. She, too, rejected him. Three weeks later, he'd married George. She knew he considered her 'serviceable.' A bad start. Thinking fast, she offered a carrot he couldn't ignore. As the poet brooded over his Gonne Girls and wondered if his marriage was an error, right there at a desk in their honeymoon suite in the Ashdown Forest Hotel, George suddenly 'received' a spirit memo.

"Look, my darling, the ghosts are speaking to me!" She scribbled some phrases on a page. Versed in Medieval Latin, the occult, and ritual magic, she tapped into her varied vocabulary. Yeats watched the rambling sentences form, astonished by George's apparent ability to scribe from apparitions worldwide. She was *better* than 'serviceable.' She could be his medium *and* his muse. Their newlywed game launched an extended venture into automatic writing. They held more than 400 sessions, many of them right here in this room.

But here's the rub:

George would later admit she'd faked the honeymoon notations. I guessed she didn't anticipate that her little trick would become a daily task. For years! Still, better a throuple with 'strangers' she controlled than with a Gonne girl.

The Yeatses devised a routine. W. B. asked leading questions and George 'received' the answers. The Others told Yeats they would further his career—just what he wanted to hear. They confirmed his choice in a wife. (Clever George.) He'd worried that sexual consummation would block inspiration, but the spirits said it opens the portal. To achieve his best work, he must satisfy his wife. (*Very* clever George.) Yeats was thrilled. He'd get sex *and* phantom memoranda.

He immersed in the cryptic notes, developing theories about infinite numbers of possible lives. George corroborated everything. Yet, if she were faking these spirit dispatches, then Yeats was mistaken about a mystical infusion. Their AW was just the product of her imaginative mind. I thought Dad would have realized this, but he'd included their work in his database.

Dad had even done his own AW sessions. In fact, he'd gotten *me* to try it, 'though I'd turned out to be a brick. He'd tell me to relax, "it's inside you," but only some weird gibberish had moved through my pen to the page. I thought it came from my wish to please him.

Dad's notes told me he'd focused most keenly on AW 'hallucinations.' Maybe that's what George had produced. In some AI predictive models, hallucinations are false data that get stated as fact. That is, I could prompt the program with a request for my bio and it might mix false credentials with true. They'd look the same and only I would know which creds were genuine.

Developers of AI products create 'guardrails' to minimize such lies, but Dad thought AW hallucinations weren't *false* data but *coded* data. If his program generated them, then 'something' was trying to communicate. For years, he'd worked with five colleagues on the AWAI project. Then two went missing, including his mistress. I suspect he thought they'd cracked the code, found a portal, and slipped through, vanishing, so to speak, into thin air. He hoped to learn what they'd discovered.

I pulled out my phone. Time to work. If the app confirmed a thin place here, I'd found the first location for my map to Dad. I lifted a finger to tap it.

"Stop!" A petite, gray-haired woman in a belted blue raincoat stood at the door, her hand raised. "Don't!" She strode toward me, dripping water, and reached for my phone. I jerked it away.

Driscol McKeer, looking flushed, entered and hovered behind this woman. Obviously, he'd called her.

"This is *my* phone," I insisted. "I'm allowed to take photos."

"We know who ye arre," the woman said. Her accent sounded like north Dublin. "Yeer Lang Hunter's daughterr. Yeer tryin' ta destroy dee aura."

I made a face. "I'm doing no such thing."

She lunged for my phone. I held it behind me and moved toward the wall, then stopped. The top of the murder hole was in here somewhere, with a lo-n-g fall to the bottom.

"The Thoor Conservancy prrotects dis place," Driscol said. "Don' open dat app."

Since they obviously knew about it, I said, "It's just a decoder."

"With emergent prrroperties!" Driscol came toward me. "It's a prrrogram, set up to tink fer itself. It *generates* tings yer da didnah expect. He opened it here. It tried ta transforrm de air."

So, Driscol *had* known what the Strangers were.

"My father's a researcher," I said. "He's just gathering information."

The Dubliner's mouth became a thin, menacing line. "He's gatherin' *portals*. His app's transmutin' 'em, *absorbin'* 'em."

I shook my head. "That's not possible."

"It's prrrogrammed," Driscol shouted. "De app lacks values. *Our* values. Lang failed ta build 'em in, so the prrrogram pleases itself. Da more it learns, da more it wants. You mus' get rid ah it."

The Dubliner leaned toward me. "He *infected* you. Oi see it. De app's usin' ya. Yer not da first guarrdian ta come. It brings 'em here. It wants ta take morrre."

"It didn't—"

"If ye did dee exercises, ye got sucked inta serrvin' it."

I had no comeback. I'd done Dad's AW exercises. I felt an urgent need to open the app, just to prove they were wrong. Or to reassure myself. But…maybe it *wanted* that. I gripped my phone's rubber case. It felt warm. "I'm not a guard—"

"Sure, an' y'are. He built dat in. Da ting *makes* ye shield it, like yer doin' roight now. Show us we're wrong. Hand over da phone."

I shook my head.

"Ye don' know what happened. It nearly torrre up the porrrtal. He troied ta undo it, but he failed. Den he lost control an' fled. We're troyin' ta rebuild it. If ya carrre about da legacy here, yu'll give it t'us."

I stood still, frozen.

The Dubliner pushed me while Driscol grabbed my phone. I tried to grip it, but he wrestled it away.

"Stop!" I shouted. "Give it back!"

Driscol's face registered shock. He dropped the phone as if it had burned him.

I stooped, grabbed it, and ran through the green door to descend the treacherous stone steps. I heard the Dubliner yell, "Destroy it! Ye canna carry it away!"

I hit the ground floor, raced through the shop, and pushed through the door. Rain slapped my face. I crossed the stone bridge and ran down the narrow lane to my car. Jumping in, I sped away.

Once I was a few miles away, I slowed down to catch my breath and think. I glanced at my phone on the seat next to me. What had Dad *done*? Had he fed *my* responses to his monster? Did this thing *know* me? Is that why I could make it work? I didn't like this. I wondered if I should just throw it into the river and send back to Yeats his silly communications.

I considered my options. Dad was scared of his own creation. These people said it was dangerous. But...hmmm. Now I had a guide. It was inside me, like Dad had said. He'd *infected* me. Dumping the phone wouldn't purge that. Only Dad could do it. I had to keep going. I had to find him. I stepped on the gas.

Next stop: the Vanishing Triangle.

* * *

Katherine Ramsland pens the Nut Cracker series that features Dr. Annie Hunter solving mind-twisting crimes with her PI team. The author of 71 books, Ramsland is also an executive producer of *Murder House Flip* and *Confession of a Serial Killer*. A respected true crime commentator, her latest books are *The Serial Killer's Apprentice* and *In the Damage Path*.

Lost at Sea

By Cathi Stoler

Western Mediterranean

I was standing on the forward deck of *The Allure*, the Wanderlust Company's newest ship, looking out at the sea thanking its gods for my good fortune. I'm Monica Delmar, Director of Passenger Events. And to say I've seen many unusual things occur onboard a ship would be like me telling you the water isn't blue. You might not believe me until you dove in and saw that it's not that color at all. Perceptions can be deceiving and not always entirely trustworthy. I was hoping this time perception and reality would match and that nothing would spoil the splendors I'd planned for the ship's three-hundred well-heeled passengers on this voyage from Monte Carlo to Lisbon.

The ship itself was beautiful. New. Sleek, elegant, luxurious—all the upscale adjectives complemented by huge oceanfront-only suites, gourmet dining, pampering spa treatments, and any other outrageous extravagances the passengers could imagine.

The select high-end merchants whose jewel-box shops lined the Grand Salon were ready, smiling as if they'd discovered bulging chests brimming with buried treasure. Who could blame them? I knew they'd have quite the time swiping those black American Express cards the passengers would be eager to present.

It was to be a perfect cruise and, for me, what I hoped would be the start of a very lucrative career with the Wanderlust Company.

I'd been extremely lucky to get the job, coming from a more proletarian cruise line whose passengers generally numbered in the thousands rather than the hundreds. There, I was the low woman on the totem pole of four social directors, responsible for the lounge entertainment: mostly performers past their prime, tottering onto the stage on their last legs. I'd done my best and my supervisor appreciated my work. When I told her I needed a change, she recommended me to Wanderlust's Human Resources department. Believe me, it wasn't difficult to say goodbye.

* * *

Now on *The Allure*, I was responsible for all the passenger events and had a staff of four to assist me. It was a bit daunting, especially dealing with celebrity passengers like Elena Holden, a movie star with a capital 'S' who attracted trouble with a capital 'T'.

Elena, now perched on the edge of fifty, was still stunningly beautiful. If she'd had work done, it was very good. She'd joined the ship two days ago before we were scheduled to leave on our route to Lisbon. She wanted to relax and rejuvenate after her latest divorce, her third I think, and believed a few days alone would do the trick before she encountered her adoring public on board—of course, her press agent leaked the news weeks before that she'd be on *The Allure*'s maiden voyage. The Wanderlust Cruise Line was happy to accommodate her. I'd had strict orders from the head of the line, to "afford her every convenience and make sure she was pampered and protected."

The last was emphasized with a low growl that let me know he meant business. *Aye, aye, sir,* I replied to myself while assuring him I would do my best to ensure Ms. Holden got the royal treatment.

Captain Brigman had joined me as we greeted the star at the gangway and escorted her to the penthouse suite. It was gorgeous, with its glassed-in verandah overlooking the ocean, private soak pool, and amenities too numerous to list. She seemed pleased as she glanced around. I knew I would be. Even though my title may have sounded grand, my quarters were less so and located on a much lower deck. I had been fortunate to be able to invite my best friend from my previous job, Irene Waxman, on this cruise. She was due to arrive later today. She'd hold my hand as I made my way through this first voyage of *The Allure*. Maiden sailings were tricky and I was still wary there might be squalls or surprises ahead, especially with Elena Holden on board.

Ms. Holden was traveling alone, unless you counted her oversized jewelry case, which was as large as a small child, and which I was sure held the famous, and huge, pear-shaped ruby and diamond earrings given to her by her first husband. Her most generous, I'd heard. She asked for the location of the suite's safe the moment we entered and excused herself as she left to deposit her jewelry in its confines. Smiling happily, she returned to the living room a few minutes later, now attired in a Dior sundress I recognized from the latest collection, and of course, those earrings. They were truly magnificent, and I had to stop myself from staring, as I was certain everyone did.

I sent for the suite steward to unpack for her while the Captain escorted her on a tour of the ship. I had other details to attend to, such as welcoming the quartet of single men I'd engaged as dance hosts and companions for any of the single women onboard.

* * *

If you've ever taken a cruise, you know about these gentlemen. Usually, between thirty and sixty years old, they receive a free cruise in return for this service. But as we all know, nothing in life is truly free, and often they more than danced for their supper. I was sure the single female passengers, or those on a mini marriage break, would put them through their paces.

These four appeared for inspection and instructions in the aft bar and lounge, The Quartermaster. All were tall, trim, and handsome enough. They presented themselves in their tuxedos, which they'd be required to wear every evening. I just hoped they could dance, as the talent booker for the Wanderlust Line had assured me by email that they could.

One of them in particular, Derrick Robson, stood out. There was something about the look in his blue eyes, which were as bright as the sky over the ocean, that signaled trouble. His black hair and chiseled features on his café-au-lait face added the slightest touch of menace to his six-foot-plus model-perfect appearance but disappeared the moment he smiled.

He'd also arrived with a walking stick, which gave me pause. Was it a prop or a necessity?

"Thank you, gentlemen, it was lovely to meet you. Please settle into your cabins, change into something comfortable, and then proceed to the Magnifique Ballroom at four p.m. Carmen and Orlando, our resident dance team, will meet you to discuss and demonstrate the dances you'll be expected to perform. Enjoy the ship and I'll see you tomorrow evening at dinner."

As they rose to depart, I asked Mr. Robson to stay behind. "Mr. Robson, I just want to make sure your walking stick is merely for effect, and not something that would keep you from your dancing duties."

He smiled. "Of course not, Ms. Delmar." He pronounced my name as if he was asking a question, almost as if he were insinuating it might be made up. I didn't rise to the bait but ignored his jibe, waiting for him to continue. "I believe it adds to my look. Don't you agree?" He spoke in one of those hybrid world accents, like the one Madonna adopted when she lived in England. I just stood there as he raised the silver-tipped handle of the walking stick in my direction then left the lounge.

I rolled my eyes. Oh boy, had I made a mistake in hiring this one? I'd have to talk it over with Irene as soon as she arrived.

* * *

The afternoon flew by with me checking on a hundred little details that, while seemingly insignificant, could make or break the voyage. My staff was efficient and proactive and had everything well in hand. The schedule of lectures, events, and entertainment was complete. The place cards and seating arrangements for the Captain's Dinner tomorrow evening were settled and the menu fixed. I checked over the daily program of movies, spa, and sporting events and was satisfied.

By the time Irene arrived on board from the airport in Nice, I was beat. Once I got her things stowed away in my cabin, I ordered a bottle of Cristal champagne to celebrate seeing her, my new job, and the delights I planned to encounter in our European ports of call.

"Cristal?" she asked as I popped the cork and poured the sparkling liquid into two elegant flutes.

"It's the house Champagne," I replied and we both started laughing. On our other cruise line, Korbel was about as good as it got. "I think I'm going to like it here," Irene said, clinking her flute against mine, then finishing what was in it and holding it out for a refill.

We chatted for a while as we sipped our Champagne. "Let's give you a tour of the ship," I said. "There's something I want your opinion on."

* * *

We spent the next hour going over every public room of the ship and some of its most luxurious cabins. "Monica, I beg you!" Her hands were clasped in front of her as though she was praying to highlight her words. "Hire me. I want to work here." She looked around the Starlight Dining Room with its gilt fixtures, moiré silk-covered walls, and beautiful table settings and sighed. "Three hundred guests instead of three thousand, and all of this."

I led her to a table under a window banquette, which was set with *The Allure*'s signature sterling and crystal. Irene gently patted the crisp white tablecloth as I asked one of the waiters to bring us tea.

"It's not all fun and games," I told her as she bit into a freshly baked scone dotted with raisins and slathered with jam and clotted cream.

"You could have fooled me," she replied as she licked a smidge of jam from the corner of her mouth.

"I'm being serious. I need your opinion about one of the dance hosts I hired."

"What about him?"

"Well, he's too handsome—" I began only to be cut off in mid-sentence.

"—Are you nuts? Isn't handsome a plus? Especially with the clientele *The Allure* will attract?" Her eyes were squinting, and she was looking at me like I was crazy.

"Yes, but there's something a little sinister…or, I don't know what too…" I shook my head at my inability to articulate my misgivings. "C'mon," I said. "I'll show you."

I took Irene's arm and edged her out of her seat as she protested she wasn't finished. "The dance hosts should still be in the ballroom with Carmen and Orlando, reviewing the dances they need to know." We left the dining room and walked along the port side until we came to the Magnifique Ballroom.

As Irene and I peeked through the entrance door, I heard a voice behind me.

"Ms. Delmar, what's going on in there?"

It was Elena Holden who had observed us observing the dancers. I explained that the dance hosts were rehearsing and introduced her to Irene, who murmured all the right things, which the actress brushed off with a "Lovely to meet you, as well." Her attention was obviously elsewhere. "Now why don't we step inside and join the fun." She swept ahead of me and marched into the ballroom. It didn't take long until all eyes were on her, as I suspected she knew they would be. Once again, I made the introductions. She nodded to everyone politely until she came to Derrick Robson. She held out her hand to him. "I performed all the dance routines in my movies myself," she said, taking his hand and leading him onto the dance floor. "Now, why don't you show me your moves?"

Orlando threw me a look but turned up the music they'd been practicing to. And Elena and Derrick were off, in a tango that was looking more torrid by the moment.

Irene whispered in my ear. "Your celebrity guest seems to like what she sees. Those dimples and square jaw are very attractive, not to mention the body that goes with them."

"Damn," I hissed, as I watched Elena smile and tilt her head up at him, those humongous ruby and diamond earrings sparkling with fire as they moved in and out of each other's arms. *The trouble had arrived,* I thought. *This was going to be bad.*

* * *

That evening, Captain Brigman had invited Ms. Holden to be his guest at dinner in his private quarters. He'd also asked me to come along so I could explain all the unique touches our beautiful ship had to offer.

When I arrived a few minutes before eight, I noticed the table was set for four. The Captain caught me looking and shook his head. "Ms. Holden asked that I include Mr. Derrick Robson, one of our dance hosts, as well." He paused and tugged on his short white beard. "So much for her wanting to be alone," he added. "I trust you can handle this situation."

Me?! I wanted to say. How could I separate her from her heart's new desire? And who was this Derrick Robson anyway? I'd vetted him with the cruise line's department that supplied our dance hosts. and he had great references. And no criminal history. What about gigolo, lothario, and con man? Was that anywhere on his resume? He hadn't wasted a second getting close to Elena Holden.

After dinner, I grabbed Irene. "What am I going to do?" I hung my head in my hands. "What if he's after her money? What if tomorrow she decides she doesn't like him anymore and complains? I'll be out of a job before I even get started."

"Oh honey, I don't think there's anything you can do." She patted my back and extinguished the light. "I need to get to sleep. I have a spa appointment first thing in the morning. It's on you, by the way."

* * *

The next day, it was full speed ahead. I welcomed as many of the guests as I could and had my staff show them to their cabins. So far, all I'd heard was praise for the elegant accommodations.

We set off from the Nouvelle Digue de Monaco port at five p.m. on our route to Lisbon, sailing into a magnificent sunset that brought 'oohs' and 'ahhs' from the passengers who were enjoying a bon voyage toast on the bridge deck. It was the beginning of a wonderful adventure that would introduce our guests to three ports along the way, Barcelona, Tangier, and Casablanca, where they could disembark and tour each city.

During the voyage, Elena Holden and Derrick Robson were inseparable. Holding hands at dinner, canoodling on the deck under the moonlight, dancing until the wee hours, those ruby and diamond earrings catching whatever light was available and sparkling for all they were worth, which I'd have to say, was a considerable sum.

* * *

Robson was a very good dancer, which also ticked me off. I was down one dance host thanks to Ms. Holden, and several ladies had complained they were lacking a partner. There was nothing I could do about it now. The other three hosts would just have to step up and dance a little harder.

The last stop before Lisbon was Casablanca where we were to dock overnight, so our guests would have plenty of time to enjoy the city's exotic souks and bazaars.

Elena Holden and Derrick Robson were foregoing the tour planned by the ship, i.e. me, in favor of "exploring this beautiful place on our own," as Ms. Holden put it while beaming up at Robson. "Derrick knows all the interesting sites," she added. "It's going to be so much fun,"

I'll bet, I thought, as I watched them walk toward the dock and be swallowed up by the crowd of merchants and vendors hawking everything from baskets and beads to spices and souvenirs.

Well, I had my group of tourists to take care of and couldn't concern myself with those two. Irene acted as my second in command and helped me round up the cluster of ten who'd signed up for the excursion and get them settled in the Mercedes bus waiting for us.

It was an exhausting day, with stops at Rick's Café, the Hassan II Mosque, Chellah, and the Kasbah of the Oudayas, a 12th-century fortress, plus breaks for shopping, and lunch at the city's finest hotel. At each stop, I looked around for Elena and Derrick but hadn't caught even a glimpse of them. They must truly have wanted to be alone.

My passengers were happy and content as we made our way back to *The Allure*. When we were once again on board, I found Captain Brigman waiting for me just inside the gangway. "Monica, may I have a word?" He strode off toward a personnel-only elevator that led toward the bridge before I had a chance to answer. I followed meekly, shooting a glance over my shoulder at Irene, in a 'What now?' look.

"Ms. Holden and Mr. Robson arrived just a few minutes ago," the Captain began as he led me toward his office behind the bridge. "It seems he saved Ms. Holden from a very dangerous situation."

He opened the door and gestured for me to enter. The two people the Captain had been referring to were sitting on a small settee. Derrick had a huge bruise on the left side of his face and his right hand was bandaged. He was bending over Elena holding her shoulder with his left hand and she was staring up at him in what could only be described as adoration.

I turned to the Captain. "What happened?" I asked, unsure of what to say.

"Perhaps Ms. Holden can tell you."

Elena finally looked at us, tearing her eyes away from Derrick with difficulty. "Derrick saved my life and my ruby earrings." She held out her hand in which rested her prized possessions.

She took a deep breath and then began. "We heard footsteps and voices behind us as we were leaving a café near the souk where we'd stopped for drinks. All of a sudden, three men in robes and face coverings surrounded us. Two of them attacked Derrick while the other one grabbed me from behind and held a knife at my throat. He insisted I remove my earrings." She touched her throat as if she could still feel the cold steel of the blade.

"Derrick managed to fight off the two men, beating them with his cane until they ran away. Then he turned toward the man with the knife and shoved him away from me, knocking the knife from his hand." She shivered at the memory. "It was all so horrible. He and Derrick fell to the ground and tumbled everywhere. The thief was trying to retrieve his knife and I was sure if he did, he'd kill both of us." She paused again and touched Derrick's bruised cheek. "Derrick finally managed to scramble close enough to grab it and lunged at the man. He dropped my earrings and fled, knowing he'd lost."

She glanced down at the gems resting in her palm, the earrings that had almost been stolen, then up at Derrick.

I fully expected her to add "my hero" to the end of her tale, but she spared us that sobriquet. I looked at Derrick and thought I saw a flash of an evil glint in his baby blues. The one I had first noticed when we met. It was gone before you could say rubies, but it had been there. I twigged to what had really happened, but there was no way to prove it unless I could examine the earrings myself.

"That's wonderful," I said. "You were so brave." I hoped the sarcasm in my voice was subtle enough that only he would notice. If he did, he didn't react. Instead, he just patted Elena's arm.

"Well, I'm glad that's all settled," said the Captain. "Please let me know if there's anything I, or Ms. Delmar, can do for you."

I knew what I wanted to do, but smiled at the pair, keeping my thoughts to myself.

The couple left the Captain's office and he turned to me. "We can't have this type of incident happen again," he said.

He was blaming *me. Again.* I couldn't believe it. "Yes, sir," I replied and left the room. This was not over, not by a long shot.

* * *

I knew finding out the truth, and getting Derrick to confess, wouldn't be easy. I'd have to separate the happy couple while I accosted Derrick with the scenario I'd figured out.

The next morning, I sent Elena Holden an invitation "to experience an intimate, restorative, total body indulgence" at our world-famous spa to make up for the inconvenience she'd gone through yesterday. It would be something she wouldn't be able to refuse.

While she was being patted and pampered, I sought out Derrick Robson. "I know what you did," I said with no preamble when I found him on the aft deck enjoying his morning coffee and checking his email—probably boasting about his score to one of his confederates. I strode over and stared down at him. "You knew Elena Holden was sailing with us." Everybody did thanks to her publicist. "You planned this ahead of time and switched the real earrings for copies during that fake attack." *Excellent copies,* I thought to myself, *probably made by a shady jeweler in Amsterdam.* "I know you did it." I paused. "And now you're going to switch them back."

He looked up at me and laughed. "You have a very fanciful imagination, Ms. Delmar, or should I call you Ms. *Delmarino?*"

His barb had struck home. I'm sure I looked like a fish gulping for air with my mouth opening and closing silently. How had he found out my real last name? The one my father had changed to disassociate himself from his former, well-known New York crime family.

"Do Wanderlust Cruises know who you really are?" He raised an eyebrow as he looked up at me from his chair. "If you go around making such serious accusations about someone you employed, and they find out, it might seem like you were the one who committed a crime."

He was right. If they found out about my family connection, they'd never believe I didn't have anything to do with his scheme.

"I...I..." I sputtered. "Just put them back before we dock." Then I turned on my heel and left. I could hear the sound of his laughter trailing me as I walked across the deck.

I thought about searching his cabin, but he was too clever to hide them where I might easily find them. I was royally screwed. I went back to my cabin and plopped down on my bed to think. It suddenly occurred to me where he'd stashed the earrings and I thought I might have a way to get them back.

I texted Irene who I knew was at breakfast. **Stop eating. Go to the aft deck & watch Derrick Robson. Text me immediately if he leaves. Will explain later.**

* * *

After a visit to our maintenance department and the exotic plant green-house, I made my way to Elena Holden's cabin. I used my passkey to enter—an action for which I'd be immediately fired if caught. I found what I was looking for, smiled to myself as I fiddled with it, and left. They'd never know I'd been there.

* * *

The next day, as the ship docked in Lisbon, Irene and I were on deck watching the passengers disembark. She'd be leaving shortly herself before *The Allure* set sail for South America later that afternoon.

I pointed to Derrick Robson ambling down the gangway, heading to the waiting Rolls parked on the dock, swinging his cane and looking like he didn't have a care in the world.

"He told me he didn't take them."

"And you believed him?" Irene asked, not able to hide the incredulity in her voice.

I considered before answering her. "Mmmm." I finally replied. She just looked at me and shrugged.

"Was that a yes?" Irene persisted.

I turned toward her, the wind whipping my long black hair across my face. "What can I say? He convinced me." I hoped she'd leave it at that.

No such luck. "But why didn't you call the authorities and confront him?' Her question snapped at me like an accusation.

"There are no authorities in the middle of the ocean. Except for the Captain. He wouldn't have wanted to know about my suspicions. It was better this way."

Irene knew the old me would have sprung on him like a tiger and held him down until the police came. "You were never this way before." Her face took on a perplexed expression as if she'd encountered a sea creature she hadn't believed existed.

She couldn't wrap her mind around why I said I believed him and hadn't done more to get Derrick Robson to confess. I'd asked her to watch him after all. What was that about? I told her I'd made a mistake.

"Well, it's done now. Over." What I didn't tell her, and what she could never know, was that I switched out the earrings, which Derrick had hidden in his walking stick. If I told Irene the truth now, our friendship would be over.

* * *

While he and Elena were otherwise engaged, I'd used the small pliers I borrowed from maintenance and removed the silver handle on top of his walking stick. As I suspected, the earrings were nestled inside, wrapped in a soft jeweler's cloth. I replaced them with two stones of a similar shape and weight I'd taken from the greenhouse and wrapped them back in the jeweler's cloth. Then I replaced the fancy handle on his stick, wiped off my fingerprints, and left it exactly where I found it.

The ruby and diamond earrings were now in my possession, and I knew what to do with them.

Derrick's threat of exposure had rattled me. My dad *had been* the head of one of New York's crime families years ago, and while I was never involved, I was a very observant child. I'd learned a few things about how the business worked while I played on the floor of Dad's study.

After my mom died, my dad had a crisis of conscience and decided to go straight. He changed our family name from Del Marino to Delmar and left the business to his brother-in-law, Louie Patrone, who'd since transitioned it into legitimate enterprises. Dad was well-respected, and the other families knew he meant it when he said he was getting out permanently.

By the time Derrick Robson got the message he'd been had, my Uncle Louie would have contacted a former associate to swing by Elena's L.A. mansion and switch back the real ruby earrings for the fakes.

Of course, I could never let Dad find out what I'd just done. He'd never forgive me for taking them in the first place. But, as you might imagine, Uncle Louie was very good at keeping secrets. And so was I.

* * *

Cathi Stoler is an Amazon bestselling author and Derringer winner. She has written four novels in her Murder On The Rocks Series: *Bar None, Last Call, Straight Up,* and *With A Twist,* as well as the Nick Donahue Adventures, the Laurel and Helen NY Mysteries, and multiple short stories. She is a member of MWA (NY), SinCNY/TRI-State. and International Thriller Writers. Find her at www.cathistoler.com, at facebook.com/CathiStolerAuthor, on Instagram @cathistolerauthor, email: cathi@cathistoler.com.

Big Vuto in Lusaka

By Lorraine Sharma Nelson

Lusaka, Zambia

"The autopsy reveals that it was definitely death by poisoning," I said, skimming the sheet of paper Uncle Manish had handed me. "Oramorph."

"Dr. Banda did the autopsy," Uncle Manish said. "He said Oramorph is the technical term for liquid morphine." He looked at me. "I know Narin had his enemies, but…to poison him? Who would do something like that?"

"Was he in financial trouble?" I asked.

Uncle Manish snorted. "When was he not? He hated working, but loved living in the lap of luxury. He went through money like running water. Never understood the value of a kwacha or a good, honest day's work." He sighed, shaking his head. "I'm partially to blame for that," he admitted. "For years he'd come running to me for money, and because he was my younger brother, I indulged him. Until he began asking for more and more, and in increasingly larger sums. Finally, last year I cut him off." He looked at me, his eyes bright with tears. "We hadn't spoken since. Maybe if I hadn't cut him off, he'd still be alive today."

"You can't blame yourself for Narin's death, Uncle. You did what you thought was best."

"I'm… I was…his big brother. I should have protected him—"

"Hush, Manny," Auntie Zohra said, walking into the living room with a platter of Indian snacks. "Narin's death has nothing to do with us. He was a bad seed. We all knew sooner or later something bad was going to happen to him."

"Zohra, stop. It is bad luck to speak ill of the dead. Especially a family member."

Auntie Zohra shrugged as she set the platter of freshly made mince *samosas* and *bhajia* on the coffee table. "I'm just speaking the truth." She smiled at me. "Your favorites still, right?"

"My absolute favorites," I said, biting into the hot and spicy triangular pastry. It was hard to believe that only a few hours ago I'd landed at Kenneth Kaunda International Airport in Lusaka, Zambia.

I had shifted from foot to foot as I waited to disembark, eager to step foot on Zambian soil again. The Zambia Airways flight attendant, who had served all my meals and drinks during the long ten- hour flight, smiled at me.

"Eager to be back home?"

"Well, in a way," I said. "I spent my childhood years in Lusaka, before my family moved to England, so I guess Zambia will always be home to me."

"How long has it been since you last visited?"

"Twenty years."

She raised a perfectly plucked eyebrow. "Twenty? You'd better brace yourself. This is not the Zambia you left behind."

"I know. I keep telling myself that, but deep down I'm really hoping that everything I remember and love is still the same."

Her smile broadened. "Good luck. I hope you're not disappointed."

"Never," I said, giving her a little wave before stepping on the flight stairs leading down to the tarmac. As I took that step, I was hit in the face by a blast of heat so intense it momentarily stunned me.

Welcome back, Nalini Naicker.

"Nalini? Nalini? Up here."

As I strode toward the airport terminal, I looked up at the enormous balcony that overlooked the airport tarmac, and saw two people frantically waving at me. They were among the last remaining members of my family still in Zambia.

Most of my relatives had emigrated around the same time my immediate family did—to Canada, the United States, England, and Australia. My mental scrapbook was filled with happy memories of big family gatherings, intricate and delicious Indian meals, and running around with my cousins in shorts and tee shirts every weekend.

When I was a little girl, Zambia had had a notable Indian population, as well as expats from several other countries. I'd gone to school with girls from Germany, Sweden, Italy, Japan, Canada, the United States, and, of course, England.

Now, a number of Indians, like my own family, had left Zambia for countries that offered more opportunities, more stability. In addition, the number of expats dropped considerably since the heyday of the sixties and early seventies.

Back then, Zambia was a newly-independent country, rich with opportunity, and eager to grow. And people from all over the world responded with enthusiasm, willing to live and work in Zambia for a set number of years.

On the drive to Auntie Zohra and Uncle Manish's house in Lusaka, I'd been shocked to see all the developments that had sprung out on either side of the Great East Road. I'd expected progress, of course, but it was still sad to see the miles and miles of maize that I remembered from my childhood supplanted by shopping strips, housing developments, and businesses.

Despite all the changes, though, my excitement at being back in Lusaka couldn't be contained.

Too bad I wasn't here for a relaxing vacation.

"So, is it like you remembered?" Auntie Zohra asked, bringing me back to the present. She watched me intently as I chewed.

"You and Ma always made the best *samosas*," I said, reaching for another.

She laughed. "I'm so happy to see you again, *baba*. I'll make all your favorites while you're here."

"Watch out, Nalini. She'll send you back twenty pounds heavier," Uncle

Manish said.

Auntie Zohra scowled at him. "Don't be ridiculous, Manny. And how many times must I tell you to use a coaster for your tea."

A little bit of bickering ensued between the couple, and while they were otherwise engaged, I re-read the autopsy report on Uncle Narin. From what Uncle Manish told me, he and Narin were never very close. They were polar opposites, and as a result rarely spent much time together.

Manish was extremely intelligent, ambitious, and successful. He owned a chain of hotels in Zambia—the Yamuna Hotels, named after the river beside the Taj Mahal in Agra, India—that were very popular with tourists coming to Zambia on safari. But, despite his massive success, he was also one of the kindest, most generous people I've ever known.

Narin was the opposite. Although also very intelligent, he had no interest in having to work for a living, and always looked for the easiest way to make a kwacha. And he rarely turned up for family gatherings when I was growing up, so I didn't really know him. However, I did love his wife, Radha, who always showed up.

* * *

"Forgive me, Detective Naicker, but I am still at a loss to understand why you expect to be involved with this case. It is a matter for the Lusaka police, and has nothing to do with you in a professional capacity." Police Detective Melo Makungo reached for his tea without breaking eye contact. "Your jurisdiction ends at the London city limits and the last time I checked, Lusaka is a long way from London."

"You are correct, of course, but, please understand, Detective, that I am here in Lusaka at the request of my uncle—"

"The owner of the Yamuna Hotel on Haile Selassie Avenue," Makungo said, sitting back in his chair. "Yes, I know of him. He is a very well-respected man in Zambia."

"He's earned that respect," I said, leaning forward in my chair. "He's very invested in education, and donates a good deal to schools across Zambia.

He also raises money for hospitals, and—"

"Yes, I know how altruistic he is, but that still doesn't explain why *you* are here." Makungo's eyes narrowed. "Does he not have any faith in the Lusaka police to solve his brother's murder?"

"That is not it at all, Detective. Narin's murder has shaken the entire family, and they all expect me to be involved in the case. You see, I'm the only family member in law enforcement."

"Detective Naicker —"

"All I ask is to accompany you in your pursuit of answers. I give you my word as a fellow detective that I will not overstep my bounds." I met Makungo's skeptical gaze. "I have to do this, don't you see? My family is depending on me."

Makungo stared at me for a long moment, his teacup still in his hands. Finally, he sighed, setting his cup back down on the table. "Very well, Detective. You may accompany me as an unofficial observer—"

"Oh, thank—"

"But if at any time you forget that this is *my* case, I will, as they say in England, cut you loose."

They don't say that, but I wasn't about to correct him. Instead, I rose, and extended my hand. "Thank you, Detective Makungo. You won't regret it, I promise."

"Let's make sure I don't," he said, taking my hand in his. "Mr. Naicker's death is big *vuto*. Big, big *vuto*, and the sooner I solve it, the better."

At my obviously puzzled expression, he explained. "In Nyanja, it means *trouble*. So, don't cause any, or it's not just my job on the line. Understand?"

"Perfectly. When and where do we start?"

* * *

"Please proceed, Mrs. Naicker. "Your husband played golf, then had drinks with his golfing partners before coming home. Is that right?"

"Yes."

"Their names, please?"

Auntie Radha took in a shaky breath. "Let's see… Samuel Sakala, and Ed McCloud. Oh, and my brother, Raju."

"Thank you," Makungo said.

"Anything to help," Auntie Radha said, then turned to me. "Have you eaten, lovey? I have some chicken *Briyani*—"

"This is not a social call, Mrs. Naicker," Makungo said, before I could answer. "You say your brother drove him home?"

"Yes. Narin was in no condition to drive."

"And, how soon after that…?"

"Minutes," Radha said quietly, staring out the window. "I didn't even get a chance to talk to him."

* * *

"Where to now?" I asked, as we drove off. I glanced at the side mirror, and saw Auntie Radha standing on the verandah, watching us drive away. She had both arms wrapped around her midriff, and her shoulders were stooped, as if she had the weight of the world on her shoulders. I had an almost irresistible urge to run back and comfort her. Despite all her grief, she still wanted to make sure she fed me. That was such an Indian family thing to do that it made my heart ache for her loss.

"We'll start with my fellow Zambian, Samuel Sakala. I have a lot of questions for Mr. Naicker's golfing friends."

So do I, I thought. These men were the last people to see Uncle Narin alive and well.

* * *

Samuel Sakala rose from his seat as Makungo and I pushed past the secretary, who was trying to bar our entry into the office.

"What is the meaning of this?"

"*Mwakabwanji*, Samuel," Makungo said, pinning a smile on his face. "Greetings. May I present my colleague from London, Detective Nalini

Naicker."

Sakala's eyes widened. "Naicker? Are you related to Narin?"

"He's my uncle," I said. "Detective Makungo has very kindly allowed me to work with him in solving Narin's murder."

Sakala winced at the *M* word. "If you're here to ask me about that, you're wasting your time. I know nothing."

"On the contrary," Makungo said, easing himself into a chair facing Sakala, and indicating for me to do the same. "You were with him the day he died. One of the last people to see him before he died, in fact."

"I wasn't alone with him. There were others there. You should talk to Ed McCloud. And Raju Pillay, his brother-in-law."

"As much as I'm sure they'll appreciate you giving up their names so easily," Makungo said, "it's you we're interested in right now." He looked at me, and I realized with some surprise that he was giving me first crack at Sakala.

"How well did you know my uncle, Mr. Sakala?"

"Not that well. We met about six months ago."

"Where did you meet?"

"At a friend's house."

"And who is this friend?" Makungo asked.

"An investor from Hong Kong. He moved back there a little while ago."

"Did you and Narin invest with him?" I asked.

"I invested a little, but Narin got excited. He invested a sizable amount with him."

"Did it work out for both of you?"

Sakala grimaced. "It was a very bad investment. Luckily for me, I did not invest much. But for Narin…*ai ai ai*… it was a big loss. He was very distressed."

"Did you loan him the money?" Makungo asked.

"Me? No. I am not that rich. At least, not yet."

"Who did he borrow it from?"

Samuel shrugged. "I have no idea."

"We'll need the name of this Hong Kong investor," Makungo said.

"I already told you, he doesn't live here anymore."

"We'll still need his name, Samuel."

* * *

"What do you think?" Makungo asked, as we drove away.

"Could be a lead," I said. "From what I'm told, Narin was broke most of the time. Even the country club membership is Uncle Manish's."

"He could have gotten the money from him. Manish Naicker is a wealthy hotel magnate."

"No. Uncle Manish told me he cut Narin off a year ago. I think he borrowed the money from someone to make this investment, and when it didn't pan out, the lender came calling, most probably demanding his money back *with* interest. And, when Narin couldn't pay it back…" I couldn't finish the sentence.

"That's certainly a motive for murder," Makungo said, pulling into the parking lot of the Radisson Blu Hotel.

When I looked at him, he smiled. "I thought perhaps we could have a spot of lunch and discuss what we have so far. The food at the *Chuma* Grill is very good. Afterwards, we will pay Raju Pillay a visit."

"Fine with me," I said, "as long as I pay."

"It is not necessary, Detective—"

"I insist. And can we drop the formality? Please call me Nalini."

"In that case, you may address me as Melo."

* * *

"I didn't know he was a cardiothoracic surgeon?" Melo murmured, as we were ushered into a very plush-looking office by a somewhat flustered secretary. "Impressive."

"Detective…Makungo, is it? And Nalini? My goodness, look at you? All grown up." Uncle Raju smiled as he rounded his desk to greet us. He shook hands with Melo, and, before I could say anything, gave me a quick hug.

"The last time I saw you, you were…what… Nine? Ten? And now, look at you. A detective, I hear. Ma and Papa must be so proud. "

I smiled. "They would rather I went to medical school. Like you."

Raju nodded. "Every Indian parent's dream for their child, right? Become a doctor."

Melo cleared his throat. "We appreciate you seeing us at such short notice, Doctor Pillay," he said, taking a seat.

"Anything to help solve my brother-in-law's murder." Raju glanced from me to Melo. "Has there been any progress?"

"We're still gathering information," Melo said. "Conducting interviews. It's why we're here."

Raju's eyebrows shot up. "Oh, okay."

"You seem surprised," I said.

"I am. I thought you'd come by to give me an update on who killed him." His brows creased. "Does this mean that I'm… You can't seriously think that I'm a suspect?"

"Everyone is a suspect until we solve the case," Melo said, calmly. "We would appreciate any information that may shed some light on his murder."

Raju's eyes widened. "What can I possibly tell you?"

"You gave him a lift home from the golf course, did you not?" Melo leaned forward, resting his forearms on his knees.

"That is correct. Narin had a habit of…imbibing… just a little too much sometimes. Didn't know when to stop. I try…tried…to keep an eye on him, for my sister's sake, you understand?"

"Of course," I said. "We talked to Auntie Radha. She looks really good. Despite everything."

"I'll tell her you said that. It'll brighten her day. Watch. She'll probably make you some elaborate dessert for saying that."

"Tell her I like *gulab jambu*," I said.

Melo cleared his throat. "If we can get back to the issue at hand…" He raised an eyebrow at me, which had the same effect as being reprimanded by the school principal.

"By all means," I said, feeling my cheeks burn.

"Did anyone at the table have access to Narin's cocktail before he drank it?" Melo asked.

Raju's eyes narrowed. "Someone who might've had a chance to dose his drink, you mean?"

"Precisely."

I shifted in my chair. Did Melo really think there was a chance Raju killed his own brother-in-law? Why? To what end? He was one of the most respected heart surgeons in the country, if not *the* most. And lived a very luxurious life in a beautiful country.

Why risk losing all that?

Raju shook his head. "No. I don't recall Narin leaving his drink unguarded… Oh, wait. He did go to the bathroom at one point."

"Leaving the rest of you at the table?" Melo asked.

Raju frowned. "I went up to the bar for a refill. And Samuel came with me. So, Ed was at the table by himself for maybe five…six minutes."

"One more question," I said, as Melo rapidly wrote down everything Raju was saying. "Did you lend Narin the money to invest?"

"No. I don't have that kind of money readily available in cash."

"Do you know who did?"

"Sorry. I don't."

* * *

"Ed McCloud," Melo said, as we walked to the car. "I know him. He works at the Canadian Embassy. He is a good man. I will be very disappointed if he is the one responsible for your uncle's death."

"So, we're going to see him now?" I stifled a yawn. I was able to forestall jet lag for a few hours this afternoon, mainly thanks to the double espresso I had at lunch, but the effects of the caffeine were wearing off, and my eyelids were getting droopy.

"No," Melo said, addressing me over the roof of the car. "He will have to wait until tomorrow morning. Tonight, my wife and I are taking our son out for a celebratory dinner."

"What are you celebrating?" I asked, as I slid into the passenger seat.

"His graduation from Oxford University."

"Oxford?" I must have looked surprised, because Melo bristled.

"Yes, Nalini. Oxford. Even in a small African country like Zambia we have students who are smart enough to get into fancy universities like Oxford and Harvard."

I felt my cheeks burn. "I'm sorry, that's not what I meant. I was just surprised to hear that you and Mrs. Makungo have a child that's graduating from university."

Melo sighed, giving me a weary smile. "Forgive my defensiveness, Nalini. I've had to endure too many shocked expressions and comments from expats once they learn that Mulubwa—Mulu for short—is a new Oxford grad. It is most insulting."

"Of course it is. People can be very ignorant. Those that venture beyond their own shores, as well as those who remain behind."

Melo turned to me, a deep frown creasing his forehead. "You sound as if you speak from experience?"

I laughed. "Of course I do. My family experienced our fair share of racism after emigrating to England in 1971. *'Go back to India'* was a common refrain. Ironic considering the British ruled and occupied India for two hundred years. Anyway, things got worse a year later when the British government accepted a fair number of displaced Asians—all Indians— who were kicked out of Uganda by Idi Amin. Remember all that? He said the Asians were sabotaging Uganda's economy, and decided to rid his country of them. All eighty thousand Asians, many of them third generation Ugandan citizens, were forced to leave their homes, properties, businesses. All of them suddenly homeless, country-less."

"I know the history of Uganda. That was a very bad time for Indians there."

"Yes, it was. Anyway, when the Ugandan Asians arrived in Britain, it caused resentment from many—not all, but many—Brits. It didn't matter if you were a Ugandan Asian or not. Just being Indian was enough to be subjected to some form of racism.

"But, on the flip side, we've also met a good amount of wonderful British people that have become very close family friends over the years. For every ignorant or racist person, there are many more good and decent people."

"My son experienced some racism at his dorm at Oxford, but found most of the academic population to be friendly, but curious. He told me once that being black, from a small African country, meant that he was always subjected to questions. *Where are you from? What is your country like?* That sort of thing. He did not mind that. He said questions gave him an opportunity to enlighten people."

"There's always the good and bad, wherever you go," I said.

Another sigh from Melo. "I suppose. Still, it gets really old, dealing with narrow-minded, colonialist attitudes." He slowed down in front of a car, which I realized was one of Uncle Manish's that I borrowed this morning. "Here you are. I will see you tomorrow, bright and early."

My eyes narrowed as I turned to him. "How bright? How early? I'm not really a morning person."

"I'll pick you up at your uncle's at 8 a.m., promptly. Best to get started before the heat of the day gets to us."

* * *

I was still yawning the next morning when Melo's black sedan pulled into the long, winding drive. Auntie Zohra had plied me with *dosas*—a type of Indian crepe, which I have a particular weakness for—and plenty of strong, sweet *chai*, but I still felt groggy and sluggish. One day of sleeping in, and lounging around, would have been perfect.

But, as I kept reminding myself, I wasn't here for rest and relaxation.

"Good morning," Melo said, as I slid into the passenger seat. "We have another lead. I have the name of the investor from Hong Kong." He held up a piece of paper.

"I take it you haven't called him yet?"

"I left a message for him to call me back at his earliest convenience."

"We already know that Narin invested a sizable amount with him," I said, as Melo pulled onto Leopard's Hill Road. "What more are you expecting to learn?"

"Hopefully, who the lender was, since no one else seems willing to divulge that tidbit."

* * *

Ed McCloud was in an embassy staff meeting when we arrived at the Canadian Embassy, so Melo and I waited in the elegant lobby, speaking in hushed tones. Someone was nice enough to bring us some fresh, hot coffee, which we got to enjoy, before McCloud himself appeared to greet us.

"These Canadians are very friendly," Melo said, softly, as McCloud approached us with a warm smile.

"It's what they're known for," I replied.

"Detectives Makungo and Naicker. I'm Ed McCloud." He extended a hand, shaking each of ours in turn, with a firm, confident grip. "I wish I could say that it's pleasure to meet you both, but, under the circumstances, it would be a bit tactless."

"So, you know why we're here, then?" Melo said.

McCloud nodded as he gestured towards a hallway. "Please, let's go into my office. We can talk comfortably there. I'll have my secretary bring in some tea and pastries."

When we were comfortably seated in his office, McCloud glanced first at Melo, then at me. "I'm hoping you're here because you've solved Narin's murder." His voice was solemn, his hands clasped in front of him on his desk.

"I wish that were the case, Mr. McCloud, but..." Melo shook his head, "we are still investigating it."

"I'll come right to the point, Mr. McCloud, if I may," I said, ignoring Melo's glare.

"By all means. Please, go ahead."

"We understand that when the four of you were having cocktails together at Makeni Hills, you were at the table by yourself for a few minutes at one point."

McCloud looked taken aback at first, then he frowned. "I don't recall being at the table by myself… Oh, wait… Yes, I was. But not for long. Raju and Samuel went up to the bar for another round, but Narin was already on his way back to the table. In fact, he called out his order to them as he passed."

Melo and I exchanged glances. "So, you were never alone at the table for, say, five or six minutes?"

He shook his head. "At the most I'd say I was by myself for about thirty seconds, give or take a few. Why? What's so important about that? What's that got to do with… Oh, I see." The color drained out of his face. "You… you think that I had something to do with Narin's death."

"Sir," Melo said, "all we are trying to do is eliminate you as a suspect—"

"Bullshit. You think I killed him." McCloud's eyes filled with tears. "He was my friend. I'm not in the habit of murdering my friends."

"Mr. McCloud," I said, "we're not accusing you of—"

"Just ask what you came to ask, and go," McCloud said, quietly.

Melo looked at me, nodding. I took a deep breath. "Did you lend Narin the money to invest?"

He shook his head. "No. All I know is that he was excited about the initial investment. And then, when the stock tanked, and he lost it all, he was so depressed I was worried he would hurt himself in some way." McCloud grimaced. "I needn't have worried, right? Because someone took care of that for him."

* * *

Back at the station, Melo called the Hong Kong investor, while I paced. If McCloud was telling the truth, and I believe he was, it meant Raju exaggerated the time that the Canadian was by himself at the table. Why would he do that, unless he wanted to deflect suspicion away from himself? Was it because he was guilty, or because he was afraid of being a suspect?

Melo finally said goodbye and hung up the phone. He looked at me, and I felt my stomach twist. "Well?"

"It was Raju who lent Narin the money."

* * *

"Yes," Raju said, head bent, hands clasped between his knees. "I did. I'm so sorry I lied to you." He raised his head, his eyes red-rimmed. "I poisoned Narin's drink. I'm so very sorry. I'm ready to face the consequences."

I stared at him. "Uncle Raju, yesterday you were ready to shift the blame to another man. And today you're turning yourself in?"

He shrugged, his face haggard. "Why fight it any more? What's done is done, and I am ready to pay for my sin. You do not have to look any farther, Detective Makungo. I am the man you want."

I watched Raju closely as he spoke. And of one thing I was absolutely sure.

He was lying.

Raju did not murder Narin, despite his insistence that he did. But, if he didn't, who did? Who was he protecting? It had to be someone very close to him. He had no wife, no children. And then the answer hit me so hard, I had to sit down before my legs gave way.

Radha.

He was protecting his sister.

* * *

"Raju lied to us about the time he and Narin arrived at your house, because he realized that you poisoned Narin's drink *after* he got home from the club," I said, standing with Melo and a police constable in Radha's living room. "Where did you get the Oramorph from?"

"I visit Raju so often at the hospital that no one keeps tabs on me. It was easy enough to steal the drug."

"How did you administer it?"

"I put it in his tea," Radha whispered, her voice shaking. "I had to, don't you see?" She looked at me with swollen, red-rimmed eyes, thick eyelashes spiked with tears. "He destroyed everything he touched. Including me. Do you know he sold my *thali?*"

Stunned, I shook my head. At Melo's puzzled look, I explained. "A *thali* is a gold chain with a pendant on it that the groom puts around the bride's neck at the wedding ceremony. It symbolizes the sacred bond between husband and wife. It's like wedding rings in western marriages."

"I never take it off. Never. You know what the *thali* means to a married Indian woman, Nalini?"

I nodded, my throat swelling.

"He removed it from my neck one night while I slept. When I woke up the next morning, and realized it was gone, I went into a panic. But, all he said was that I had misplaced it somewhere. And I knew." She started to cry, deep, heart-wrenching sobs that tore through me. "I knew then that the bastard had sold it."

Radha turned to look out the window, her voice dropping to a whisper. "Then, there were the nights he'd come home so drunk he could barely stand, reeking of cheap perfume." Tears coursed down her cheeks, and all I wanted to do was put my arms around her, and comfort her.

But I couldn't.

So, I stood beside Melo, spine stiff, stomach roiling, so full of angst I thought I would burst.

"The last straw was when he convinced Raju to give him two hundred and fifty thousand kwacha, promising him an outstanding rate of return. Then, he lost it all." She gave a choked laugh, shaking her head. "Raju was swindled by him. Just as I was."

Radha stood then, and allowed herself to be led away by the constable. At the front door, she turned, forcing a smile that almost broke my heart. "Raju mentioned the nice things you said about me, lovey. I made the *gulab jambu* you wanted. It's in a container in the fridge. Take it back home to share with the family in London. And tell them I love them."

* * *

Lorraine Sharma Nelson is of Indian ancestry, and grew up globally. She is a wife, mom, travel bum, Tai Chi fanatic, and coconut cupcake lover. Lorraine has twenty-one short stories published in horror, fantasy, crime, and sci-fi anthologies, and has won two sci-fi awards. She was the 2022 President of Sisters in Crime New England, and is a UNICEF New England Regional Board member.
Website: www.lorrainesharmanelson.net
Instagram: instagram.com/lorrainesharmanelsonauthor/
Twitter: twitter.com/loneriter

Reynisfjara

By Kristopher Zgorski

Iceland

Reynisfjara is a three-hour drive from Keflavík International Airport on the beautiful island nation of Iceland. On our first visit two years ago, it was just a brief stopover on our way to the village of Vik and locales in the South, but today, it is our main destination.

"You know you've created a monster, right?"

He laughed. "Oh, is that right, Ernst? Is this another *Frankenstein* reference?" Tram asked.

"No, I'm serious. This isn't about my term paper, you doofus. Although I do recall a certain professor who is in this car saying I should consider publishing it someday," I said, lightly punching him on his upper arm. "What I mean is a travel monster. Before our first Iceland trip, I hadn't been anywhere. Now look at me. In just this past year, I've been to Iceland, Hawai'i, and the Florida Keys."

"Lucky for me, you—'Ern the explorer'—allowed me to accompany you," Tram said as he lifted our entwined hands from his leg and proceeded to kiss the back of my fingers.

"Let's see how you feel after we get this task done," I said.

The drive south on Iceland's iconic Ring Road made the journey to Reynisfjara quick and easy, something that is not always true about the less-traveled secondary roads across the island. Iceland is known for the treacherous crosswinds that can make navigating around the island a bit like a solo race on a deceptively complex obstacle course with invisible impediments forcing you off the path at random intervals. Success feels like it depends on some mythical combination of concentration, perseverance, and a bit of luck.

The blurred landscape out the passenger-side window hypnotized me, making me think of H.G. Wells' time machine, transporting me back to that first journey to the foreign environs of Reynisfjara Beach. It had been almost a year ago to the day, but the novelty of it being my first serious travel kept it as a treasured memory in the forefront of my mind. Well, that and a few other things, of course.

* * *

Bertram and I stayed in Vik on our original trip. Our binge sessions watching this bizarre but fascinating science fiction-esque Netflix series set in the small village dominated by the specter of the Katla volcano served as inspiration for our first adventure together. Reynisfjara Beach featured prominently on that streaming show, so it naturally helped dictate the agenda.

Since the route to Vik took us past the famous black beach first, Bertram insisted we tackle that before checking into our hotel, despite the exhaustion of all the day's travels.

"I can't believe we'll soon be standing on such a strange and unique beach, just like on the show," I said as we took the side-road turn that would lead us directly to the parking lot.

Once we parked the car, the short path to the main beach didn't even lend itself to anticipation. Just a short distance and BAM! your life view is instantly and forever altered.

"Holy smokes," I said, probably looking as shaken as I felt. "I've never seen anything so weird and beautiful at the same time."

In the distance lay a vast canvas of sand and stone, various shades of black and grey occasionally spotted with a brief glimpse of an off-white pebble. The fierce assault of the Atlantic waves was undeniable, pummeling the shoreline, looking for all the world like Poseidon's horses bursting out of their watery stables, ready to trample anything in their path.

Off to the left rose the huge basalt cliffs that closely resemble something one might expect to find in Middle-earth.

"Are you taking all this in, Ernst?" Bertram asked as he grabbed my shoulders and spun me around for a three-hundred-and-sixty-degree view.

We must have spent an hour or more walking the beach, basking in the majestic nature around us, never straying too close to the incoming tide, obeying the signs in the area that warned of danger.

I don't even remember when I first spotted it. Or even what it was that caught my eye. Somehow, I had found myself separated from most of the crowd on the shoreline that day, so I was free to explore unimpeded. Unjudged.

The moment I kicked the thin layer of black sand—the result of years where the powerful waves pulverized the dried and hardened lava flows from the nearby volcano—the shiny surface of this small stone called to me. I bent to pick it up; the small black rock seemed harmless in my hand, the smooth surface not so much reflecting the afternoon sunlight as absorbing it like a terrestrial black hole. I knew immediately that I would be taking it home with me. A while back, my best friend Jason had got me started collecting fossils and unique gemstones, so it was inevitable that I would crave this for my stash. I wouldn't realize why until some time later.

* * *

Back in the present, next to Tram on a journey to that beach once again, I marveled at life's strange trajectory.

"I can't believe how quickly things started to go wrong after I took this," I said, pulling the simple stone from its hiding place deep in the pocket of my faded jeans.

Tram gave me that look. "There's no such thing as a cursed rock. But it was stupid of you to take it. Everything else is just a coincidence you have manifested with an overactive imagination."

"Riiiight," I said, while thinking two things: *'You're full of shit'* and *'Little do you know.'*

By the time we'd gotten back to our car in the parking lot on that initial visit, most of the other tourists had moved on for further sightseeing. Bertram was the first to notice the flat tire. Thankfully, the rental car came with a spare, and my hunky travel companion knew how to change a tire.

Then the Vik hotel couldn't find our reservations. I'll admit, for a moment, I thought maybe Tram had made the error on purpose, just to give me a fright. But the Icelandic residents are so kind that the issue was resolved quickly.

It continued with little things like that throughout our stay, small inconveniences that seemed unusual and random. I mentioned them each time, even saying maybe I should put the stone back, but Bertam—*ever rational Bertram*—said I was being ridiculous and foolish.

The encroaching warnings of real trouble continued on the way back to the airport at the end of our stay. A warning light came on, indicating the car needed AdBlue, which neither of us had ever heard of. Turns out, it's a special additive motorists add to diesel fuel to help prevent it from freezing in colder climates. *Who knew?* The car rental people had not thought to leave some of that in the trunk for emergencies, so we almost missed our flight home.

Honestly, I guess I should be thankful that our plane didn't drop out of the sky. Maybe I should have left the stone on the island of its creation. Perhaps the foregone conclusion could have been avoided. Certainly, things might have progressed differently if not for that cursed rock. I think MeMaw would agree.

* * *

Our car conversation on the way to MeMaw's house that Sunday more closely resembled a first date than a relationship at the stage of meeting relatives, but there you have it.

"Do you think your grandmother will like me?" Bertram queried. "Who am I kidding? Everyone likes me." Bertram followed this with a half-hearted chuckle, a shade closer to affirmation than it was to jest.

We had been over this many times already. "Yes, MeMaw is going to love you," I said, despite knowing the age difference was going to be a challenge for her. In our normal circles, the twenty-year age gap was never questioned… Well, honestly, I'm not sure we really even had a 'circle.' It was mostly just us. All the time. The fact remained that I've always related better to people older than I was. Even my best friend—my only friend—growing up, Jason Johnson, was five years older. We were like brothers until he went away to college. Over the course of two years, his visits back to the neighborhood became ever more infrequent. Sadly, I came to realize that sometimes people leave and can't come back, shattering my idealized view of the world. It was at that point that I began to rely on humor to deflect everyone about everything, including my May-December romance.

"You know what would be funny," I said. "Let's tell MeMaw that we are calling ourselves Bert and Ernie."

From the tone of his pseudo-laugh, I could tell Bertram was annoyed.

"What the hell is wrong with you? You know you have a few screws loose, right? Doesn't that seem a tad bit childish to you?"

"It was just a joke," I said, trying to smooth things over. "She's the only family I have, so I need her to like you."

* * *

Dinner with MeMaw went swimmingly. She really did seem to find Bertram interesting and kept any concerns she might have had to herself.

"So, Mrs. Ziegler, what do you think about these nicknames for your grandson and me? We have taken to calling ourselves Tram and Ern. That's got a ring to it, don't you think?" Bertram said, shooting me a side eye worthy of its own Tik-Tok meme.

MeMaw shook her head. "Oh gosh, younger generations have the strangest priorities. It's just silly. What really matters for a relationship to stand the test of time is love, respect, and always listening to each other."

As I poured some coffee for everyone, I hoped that Bertram was picking up what MeMaw was laying down. "Why don't you grab the brownies you made while I show MeMaw the rock I stole from Iceland," I said to Bertram...*or rather to Tram*...after I collected the dirty dinner plates. "We need to head out soon."

The shifting shades of red on Bertram's face were visible. "How many times do I have to tell you that is a skúffukaka, a very traditional Icelandic dessert that may look like a run-of-the-mill brownie, but requires a more complex preparation resulting in better flavor," he said, dripping condescendingly with pride and indignation.

That blunt correction suitably delivered, Bertram slipped into the kitchen, but not before I heard him say "Please don't bore her with that ridiculous theory about how the stone is somehow cursed. As if."

* * *

A short while later, Bertram carried the Pyrex casserole dish in from the kitchen, humming a little tune. "Who wants dessert?" he said.

Watching my boyfriend wield the knife to cut his ultra-fancy brownies made me wary of getting too close. "If you aren't careful, you are going to hurt yourself or someone else with that thing," I said.

As MeMaw enjoyed the sweet after-dinner treat, I could almost see the past as it flashed behind her eyes. "You know, this reminds me of a dessert Mrs. Johnson used to make. Do you remember her, Ernst?"

"I do," I said, not wanting to continue on that particular memory stroll.

MeMaw came back to the present. "It's a shame. She was never the same after her only child succumbed to suicide. He had such potential."

The room took on a stillness that felt heavy. "I find it's best not to dwell in the past. We have to live for today," Tram said with compassion, not wanting to end the evening on a downer.

Turns out his words were almost prophetic. The police would tell us later that when we left MeMaw's house, it looked as though no one locked the front door, allowing access for some maniac to ransack the house looking for valuables and brutally stab MeMaw to death in the process. The curse of the Icelandic rock would rob me of any future dinners at MeMaw's house.

* * *

Tram gave my hand a squeeze. "Are you thinking about your grandmother?" he asked.

"I'll never understand why she didn't lock the front door," I said. "She was never that careless."

As the unique landscape loomed outside the windshield, tears made their way down my face like tributaries seeking an outlet. I heard Tram's comforting voice, but all I could understand were the words tragic and accident. But my true feeling was that it was neither of those things.

"Hey, look, there's that stop-off for that waterfall where visitors can walk behind the majestic falls. Let's be spontaneous and go on an adventure," Tram said.

The Seljalandsfoss is one of the tallest waterfalls in Iceland and the only one where it is possible to view nature's infinite beauty from both in front of the cliff and from within the falls themselves.

The trek to the top of the falls was not as strenuous as one might expect, but it certainly was slippery. I had to stop a few times to center myself, avoiding what certainly could have resulted in a broken limb if not careful. But that was nothing compared to the thin coating of water that made the rocks behind Seljalandsfoss so slick.

Tram grabbed my shoulders and positioned me so that the cascading water was behind me. "Lift your arms like you are Loki, controlling the elements," he said.

As silly as it sounds, I knew this would make an awesome photograph, between the falling water and the vast wildness stretching into the distance as far as the eye can see.

"You do realize that Loki has nothing to do with the elements, right? Have you ever even *seen* a Marvel movie?"

Tram got a look on his face. "I think you need to move closer to the edge for the angle of this shot to work properly."

I could feel my feet sliding across the slimy rock face as I took timid steps backward. "How's this?" I queried.

"Perfect. Got it!" Tram said before lunging forward to pull me safely into his waiting arms. "I've got you, babe, don't worry. I would never let anything happen to you."

Our voices echoed off the cavernous walls as we began our trek out from under Seljalandsfoss. Like countless times before, Tram to the rescue.

* * *

"Ern, it's not exactly a practical car," Tram said, looking at the vintage cherry red Mustang with the dramatic racing stripe down the hood.

"I'm still young and adventurous, practical is over-rated," I said, an edge to my voice.

I could see the confusion on the face of the gentleman selling us the car. *What is the deal with these two weirdos?*

"Aren't you tired of having to drive me around, Tram? Or do you like having that level of control over my whereabouts?"

Bertram tried to hide his indignation behind a grunt, but it was clear my words had touched a nerve. "That's not it at all. Do what you want," he said. "But let's at least look under the hood, shall we?"

As Bertram and I checked out the car, I couldn't help but notice a shift in the seller's demeanor. "You know, I'm thinking maybe I underpriced this beauty. Let's make it seven thousand."

"You can't do that," I said, deflating. "I only have the forty-five hundred you quoted me over the phone."

Hearing the exchange, Bertram stood to full height. Walking away from me and the car, I knew this stranger was in trouble. "What is it, can't bear to sell your precious vehicle to a couple of queers, much less a queer couple?" Tram said, the anger apparent in both volume and tone. "That's unacceptable."

"My car, my price." There was no negotiation.

Bertram came back to the front of the car and pushed me aside before slamming the hood with more force than was necessary. "It's all right," he said, glaring at the man. "We'll find you a better car somewhere else."

I took Tram's hand in mine as we turned and stormed away from the homophobe.

Had we watched the news over the next few days, we might have heard about the car driving off the road and into a ravine that evening. The newscaster would say that it appeared to be some critical mechanical error and that it was likely the Mustang's driver had no time to even panic. I remember picking up the Reynisfjara stone from the nightstand and unconsciously stroking it to soothe my nerves. *Some things have a way of working out just as they should.*

* * *

The feeling of déjà vu as we arrived at Reynisfjara Beach again was palpable. Sure, the sky this time was overcast, with the threat of damp, chilly rain ever present, but somehow that seemed appropriate.

Tram and I walked hand in hand to the edge of the sand and watched in silence as the waves pummeled the shoreline and cliff face. Out in the distance stood the iconic rock formations rumored to be petrified trolls. I couldn't remember if they were supposedly guarding the coast or attacking it. Seemed irrelevant either way; today, they would simply be witnesses. Nothing was going to alter the decision I had made.

I turned to Tram—perhaps with tears in my eyes, but let's face it, the wind was strong that day. "This ends here," I said, with a seriousness in my voice that could not be downplayed.

"What the hell are you talking about? Are you saying you want to end our relationship?" Tram turned to face me and saw the bleak look in my eyes.

298

I made a sound that was a cross between a huff and a laugh. "Oh, not the relationship…you!"

The shock on Tram's face confirmed my decision. Such arrogance, as though no one would ever think badly of the great Bertram Bannister.

"What the hell are you talking about?" His confusion was as pathetic as he was.

We began to stroll towards the basalt wall that stands to the left of the beach. "Are you kidding me? Do you really think I am that clueless? I saw how you looked at that twink in the front row of your *Intro to Lit* seminar last week." Keeping the anger from my voice was imperative. It had to look like we were joking to the few other tourists around us. "I'm not as stupid as you like to think."

"I never said you were. And I would never get involved with a student." Tram placed his arm around my shoulder, and despite my disgust, I allowed it.

"Never?" I laugh. "Uh…ya did! I'm standing right here."

"I meant other than you, of course. I love you."

In the hollowed-out cave along the basalt wall, the cold of the whipping wind diminished, but the chill remained in my voice. "Please. Don't make yourself look so pitiful. The player got played. You will do what I say, or the whole world will know how you manipulated a poor, innocent freshman. How you abused your power. And it wasn't the first time."

"It wasn't like that, and you know it," Tram said, confused.

It was time to bring out the big guns. I'd been holding this secret so long that I struggled to open up. Looking around to make sure no one could overhear us, I stood face-to-face with Tram.

"Remember Jason Johnson? He was an older kid in my neighborhood…I idolized him. I loved him. And you destroyed him. What you did drove him to suicide. He put it all in his diary, which he left in my possession. I carried that diary around with me for years until I could arrange our meeting. From that moment, I knew I would make you pay." The cathartic power of truth coursed through my veins.

I could tell this revelation shook Bertram to his core.

"Have you gone insane?"

But I wasn't going to stop there. "And if threatening to ruin your reputation isn't enough incentive, don't think I won't tell the police how I suspect that you killed MeMaw."

The color drained completely from Bertram's face. He was a ghost of his vibrant self.

"Yeah, I set you up, my love! You should have seen MeMaw's face when I used my spare key to open the door that night. I proceeded to stab her with the kitchen knife you used to cut your precious brownies. Just more collateral damage of your toxic nature. Hey, and a financial windfall for me." My laughter was more performative than authentic.

"This can't be happening." Tram stood in disbelief, his chin quivering. *Was it denial or respect? Did I care?*

I just nodded. "Oh, it very much is happening. And remember when I wanted that Mustang? If I wasn't going to get that car, no one was. Fortunately, I hung out with some troubled kids growing up. This one delinquent, Scott, taught me how to cut a brake line in minutes with the tiniest tiny hacksaw you ever did see."

That seemed to be the last straw.

"You're a monster."

Fortunately, there was no one else around to hear this accusation. "Didn't I tell you that earlier this morning? You really should learn to listen more closely. Wasn't that MeMaw's advice?"

It was time for my coup de grâce. Or, as I learned in Professor Bertram Bannister's *Literary Terms 101* course—the denouement.

I faced Bertram with my steeliest look. "You are going to walk out into that water and meet your maker—or whatever stupid cliché you'd like. If it makes you feel better, you can just blame it on this cursed rock." I tossed the worthless pebble toward the shoreline, its purpose complete. No longer needed.

I saw a moment of hope glimmer on Bertram's face. "Exactly! This is not necessary. You have returned the stone to the beach. The curse has been broken. We can get past this."

"If only that were true, Tram. Doesn't the idea of a curse seem just a bit childish to you?"

With resignation and perhaps a shattered ego, Bertram turned to the tumultuous water. His silence spoke volumes.

"You need to walk into that water right now. We are about to see if my decision to change majors to the theater department was a good call. I'm ready for my close-up, Mr. DeMille."

"You are going to rot in hell for this."

"I'll see you there!"

I pretended to be distracted by the complex patterns of basalt columns, but I kept an eye on Bertram's death march. I knew it was only a matter of time before one of the legendary sneaker waves grabbed him and pulled him to a watery grave. Once that happened, it was my moment to shine.

"Help, help. Oh my God…this can't be happening. Someone save him!"

* * *

Kristopher Zgorski is the founder and sole reviewer at the crime fiction book blog, BOLO Books. In 2018, he was awarded the MWA Raven Award. That same year, the blog was nominated for the Anthony Award. Kristopher writes a column on digital crime fiction resources for every issue of *Ellery Queen's Mystery Magazine*. Appearing in 2023, Kristopher's first published short story—"Ticket to Ride"—(a collaborative work with follow blogger Dru Ann Love) was nominated for an Agatha Award.

Arsenic and the Shepherd

By Nev March

Bombay, India

Eyebrows knotted, Superintendent McIntyre said, "Mee-thay?"

My superior officer's grasp of the vernacular was questionable, even after a decade in charge of the growing Bombay police force. 1892 had not been a good year for him—the hot summer air that the three-bladed punkha fans barely circulated, complaints from the Governor's council, and constant interference from Home Office left him red-faced and steely eyed most days.

"*Mithai*, sir," I said. "Sweetmeats. He found a box of sweets at the scene of the crime and secured it." I nodded at Sub-inspector Sabrimal with an encouraging look. "Go on."

Despite my urging him in English, he launched his explanation in Hindustani.

"Captain Agnihotri!" Superintendent McIntyre's growl held a note of exasperation.

Sabrimal was my junior by seven years but already the father of four. He would have taken the confections home to his family but my insistence that it be analyzed had brought us to this juncture.

I prompted him. "You took it to the Medical Examiner, yes?"

He protested in his mother tongue. "But Captain saheb, *you* sent me to him!"

I clicked my tongue. "Tell the chief."

Sub-inspector Sabrimal straightened to attention and gazed above our heads. He'd begged for more work in the hope of advancement. I could have told him that was useless—he was too damn well-meaning. A good detective needs a healthy dose of skepticism. Sabrimal had not an ounce of it on his well-padded frame.

I cast a look over his pillow-like posture, eyes bulging with effort, as he assembled some English. "Doctor said, poison!"

McIntyre's eyes snapped to me as I added, "Arsenic, Jameson said, in sufficient dozes to 'fell a small elephant, or a good-sized rhino.'"

McIntyre's gaze sharpened. "Where was the box found?"

"It lay near the victim, Bhanu Kamgar, who owned the tea stall. He'd retired from a Bombay Infantry division some years ago." That the deceased was an ex-serviceman, however humble, had elevated this ordinary crime to my attention.

Pre-empting his next question, I added, "Sweetmeats are usually wrapped in old newspaper. The fancy box could give us a lead. Two pieces were missing, presumed consumed by the victim. He died quickly. Frothing at the mouth and rictus witnessed by a customer."

"Did he see who delivered the sweets?"

"Apparently not. I'll question him again this afternoon."

McIntyre's mouth twisted as though he'd tasted something sour. "Wrap it up quickly, Agnihotri. We've got real work to do."

Real work. I wondered why, if he disliked policing so much, he'd refused a much-touted promotion back into the British army in Africa. Who was supposed to watch over the populace of Bombay, if not us? How many insidious little crimes escaped justice because we were too busy with the grand work of empire?

'The chaiwallah case' brought grins and chuckles from my colleagues. I'd been expected to promptly file it, since it was too minor to merit much investigation. But a peculiar sensation crept down the back of my neck each time I glanced at the thin file, like seeing the tail of a snake sticking out of the ground. Where was the rest of it?

I snatched up my coat and tracked down the witness, an elderly watchman, in front of a brick factory.

"Did you see who gave Bhanu the box?"

"Bhanu?"

"The chaiwallah."

His reply was a downturned mouth.

"What was he like?"

"Who?"

"The chaiwallah!"

The watchman only shook his head and shrugged in answer to each question. I squinted at his squat nose and pudgy chin, pondering how to pry loose some intelligence. A carriage approached, so he hurried to open the gate, raising a hand to his forehead in a sloppy salute that, in the army, would have won him three sprints around camp and a hundred pushups. A dozen questions later I gave it up as a lost cause.

Hours later I still had no leads. The box of deadly sweets lacked any distinguishing mark, and resembled hundreds sold each day in Fort market. The victim had no family, his wife having died the year before. He lived at the chai stall, so there was no home to examine.

As I prowled through the hovels neighboring the stall, a bicycle repairman was pumping air into an overly patched tube. He looked up at my approach.

I pointed toward the deserted chai-stall where crumpled newspaper and dry leaves already accumulated. "Do you know the chaiwallah?"

He glanced away but not before I caught his lips pucker with dislike. Then he said, "He died yesterday."

Wondering at his grimace, I probed. "Will you attend his cremation at the *shamshan ghat*?"

In answer he spat to one side. I took that as a no. So he didn't like the chaiwallah and wasn't particular who knew it.

I asked, "Tell me, how did his wife die?"

"How? She vomited blood. And fell down. And died."

But that did not explain his tone of disgust. "You think the chaiwallah…?"

He met my gaze. "What happens at home is private. But neighbors hear. We hear crying. We hear beating. He beats too much, she vomits blood."

But other neighbors disagreed. The carpenter next door said, "Bhanu and his wife argued a lot, but he could not be ten minutes without her. Always keeping her in sight, he was. Where is she going? Why is she taking so long. Married five years, they were."

Both husband and wife dead in the space of a few years? Disturbed, I spent the next few hours poring through Records Hall on Esplanade Road. Eventually a clerk brought down a stack of files from 1887 and thumped the dusty bundle before me.

Leafing through, I found Champa Kamgar's death in the register: her cause of death was listed as Natural Causes. I frowned. At the age of twenty-five?

Years ago, a sepoy in my company had collapsed and died during our morning drill—an autopsy found he'd had a brain aneurism: natural causes. So, it could happen, I supposed, but the cyclewalla's words made me doubtful. Champa had no known relatives. Her maiden name was not listed. Her cremation was paid for by Bhanu Kamgar, chaiwallah at Warden Road.

Another dead end. I sighed, returning the file.

Back at headquarters, my colleagues grinned at my bachelor's meager dinner of *vada-pav* from a street-cart as they departed for their bustling homes. I added my notes to the chaiwallah file and feeling morose, went to the drawers that contained Bombay's unsolved cases. They were filed alphabetically but that didn't help at all, because each officer named his file whatever he wished. I frowned, undecided. Should I place it under B for Bhanu, or K for Kamgar? S for Sweets? P for Poison or A for Arsenic?

Labelling the file MITHAI, 1 pulled open the drawer marked M.

There, among three Military murders, seven Meat-market robberies and a Milkman's arrest for assault, I found an old file marked MITHAI-SWEETS.

Staring, I grabbed the file and took it over to my desk. The story was spread over a few scant pages: A week before last Dussehra, a low-level clerk of the P&O shipping office had been poisoned. Just before lunchtime, an urchin boy delivered a small package to his desk and ran off. The red and gold box contained almond burfi, a popular confection. The clerk ate some and died within minutes. The report noted in a postscript that his widow and child had moved to Dehra Dun to be with her family.

No point swearing, since no one could hear me. Silence pressed against my ears. No one would complain if I stuffed the file into a drawer and went off to bed. But no, it would not do. I'd have to check the hodge-podge files.

Starting at the drawer marked A-C, I riffled through the file labels and scowled. No, it would not be easy. I yanked out a batch and took them to my desk.

Four hours later I'd found a file parked under B: BOX OF SWEETS and another under H HARVANTRAI. For both, cause of death was listed as: Arsenic poisoning. I shooed away a mouse nosing at the crumbs under my desk and compared the different cases.

At one o'clock, the station guard came to check if someone had left a gas lamp burning by mistake. Later, some inmate in the jail room below made a ruckus. I debated going through to find out what the trouble was, but it quieted down, so I returned to the misnamed files.

Around three, the fire truck next door harnessed horses and went out on an alarm just as I found a file under S: SWEETMEATS; a milkman had died after consuming *halva mithai* from a red and gold box.

At five, the temple bells chimed next door. Under P: PATIL, a thin folder noted that a law-clerk named Bisvas PATIL had also been poisoned with sweetmeats from a red and gold box before the Ganesh-Chaturti festival.

All five deaths had occurred in the last three years. Six, if you included my chaiwallah.

Sometime later a muezzin called his mournful song in the distance. The water pipes made a ruckus as the mali began the lengthy process of watering the street outside to keep down the dust. The water wagon would not arrive until noon, spraying from hoses to cool the sidewalks. Light glimmered along the windows as cool night gave way to humid day. Our station's stone walls were usually pleasantly cool, but already a warm gust blew through my window.

Mopping my forehead, I gazed at the slim files on my desk, their yellowing pages containing meager details. The victims had all lived in the northern parts of Bombay but that meant nothing; the elite south held mostly British residences. They had different occupations. Some had families, others did not. Their ages ranged from thirty to sixty-seven. Five were male, one female. Different religions, ethnicities, occupations. Some were born in Bombay, others hailed from different cities. Nothing in common.

Setting out a foolscap sheet, I marked out six columns down the page and began to fill in the comparable details. When it was full, I started another sheet. Studying these, I stifled a groan. What little information I gleaned for one victim was frequently missing for others. It seemed a vain exercise, but I could not stop. I was focused on the puzzle like a mongoose pawing at a snake-hole. Perhaps some part of me relished the obsessive oblivion, for I could see nothing else.

Daylight brought my colleagues, but some tacit understanding kept them from disturbing me. The chaiwallah boy silently placed a tiny glass on the corner of my table and departed without his usual chatter. I turned over my handwritten sheets, troubled by the gaps that littered the columns. A cough somewhere above me drew my attention.

"Well?" McIntyre asked with a narrowing of his eyes.

I tapped my page. "At least six people were poisoned with arsenic-laced *mithai* in the last three years. Not counting those poisoned with tainted milk, or other things ingested. No connection that I can see, except that in each case a red and gold box shows up."

"Hm," he said, and walked away. For him that was high praise, indeed.

Sub-inspector Sabrimal was staring at me, so I said, "Yes?"

"Captain saheb, You didn't salute!"

I stretched and shrugged the ache off my shoulders, then went to clean up and see Dr. Jameson, the medical examiner.

* * *

"Arsenic isn't that rare," said Doctor Jameson, military physician and our de facto Medical Examiner, leaning back in his chair. "It's used in all sorts of things. Ladies' face powder, dyes, wallpaper, chemicals that kill bugs and weeds…"

"Face powder!"

"Oh yes. Lightens the skin. Did you know Queen Elizabeth used a paste of lead and vinegar called Venetian ceruse, or the spirits of Saturn. Awful stuff, lead."

"But arsenic?"

"Well, it's sold to American women as wafers, a sort of biscuit."

"They consume it?"

He smiled at my incredulous tone and rattled off a call like a hawker in Chor Bazaar, "Dr. James P. Campbell's Safe Arsenic Complexion Wafers! Good for dyspepsia, constipation, malaria, neuralgia, rheumatism, loss of appetite, lackluster eyes, low spirits, want of vitality, mal-assimilation of food, headache, hay fever. Le-ja-oh, Lejaoh!"

I stared.

Chuckling, he said, "I met the inventor on a steamer in 1890. My last trip home."

"And it doesn't kill the ladies?"

His eyebrows climbed toward his hairline. "Well, I suppose they imagine a little might not cause harm. In sufficient doses, it could be very nasty indeed. It would have to be concentrated, dissolved and the water boiled away, perhaps. Planning to poison someone?" he said idly.

"Could one buy Arsenic wafers here?"

"Possibly. You'd have to consult a chemist."

"Right." I got to my feet.

"And Agnihotri!"

I stopped at the door.

"Get some sleep for God's sake. You can't go around like that. What if you bump into the Framjis?"

Not likely, I thought, touching my forehead and bowing like a lowly orderly. He grinned at my salaam, and I went back to my new digs, still cluttered with boxes I could not find the will to unpack. It was part of what I was determined to avoid so I bathed and shaved, and even went down to lunch with my fellow boarders. But that was as far as my return to human society would go: scarfing down the Goan fish curry and white rice, the *masala bhurji* and fried plantains. At another time I'd have savored the deep curry spice that could make a Hyderabadi sweat, but not today. Ignoring the wide-eyed looks around the table, I hurried back to my room.

The small stack of files was as mulishly untalkative as before, but feeling refreshed, I glared at them and started over with my interrogation.

Hours passed. Sighing, I leaned on my forearms. I was going around in circles. By now I knew each page as well as the rooms of Poona Cantonment Hospital where I'd spent months recuperating.

Feeling lightheaded, I glanced at the light fading in the window. I'd turn in early, I promised my aching shoulders. One more shot at the bugger and then I'd rest, I thought, returning to my handwritten pages.

And then, I saw it…

Scrawled in my own hand, sitting there as pretty as you please on page three. DEATH REGISTERED BY: Two columns contained the same name. Dr Mehra, and Dr A Mehra. His address was given as Plot #7, Agiyari lane, Fort market.

He'd recorded two of the poisoning deaths. It was late, almost sunset, but I scampered down the stairs like Romeo off to see his girl.

* * *

Plot #7 Agiyari lane was a small house sandwiched between the Parsi Fire temple on one side and a two-story chawl whose balconies were festooned with wash drying on clotheslines. Twilight hung over the narrow lane, bathing it in indigo and violet. Windows flickered with candle or gaslight as families prepared for supper. The gate of #7 creaked as I entered and stepped toward the old bungalow.

It must have been pretty, once. The bamboo lattice work was now the color of wet sand, the shingles bleached to grey. The top floor was a residence, I saw, one window lit by a kerosene lantern. So, Doctor Mehra probably had rooms above his ancient clinic. Brown moss covered an old mounting block that stood by the rusted wrought-iron railing. Peeling paint on the crooked shutters. Old brick stairs, still serviceable.

I headed toward the wooden door that stood ajar, and almost didn't see the old man on the front porch. Swaddled in an oversized shawl, he looked up from his tiny desk and laid down his fountain pen, his white beard bobbing. "Yes, Saheb?"

"I want to see Dr Mehra."

"Doctor-ji…" he began.

A young woman wearing spectacles swung open the door and cut him off. Speaking in Hindustani, she said, "Vasant babu, you carry on home. I will close up the clinic."

Mumbling goodnights, the old man shuffled away. The woman retreated into the clinic, so I followed, entering a room lined with bookshelves. A row of chairs cluttered one side and a corner was screened off into a little nook. Here, a window cut in the wood screen had a small shelf to dispense syrups and powders.

After closing the rear windows, the woman returned. Her sari was blue washed to grey, but she did not wear it in the old-fashioned way over her hair, which was parted in the middle and braided. Neither overtly traditional nor modern, she moved with natural grace, arranging objects with practiced ease as she closed up the clinic.

I asked, "Where is Doctor Mehra?"

The women sent me a glance. "Do you need treatment?"

"No, I have some questions. I'm Captain Agnihotri, Bombay police."

"Police?"

"Are you his daughter?"

She smiled and gestured at a chair. "Please."

I sat. "Your mother…?"

"Died when I was born," she said, completing my sentence.

"Is the doctor called away, then?"

She stood to one side, clasped hands resting over her sari and said, "People seek a physician when they have trouble. And trouble does not keep banker's hours."

"No," I agreed, wondering whether to postpone my visit for the morning. But the poisoner must be someone with a close understanding of chemicals, so I questioned the woman. "Where does the doctor live?"

She raised a finger, pointing to the floor above.

I tilted my head in the direction of the old man's departure. "Vasant babu, who is he?"

"Our compounder. He has been with us more than forty years."

He compounded medicines. Wouldn't he know about chemicals and their properties? With only an old doctor and his daughter around, how hard would it be to siphon some of the physician's supplies for his own needs? The room's silence pushed at my skin. Miss Mehra stood with her hands modestly before her, waiting.

"Is this a busy practice?"

She shrugged. "No more than most, I suppose. We have been here for decades, so we get to know the families. They bring their neighbors, the new daughter-in-law, her child. Then the child grows up and marries. And it goes on."

Her voice had a pleasant intonation. Calm, but also competent, instilling confidence. But someone was poisoning the old doctor's patients. I paused, watching the physician's daughter quietly worry. Had age eroded the old man's mind? Yet that would not explain the deliberate use of arsenic in sweets. I was willing to bet all six boxes were prepared by the same hand.

"So Dr. Mehra is popular?"

She smiled. "A shepherd. Tending the flock."

That was a curiously biblical allusion. "And he tends the wolves too?"

Her eyebrows rose in surprise. "How can you tell them apart? You are police, yes? How can you tell innocent from guilty?"

I smiled. "That's a job for the court. I see victims and…suspects."

"Is Dr. Mehra suspected of something?" Her demeanor was calm, but a sort of strain gathered around her eyes.

"He may be able to help me. Two of his patients died of arsenic poisoning."

"Oh!" She frowned. "Recently?"

"No, last year." I searched her troubled face. "But he signed the register for both deaths, so the two victims may have known each other. And possibly, also…the one responsible."

"It cannot be a mistake. Vasant babu checks all the prescriptions with great care."

I shook my head, then nodded at the rows of bottles behind the nook. "Who else has access to these chemicals?"

"Me. But I do not dispense the pills and powders. Sometimes I fetch them from the chemist, sometimes Vasant babu."

Jameson had said the sweets were not just laced with arsenic but prepared with a large dose of it. That was six deliberate acts, spread over three years.

"Dr. Mehra must keep a record of his patients?" Reading the reluctance on her face, I added, "Their occupations?"

"What work they do? Oh, we don't ask that. What does it matter? Most Indian names denote some ancestral occupation. Mehras were once weavers, in Punjab."

"Can you recall a *'mithaivala'* among the patients?"

It was a long-shot and it went wide. She smiled, shaking her head, hands wide.

Returning her smile, I picked up my hat and said, "I'll take no more of your time, Miss Mehra. Thank you for seeing me. Please tell you father I will return at another time."

* * *

The next day, as I crossed toward Dhobi Talav, I saw the peeling, crooked sign of a chemist hung over a store, so I walked over.

The counter was empty of customers. An elderly attendant nudged his glasses higher and greeted me. "How can I help, *Afsar-saheb*?"

Afsar...Officer. Even in civilian garb, he'd taken me for a serviceman. "Are you the chemist?'

"Yes, come, come," he said. "If you want a good doctor, I can tell you where to go. We also have cures for common ailments. Hemorrhoids?" he asked, kindly.

"I want to know about arsenic. Have you sold any in the last three years?"

He looked surprised. "Of course, saheb. It is an ingredient of many Arurvedic medicines. Native Indian *vaids* use it all the time."

I asked for the addresses of the nearest three practitioners and jotted them down in my notebook, then asked, "Does Dr. Mehra get ingredients from you?"

He took off his glasses and polished them. "Aahh. There is a compounder, Vasant babu. He comes for the usual hydrogen-peroxide, mercurochrome, iodine, ammonia."

"Arsenic?"

He shrugged. "Yes."

"Other doctors too?"

He nodded, looking anxious. "Some."

"Dr. Mehra. When did he last order it?"

"He?" The chemist put up his glasses and peered at me. "But old Dr Mehra died 4 years ago!"

* * *

I returned to the clinic with long strides, only to find a crowd gathered around the gate. Clad in traditional dhoti and shawl, the old compounder seemed besieged on all sides. Palms out, he seemed to be pleading with unhappy customers.

"What's the matter?" I demanded over their crowded heads.

A pathway miraculously cleared in front of me. As I approached, the lines in the old man's face seemed deeper, his stoop more pronounced than yesterday.

He opened the gate to admit me. "Saheb, I am telling them, but they are not listening. Doctorji cannot see any patients. She cannot see anyone. She has gone away."

Doctorji. She.

Bollocks.

Now I recalled his initial words to Miss Mehra. "Doctorji…" And she'd cut him off, saying she would wait and close up the clinic. Bloody hell.

I stepped close. "Where did she go?"

He pressed his folded hands together, the skin creased around his eyes. "Where?"

Realizing that he would not reply until I'd disbanded our audience, I turned and announced, "The clinic is closed. See another doctor."

The crowd replied with protests. "But saheb! We cannot afford them! Where shall we go? My son has fever!"

"The gora doctor is too far! We cannot pay his fees! Only Doctorji comes when we need her. Hai hai! What will I do?"

I set my shoulders back and gave them my best impression of Chief Superintendent McIntyre. Grumbling protests, they shuffled away. A woman doctor who didn't charge much would be hard to find.

Then we were alone in the small green courtyard with its jasmine and ferns, glossy leaves of elephant-ear waving under the drooping roots of the old peepul tree like ropes hanging from an abandoned sail.

I turned to the old compounder. "Well?"

He shuffled away taking small steps on the flagstone path.

No, not this time. I stalked after him, preparing a choice rebuke. Before I could deliver it, he handed me an envelope.

It was marked, CAPTAIN AGNIHOTRI in a neat flowing script.

My heart jerked a beat, then settled into a warning pace. Careful; this is dangerous terrain, a thin veneer that may not take our weight.

Somewhere above me a koyal cooed, "Who-oo? You-oo?" A hot breeze brushed my forehead. Taking out the pages, I knew what they would say before I read them.

Captain Saheb, I did not mislead you. No, I admit, I allowed you to mislead yourself. But everything I told you was true. We few native doctors treat whoever comes to our door. We see the pieces, the ragged torn flesh, the bruises, the burns, the tears. Papa sewed them up and treated the pain. Vasant babu Compounder served him for decades, and I helped since I was ten years old.

Factory accidents, falls, broken bones. Colds and aches and fevers. Scrawny women depleted from multiple childbirths. Women with broken noses and black eyes. Burns and bruises. So many bruises.

Papa would worry there was internal damage. "Is there blood when you make water?" he would ask. We feared the answer, sometimes, for there is only little we could do. And next month we'd see another broken bone, a finger that "got caught in the rope of the well." We questioned them; the women's haunted eyes spoke such awful truth they could not look at papa. So they cast sideways glances at me, begging me, to answer for them, to make excuses, to hide their shame. Before I was thirteen, I learned the language of their silence.

You assumed that papa was Doctor Mehra. He was.

By now you know he has been dead four years. Since you are reading this, I know someone has blabbed to you. Our chemist? If you turned your eyes upon him, no doubt he would keep talking until you looked satisfied. But you know the power of your official vardi, and your stare.

Let me explain. I had assisted papa since childhood, taking on more duties as he grew infirm over the last decade. He died when we were traveling in Ajmer, and no one questioned it when I continued his practice.

But how could I keep on treating broken ribs and cigarette burns? In the bruises I could see the shape of the husband's fist, the imprint of his shoe.

Many years ago, an English customer gave me her face powder—a gift, so I could someday claim a handsome husband. Papa scoffed, shaking his head and would not let me apply it, because it contained arsenic. Still, how could I throw it away—it was so expensive! Later I found a use for it after all.

Captain Saheb, I did not kill indiscriminately. Some wives would have become destitute without their abusive husbands. So I waited. Others would be on their way to the shamshan burial ghat if I did not act. Who can know the future? I agonized over each one. Each year at festivals, grateful patients gifted papa laddus in pretty boxes. Papa was so thrifty. Each page, newspaper or brown paper used over and over. Magazine covers and cardboard I cut into tapers to light the chulha. Somehow, we had saved a stack of seven mithai boxes.

So, I made good use of them. The face powder, sugar and almond paste concentrated into a tasty burfi. Then I ran out of arsenic and had to get some from Chemist Babu. He was surprised, because I usually do not make ayurvedic preparations.

The shepherd must use whatever means are at hand.

I have no regrets. By the time you have read this, I will be on a ship to Shanghai. I have joined Christian missionaries who care for the poor in rural China.

Who will protect my flock now? Captain Saheb, in another time and place, we might have been friends. This lifetime, it is not to be. I can only remain,

your devoted,

Dr. Mehra

Something inside my chest twisted as I folded the letter and inserted it into the envelope. I would not hand it to McIntyre. All those "little" crimes he'd overlooked…some had not gone unpunished. Would I have arrested Miss—Doctor Mehra? I wasn't so sure. The shepherd had left her flock.

* * *

Nev March is the first Indian-born author to receive the Minotaur Books/Mystery Writers of America Award. Her debut novel, *Murder in Old Bombay*, won an Audiofile award and was an Edgar and Anthony finalist. *The New York Times* listed it among the "Best crime novels of 2020." Nev's historical mysteries deal with issues of identity, race and moral boundaries. She teaches at Rutgers University's Osher Institute and is the NY chapter President of MWA.

The Package

By Anne Hillerman and Dave Tedlock

Mexico

Most of the trouble started when his brother and Sally, his brother's girlfriend, changed the plan. "Never mind about taking a bus back to Santa Fe from Mexico City," his brother said.

"We want you to go with us to Guadalajara."

"Why?" the kid asked.

In their family, the family nickname for his brother was The Genius. His brother was 12 years older and extremely intelligent. The kid had just turned 17, and he didn't have to be a genius to know that his brother was up to something.

Well, for an answer to the question, The Genius pushed his wire frame glasses back up his nose and said, "We would like to have you with us for another day, Guadalajara is beautiful, and we think we can find the perfect chess set for Dad there."

The kid waited for more of an explanation, but The Genius was done talking and Sally didn't add anything. The kid had a long, boring summer ahead of him before his senior year in high school. He figured The Genius was planning something, so the kid said, "Okay."

Throughout their week of travel into the heart of Mexico, the kid had enjoyed exploring street markets with The Genius and Sally, but he'd seen countless chess sets already, most of them made from onyx. They were all pretty much the same. While he was stuck looking at chess sets and t-shirts with *loteria* designs, and wooden carvings of Don Quixote, his brother was busy engaging different street vendors in complicated, rapid-fire conversations that the kid couldn't follow with his high school Spanish. Every one of these encounters ended in heads shaking and "no," until, in Mexico City, an answer came that was not a "*si*," but was less than a "no."

After the long trip to Guadalajara the three of them went to another beautiful, open-air marketplace, this one filled with flowers, food, ceramics, tourist souvenirs, silver jewelry, textiles and more. The crowd included tourists as well as local Mexicans, and plenty of children. The kid noticed one man who showed up at the same booths they visited as they went through the market. The kid found it impossible to get a good look at him. He wore mirrored sunglasses and had black hair starting to gray and a beard.

After about an hour at the market, his brother abruptly said that he and Sally were finished shopping. The Genius put a bag in the trunk and they returned to the hotel. The three of them shared a room to save money, and his brother announced that he and Sally needed some private time. "Why don't you check out the pool?"

The kid started to tell The Genius what everyone in the family already knew. He didn't like pools and was a lousy swimmer. But he went.

Then, early the very next morning, The Genius said that their parents had called and wanted the kid home. At the bus station, The Genius bought him a ticket to Juarez and another from there to El Paso and on to Santa Fe. He handed the kid a package wrapped in white paper with what felt like a lot bubble wrap underneath, and plenty of strong tape all the way around.

"It's a gift for Mom and Dad," his brother said. "The perfect chess set for Dad. Plus one of those Don Quixote sculptures for Mom. Promise me you won't open it until you get home. It was a bitch to get all the bubble wrap taped in there. Promise?"

"Sure, I promise."

"Great. Let Mom and Dad open it. Don't spoil their surprise, All right?"

"I already promised," the kid said. "I've already seen too many chess sets and too many Don Quixotes."

The package was heavy, but the kid's backpack was sturdy and he was traveling light, so he stowed it between his jeans and t-shirts, and hugged his brother and said goodbye to Sally. As he walked toward the bus, his brother said, "Em. Remember what I said about riding on a Mexican bus. Don't sit in the front. And don't let that backpack out of your sight."

His brother seldom called him "Em," his family nickname, short for Emmett. On the way to the station, his brother also had told him, "Listen, guard that backpack like it's worth a million bucks."

Em started out on the bus trip home doing exactly what The Genius told him NOT to do. He took a seat in the front row, not behind the driver, but on the other side of the aisle for the best view out the front. He put his backpack on the floor between his knees, not because The Genius told him to, but so he could reach his book, his phone and his snack. He had a long ride ahead of him. Long and probably boring.

To his surprise, for once The Genius had given him good advice—at least about where to ride on the bus. In the first hour alone, he thought he was going to die multiple times. The bus driver was insane. The highway became two lanes not far out of Guadalajara because of construction, and the driver routinely passed slower vehicles when there were cars or trucks or even other buses coming the other way. And the bus driver seemed to think that every vehicle in front of them was a slower vehicle.

The kid quickly surmised that something like a game of chicken he'd played riding bicycles with friends was taking place on the highway, only the bus driver had 60 lives in his care and seemed to enjoy putting them at risk every 10 minutes. Finally, around noon the driver brought the bus to a stop and yelled something over the PA system in rapid Spanish about a lunch break for *vente minutos*.

The kid wasn't sure exactly what else the driver said because his Spanish was marginal, but he knew the bus would leave again in 20 minutes. So he got off with his backpack, went into a little store there and bought some wrapping tape and put a toilet stall to good use. Then, he stood in line along with everyone else, purchased something hot and fresh to eat and got back on the bus

This time he selected a different seat, a spot on one of the middle rows. He settled in by the window behind an enormous lady whose body spilled over into the seat next to her, where her companion, an incredibly skinny man, sat. There was no way the kid could see past the lady and have any idea of what the driver was up to.

Em made one other change. He was tall and had big feet so his backpack didn't fit comfortably on the floor. Before he sat down, he shoved his pack into an overhead bin directly across from his seat. He had some trouble getting the heavy bag up there. But he figured it was safe. He could access it quickly if he needed to, and his dirty, worn backpack looked less appealing to a potential thief than the other stuff crammed in the bin. Because he was six feet tall and weighed two twenty, people assumed he was older and not a guy to tangle with. Besides, nobody on the bus looked especially sinister. After the large lady in front of him, the kid was the biggest person there.

Once Em was settled in his seat, he inspected his meal, a taco made from a soft corn tortilla. It smelled great. He wasn't sure what all was in it, but it looked mostly like onions and steak. The vendor called it *un saudero* and he took a chance on it because it resembled sliced beef. Now, he pondered whether it would give him Montezuma's revenge.

Some commotion outside his window caught his eye. He watched as a black Cadillac SUV pulled into the parking lot at high speed and squealed its tires as it came to a stop alongside the bus. Then a man wearing a handsome suit and navy-blue tie jumped out of the SUV and ran for the bus, the guy's backpack bouncing around on his shoulders. It was an odd combination, the kid thought. He would have expected the man to have a suitcase with wheels and to be headed to the airport, not a bus station.

The new passenger barely made it onto the bus as the doors closed. He came down the aisle and stood there smiling at Em. He said, with a kind voice, "*Perdoname.*"

Then, upon studying the kid's face, he switched to English and said quite clearly, "Is this seat taken, *señor?*"

Em liked the *señor* part, which made him an adult. He also noticed the way the man had switched to English when he recognized that Em was an American. He looked at the man as the guy stood there and caught his breath from the run onto the bus.

"No," the kid said. "Please, uh…" He thought for a moment. "*Sientase. Por favor.*" There were plenty of other empty seats on the bus, even a few by windows, but the guy was choosing to sit next to him.

The man was maybe 50 and had a pleasant face. He had short black hair parted on one side with a touch of gray working its way to prominence and a neatly-trimmed goatee.

"Thank you," the man said in English.

"*De nada,*" Em answered.

The man sat and said, "Your Spanish is very good."

"*Gracias.*" Em's Spanish wasn't very good, but it was nice of the man to exaggerate.

As the man settled into the aisle seat, he asked, "Where are you going?"

"Juarez," the kid said with an excellent accent. Then he added, "Then El Paso, and then onto Santa Fe, New Mexico."

"Our little *hermanitos,*" the man said in a gentle way, though the kid doubted that Santa Feans would like to be thought of as the little brothers of Mexicans. "Many lovely museums there."

"Where are you going, *señor?*

"Oh, I am going back to my hometown," the man said. "Ah, but I fail to introduce myself. I am Rodolfo Martinez."

He stuck out his hand and the kid shook it, saying, "Mucho gusto, Señor Martinez. I'm Emmett."

"Emmett. Please call me Rodolfo."

"Please call me Em, Rodolfo. Short for Emmett."

For the kid, instead of feeling like death was imminent from a bus wreck, the journey toward Juarez instantly became more engaging with Rodolfo in the seat next to him. Their time on the bus passed quickly as they talked. At first, Em did most of the talking with Rodolfo asking questions.

"Why are you, such a young man, traveling on a bus from Guadalajara to Juarez? That is a very long way."

"Well, my brother and his girlfriend took me along with them as they drove all the way down here from Santa Fe, but…" He thought of how to position himself. "Well, I had such a good time I was running out of money, so it was time to go home. And I promised to bring back a chess set my brother bought for our dad and one of those Don Quixote carvings for my mom.

"So are you going to Juarez too?" He noticed that Rodolfo had placed his own backpack between his legs and kept glancing at it nervously.

"No, my friend." Rodolfo explained that he was traveling back to his beloved little hometown because he had gotten a letter from his sister saying there was trouble there. Strangers had come to town and shot and wounded two of his sister's neighbors.

"Right there on the street. Then the two men walked up and down the village roads telling everyone that they were looking for a man, and they would hunt for him, house by house, until they found him."

"Jeez," Em managed. "That's awful. Did your sister or her neighbors call the police?"

"No. They could not do that. My sister says the two men told everyone that the police would not be coming to help them. Mexico, as you have seen, is a beautiful country, but also a place with a few *problemas* and some bad *hombres*." Rodolfo's eyes were sad.

"So, why go back to your hometown now? I mean, isn't this a dangerous time to show up?"

"Yes, it is a very dangerous time. But I love my sister and her little ones. She has four children, twin boys and two girls. Her husband is an archaeologist, working in the jungles of the Yucatan for a month. I need to help her and the *hijos*."

The kid took another look at his seat mate. "Are you a cop? I mean, no offense, but you don't look like a cop."

"You are right," Rodolfo said. "I am not with the police. But, like a good officer, I understand my duty to my family. The same as you, delivering the gifts to your dear parents."

The kid hadn't thought of himself as doing his 'duty,' exactly, in taking home his brother's package.

"Em, are you happy about these gifts?"

"Not especially. At every single market in Mexico vendors sell those chess sets. They are all about the same except the pieces might be black and white, of course, but maybe in grays or greens." The kid shook his head. "And those Don Quixote carvings? They're corny. But it's what my brother bought for our parents. Go figure."

Rodolfo said, "Did you help to pick out this chess set with your brother and his, uh, girlfriend?"

"No, no. He just handed the package to me." The kid had an idea. "Maybe if we get bored later on, I can unwrap it and we can play a game. Do you enjoy chess?"

Rodolfo chuckled. "I like strategy, but I never learned the game. We should leave your chess set in its package."

The kid looked out the window at the growing darkness and the lights of the vehicles the driver passed and thought for a while. He was good at figuring things out.

"What are you going to do when you get to your sister's house?"

Rodolfo ran his hands through his hair. "We do what we have to do. I am grateful that when my sister married, she took her husband's name. She is no longer a Martinez. Instead, she is Maria Lopez. Our family always thought Maria Martinez was such a lovely name."

"Why? I mean, why be grateful her married name is different?"

Rodolfo sighed. "Because the bad men do not know she is a Martinez. They have been going through the neighborhoods, pounding on doors, asking questions, but they don't seem to know much about who they are looking for."

"So, who are they looking for, and why do they want to find him so badly?"

"They can't find the man because he is not there yet. They cannot find him until tomorrow," Rodolfo said. "As for the 'why,' that is another part of the story."

The kid glanced at his phone. It was 10:14 PM. He thought for a moment.

"You said your stop was in about three hours?"

Rodolfo nodded.

Em pulled the schedule out of his back jean's pocket and said, "So is your town, I mean your hometown, Sanditas or Novenas?"

Rodolfo said, "Sanditas. The most beautiful town in all of Mexico. Sanditas." He smiled as he said the name again, but looked worried at the same time.

The kid was tired. He'd hardly slept in Guadalajara because of the excitement of being somewhere new and putting his Spanish to use with that cute girl he met at the hotel pool. But Rodolfo's story had his mind racing.

Em said, "So the bad guys can't find the Martinez they're looking for because you're that guy and you're not there yet."

"You catch on quickly. I am sorry to say that you are right. They are looking for me. Perhaps not so much for me, as for something I have. Something they believe can make them *ricos* with fancy cars and gold chains on their necks. They know I am coming."

"So what you have is valuable enough to make them rich?" Then the kid changed the tone of his voice. "Is this about drugs?"

"No. No." Rodolfo looked offended. "Our family detests drugs. This concerns Mexico's history. Our heritage. *Cultura y patrimonia.* It is something they are willing to kill for and that I am willing to die for."

The kid turned in his seat. He was wide awake now. "You'd better tell me the whole story."

Rodolfo hesitated. He looked torn, as if he wanted to tell someone and at the same time thought he'd better not.

Then the kid said, "Look, when we get to your town, you can't get off the bus. The bad guys could be watching the bus station. We have to figure out how you can arrive in Sanditas and help your sister without them knowing you're there."

"What is this 'we' you are talking about? You are going to Juarez."

"Well, sure, but I can afford to stop in Sanditas first and then catch the next bus. Those guys aren't looking for me. They're looking for you. What can I do to help you keep your sister and her children safe?"

Rodolfo looked at Em for a long time, started to say something, stopped, and then said, "I will tell you a story and then we can talk about getting off the bus together."

The kid nodded.

"I will tell you about the earthquake, but the story must begin with Papa. My father was an educated man and devoted to helping people understand our nation's rich heritage. He worked as the director of Sanditas's museum. Sanditas is a poor village, so he used his charm and his wits to bring in visitors to keep the museum open. People in our town admired him and so, when the time came, they would leave their family's treasures to the museum."

"Treasures? You mean like jewels? Gold?"

"Ah, that word treasure isn't quite right. I mean the things these good people had collected and valued, especially old things from the Maya, the Aztec, the others. My father displayed these gifts so everyone in the village, surrounding towns and our tourist visitors could enjoy them. Our mother was long dead, but my sister and I helped at the museum when we could."

The kid wasn't a museum goer. He preferred playing football and basketball, and watching sports on television. But Rodolfo's story intrigued him. "What was the best thing your father collected?"

"The museum's prized possession was an onyx statue of a sacred Jaguar carved many centuries ago. Our Mayan ancestors held the animals sacred as rulers of the night sky. And this is a black jaguar, very rare in life and in art. Do you know about jaguars?"

"A little." Em had seen caged jaguars at the Albuquerque Zoo and he loved the sleek look of the Jaguar sedan. He said, "So the jaguar you have is unique, right?"

"*Correcto.* The museum's jaguar carving drew much attention including, unfortunately, some from those who wanted to steal it."

Rodolfo fell quiet and the bus rolled on, slowing down for additional highway repairs and construction. The kid noticed his seat mate glancing out the window more and more often. The man seemed nervous and the kid had more questions about the jaguar.

"You mentioned something about the earthquake," Em said. "Is that part of the story about you and your sister and the jaguar?"

"But of course. I forgot to tell you about that." Rodolfo smiled. "Mexico is subject to earthquakes. One day our village was near the epicenter. Some buildings were destroyed and many more were damaged, including our beloved museum. Not only the structure. Priceless objects fell off the walls and much was ruined. That was terrible, but what happened next was even worse."

"What?"

"My father went to the museum to assess the damage. Looters were there. He managed to find our sacred Jaguar sculpture and hide it, but they shot my father, and…"

Rodolfo fell silent and the kid saw the tears, the first time he'd watched a grown man cry.

"So, your father died?"

"*Si.* My sister and I had gone to the museum to help him. We were hiding in the back room and heard the shots. Eventually, all was quiet and I'll never forget it. *Mi papa estaba muerto.* He was dead and most of the treasures in the museum were gone. But the sacred jaguar was beneath his body. He had died but this treasure of all treasures was safe."

The man fell silent and the kid thought about what he had learned.

The kid remembered the lime drinks in his pack. He retrieved the backpack from the overhead compartment and sat down again. He shoved the pack between his feet, unzipped it and carefully removed the package his brother had given him and placed it on his lap. Then he pulled out two bottles of the *limonada* and offered one to Rodolfo. His seatmate accepted it and took a long sip. He removed another *limonada* for himself.

Rodolfo motioned to the package the kid had placed on his lap.

"Is that the gifts you are delivering to your parents?"

"Yeah, that's right. Chess set and Don Quixote. Tell me about your package."

Rodolfo glanced at the pack between his feet and didn't answer right way. Then, he lowered his voice to almost a whisper. "It is, how you say, an odd coincidence that the sacred jaguar my father saved is onyx too."

"What does that black jaguar of yours look like?"

Rodolfo seemed to check out the other passengers before he spoke. "An Olmec artist carved it and it is both old and rich in detail. Like your package, it is wrapped for safety. My father understood its value. He wanted it to go to a museum in Mexico City, where more people could appreciate its beauty and importance. He spent years making the arrangements with Señora Rosa Flores. But Señora Flores passed away before he could get it to her. So, when I was 18, about your age perhaps, I left Sanditas and took the sculpture with me. I have safeguarded it ever since. And now, after all these years, for some reason, bad men are looking for it again."

"Whoa," the kid said. "The curse of the jaguar."

Rodolfo's lips turned up in the trace of a smile. "No, my friend. We see it not as a curse, but as a responsibility. We had hoped to follow my father's wishes, but now, well, my sister's life is in danger." He stopped a moment and studied the nearby passengers as if checking for eavesdroppers. When he resumed speaking, his voice was even quieter.

"I need to act with caution. I do not want to give in to terror, but my sister and her children are *muy preciosa*, of more value to me even than the sculpture my father died to save."

The road had grown smoother and the bus driver sped up to compensate for the time he lost driving through the construction. The kid drank some limeade and spoke softly. "So, are you going to give it to them when you get to Sanditas?"

Rodolfo looked surprised. "How did you know that I had it with me?"

"The way you looked at your backpack when you put it between your feet after you took off your sunglasses. You are so careful with it. Kids my age throw their backpacks around like a bag of potatoes. You acted like yours was full of nitroglycerine. And, your pack looked heavy just like mine."

Rodolfo said, "I wrapped the jaguar in those padded packages people use for mailing, and then sealed it up with tape. I have to give it to the, as you say, bad guys. My sister, she tried to talk me out of it, *pero,* it's not worth her life, not worth leaving her sweet *niños* without their mama. Her family is ready to leave Sanditas with me the moment the *banditos* have the package."

Rodolfo sighed and glanced at his fancy wristwatch. "You are a smart young man, good at solving problems. The bus will be at Sanditas in an hour. Can you think of a way I can keep both my sister's family and the statue safe?"

The kid sat in silence for a long time. Finally, he whispered to Rodolfo. "Maybe… You want to get your sister and her family out of town, right?"

"Well, yes, of course."

"And you want to keep the statue."

"I have spent my whole life protecting it."

"All right. Does your sister have a phone and a car?"

"Yes, of course she does. *Claro que si.*"

"Okay. So you get off at Novenas, the stop before your home town. You call your sister to come there to get you. Tell her first to take a walk with her family past as many people as she can, especially the bad guys. And every time anyone can hear her, she tells her children a little too loudly that she has heard that the man with the statute is arriving on the next bus to Sanditas."

"Senor Em, I do not understand."

"You can't get off the bus in Sanditas. It's too dangerous. The bad guys will come to meet the bus, right?"

"Well, yes, I'm sure they would."

"And they want the statue. Let's make it easy for them."

Rodolfo's eyes began to shine, but he said, "I still am confused."

"I can hand the bad guys a package through the bus window. I will tell them a man asked me to give the package to them. I don't even have to get off the bus. If they have questions about anything, well, I don't really speak Spanish. Meanwhile, you get your sister and get her family the heck out of town."

The kid looked at Rodolfo and hoped he comprehended the English. Maybe he shouldn't have said "heck."

Rodolfo was shaking his head. "You are kind, but I cannot just give my statue away. I have spent my whole life guarding it. My papa died for it."

"I understand that," the kid said. "*Comprendo.* But the bad guys aren't going to get the jaguar. They're getting that stupid chess set my brother bought. We'll make a switch."

"Ahhhh!" Rodolfo said. "And I keep the statue?" His eyes gleamed.

"Exactly. I'll explain to my parents that the package got stolen. My mom's not going to care about missing out on a Don Quixote statue and my dad has other chess sets. Or maybe I can buy one for him in Juarez. My brother told me to keep an eye on my backpack, but he knows I never do half of what he tells me."

Rodolfo smiled hugely and patted the kid on the shoulder. "You are a very smart young man. But, to be fair, I should pay you for the chess set."

The kid thought about that. "Well, okay. Forty bucks should cover it and the Don Quixote."

"Bueno." When Rodolfo opened his wallet to give him the money, the kid noticed that the man had pesos and American dollars and plenty of both.

They went over the plan a couple of times. Then they waited. Not very much later, the bus stopped in Novenas and the kid said, "I'll leave with you so we can swap out the packages."

Once they got off the bus together, the kid pulled his package out and told Rodolfo to do the same.

"Here," the kid said, "see if you think they're about the same weight." He handed his package to Rodolfo who hefted both packages, one in each hand.

"Esta bien," Rodolfo said excitedly. "They weigh about the same. Very good. Here. See for yourself."

The kid took both packages and said, "You're right. But there's one last thing. Yours looks old, exactly like the jaguar package your father would have prepared. It's what they'll be expecting. But look at mine. It looks new, right?"

The kid's package was wrapped in fresh white paper that had the name of a famous Guadalajara market stamped on it. The brown paper on Rodolfo's package looked very old, even though the tape seemed new. Rodolfo frowned and, the kid thought, looked anxious.

"Don't worry," the kid said. "I'll swap out the wrapping paper in the bathroom while you stall the bus driver."

"But…"

Without waiting for an argument, the kid said, "I have to use the bathroom anyway," and ran off with both packages.

Rodolfo blurted out, *"Esperate!"* but the kid didn't stop.

Em came running back a few minutes later and heard Rodolfo in the middle of a shouting match with the bus driver about the delay Em had caused.

When they saw him, they both looked relieved.

"Perdoname," the kid said to the driver as he headed up the steps up into the bus. "I had a case of Montezuma's revenge." Then Em stopped abruptly, turned and said, "Señor Rodolfo, don't forget your package."

Rodolfo grabbed the package from Em. By then the bus driver was practically pulling the boy onto the bus so he could close the door. Rodolfo ran down the side of the vehicle, looking relieved and happy. He watched and when the kid stopped at an empty row, Rodolfo gestured to the kid to open the window.

"Be sure to hand it off through the window, my friend. Be very careful. Don't tell anyone what happened."

The kid smiled and nodded. As the bus began to pull away from the station, the kid could see Rodolfo putting the package into his backpack. Then he was waving goodbye, and smiling hugely as the bus drove off.

In about ten minutes the bus slowed for the next station, but there was no one there waiting to get on the bus at that stop, and no one who wanted to get off. The driver knew the kid had put him behind schedule, so he kept right on going. The small sign the bus zipped past read *Sanditas*.

Em worried a little about what might happen at the next stop or at the stop after that, so he didn't get off the bus between there and Juarez, just to be extra cautious. He observed that the only new passengers to get on the bus were peaceful souls who paid no attention to him. No one seemed to be looking for him. After about an hour of vigilance, the kid finished his lime drink, ate a few snacks, and then had a long deep nap. He awoke refreshed hours later when the bus encountered the heavy traffic outside of Juarez. As he watched the city go by, he gave himself credit all over again for not always doing exactly what The Genius told him to do.

On the Juarez side of the border, the timing of the buses was perfect. He strolled through the bus station and before he climbed onto a bus bound for El Paso, he stopped at a little shop and used Rudolfo's money to buy an onyx chess set and a Don Quixote. When he was passing through customs he had everything unwrapped and he showed the agent what he had. The border agent looked bored and said, "Walk on through," and that's exactly what he did.

It took most of a day to get home to Santa Fe from El Paso after that but the bus trip was uneventful with no Rodolfo to chat with. His parents picked him up at the station. His father said, "Your brother said he found a present for us and you have it in your backpack. He hefted the package. "This is heavy."

"Yeah. The Genius said you'd love the chess set." Then he added, "Sorry to spoil the surprise."

His father gave him an odd smile and said nothing.

When they got home, his mom said, "Let's see the package!" so he took it out and set it on the dining room table.

He said, "I can't figure out why he wanted you to have a chess set, Dad. You've already got one."

Meanwhile, his mom was unwrapping the package carefully as he and his father watched, but when she saw Don Quixote and the chess set, her face fell. "This is what your brother sent?"

His father sat down heavily in a kitchen chair. "Oh my God! What happened. What the hell?"

The kid reached into the backpack, down past his laundry, and pulled out another package. "Maybe this is what you're expecting." He placed the package on the table.

His mother looked shocked and then laughed as she removed the wrapping paper. His dad said, "I don't know whether to punch you in the arm or hug you."

His mom said, "You knew about your brother's gift, didn't you. You weren't even surprised to see me unwrap a jaguar."

Em smiled. He thought, 'The guy with the surprise package is a con man named Rodolfo.'

* * *

Anne Hillerman, the author of *nine New York Times* bestselling mystery novels, switched to fiction after publishing half a dozen non-fiction books. She is the daughter of novelist Tony Hillerman, and continued her father's popular Joe Leaphorn-Jim Chee novels following his death. To make it her own, Anne elevated Officer Bernadette Manuelito to full partner in solving crimes. Anne is an executive producer of AMC's award-winning *Dark Winds* series based on the Hillerman stories.

Dave Tedlock's short stories have appeared in *Southwest Review, Kansas Quarterly,* and elsewhere. He wrote columns for *The Ames Tribune*, the *Tucson Citizen* and more. His essays appeared in *College English* and *College Communication and Composition.* He was an advertising agency copywriter for 14 years and holds a Master's in Fiction Writing from Brown University. He lives in Tucson and Santa Fe with his wife, Anne Hillerman.

The Diamond Caper: An Alternate History

By Verena Rose

Austria and Germany

1907 - Vienna

Admiring the painting on the wall, Herr Bloch-Bauer turned to his beautiful wife, Adele, and said, "Herr Klimt has captured you perfectly."

"Thank you, Ferdinand, I am so pleased you like it."

"I'm especially pleased with the representation of the necklace."

Adele agreed. "It truly is a thing of beauty–so much gold and the diamonds sparkle around my neck."

January 24, 1925 – Vienna, Austria

Ferdinand Bloch-Bauer was bereft. His beautiful Adele had succumbed to meningitis at only forty-three. He had all of the Klimt paintings, including *Portrait of Adele Bloch-Bauer,* hung in her bedroom, creating a shrine to her memory.

1928 – 1937

The Klimt paintings owned by the Bloch-Bauer family were loaned for exhibition at various events.

December 9, 1937 – Vienna, Austria

Maria Bloch-Bauer, Adele and Ferdinand's niece, and Fritz Altmann were married. Ferdinand gave Maria the diamond necklace and matching earrings as a wedding present.

"Oh, Uncle Ferdinand, I never dreamed these would someday be mine," said Maria.

Ferdinand, with tears in his eyes, said, "They were always meant for you. It was your Aunt Adele's wish that I give them to you on your wedding day. And I hope that you and Fritz will stay here in the apartment with me. Our world is starting to collapse, and I'd feel more comfortable with you here."

"Of course, Uncle Ferdinand. We will stay with you."

* * *

June 1938 – Vienna, Austria after Nazi annexation

Early in the morning there came a loud banging on the door of the Bloch-Bauer apartment. Tightening the belt on his robe, Ferdinand went to see who was visiting so early in the day. He opened the door to six uniformed soldiers. Pushing past Ferdinand, the soldiers entered the apartment. The man in charge demanded, "Are you Herr Bloch?"

"Ja, I am Ferdinand Bloch-Bauer."

As Ferdinand answered, the other soldiers spread out and started going through the apartment.

"Herr Bloch, under orders of the High Command we are here to take possession of all of your valuable property."

Disturbed by voices and men moving through the apartment, Fritz and Maria Altmann came out to see what was happening.

"Uncle Ferdinand, they are ransacking our rooms and taking our belongings," said Maria.

"My darling Maria, they have orders to confiscate our valuables. Please stay calm. I've been told we can remain in the apartment."

Over the course of several hours the soldiers brought out the Bloch-Bauers' most prized possessions. Many artworks, several by Gustav Klimt including the portrait of Adele Bloch-Bauer, the silver service and china, antique furniture, and all of the jewelry, including Maria's special wedding gift—the diamond necklace and earrings. When one of the soldiers showed it to his commanding officer, he ordered the man to put it aside.

"Keep that separate from the other items. Reichsmarschall Goering will want this for his collection. Also, isolate the paintings for him to make selections."

* * *

Later in 1938

Ferdinand hugged his niece and her husband.

"I wish you both would come with me to Switzerland," said Ferdinand with a sad look in his eyes.

"I cannot leave yet, Uncle. I have to try to retrieve Aunt Adele's necklace and earrings," said Maria.

"Those diamonds are not worth your life, Maria. Your Aunt Adele would not want you to sacrifice living for them."

"I have to try. We know they are at Carinhall north of Berlin near Brandenberg. We have some friends who are going to help us out of Vienna and we're hoping that with our fake passes and by dressing like middle-class Germans we will be safe."

"All right, my darlings, my prayers go with you." Hugging Maria and

Fritz one last time, Ferdinand left the home he had shared with his adored wife, Adele, never to return.

That night Maria and Fritz dressed in their most sedate clothes, packed a small amount of food, and left the apartment in the Palais Adele Bloch-Bauer. Maria's family had lived there for almost 100 years. Fritz held her close as she broke down in tears, knowing they would never be able to return.

Under the cover of darkness, Maria and Fritz made their way to the motorcar their friends the Schmidts left for them. Elsa and Max had risked a lot giving them the car. Now they planned to travel north to Berlin and then on to Carinhall. But the first obstacle was to get out of Vienna and onto back roads. In the car, Fritz turned to Maria. "Are you sure you want to do this? We can head south and into Spain where we'll be relatively safe."

"I know you and Uncle Ferdinand think this is foolish, but I must at least try to retrieve Aunt Adele's beautiful diamonds."

With a sigh, Fritz started the motorcar and said, "Okay, my love, let's see how far we can get before daybreak."

Maria and Fritz had agreed they would only drive at night and try to stay on secondary roads as much as possible. While the trip should only take about eight hours, they knew it would probably take them two or three days.

Just before the sun was about to rise, Fritz found a suitable place for them to pull the motorcar off into the woods. He got out and positioned some large tree branches over the motorcar to disguise their whereabouts.

"Darling, let's eat a bit of bread and try to get some rest," suggested Fritz.

"That sounds fine, but I'm not sure I'll be able to sleep."

Even though they'd been traveling on a secondary road, they had heard quite a number of motorcars that day. Fritz peeked through the branches a few times and saw military transport trucks loaded with soldiers, most of them headed south.

Once the road traffic had subsided and it was pitch dark, they returned to the road and continued their journey north.

Turning to Fritz, Maria said, "We need to talk about what we're going to do once we get to Carinhall. I have information that the Reichsmarschall and his family are not in residence. They are at their home near Berchtesgaden. I'm praying that there are only a few household staff on site. I've also heard that he's given Aunt Adele's jewels to his daughter, Edda, who is just a baby. So I think the first place to look for them is in her nursery."

"Do you really think that he would actually give a baby diamonds?" asked Fritz.

"Of course I do. Goering is so self-absorbed and egotistical that he'd never imagine anyone breaching the walls of Carinhall to steal any of the treasures that he himself has stolen."

"Have you thought of a plan?"

"Indeed, I have!" answered Maria with a smile.

All of a sudden Fritz veered the car off the road into the field by the side of the road. In a few moments Maria knew why. Heading toward them from the north they could see headlights. A large motorcade passed them at such high speed, their car wasn't noticed.

"Darling, I think we should find some place to pull off for the rest of the night. We'll soon be getting close to Berlin and I'm going to have to find more remote roads to travel," Fritz said.

"I'm sorry I dragged you into this."

"I wouldn't have had it any other way. If something happens and we get caught, we will be together. That's all that matters to me."

* * *

After another day of hiding in the woods, Maria and Fritz started off again. Fritz had managed to locate a remote road, badly maintained, heading due north.

"Okay, let's discuss your plan." Fritz glanced over at his wife.

"When I dressed to leave, I put on a maid's uniform and then my traveling clothes over top of them. Once we find a good place to hide the car near

Carinhall, I'll change clothes and you and I will walk through the wood to the edge of the property. I think we should watch and observe for at least a day before I try to enter the estate."

Fritz looked at his wife in utter astonishment. "You can't be saying you're going in there alone, are you?"

"It's the only way."

The next couple of nights were terrifying the closer they got to Berlin. Even the secondary roads were busy with motorcars and transports well into the night.

God, in his infinite wisdom, must have taken pity on these foolish children. On their fifth night on the road, they made it to within walking distance of Carinhall. Fritz pulled the motorcar well into the woods and covered it with branches.

"Maria, do you want to rest for a while before we start our trek to the estate?" asked Fritz.

"We can rest once we are within sight of the estate. Let's find a good place to lie down and observe. Then we can take turns resting," answered Maria.

Fortunately, they didn't encounter any trouble during their walk to Carinhall. The weather was mild and, even though the terrain was rough, they didn't need to rush. Once the estate was in sight, they found a safe hiding place where they could see all of the comings and goings. They settled in for a long wait.

"Fritz, I want you to take the first rest break. You've done all the driving and I'm too keyed up to sleep anyway."

Several hours later it was full dark, and Fritz finally awoke. "I'm sorry I slept so long. What's been happening while I was asleep?"

"You needed the rest, and nothing has been happening. I believe I saw either the houseman or butler come out to smoke but that's all."

"Darling, you need to get some sleep. You haven't rested in days," Fritz said with a worried look on his face.

"I can rest once we're free. It's dark and now is the best time for me to make my way into the house,"

Removing her coat to reveal the maid's uniform, Maria turned and fiercely hugged her husband.

With resolve on her face Maria said, "Promise me that if it appears I've been caught, you will leave and get yourself to England just as we planned."

Before Fritz could respond to this request Maria left their hiding place and walked toward Carinhall. When she got to a door off to the side of the front of the estate, she turned and looked to where her husband was hiding and nodded her head. Petrified for his wife Fritz settled down to wait.

* * *

Once inside Carinhall, Maria looked around to make sure she hadn't been observed. She saw a door a short way down the hall and gently turned the knob, hoping there wasn't anyone in the room. Taking a deep breath, she opened the door and looked in. The room appeared to be a small office, so Maria pulled a chair close to the door and settled down to wait until it appeared everyone was in bed for the night.

Once the moon had risen, Maria left the office and started exploring the corridors of the house. All of a sudden, she heard what sounded like footsteps and frantically looked for a place to hide. Just in time she ducked behind a tapestry hanging on the wall. Breathing shallowly, she listened until the sound of the footsteps receded into the distance.

When she emerged from her hiding place, she noticed a door across the hall with a beautiful pink plaque. In beautiful script, it said "Das ist Eddas Zimmer." Crossing the hall quietly, she opened the door to the most beautiful nursery she'd ever seen.

In the faint moonlight from a high window, she could see, on a child-sized rocking chair, a stuffed bear and it sparkled.

With a soft cry of surprise, she hurried over to pick up the bear. Around its neck hung her aunt's beautiful necklace, and the matching earrings adorned the bear's fuzzy ears. As she stared in disbelief at her luck, her hands stroked the bear, feeling the familiar touch of the fur, even…even a rough patch on its arm. This was HER bear! The Gund bear her Uncle Ferdinand had given her when she was a child.

Tucking the bear under her maid's apron, Maria knew she must get out of Carinhall as soon as possible. Retracing her steps, she made her way back to the door where she had entered, encountering no one. Safely out into the night, without hesitation she hurried to their hiding place and Fritz.

$$* * *$$

After what seemed like an eternity but was only about two hours, Fritz saw Maria running his way. It looked like she had something bulky under her apron. Pulling her close into the safety of their hiding place, Fritz asked, "Were you successful? And what is that under your apron?"

Maria pulled the apron up, revealing the beautiful Gund bear with its glorious ornaments. "I didn't realize that the Nazis had taken my childhood bear. I was correct, Goering did give the diamonds to Edda. He attached them to my bear."

Redressing in her other clothing, she hugged Fritz and said, "Let's get out of here. We have to get back to Vienna before the 21st."

Fritz and Maria made their way back to the motorcar and decided to drive as far as they could before daylight.

Each day, there seemed to be much more traffic on the roads going south. One night they were stopped at a roadblock. Thankfully, their fake papers were accepted and they were allowed to drive on with a warning to watch out for the resistance fighters that had been attacking lone cars on the roads.

Fritz and Maria made it back to Vienna by the night of October 20th. They were able to meet their contact who was tasked with getting them out of the Reich and to safety. After several unsettling days they finally made it to Liverpool, England.

"Fritz, thank you so much for helping me retrieve Aunt Adele's diamonds. I know you thought it was a fool's errand, but you never tried to stop me."

"My darling, I could do nothing else."

* * *

AUTHOR'S NOTE

All of the characters in this story are real; however, these events are the creation of the author.

Adele Bloch-Bauer is best known for having her portrait painted by Gustav Klimt. In fact, Klimt painted her several times. She died in 1925 of meningitis.

Ferdinand Bloch-Bauer was Adele's husband and the uncle of Maria Altman née Bloch-Bauer. After the annexation of Austria, he managed to escape to Switzerland. Charging tax evasion, the Nazis seized his entire estate, including his Bohemian sugar factory, the Junger Castle in Brazen, and his personal property, including the Klimt paintings. He died in 1945 and is buried alongside his wife in Vienna.

Maria Bloch-Bauer Altmann was the niece of Ferdinand and Adele Bloch-Bauer. Her Uncle Ferdinand presented her with the diamond necklace and earrings on December 9, 1937, upon her marriage to Fritz Altmann.

In October of 1938, Fritz and Maria escaped to London. By 1942 they had settled in California. Maria received U.S. citizenship in 1945. *The Lady in Gold* is a movie starring Helen Mirren as Maria Altmann. It chronicles Maria's life and particularly her fight to acquire the return of the Klimt paintings. She was ultimately successful.

Reichsmarschall Hermann Goering was a voracious collector and vandal who stole artwork, jewels, and other antiquities from the homes of Jews who were evicted and deported. There is some information that he did acquire the Adele Bloch-Bauer necklace and earrings and gave them to his second wife, Emmy. To date they have not been recovered.

Carinhall was Goering's estate near Brandenburg. It was originally a hunting lodge, but over the course of the twelve years of the Reich, he expanded it to mansion proportions. He was very proud to display the artwork he pilfered.

I wrote this story as a caper because I wondered 'what if' Maria decided to go retrieve the jewels before they left for England. Like so many other unsolved mysteries, I'd love to know what happened to that beautiful necklace. The closest I got was at the Neue Gallery in New York City. *Portrait of Adele Bloch-Bauer* (*aka* The Lady in Gold) is on display there. No photograph will ever do it justice.

** * **

Verena Rose is the co-owner, chief financial officer, and acquisitions editor for Level Best Books and as their representative, Verena is a member of the Crime Writers Association (CWA) and the Crime Readers Association (CRA). While she loves all mystery subgenres, she has a preferred fondness for historical mysteries. In addition to her other duties at Level Best Books, she hosts a podcast: *Sunday Tea with V at the Hystery Chronicles.* She is the Anthony Award-winning co-editor of *Malice Domestic 14: Mystery Most Edible,* and has co-edited numerous other short story anthologies, many of which include stories she has written. Verena is a member of Mystery Writers of America (MWA), Sisters in Crime-National and Chessie Chapter, and the Historical Novel Society.

Sins of the Father

By Kerry Hammond

Rome, Italy

I sat in the wooden chair on the hotel balcony and leaned my head back, turning my face toward the sunshine. I closed my eyes and listened to a string quartet play Autumn from Vivaldi's Four Seasons. It has always been one of my favorite pieces of classical music.

When I'd first arrived in Italy, I was hesitant; I wasn't sure what to expect. Was it really all pizza and pasta? Now that I'd been here for six months, I could easily see why people loved spending time in this part of the world. My new employer wanted me here, at least for now, so I decided to give in and enjoy it. I was kind of in his debt, so I had every reason to go along with his wishes. Maybe once he came back from his honeymoon we could re-evaluate. I'd been thinking about retirement anyway.

I honestly hadn't anticipated a problem with the job I came to do, but hindsight analysis had shown a few yellow, if not red, flags. I had underestimated the man I had been paid to kill and I hadn't listened to my inner voice, two very dangerous things. Maybe it was because business had been slow and maybe I was just getting tired of the rat race—in my line of work, forty-three can be considered old. Either way, things had nearly ended badly for me.

Six months ago, I had walked out of Rome's Fiumicino Airport into the bright sunshine and immediately reached in my bag for my sunglasses. I had never set foot in Italy, but had come prepared. I had everything I needed to blend in as a tourist: sunglasses, shorts, sandals, and a mobile phone to use as a camera. I knew some tourists would have hefty, digital cameras, but in this day and age, using a phone to take photos helped you blend in better. I wanted to look like a tourist, but not a memorable one.

I have always been great at languages and prior to my arrival I took an online course in Italian. I would pretend no knowledge of the language, but in order to do the job I came to do, I would need to understand it. After only six weeks of study, my comprehension was great and I found myself eavesdropping on conversations just to test myself.

I walked up to the taxi stand pulling my nondescript black suitcase behind me, feeling a trickle of sweat as it made its way down the small of my back. I said the obligatory, 'I'm sorry, I don't speak Italian, do you speak English?' before directing my driver in my practiced flat and unrecognizable mid-America accent to take me to my hotel. He nodded and pulled out into traffic, as uninterested in conversation as I was.

The hotel I'd chosen was within walking distance to everything I needed. It was important that there be no record of a cab ride, other than back and forth to the airport. My check-in experience was a breeze and I handed the clerk a credit card and passport in the name of Teresa Baker. Not as nondescript as Jane Smith, but less memorable because of it. When I got to my room, I pulled out the phone I bought at the TIM Tourist shop at the airport. I bought it specifically for this job, a prepaid smart phone with an Italian telephone number and enough data to get me through the long weekend.

I kicked off my shoes and dialed my client's number from memory. I rarely, if ever, wrote any pertinent information down. A good memory—and mine was near photographic—was a must in my line of work. "Hello, Mr. Ferrari," I said when I heard the familiar voice answer. My client was a bit less creative on the code name front, but it wasn't a problem since he was only using it to stay anonymous to anyone who might be listening in. I knew his real name, but he would never learn mine.

"Hello, Miss Baker," he said, in heavily accented English. "I assume that you are calling to tell me you have arrived in Rome."

I told him that I had indeed arrived and would follow the schedule to pick up the package at the location as planned. The schedule was this afternoon at two o'clock, the package was a Glock 9mm handgun, and the location was behind a pizzeria next to a trash can. I already had the address.

Everything seemed to be in order and I hung up after promising to call one more time, from the airport before my flight out. Two phone calls were as much communication as I was willing to allow. One to make sure I was still comfortable that the job wasn't a setup and that the Carabinieri weren't going to be waiting for me at the drop point, and then one to let the client know that the job was done and the final payment could be wired to my offshore account. If a client made additional contact it would be to warn me off or cancel the transaction. In the latter case, their first payment would be non-refundable.

I had a few hours to kill before the pick-up time, but I needed to get some supplies; I never traveled with any tools of the trade. I kept the prepaid phone in a hidden pocket I had specially sewn into my favorite jacket. If I was ever stopped and searched on my way, there would be nothing to tie me to my client or the target. The phone was securely stowed, but could easily be pulled out to take a photo of some landmark, in the event I needed to blend in with the other tourists.

The research I did ahead of time told me there was a store located four blocks from my hotel that sold the items I needed. It was a combination of a grocery store and a hardware store. It was located in a touristy area, so one more American wandering around the aisles wouldn't look out of place.

As I walked, I enjoyed the warmth of the afternoon and noticed that I wasn't the only one wearing jeans. Mission accomplished. What people don't realize is that wearing the wrong clothing is the easiest way to stand out in a crowd. Before I go anywhere for a job, I scour the internet for street cameras in the neighborhood I will be visiting. I take note of how people are dressed in the daytime, nighttime, weekends, and weekdays. It's the best way to prepare.

As I walked, I thought through the plan for the job I was there to complete, something I would do a couple of hundred times before tomorrow night.

Much like an athlete pictures the game-winning shot over and over in order to increase the chances of actually making it, I visualize myself completing every step of a job over and over to ensure that there are no glitches in my plan. When I finally perform the work, it will go as smoothly as it has in my head.

Once I purchased the items I needed, I headed back to the hotel for a nap. I usually power through jet lag, but I have a hard time sleeping on airplanes and was in need of some rest.

At the allotted hour, I walked the seven blocks to the pizzeria, which was busy enough that I felt comfortable walking past it twice before I slipped into the alley behind the building and located the dirty duffle bag tucked away behind the trash can next to an even dirtier rolled-up sleeping bag. I had instructed that the scene be set in just this way. I found that people were loath to touch anything they thought was left by someone living on the street.

No one was around, so I slipped on a pair of gloves from my bag, stepped behind one side of the large trash can, grabbed the duffle, and exited the other side in one smooth movement. I peered inside and saw both the gun and a box of ammunition. I slipped them inside my shoulder bag and threw the duffle in the trash a block away. I made my way back to the hotel feeling confident that everything was in place and that no one had given me a second glance. I am a very average looking woman, not too young and not too old. I am neither pretty nor homely, short nor tall. My looks suit my career just fine and I have never been hindered by them; not turning heads is an asset in this line of work.

By that evening, I had run through the logistics in my head so many times I could do it in my sleep. Before bed I took some time to run through my client's information and our contact thus far. I like to make sure I am comfortable with everything before I figuratively, and literally, pull the trigger. I want to make sure that there is not a shred of doubt in my mind that the job is legitimate. I can't afford to make a mistake. It would not only end my career, but could get me thrown in prison, or killed.

Mr. Ferrari contacted me through the usual channels. When asked, he provided me with a reference: the name of the person who had recommended me. I did my due diligence into his background and everything I found checked out. He was the only child of a wealthy and elderly Italian businessman. He would inherit his father's entire estate when he died since his mother had been dead for ten years and his father had never shown interest in remarrying. Until now.

There had always been women sniffing around dear old Papa, it happens when a widower is rich. But just last month the old man had announced that he intended to marry the most recent sniffer and change his will, leaving her everything. Since Mr. Ferrari was heavily in debt from some bad business deals, this was not an ideal situation for him. Papa had lived a long life and his son was ready for that life to come to an end. That's where I came in.

Some people think that hired killers will take any job and kill anyone. I wasn't so much picky about the *who*, but I did have some rules when it came to the *how*. Many in my line of work have their specialties, and mine was what I liked to call the robbery gone wrong, or RGW. There are acronyms for everything, so why not? I had perfected the break in, steal a few items, and kill the homeowner job. This way no suspicion falls on the family members, who are usually the ones who hire me.

I re-analyzed the financial portion of the transaction; it had gone smoothly. Half the money had been paid up front, wired to my offshore account and then moved to my other offshore account to keep it safe. The second half would be wired after my airport call. I couldn't put my finger on it, but there was still something that just didn't sit right and my Spidey senses got a slight tingle. It was low intensity and I suspected that it stemmed from the fact that my client was a slimy individual and rubbed me the wrong way. It happens. Since it was such a low intensity tingle, I had to make a call and I chose to ignore it.

The next morning was my workday. I went through my usual ritual; I got up at six o'clock in the morning and ran five miles. I showered, drank an espresso, ate breakfast and then meditated. I don't like to be pigeonholed. Hired professionals aren't just gritty, dirty men who smoke cigars and drink too much. Some of us are health-conscious people who like a little bit of Zen in our lives.

The deal was set to go down at ten o'clock that night. At that time my client's father would be pouring a Scotch and ready to sit in front of his fireplace to read the paper at his villa in a swanky part of the city. I would make it look like a robbery gone wrong, and the police would find not only a dead body but a missing Rolex watch and a few other trinkets of my choice. Junior would then be the heir to Papa's wealth, his debts would be paid off and his own trophy wife kept happy enough to stay married to him.

At nine o'clock I put on my black leggings and sweater. The sweater was baggy enough that it hid the tool belt I wore around my waist. This was my most precious possession and the items I stored on it had gotten me out of quite a few tight spots. Without tools, it looked like a designer belt that could be worn over a long shirt. The fact that it could be camouflaged underneath an oversized garment was another bonus to being female.

Getting into the old man's house wasn't difficult. I'd been picking locks since I was ten years old. It's what happens when you grow up in a dysfunctional family with an uncle who is a con man and a father who is a thief. Junior had assured me that his father walked his Chihuahua at exactly ten o'clock every night and came in and fed him a snack immediately afterward, not turning the alarm on until after he took care of the little canine, poured his drink, and lit his cigar. I had a small window, but it was enough.

After some quick recon, I chose to enter via the French door in the study. Not only would that room be dark and empty, but French doors are the easiest to pick. This model was clearly lacking a deadbolt—the nicest ones always are. I slipped in and closed the door behind me. I stood just inside for a beat of ten while I listened. My hearing has always been the strongest of my five senses. It was unfortunate in my childhood because it meant I heard every argument my parents ever had, in detail. After my father left, I then heard everything my mother did in her bedroom with her long string of boyfriends. Just the thought made me shudder.

Hearing nothing, I crept through the study, admiring a large floor-model globe in the corner; the old guy had taste. The door to the hallway was open and I could see a light was on at the end. Junior had given me a detailed sketch of the floor plan and I knew the light came from the kitchen where the dog was eating his late-night snack. I reminded myself how happy I was that the dog in question was a Chihuahua and not a Doberman.

I wasn't rushed, but I didn't have all the time in the world either. I needed to finish the job before the old man had a chance to activate the alarm. Walking on the balls of my feet, I made my way down the hallway. I knew my target would be in the living room choosing which cigar to smoke; I was told it was his evening habit. I pulled out the Glock, made sure the safety was off, and rounded the corner.

Standing by the built-in humidor was the old man I recognized from the photo. His grey hair was so thin that you could see his scalp beneath it. He wore a Mister Rogers cardigan sweater that looked rather tatty considering his net worth, and he had a newspaper under his right arm. He also had a gun in his hand. It was aimed at me.

"I did not expect you would be a woman," he said in English. "I did not think Terry was your real name, but I thought that it would be a nickname for Terrance."

His choosing to use English told me he had done his homework. The fact that his English was flawless left no room for misunderstanding. "Why don't you sit down, Terry." It was an order, not an offer.

I have to admit that I was stunned to find the old man not only expecting me, but armed. I didn't have many options, so I sat. I have one of the best poker faces around, and it has come in handy. On one specific occasion it had saved my skin by leading the police in the wrong direction. 'I'm sorry officer, I didn't get a good look at the man who ran past me. I just know that he had brown hair and a gun.'

As good as I was, I couldn't help my surprised reaction to what he did next. He offered me a glass of Scotch. I accepted, if only to delay things a bit. He got up from his chair with the ease of a fifty-year-old rather than the eighty-two that I knew he was. He poured me two fingers of single malt, handed it over, and returned to his chair.

"I know my son paid you to kill me." There would be no beating around the bush with this guy. "I also know why," he continued. "I plan to get married and he will not be inheriting my money. That makes him very angry.

"Now, I am a reasonable man. I was willing to continue to support the lifestyle of my son, including some of his bad habits. But when my son tries to have me killed, this is where I need to draw the line." I really couldn't blame him on that count. I sipped my Scotch and let him talk. I honestly didn't feel I had much to add.

What came next shouldn't have shocked me, but it did. "I don't put the blame on you Terry, I really don't. You are a businessman, excuse me, businesswoman. And this, for you, is a business transaction. I did not get to be as rich as I am without understanding the business transaction." He paused to sip from his own glass. "I also understand that not every transaction needs to be, how do you say, strictly legal."

I couldn't help myself. "That's putting it mildly," I said. At this he smiled, and it appeared to be a genuine smile. I decided I liked the old guy.

"I won't continue to beat about the bush, my dear." This guy really had a handle on his idioms. "I will tell you the business proposition I have for you. But I will warn you, it's non-negotiable." He smiled and waited while this last part sank in. "The reasons for this should be understandable to you," he said. I nodded.

When he finished laying out his terms, I didn't hesitate. You might think it was because I had no choice, but the deal was actually fair. The smirk on his face as I paused before accepting told me that he knew what I was thinking. He knew he'd given me an offer I couldn't refuse and he enjoyed watching me realize it.

* * *

Unlike his father, when I broke into Junior's house to kill him, he wasn't expecting me. The look on his face was priceless and I couldn't help telling him who I was, why I was there, and whose payroll I was now on. His shock turned to anger right before he launched himself out of bed and took the bullet I'd brought for him. His reaction actually played into my plans to make the whole scene look like a robbery gone bad.

I had been instructed to schedule the job on a night when Junior was supposed to be attending a charity gala with his wife. The old man knew that his son wouldn't show, but anyone following what passes for a society column in Italy would have expected him to be there, so planning to rob him that night was understandable. I guess the guy's bad habits really did get him in the end.

The wedding was postponed while Junior's father grieved the loss of his only child, but only by a few months. It really was a nice ceremony. I kept my distance, but followed it in the aforementioned society pages. He spent his honeymoon traveling through Europe and riding the Orient Express, but before he left, we negotiated an extension of my contract to keep an eye on his businesses while he was gone. I was enjoying my extended stay in Italy, as well as the healthy increase to my bank account.

If Junior had known that he and his father were so similar, perhaps their relationship would have taken a different turn. As it was, I was happy to have been in the right place at the right time.

Now, about that retirement.

* * *

Kerry Hammond is a recovering attorney now working for a nonprofit in Denver, Colorado. She is a lifelong mystery fan and several of her short stories have appeared in mystery anthologies. Her most recent, "Strangers at a Table," was included in *The Mysterious Bookshop Presents the Best Mystery Stories of the Year 2023*. She spends her free time writing, traveling, and leading the Crime & Beyond book club, which is so hard core they have a Wiki page.

353

From Hunger

By Robin Hazard Ray

Nassau, Bahamas

June 12, 1962

Dear Mother,

We arrived safely at Nassau yesterday, glorious weather. We have (appropriately) the honeymoon suite at the Grand Colonial, so you can write to us there. Ginny is already getting a little tan, the first time I have seen her thus! It suits her coloring beautifully and makes me an even happier man, if possible.

Please <u>don't worry</u>. I talked with the chef at the hotel and explained matters. He's been very diligent about meting out the portions, 2,400 calories a day in three lots, with vitamin and protein balance etc. as the doctor dictated. It's no worse forcing myself to ingest meals here than it is at home. Ginny, at least, is able to enjoy the tropical dishes that they trot out with great flair, very colorful, some with flaming skewers, though of course they mean nothing to me. I hope our children will inherit her gusto for food.

Could you be a dear and run over to the house to see that it's getting on as it should? I'm most concerned that the screen of cypresses is planted in time for our return. Ginny is very particular about privacy, I find.

Having a delightful time, see you in two weeks,
Malcolm

* * *

June 19, 1962

Dear Malcolm and Ginny,

I hope things continue well for you both on that sunny isle. It has done nothing but rain here since you left.

Penn called this morning, mentioned that he had not heard from you since the wedding and did I know a cable address. Malcolm, please don't be neglecting business just because you are now a married man! I gave him the address of the hotel, I hope you don't mind.

The house looks very nice, now. The painters and drapers are done, and the garden staff is doing their best to lay out the annual beds in the pouring rain. The tennis court is nearly flooded, but I have Harry working on the drainage. It should all be in great order for you to carry your bride over the threshold.

Dear, since I wrote the above, Penn has called again. He says the hotel cabled that you were no longer staying there.

Please, darling, let me know where you are and <u>that you are eating</u>. You know how I fret when you don't have Winnie to cook for you and make sure you are getting enough. You will remember what happened to you at Princeton. We can't have a repeat of that, risking your poor kidneys and such. You're skinny enough as it is!

All my love, Mother

* * *

June 24, 1962

Dear Mother – if I can call you that now!

I hope we haven't neglected you, dear Mother, we have been having such a lovely time!!! We have moved to a little villa outside Nassau with its own pool as well as a beach, quite enough swimming for all! and much more seclusion. We have a cook and she's quite nice and keeps Mac in good fettle, though it was quite a time explaining his lack of appetite, etc. I'm sure I needn't tell <u>you</u>!!!

The place is very new – plaster practically still damp! – so there's nothing like an address let alone a telephone. Just write us c/o American Express, where we'll be sure to get our mail at least twice a week.

We've wired to Penn. He won't mind us being another few weeks on our honeymoon, will he? After all Mac has done to turn the business around.

Cheerio, Ginny

* * *

July 1, 1962

Penn Walker, Walker & Sims, Co. Ltd., Boston, Mass., to Malcolm Sims, c/o American Express, Nassau, Bahamas. Telegram.

Merger imminent need you back please wire immediately, Penn.

* * *

July 5, 1962

Dear Malcolm and Ginny,

Please don't think me an interfering mother, but <u>please please</u> can you get in touch. I've had Penn on the phone three times today, saying he's written and wired and heard nothing. Then this morning I had a call from Mr. Beacham at First National, saying that you had wired a large sum to a bank in Nassau! Are you buying a house, or a yacht or something?

I tried to get in touch with Ginny's family, who we were so sorry not to see at the wedding. But there again, the letter came back with "addressee unknown". Have they moved as well?

You know I don't like to pester you, but please, darling, just drop me a line so I know you are well and what all this money is for and when you are coming home.

Your loving Mother

[Unclaimed at American Express]

* * *

July 6, 1962

Postcard, "Great Fishing in the Bahamas!"

Dear Mother,

Everything is going wonderfully here!

Love, Ginny (& Malcolm)

* * *

July 7, 1962

Penn Walker, Walker & Sims, Co. Ltd., Boston, Mass., to U.S. Consulate, Nassau, Bahamas. Telegram.

Urgent seeking Americans Malcolm Sims and wife Virginia of Brookline, Mass., on honeymoon stop last known at Grand Colonial Hotel stop kindly wire for details family frantic Penn Walker

* * *

July 8, 1962

U.S. Consulate, Nassau, Bahamas, to Penn Walker, Walker & Sims, Co. Ltd., Boston, Mass. Telegram.

Inquiry hotel indicates nothing amiss Sims couple stop no record of departure from Nassau stop will likely turn up once money spent

* * *

July 12, 1962

Incident report, Royal Bahamas Police Force.

11th inst. Pool attendant Jerry Weekes telephoned from neighbor's house reporting a foul odor from the unfinished villa called "Winsome Sea" on the new road platted as "Pebble." Constable was dispatched and found the decomposing remains of a male, age indeterminate, in a servant's room off the pool area. Inquiry of the landlord established that Malcolm and Virginia Sims of Brookline, Mass., U.S.A., had let the villa on June 18 for a period of one month, engaging a cook and a houseboy. U-drive car hired June 18. Both servants dismissed from service on June 23.

On autopsy, Dr. N– determined that the deceased, identified as Malcolm Sims, weighed 82 pounds, 4 ounces.

The U-drive car was recovered at the airport. Attempts to determine the whereabouts of Mrs. Sims have so far been unsuccessful.

* * *

Robin Hazard Ray is a crime fiction writer, historian, and essayist. She leads tours at historic Mount Auburn Cemetery in Cambridge. The cemetery provides the setting of her Murder in the Cemetery novels *The Strangers' Tomb* and *The Soldiers' Rest*. Her stories have twice appeared in the *Best New England Crime Stories* anthologies (2022 and 2023) of Crime Spell Books. In her spare time she helps tend the courtyard garden at the Isabella Stewart Gardner Museum and makes quilts. She lives in Somerville, Massachusetts, with her husband David and two black cats.

French Fried

By Lori Robbins

Paris, France

The concierge at the Hotel du Lys was the only employee who didn't answer my awkward French queries in English. With Gallic savoir-faire, Henri repeated simple phrases until I figured out what they meant. Even when it took me seven minutes to translate the baffling, Frenchified *ahMAhzon* as Amazon, he remained patient.

The multi-lingual Henri *buongiorno*-ed Signore Gallo, *guten morgan*-ed Herr Schmidt, and *buen día*-ed Elena Garcia and her grim-faced sister, Eva. Each morning, he greeted the reserved Londoner Mr. Hugh Wallingford with a respectful, "Have a nice day, sir." With me, however, it was *parle français* all the way.

I was in Paris, as one-third of Nana's birthday present to herself. She decided against celebrating in her usual way, which was at the blackjack table, counting cards. After getting banned at every Las Vegas Night at senior centers in the greater New York metro area, my grandmother graduated to fleecing unwary dealers from the Catskills to Atlantic City. This year, however, after a huge windfall at the Tropicana, she set her sights on Monte Carlo, with a stopover in Paris. It was just as well. The manager of the New Jersey casino was polite but firm in his request that she never set a single, spangled foot in his establishment ever again.

"

I was delighted with the chance to visit Paris, as I hadn't been there since a misspent summer abroad during college. My mother's reaction was less enthusiastic. Tania's astrologer advised her against long trips, and it took the combined efforts of me and Nana to persuade her to go. Although the arguments between my grandmother and mother didn't abate after we arrived, they didn't rise to the level of true acrimony until the morning of our fourth day.

Everything was as it had been for the previous three breakfasts. Mr. Wallingford had tea instead of coffee. Herr Schmidt ate two croissants. The Garcia sisters made a mess and a fuss over some spilled coffee and left to change their stained clothes. Monsieur DuPont didn't show up at all. The one variation in the morning routine was Madame DuPont's early departure, which at the time seemed insignificant.

We lingered over our meal as we debated the best place to begin our afternoon of shopping. Nana had invited Madame DuPont to join us, and we delayed a final decision until she returned.

The appointed time for our departure came and went. Impatient to leave, Nana texted her friend, who didn't answer. Nor did she respond to repeated phone calls.

Nana approached the concierge's desk and asked, "Have you seen Madame DuPont? She's not answering her phone."

Henri frowned. "I have not seen Madame DuPont since breakfast. Perhaps she is resting."

My grandmother moved aside to allow the Garcia sisters to pass. Elena and Eva were dressed for a day of stylish sightseeing, in Chanel sneakers and small backpacks in woven leather. Nana pounced on them with the same query about Madame DuPont.

Elena shrugged. "No idea, señora."

Eva pulled her sister's sleeve and added, "Haven't seen her. *No sé.*"

Nana turned to Henri and said, with greater force, "Madame DuPont promised to come shopping with us. If she wanted to cancel, why wouldn't she have called me? What am I? Chopped liver?"

Henri didn't pick up on the urgent connotation embedded in Nana's minced organ meat reference. Maybe she should have said foie gras instead of chopped liver.

Nana poked him. Out of respect for their decades-long friendship, she used the curved end of her umbrella and not the sharp point. "Do you understand what I'm saying?"

The concierge gave in, as most people did when faced with my indomitable grandmother. *"Oui, madame.* I will go to her room in a short while."

With an exaggerated groan, she turned to me. *"Vey iz mir.* I could die waiting."

Yiddish wasn't Henri's usual method of communication, but after two more *vey iz mirs* he got the message. The concierge left his post at the front desk and crossed the lobby to the newly installed elevator. It was large enough for two slender people and their combined luggage but not at the same time. Given the tight quarters in the elevator, my mother and I decided to wait in the lobby.

Tania pointed at Henri. "Julie! Do you remember what I told you? My astrologer said to beware of tall, dark strangers."

I shushed her until the similarly tall and dark Mr. Wallingford was out of earshot. "Why didn't your astrologer stop you from dating Herbert? He was tall, dark, and strange."

She gave the matter serious thought. "Herbert may have had a few quirks. That didn't make him strange."

To people like me, who didn't live on an astral plane, the relative weirdness of my mother's latest boyfriend was the least of his problems. "He may not have been certifiably odd, although I found his refusal to eat any food that wasn't white rather unusual. The main issue with Herbert was the fact that he was a con man and married to two women. Why didn't your stargazer mention that?"

My mother, as always, was confounded by my lack of deeper insight. "He had a beautiful aura."

A chime announced the elevator's arrival, which I interpreted as a divine indication to abandon logic as a means of persuasion. A second signal also came from above, although not from any source higher up than the top floor of the hotel.

When the silver panels of the elevator opened, Madame Dupont's body was wedged inside. With a cry, Nana fell to her knees. I raced across the lobby to brace myself against the automatic closing of the door, which threatened to crush my tiny grandmother.

Signore Gallo threw up his croissant and coffee on the stone steps outside the breakfast room. Tania tripped over her own feet, and poor Henri lost command of all five languages he knew so well.

* * *

Nana and Tania judged Madame DuPont's death suspicious before the police came to the same conclusion. They agreed on very little else.

Tania, still fixated on the perils of tall, dark strangers, had two suspects. One, of course, was Henri. The other was Hugh Wallingford, the reserved British guy who'd breakfasted with Madame DuPont while her husband took his daily morning walk.

Nana could barely contain her scorn. A devoted reader of crime fiction, she considered herself an expert in the field. "Tania, dear, hair color and height are irrelevant. We need motive, opportunity, and means."

I stepped between them, in an effort to prevent this minor skirmish from turning into an all-out war. In the past, these had included both stealth missiles regarding adult lifestyle choices and atomic bomb-worthy attacks that hit upon childhood grievances. "We know nothing about Madame DuPont and have no idea how she died. Perhaps we should wait before condemning an innocent man for a crime he may not have committed." I corrected myself. "For a crime that may not have happened."

Nana was more patient with me than with her daughter, although not to the point of admitting I was right. "Well said, Julie. Nevertheless, we should be prepared for the worst. I think we should keep an eye on Madame DuPont's husband. She and I had quite a long chat yesterday. The poor woman thinks he's having an affair. Aside from that possible motive, he'll inherit her fortune." She swiveled her hips in an impromptu dance and said, "Money makes the world go around."

Nana loved musical theater almost as much as gambling, and she'd made me a fan as well. Her reference to money was from *Cabaret*, but I had no ready response from that show to challenge her. I went with Cole Porter, who never let me down.

"If you want to talk money, I suggest we spend some. Let's go shopping, and you can sing 'I Love Paris' all the way to the metro."

She wavered. "That's another good idea. But first, tell me if you have any suspects."

"It's too soon. We can't determine means or opportunity until we find out what killed her. Madame DuPont was—"

I was going to say "old" but the dead woman was probably younger than Nana, who might not have appreciated the description. I amended my comment and said, "She may have died a natural death. I suggest we go on with our day and check in with Henri later."

Tania tipped the vote in my favor. She loved to shop, and we set off to visit the famous flea markets at Porte de Clignancourt. "That's a very sensible idea, Julie. I have to get away from these negative vibes."

We set off on our journey and spent a pleasant afternoon browsing tiny shops that sold vintage postcards for one euro and others that offered estate jewelry at prices far beyond our budget. I'd recently opened my own business, staging apartments before they went on the market, and I took dozens of pictures of the furniture, lamps, and vases.

At the end of a tiring day we took the metro back to Saint-Michel. Nana spent the twenty-minute ride furiously tapping at her cell phone. Tania said she was meditating, but her snoring indicated otherwise.

Before returning to the hotel we stopped by a favorite café for our afternoon coffee and patisserie. Nana can't go for more than a few hours without a meal sourced from the base of her food pyramid, which was made up of candy, cake, cookies, and ice cream. For protein, she ate peanut brittle or peanut M&Ms. Strawberry tarts supplied Vitamin C, and chocolate pudding provided, in her estimation, the minimum daily requirement for calcium.

Over coffee and an excellent cake that was studded with walnuts (high in antioxidants), my grandmother returned to the subject uppermost on her mind.

"It's time to act. We have to prevent Madame DuPont's killer from getting away with murder. We'll make our move tomorrow morning."

Tania choked down a blueberry from her fruit platter. "Even for you, that's crazy. We can barely speak the language. Let the police take care of it."

Nana plucked her phone from the bottom of a bag filled with chocolate boxes and showed us the screen. "Henri texted me. Madame DuPont had a severe allergy to peanuts. She died of anaphylactic shock."

My mother was relieved. "Then there's nothing for us to do. It's a tragedy, to be sure, but not a murder."

Nana forked up the rest of the walnut cake. She wasn't allergic to anything except opinions that differed from hers. "If that were the whole story I might agree with you, but her jewelry has gone missing."

Tania, whose belief in a higher state of consciousness didn't preclude an appreciation of fine jewelry, gasped. "Has her diamond ring been stolen?"

Pleased by her daughter's reaction, Nana said, "According to Henri the ring wasn't stolen for the simple reason that it was on her finger when she died. But that beautiful emerald necklace and matching bracelet and earrings are gone. Her husband reported the theft a few hours ago, as he was going through his wife's room. He's my prime suspect."

This didn't make sense to me. "If her husband is guilty, why would he report her jewelry missing?"

Nana's devotion to romantic Broadway shows coexisted with a decidedly less rosy view of human nature. "That's easy. He reports the theft, gets the insurance payout, and still has the jewels to sell. Should the police decide to investigate the death, that gives everyone in the hotel a motive, except for him."

My mother shook her head. "This is all speculation. You have no facts."

Nana anticipated opposition. Had she turned that great brain of hers to the law she would have been the Clarence Darrow of her generation, although her ambition was to be a Jewish Chita Rivera.

She spoke with staccato precision. "Love and money are the two most common motives for murder. As for the means, Madame DuPont has been allergic to peanuts for the last seventy years. Why didn't she use her EpiPen?" With the look of a woman holding four aces, she answered her own question. "Because the killer took it. And who was the only person who could have removed it? That cheating husband of hers."

Tania said, "Please be quiet while I think." She closed her eyes and did some deep breathing, but if any of her personal spiritual guides were available, she didn't share with us what they knew.

I could see from Nana's scowl she was going to say something along the lines of *I'm not going to sit here and wait for Jupiter to align with Mars.*

I stopped her remark with one of my own. "What did you have in mind?"

My grandmother signaled for more coffee and another piece of cake. "I'm going to set a trap with me as the bait. Think of it as a poker game, in which I'm going all in." She hummed a few bars of 'Luck Be A Lady' from the show *Guys and Dolls.*

As a child raised by two idiosyncratic women, I had far more freedom than my twenty-something friends. They suffered under the burden of family expectations regarding employment, marriage, and quality of life. Nana, who lived by her wits at the card table, and Tania, who drifted through life in a quasi-spiritual haze, put no such restraints on me.

It was time, however, to put a few restrictions on them. "I refuse to allow you to engage in any dangerous schemes. This isn't a game of cards, where you can count your wins and losses in poker chips."

I knew I was in trouble when Nana agreed with my assessment. "I wouldn't think of doing this alone. You and Tania are going to help."

My mother was still lost in thought, so I spoke for both of us. "We're not going to help. You have no evidence and it's cruel to go after a guy who's probably consumed by grief."

Tania came back to earth and said, "I still think it was either Henri or the British guy. Mr. Wallingford looked very shifty to me. And he ate breakfast with Madame DuPont while her husband was out walking, so he would have had the opportunity to poison her with peanuts and to steal the EpiPen."

I fended off Nana's fork and ate the rest of my éclair. "Neither one has any motive. The DuPonts have been coming to the Hotel du Lys for forty years. Why would Henri kill her now? And Mr. Wallingford is also a longtime visitor. I say we forget the whole thing and pack for Monaco."

The first trap Nana set was for me. "Who do you think killed her?"

I thought about each of the people who'd breakfasted with us that morning. "If we eliminate Henri and Mr. Wallingford, that leaves four suspects. Herr Schmidt and Signore Gallo were across the room from Madame DuPont and, as far as I can remember, didn't come near her. So we can eliminate them."

Tania approved. "They're also too short. And Herr Schmidt has blond hair."

I patted my mother's hand to indicate my affection for her despite my low opinion of her clues. "Monsieur DuPont was out for a walk when his wife got sick. By the process of elimination, that leaves the Garcia sisters. Elena made such a fuss over the spilled coffee. It could have been a ploy to distract people while Eva tossed some peanut powder into Madame DuPont's cup. Or maybe a capsule of something?"

Nana, although she didn't change her mind about Monsieur DuPont's guilt, was thoughtful. "They do take an unusual number of vitamins each morning."

"Right. They couldn't have used whole peanuts without Madame DuPont knowing it." I warmed to the story. "They ran upstairs to change clothes, which is when they must have stolen the jewels."

My mother said, more crisply than her usual dreamy fashion, "The Garcia ladies are guilty of carrying knockoff handbags and wearing fake Chanel sneakers but I see no plausible connection to the murder, other than the color of their hair which is most assuredly not their own. I wonder if the hair color has to be natural for them to be the strangers my astrologer warned me against."

Nana hummed a few bars of 'Just You Wait' from *My Fair Lady*. "You make a good case, Julie. Cornering the Garcia sisters will be our Plan B if it turns out Monsieur DuPont is innocent."

Yeah. That's how an old lady with arthritic knees and a penchant for chocolate truffles called my bluff and suckered me in.

* * *

My two insomniac roommates talked for half the night. The lack of sleep didn't bother them, but I was bleary-eyed when Tania woke me the next morning. By the time I stepped out of the shower, Nana had already finished her first task.

She made circular, hurry-up motions with her hand. "I invited Monsieur DuPont to breakfast, thinking we could interrogate him then, but he said he had an appointment at the police station. This will make everything easier, since he's sure to be away from his room for a longer period of time. I'll follow him and wait outside until he's done. Then, I'll intercept him and ask sympathetic and subtle questions. If I think he's guilty, I'll confront him."

I towel-dried my hair, and, succumbing to Nana's impatience, gave up on further grooming until later. "What if he doesn't return to the hotel? What if he gets into a taxi and the only thing you learn is that you've missed our complimentary breakfast?"

Undaunted, Nana said, "With his wife out of the way, I'm hoping he meets up with his mistress. Then we can nail both of them. Tania will provide backup, in case either of them gets suspicious and tries to throw me into the Seine."

On the whole, her plan seemed unlikely to succeed, but it had the advantage of being fairly tame. As long as Nana and Mom didn't confront Monsieur DuPont in a dark alleyway or deserted metro station, they'd be fine.

I yawned and said, "Sounds like fun. Let me know how it goes."

Although Nana spoke with confidence, she didn't meet my eye. "I wouldn't dream of leaving you out. While we're gone you will search Monsieur DuPont's suite for the missing jewels. You'll have to climb over our balcony and sneak past the Garcias' room. He's right next to them."

This was where I stopped her. "I'm an interior designer. Not a burglar. How do you propose I get in?"

Tania stepped onto the balcony and instructed me to lock the door. Moments later, armed with a nail file and a credit card, she was inside.

The latch on the seventeenth-century door wasn't high tech, but it was an impressive performance, nonetheless. "Uh, Mom? You told me you majored in comparative religion. Not breaking and entering. Where did you learn to do that?"

She gave me a smug smile and said, "Herbert taught me. I told you he wasn't such a bad guy."

"You told me he had a really great aura. You didn't tell me he was a criminal. Other than the bigamy and bank fraud."

My mother sighed. "Don't be so judgmental."

"I'll hold off on judging until this day is over. But since you're so good at picking locks, why don't you break into the room and leave me to protect Nana from getting pitched into the Seine?"

She turned down the corners of her mouth. "I'm afraid of heights. Those thirty seconds on the balcony had me terrified. There's no way I can climb over a railing without passing out."

I gave up on Tania to concentrate on the brains of the operation. "If Monsieur DuPont stole his wife's jewels, why would he leave them in his hotel room?"

"He's going to the police station, so if he has them, he can't carry them on him. And he's unlikely to leave a trail by stowing them in a safe deposit box. There aren't many hiding places in the room. If the jewels are there, you'll find them. And if they're not there, I bet his mistress has them."

* * *

My grandmother installed herself in the lobby a few minutes before the dining room opened for breakfast. Nana assured us the dead woman's husband was a very slow walker, and she was confident in her ability to keep him in her sights. A text in all capital letters informed me she was on the move.

I wasn't worried about catching up with Nana or Mom if they needed my help. Neither owned sneakers, and both favored shoes that added a few inches to their small stature. From a style perspective they always looked great, but neither they nor Monsieur DuPont was likely to medal in any track and field event.

Nana and Tania shared their locations with me via their cell phones. I waited until they reached the Boulevard Saint-Michel before I slipped over the railing from our suite and crept past the Garcia sisters' room. I didn't think I was as afraid of heights as my mother but climbing across the balcony proved otherwise.

When Tania showed me how to spring the latch on our balcony door, she did so in seconds. I practiced a few times before attempting to break into Monsieur DuPont's room, but his rusty lock remained impervious.

A conversation between Elena and Eva Garcia floated through their open window. I strained to hear what they were saying, hoping it concerned their immediate departure.

The deeper voiced Elena spoke first. "Finish packing, so we can get out of here before he gets back."

Eva said, "We should have left yesterday. It was crazy to wait so long."

Elena answered, "You are one thick-headed *chiquita*. I didn't want to raise any red flags by leaving early."

A brazen pigeon landed on the balcony and pecked at my motionless foot. I jerked out of its way and it swooped onto the roof of a shorter building across the street. That's when I looked down, which was a mistake. A wave of dizziness came over me, and I feared I was going to faint. Or throw up. I sat with my back against the door and silently counted to ten. Then twenty. It didn't work.

With shaking hands, I took my buzzing phone out of my jacket pocket and looked at the screen. There were five texts each from Nana and Tania.

They all said, with increasing numbers of exclamation points: **He's on his way back! Get out!**

This was easier texted than done, because one of the sisters opened the balcony door. I froze. There was no place to hide. If they came outside, I would have a lot of explaining to do. No plausible excuse came to mind, other than temporary insanity.

A ringtone called her back into her room, and she shut the balcony door. I was weak with a mixture of relief that I'd escaped detection and shame that I'd failed in my mission. Since I didn't have enough time to continue fiddling with the lock, I spent a minute or so surveying Monsieur DuPont's room. The dresser was bare. The closet was open and empty. Two suitcases stood at attention at the foot of the unmade bed.

Monsieur DuPont entered the room, which inspired waves of butterflies to start waltzing in my stomach. I again flattened myself against the wall of the building. A few thumps ensued and then silence. I got on my knees and checked to see if the coast was clear.

It was. Monsieur DuPont was gone. So was his luggage. I climbed back onto the Garcias' balcony and crouched low. I figured if they were still there, I'd claim to have locked myself out of my room.

A strong hand slammed the door into my face. It knocked me over and momentarily stunned me.

Elena Garcia put her stiletto heel on my neck. "Don't move," she said, in an unmistakable Brooklyn accent. "Unless you want to take the short way down." She had a six-inch knife in her hand.

I was flat on my back. "That's er, you've got this all wrong. I was locked out of my room, and I—"

Eva inspected me from the threshold. Speaking to her sister, she said, "Don't be stupid. If you pitch her over the ledge, it'll make a huge mess. Let's tie her up and lock her in the closet. By the time her spacey mother realizes she's missing, we'll be long gone."

Elena considered this. "No. Too risky. I say we pitch her off DuPont's balcony. The police already think he killed his wife. This will take him out as well."

I considered the odds. One on one, my chances were good. Unarmed against both sisters, one of them wielding a knife, would be tricky. "You're wasting time, worrying about me. I'm off to Monaco tomorrow with a nonrefundable hotel deposit, and there's no way I want to get held up in Paris. Let me go, and we'll forget this ever happened."

Elena told me to shut up. The pressure on my neck eased slightly, as she continued to argue with her sister. Like my grandmother, I'll go for a long shot if the reward is worth the risk. In this case, it was. I grabbed her ankle, and she fell on top of me. The three of us scrambled to get the knife she dropped. Eva got to it first. She stabbed wildly at me. I kicked and squirmed. The knife hit the ground next to my neck and clattered over the edge.

I got to my feet and tried to get away, but the combined strength of the two women pushed me, inch by inch, toward the edge.

I slammed my head backwards, into Eva's face, hoping to break her nose, but she was so much taller than I was, it didn't do much. I was bent double over the railing, yelling (in English) for help.

That's when Tania overcame her fear of heights to conk Eva over the head with a brass lamp. Nana used the pointy end of her umbrella to stab Elena, who doubled over in pain. The police, led by Henri, finished the job.

* * *

After giving our statements to the police, we celebrated over too many glasses of champagne and pieced together the events that killed Nana's friend and came close to doing the same to me.

Tania was eager to justify her faith in the stars. "My astrologer was right all along. Elena and Eva were both tall, dark, and strange. They're not from Spain, by the way. They're from Sunset Park, in Brooklyn."

I was baffled. "I thought Elena was Monsieur DuPont's lover. Why would he book a room for himself and his wife in the same hotel as his mistress?"

Nana unwrapped a box of chocolates as an antidote to her bitter tale.

"He didn't. He broke up with her, but Elena followed him from Marseille to Paris. Monsieur DuPont and I had a nice long talk after the police released him. I figured it was a good time to strike and told him point blank I thought he was guilty. The streets were so crowded, it seemed safe to confront him. He thought I was talking about his affair and confessed to infidelity. It didn't cross his mind that I was accusing him of murder."

I nodded. "If he'd killed his wife, that's not how he would have reacted to your accusation. Did you ask him about the jewels?"

"Yes. He suspected Elena took them but didn't want to say anything for fear she'd reveal their affair."

"Did the police find them?"

Nana smiled. "Oh, yes. They were in the lining of those fake leather backpacks. The clues were right in front of us, but we didn't see them."

Tania protested, "We had no way of knowing Monsieur DuPont was having an affair with Elena."

I emptied the last of the champagne into our glasses. "Forget the affair and concentrate on what happened in the dining room. I presume that after the scene they staged with the spilled coffee, they stole the jewels. We can justify not seeing through the plan, but not the fact that we missed the most obvious clue: They both pretended they had trouble understanding English, and yet they kept slipping into speaking it. At the very least, they weren't who they seemed to be."

Nana said, "I hope you're going to put that analytical mind of yours to the casino, Julie."

"I'm on it."

* * *

We had a wonderful time in Monte Carlo. And flew home first class. Despite the tragic interlude at the Hotel du Lys, the trip was, as I liked to say, *magnifique.*

* * *

Lori Robbins writes the On Pointe and Master Class mystery series and is a contributor to *The Secret Ingredient: A Mystery Writers Cookbook*. She won the Indie Award for Best Mystery, two Silver Falchions, and Honorable Mention in the *2022 Best Mystery and Suspense* anthology. Lori is a co-president of the New York/ Tristate Sisters in Crime and an active member of Mystery Writers of America. You can find her at lorirobbins.com.

Tears of the Trophy Wife

By Elaine Viets

New York, United States

I didn't mean to kill Mark. If he'd given me my prenup money, I would have walked away. Instead, he made a fatal mistake, and I had no choice.

No one will believe me, especially after what happened, but I married Mark DeMille for love. I am Mark's fourth wife, Simone. Just Simone. I went by one name because it sounded glamorous, and besides, my last name is Polkinghorne. Simone Polkinghorne is no name for a supermodel and the face of Forever Lovely Cosmetics.

I was twenty-seven when I met Mark at the New York Fashion Week. I still stopped traffic with my long blonde hair and longer legs, but I knew my skin wouldn't stay flawless forever. My cosmetic contract was up in January, and I wasn't sure it would be renewed.

All around me at the show, I could see my competition. Women who were younger, thinner, and more ambitious. Women who would gladly live on lettuce and lemon juice to maintain their face and figure. Some days, I would sell my soul for a greasy cheeseburger. Occasionally I would succumb to the lure of a good meal, and then I'd vomit it up. Bulimia was the curse of my profession, and if I kept at it, the stomach acid would destroy my teeth.

Mark introduced himself at the party of the fashion season, Neiman Marcus's cocktail celebration. I wore a short black vintage Chanel number that hugged my curves, and turned my blonde hair gold. Mark was dazzled.

Mark was fifty-seven, thirty years older than me. With his thick dark hair, blue eyes and broad shoulders, he was good-looking, but he was more than just a pretty face.

I loved his shy charm and sly wit. He was, well, 'sweet,' was the best way to describe him.

As the party guests started drifting out the door, Mark asked if I'd like to go to dinner. He seemed sort of embarrassed when he asked, "Do you like red meat?"

"Love it." I'd been dieting for weeks.

"Would you like to have dinner at Red Meat?"

Red Meat was the restaurant of the moment, located in Brooklyn. The interior was splendid, all red velvet and towering mirrors so we could admire our fashionable selves.

Somehow, Mark got us a good table at the last minute. My mouth watered at the lovely smells of charred meat. Mark and I split a Caesar salad. Mark wanted a New York strip steak and I ordered a veal chop the size of a paperback novel. I allowed myself bread and butter. Fabulous.

"I like a woman who eats," Mark said.

Tonight, I ate everything, and kept it down.

After that dinner, Mark and I did all the things that lovers do. Manhattan is a walking city, and we'd walk and talk for blocks. We ate dinner in Chinatown, at little hole-in-the-wall restaurants that had roast chickens and Peking ducks in the window. We went to grand restaurants, too, but I enjoyed the casual ones more. I was tired of being on display.

We did more than eat. At Brooklyn Boulders, we climbed the 22-feet-tall rock wall. When Mark slipped and missed a handhold, he said, "See, I'm falling for you."

We took the tram to Roosevelt Island, and I felt a tinge of fear. I was fine on the crossing, as long as I didn't look down at the East River. I held Mark's hand tightly. On the island, we arrived at the exact moment to enjoy the incredible views of Manhattan at sunset.

We saw Broadway shows, and did silly things, like ride the SeaGlass Carousel at Battery Park, a surreal experience. I rode in a fanciful blue fiberglass fish while listening to Mozart.

Mark wooed me sweetly and carefully until I felt loved and cherished. After six weeks, he told me he had a special weekend planned for us at the Swinging Sixties-themed TWA hotel, the terminal designed by Eero Saarinen, at the JFK airport.

I found a vintage Courrèges red-and-black space age dress online, so I looked like I'd stepped off a Sixties' Paris runway, and black Courrèges boots. My hair was done in the style of the time, an elegant updo with my long, curled hair trailing down my back, and Sixties' make-up that made my eyes look like black daisies.

Mark whistled when he saw me. "You're perfect," he said.

"You are too," I said. Mark wore a slim-cut suit, narrow tie, and Chelsea boots.

Together, we stepped back in time at the TWA Hotel. Saarinen caught the spirit of the Sixties with his soaring architecture. This was an idealized Sixties, with no political assassinations, protests or the Vietnam War. I was happy to live in this fantasy for a weekend.

We had vintage cocktails—Manhattans—in the hotel's red-carpeted Sunken Lounge, while Saarinen's architecture swooped and swirled around us, followed by dinner at the Paris Café.

At ten o'clock, Mark and I went upstairs to the Eero Saarinen Presidential Suite, furnished in mid-century modern. The lines of the Knoll furniture were simple and clean, and our bedroom had a view of Saarinen's terminal.

A chilled bottle of Champagne was waiting in our sitting room. I was slightly woozy from our glamorous evening, but I sipped my Champagne with my head on Mark's shoulder.

"This has been a perfect evening," I said and sighed.

"Not quite," Mark said. "I need one more thing to make my life complete."

He got down on one knee and said, "Simone, would you do me the honor of marrying me?"

"Marriage?" Mark was much-married, and his divorces were tabloid scandals. Did I want that? I loved Mark, but I wasn't sure I wanted to marry him.

"I'd like to think about it," I said.

"I won't bring it up for a week," he said.

He kept his promise too. The rest of our weekend was idyllic, and we explored the delights of the hotel. We had drinks at the Connie, a 1958 Lockheed Constellation with a storied past. Connie started her career with TWA as a jetliner at Idlewild, which later became JFK. In the 1970s, she was an Alaskan bush plane. In the Eighties, Connie was forced into drug running, and abandoned in Honduras.

We watched from the rooftop infinity pool as the planes took off. I loved being with Mark, but I desperately needed advice. Should I marry him? What happened if I refused? Would that be the end of our romance?

Saturday afternoon, while Mark was drinking at the pool bar, I excused myself and made a frantic call to my agent, Edith Winthrop, for an emergency meeting. She said I could meet her for coffee in her office at ten Monday morning.

Our magical weekend was over all too soon. Mark kissed me goodbye tenderly. I tossed and turned all night, until I fell asleep just before dawn. When my alarm went off, I had to rush to make my appointment with Edith.

Edith had known me since she signed me up at age eighteen, when I was fresh off the bus from Festus, Missouri. She'd made me the success I was today.

"You look like hell, Simone," Edith said. "You didn't get enough sleep last night. And you've been out partying nearly every night. It's showing in your complexion, my dear."

Edith was one of those ageless New York women, somewhere north of forty and south of seventy. Whip-thin and supple, she always wore black. She wasn't conventionally pretty, but Edith was so stylish, pretty would be a comedown.

She examined me carefully. "However, you seem happy. Let me guess.

You're in love." She poured coffee into two bone china cups. Edith didn't offer me cream or sugar. They were banned from her office.

"Oh, yes, Edith." I caught myself. I was gushing like a teenager. "I've met a wonderful man. He wants to marry me."

"Don't tell me it's Mark DeMille."

I must have looked startled, because she said, "I've seen photos of you two in the gossip pages and put two and two together."

"It's true," I said. "We spent the weekend at the TWA hotel and he proposed."

"Did you say yes?" she asked.

"I wanted to consult you first. I need you to be brutally honest."

Edith laughed. "Simone, I'm always honest. It's my greatest fault — or virtue."

"I need you to evaluate me and help me decide."

"Come over here to the light," she said. The windows in her office were uncurtained and the morning light was merciless. She studied my face, neck and arms.

"Hm. I'd say you've reached your peak earning years. Tiny lines are starting to form on your face, and your boobs are dropping a bit. Just a fraction, but I'm trained to notice. Take good care of yourself, and you'll be able to pass yourself off as a beauty for another couple of decades. But the camera's cruel eye will no longer treat you kindly.

"Don't get me wrong, dear. I'll rep you as long as you want. But your glory days are coming to an end. How much money have you saved?"

My silence was my answer. I doubted I had more than a few thousand in savings. New York was expensive, and so was the pampering a professional model needed.

"I should have known," Edith said. "If you want to marry Mark, I should warn you. He's repeatedly said he doesn't find women over forty attractive."

"But he's—"

"Fifty-seven." Edith shrugged. "It's not fair, but that's the way the world works."

"I'm twenty-seven," I said. "By the time I'm forty, he'll be seventy. Surely he won't be looking for someone younger at that age."

Edith burst out laughing. She patted my shoulder and said, "Look, my dear, if you want to take a chance on Mark, go ahead. Forever Lovely Cosmetics doesn't want to renew your contract. If you marry a billionaire like Mark, you'll retire in triumph. You can always come back.

"But take my advice. Save as much money as you can. Take it out of your clothing allowance if you have to. Remember, some designers will give you dresses for free if you attend major events. Encourage Mark to give you jewelry—major pieces from Tiffany, Harry Winston, and—well, you know the names. They'll be your backup if things go bad. Insist on diamonds. They hold their value."

She stood up, and I knew it was time for me to leave. She air-kissed me and said, "Be happy, my love. And call me if I can help you."

I accepted Mark's proposal two days later, and the tabloids erupted with snarky headlines. *Beauty and the Billionaire* was the kindest. Most were like this one: *I Do, I Do, I Do, I Do It Again: Much Married Mark to March Down the Aisle for the Fourth Time.*

The brouhaha had just died down when word leaked that my engagement ring was a massive eighteen-carat emerald-cut diamond that cost a record 5.5 million dollars. It was delivered by armed guards. My former colleagues were envious. They shouldn't have been. That ring seemed to guarantee my financial freedom. Except my prenup stated that Mark got the ring back if we divorced. I was too much in love to take that red flag seriously.

I also ignored the provision I could not gain more than five pounds after our wedding date. I would be weighed like prize livestock before the ceremony by a female lawyer from Mark's firm, wearing only my undies. I would be weighed every year on my birthday. I was committed to looking like a trophy wife forever: bone thin, with visible clavicles, ribs, and hip bones, and huge fake tits.

I didn't care. Mark and I were mad about each other. He would overlook that provision. I knew he would.

We were married at his Hamptons estate, Rockydale Farm, and a slew of A-listers attended, including Beyoncé, Robert De Niro, and Robert

Downey Junior. Gwyneth Paltrow couldn't make it, but she sent a hamper of fabulous Goop products. Thankfully, one of them wasn't her *Smells Like My Vagina* candle. (No, I'm not kidding. The candle is real and that's what it's called.)

Our wedding day was perfect, and I looked stunning in my Vera Wang gown. Mark was perfect in his Tom Ford suit. We danced until dawn and spent our honeymoon in the Seychelles.

The next years were blissful. We stayed in our New York apartment during the season, and summered in the Hamptons. My life was a round of fashionable charities and dinners. Mark loved to show me off. He was thrilled when I made Gotham's ten best-dressed women list two years running. Each time, Mark gifted me with a spectacular diamond necklace. My agent Edith would have been proud. He gave me more diamonds on our anniversary.

Mark's long-range private jet allowed us to travel in style. We flew to Paris for dinner, Montreal for lunch, and hopscotched across Europe, Africa and Asia.

We enjoyed the simple pleasures too. We spent Sundays in bed, making love, reading the *New York Times*, and eating bagels from Zabar's. Mindful of my weight, I scooped out my bagel's center and skipped the cream cheese. Mark made delightful gestures, bringing me breakfast in bed. He loaded my tray with roses from our garden and wrote tender love notes. I saved every one.

When I turned thirty-eight, my life began to change. I was still a showstopper with my long hair, long legs and glowing skin. But my weight was creeping up. I'd gained six pounds, and Mark noticed. "Remember our agreement," he said, and playfully patted my tummy, which was flat by any standard but his.

Soon his reminders weren't quite so playful. When I ate a chocolate bar at home, he said, "That's fattening, you know." I stepped up my exercise routine, but couldn't shed those stubborn six extra pounds.

Finally, I resorted to CHSP—chew and spit—the eating disorder of actresses and trophy wives. I was so desperate for the taste of real food, I would chew it to get the flavor, and then spit it into my napkin. I carried a paper towel in my purse so I wouldn't embarrass myself when the server picked up my napkin. I lost those pesky pounds and picked up an ugly addiction.

Mark changed too. He was still handsome—for his age. His hair was silver (a rinse) and a small toupee covered the bald spot on his crown. He had to work out longer to keep his slim figure, and he was losing the battle at the beltline.

He changed toward me too. We no longer spent long, lazy Sundays in bed. He traveled more, and didn't take me along. For our anniversary, he gave me a tennis bracelet with lab grown diamonds. He bought it on Amazon. For forty-nine dollars. There's nothing wrong with a bracelet from Amazon, but when a man as rich as Mark gives an inexpensive gift, that's a gesture of contempt.

Mark began treating me like a housekeeper. He no longer kissed me in the mornings and brought me breakfast in bed. Instead, Mrs. Cooper, the cook, would bring my breakfast, with a list of Mark's instructions, mostly for the house in the Hamptons. Rockydale Farm was more than a hundred years old, requiring constant work. We employed a second housekeeper, Mrs. Francetta, and a full-time work crew, headed by George Clement, for upkeep.

Mark would curtly instruct me:

Make sure gardener trims the south hedges properly. They look ragged.

Fix fence in east pasture.

Remove dead tree on east lawn.

No please or thank you. Not even my name. Just orders.

I supervised this work myself. That's how I discovered Mark was cheating on me. He traveled with his new assistant. Clare was twenty-four, and so pale she was almost translucent. Her long hair was ice-blonde, and she wore only white. I found six of her white dresses in the pool house's guest room closet, along with white lingerie. Skimpy, sexy lingerie. Those filmy wisps made me feel like I'd been punched in the gut.

I sat on the guest bed, and put my head in my hands. My agent Edith had warned me, and I was glad I'd listened to her. I had little over a year to prepare for my exit.

When I recovered enough to stand up, I opened a bank account in the name of Simone Polkinghorne, the woman I used to be. I had copies made of my diamond jewelry, and quietly stashed the real jewels in a safe deposit box at the bank. I shaved a few thousand off my monthly allowance, and banked it. I began selling my couture gowns on consignment. In eight months, I had a nest egg of 250,000 dollars, plus my jewelry. When Mark divorced me after I turned forty, I'd get another 250,000 from my prenup.

I could live simply on that.

Mostly, I mourned my lost love. I missed Mark. My heart was broken, but I tried not to let my sorrow show. I pushed away the happy memories we'd shared—our Seychelles honeymoon, and idyllic early years. Those lazy Sundays in bed. The romantic trips.

I was determined to leave this marriage with dignity. I was not going to be tabloid fodder, like Mark's other wives.

All that changed when I found this note from Mark on my breakfast tray:

Pool house windows are leaking. Have crew fix. Building must be airtight.

The pool house, built by Mark's father, had been featured in *Architectural Digest.* We used it for summer entertaining. It had a ballroom, a full kitchen, an upstairs guest room, and a spa. It was our special retreat. When Mark still loved me.

On a cold November morning, I was at the farm, struggling to explain Mark's wishes to George, our crew foreman. George was a no-nonsense man in his fifties with gray hair and work-callused hands. We were in the ballroom, which was closed for the winter. The glass storm windows were up, and the furniture was draped in sheets, but the old-fashioned winter-proofing didn't work. A freezing wind rattled the ballroom windows, and roared through the place. The chandeliers, covered in linen bags, swayed softly.

George scratched his head when he read Mark's instructions. "It's a pool house, ma'am. What's Mr. D thinking? It's supposed to be open."

"I know, George. Just work on the parts you can. This ballroom. The kitchen. The guest room. And the spa. Make them as airtight as you can."

"They'll need storm windows, ma'am. Custom jobs."

"That's fine. Get hurricane windows."

"Okay, but it's going to be expensive. Do you want to text him to explain?"

"No, that's okay, George." I was too ashamed to say Mark no longer answered my texts.

"My husband delegated me to supervise this job, George. Start with the ballroom, please, and then the guest room. Mr. DeMille likes the view from there." The guest room had outside stairs. I knew Mark came out to the farm once or twice a month and brought his assistant, Clare, though our paths never crossed.

Except for the curt notes on my tray, Mark and I were living separate lives. The days ticked away until my fortieth birthday, February 16. Each day, I waited to hear that Mark was divorcing me.

Meanwhile, I came out to the farm several times a week to supervise this new task. Mostly, that meant checking in with George, and drinking tea in the kitchen with Mrs. Francetta, the farm's housekeeper. On one of my first visits, she introduced me to Patty Owen, her part-time helper.

"Patty comes in to help after school," Mrs. Francetta said. "Her mother is Ida Owen, the local seamstress who does such beautiful work."

I knew the story. Ida had fallen in love with Winston, a rich kid whose family owned Summeredge, the farm near ours. Ida got pregnant and Winston gave her some money to 'get rid of it.' He went off to Yale and Ida raised her baby daughter, Patty, barely making a living altering rich women's clothes. Ida wasn't the type to sue for child support.

Mrs. Francetta interrupted my thoughts with, "Patty's saving money to go to college. She's interested in fashion design, and wants to ask you about being a model."

Patty joined us for tea that afternoon. She was eighteen, a senior at the local Catholic school, and wore her uniform: pleated plaid skirt, white blouse with a round collar, and knee socks. There was nothing girlish about Patty's face and figure. Or that platinum hair. Even the ugly uniform couldn't conceal her dazzling beauty. She had presence too.

Patty would make a perfect model.

"I want to be just like you, Mrs. DeMille," she said. I winced when I saw the stars in her eyes.

"No, Patty, you don't," I said. "You want a career. You want to be able to support yourself."

You don't want to be married to a man who'll dump you when you turn forty, I thought.

"But you get to wear such beautiful clothes," she said, and crunched a chocolate chip cookie. "You go to so many glamorous places. All we have here are crab shacks and bars. We can't afford the local fancy restaurants."

"Patty, after you go to these so-called glamorous places enough," I said, "they're like your neighborhood places. Same people. Same conversations. There's no difference, except we may be better dressed."

And many nights, I'd rather be wearing no make-up, jeans and a sweatshirt, eating bar food. If it wasn't for the ever-present paparazzi.

"Do you have a boyfriend?" I asked. It was a clumsy way to change the subject.

Patty shrugged. "Boys my age are boring. They don't have much to say."

"They'll get better once you're in college," I said.

"I prefer older men." Her eyes looked dreamy. "They have better cars and they take me to the best places. Mom says I should marry a rich man. There are lots around here."

Mrs. Francetta said, "There are, Patty, but the local rich boys will never marry a pretty girl like you. They'll use you for a fling and then marry someone from their own class."

Like what happened to your mother, I thought.

Patty set her pretty mouth in a hard line. Mrs. Francetta looked at the kitchen clock and said, "Patty, it's time to get to work."

Patty grabbed one last cookie, jumped up and said she'd change into her work clothes. I'd see her around often when I went out to the farm. I let her try on some of the evening dresses I kept there, and she enjoyed swishing around in the silks and satins, as well as checking out the dresses' workmanship. Sometimes she'd examine dresses by my favorite designers—Valentino, Chanel, Carolina Herrera, as well as Stella McCartney and Alexander McQueen. We agreed the workmanship was fabulous.

Patty and I would discuss fashion trends and career choices. I admired her brains and ambition, and encouraged her to start her own business. Never again did we talk about who she was dating. Patty seemed to be avoiding me the last week or so before it happened, but there was so much going on, I wasn't sure.

My fortieth birthday was only three weeks away, and I continued to work on the same project at the farm. Still no notice when Mark was filing for divorce, so I could collect my 250,000 dollars in cash and leave quietly. I began to hope that maybe he'd changed his mind.

That same week, I intercepted a text message on Mark's burner phone. He left it behind in his jacket on a living room chair. I heard the phone buzzing, and read the text.

The message said: *$50,000. Accident guaranteed before 2/16.*

My heart was pounding. February 16? That was my birthday. When I turned forty. Was Mark hiring a hit man to kill me and make my death look like an accident? I scrolled back to see the text history. The answers were all there:

M: You do pest removal?

A: What kind?

M: Inconvenient kind.

A: Painful or painless removal?

M: Painless. Quick. Accidental. Must be found.

A: Will text a quote tomorrow.

It was bad enough when Mark's prenup would send me away with 250,000 dollars—pocket change for a man as rich as he was. Now he wanted to get out of his obligation. By killing me.

Hell, he'd make money if I died. We both had accidental death insurance policies. Mine was for half a million dollars. His was for much more—five million.

What was I going to do? I didn't know how to hire a hitman, and I was too cowardly to kill Mark myself. I paced my bedroom hoping for a solution, but I was so upset I couldn't think. The weather had changed abruptly yesterday. It was unseasonably warm. February did that—gave a taste of good weather to the winter-weary and then cruelly yanked it away.

I drove out to the farm, where I always felt peaceful. After tea with Mrs. Francetta, I took a long walk in the springlike air, and then stopped by to see George.

"Mrs. D," he said. "I've finished the work on the guest bedroom. It's airtight. But we have a problem. That old propane space heater in there needs to be replaced. It was installed during his father's time, and it's not safe. If anyone spends the night there, they could die from carbon monoxide poisoning. I left the space heater in place for now, because it's too warm to turn it on. It will be a week before I can get a new one out here."

"I'll text Mark right now." My heart was pounding. This was the answer to my prayers.

I showed George the text: *"Mark dearest, IMPORTANT. Do NOT use the guest bedroom in the pool house. Now that the new storm windows are in, George says the airtight room could be dangerous with the old propane space heater. He's ordering a newer, safer electric heater. If you stay overnight, stay in the big house."*

I didn't tell George that Mark didn't answer my texts or take my calls any more. If Mark didn't read my text, too bad. He'd get what he deserved. And so would Clare. That would teach her to chase married men.

I left the farm. A visit there did solve my problem. I drove home with the sky black with scudding clouds. The weather was changing. Winter was back.

I didn't have long to wait. Two days later, I got a phone call from a hysterical Mrs. Francetta. She was weeping so hard, I could hardly understand her. I finally figured out there had a been a terrible accident at the farm—Mark had slept in the guest bedroom and had been overcome by carbon monoxide. So had the woman with him. Mrs. Francetta was so upset, she dropped the phone. I heard sirens in the background. I hopped in my car and started driving.

Emergency lights danced across the farm's lawn. Paramedics were treating Mrs. Francetta for shock. Most of the emergency vehicles and people were clustered around the pool house. I ran straight there, just as the bodies were brought out on stretchers. Our uniformed staff blocked my view, and I had to stand on tiptoe to see.

One body bag held a man. Mark, I presumed. The other was a woman.

"So sad, isn't it?"

I recognized that voice and nearly fainted. "Clare?" I felt dazed. Mark's philandering assistant was supposed to be dead.

"Is anything wrong, Mrs. DeMille?" she said. "You're white as a sheet."

I must have been even whiter than Clare. "I just found out my husband is dead." My voice quavered.

"Of course. Would you like to sit down?" She guided me to the bumper of a patrol car.

"Who was the woman with Mark?" I asked.

"Poor little Patty, the girl who worked here."

"Patty? The pretty blonde who wanted to be a model?"

"Yes."

"Oh, no, no."

"You didn't know?" Clare said. "I'm so sorry you have to find out this way. She was having an affair with your husband."

"But he's…he's…"

"More than fifty years older than Patty. We all knew what was going on. We thought you did too. Mrs. Francetta talked to the girl about it and threatened to fire her. Patty promised she'd never ever meet with Mr. D again."

Rage surged through me. "Why that miserable…"

"Little slut?" Clare shrugged. "Like mother, like daughter."

"No!" I wanted to say that it wasn't Patty's fault. She'd been seduced by an older, richer man. Mark might have even promised marriage.

Before I could explain, a police detective, Rob Grippando, interrupted us.

"Are you Mrs. DeMille?" he asked. "I'd like to ask you a few questions back at the house."

"I'll go with you," Clare said. "I need some coffee."

The detective led me to the kitchen, which smelled of coffee and freshly baked scones. Clare gave me strong black coffee loaded with cream and sugar. When was the last time I'd tasted those treats? I couldn't remember. What luxury. I gulped it down, knowing Mark couldn't fat shame me any more.

"What did you know about the space heater in the guest bedroom?" Detective Grippando asked.

"A couple of days ago, George told me the old propane heater shouldn't be turned on. He ordered a new electric space heater. He wanted to install it in a week."

"Did your husband know this?"

"Yes. I texted him." I showed the detective my text and didn't mention that Mark never read them.

"We found women's clothes in the closet. Were those yours?"

"Those were mine, Detective," Clare said. "I keep a few changes of clothes here. Mr. DeMille would sometimes stop by to take a client to dinner and I'd need fresh clothes."

"Were you having an affair with Mr. DeMille?" Grippando asked.

Clare looked shocked by his bluntness. "No," she said. "Mr. DeMille was seventy years old. Besides, I'm engaged." She showed the sparkler on her left hand. "Hunter and I will be getting married in May."

"What about Patty Owen?" he asked. "Was she having an affair with Mr. DeMille?"

"I didn't know," I said.

"The rest of us did," Clare said. "She was the talk of the farm."

"From what we can tell, she'd been engaged in sexual activity with Mr. DeMille," he said.

"That's terrible," I said.

"Yes, it is," he said. "I knew Miss Owen. I expected better from her."

Thanks to that text I wrote, the detective decided I had nothing to do with Mark's murder. Technically, I didn't. but I didn't do anything to prevent his death. Or Patty's.

Once the investigation was over, I had Mark cremated. I didn't attend the funeral. Everyone thought I was prostrate with grief.

I was, but not for my cheating, murderous husband. I mourned that poor girl, Patty, her promising young life cut short. I paid for her funeral and burial, and used Mark's life insurance to establish a scholarship in Patty's name.

I gave Mrs. Francetta and George a generous pension. I sold our New York apartment and the farm. I gained twenty pounds and looked much better. I could eat again, but I couldn't taste my food. I was tormented by how I'd killed that young woman.

Free, rich and friendless, I moved to Florida, far away from what I'd done. I was fine for a while, but then I saw Patty in a crowd at the beach. I certainly saw her long, platinum hair. But when the blonde turned around, I realized it wasn't Patty. Still, I couldn't stay there. I relocated to New Orleans, until I saw Patty in the French Quarter. I kept moving around the country. Chicago next, then Seattle, then LA.

I lived in Europe, South America and the Caribbean. I'd be fine for a while and then I'd see her and I'd move. I did everything I could to atone. I founded program after program for young women to become entrepreneurs.

But Patty was always with me.

So was my husband. After Mark was cremated, I had his ashes turned into a diamond. You can do that, you know. Not a flawless diamond, of course, but a two-carat with flaws so small they're barely noticeable.

Mark's on a chain around my neck.

That is Mark's punishment. I'm seventy now. Mark will never ever know the feel of young skin again. He'll be buried with me.

* * *

Elaine Viets has written 34 mysteries in four series ranging from cozy to hard-boiled: the Dead-End Job mysteries; the Francesca Vierling mysteries; the Josie Marcus, mystery shopper mysteries; and the Angela Richman, Death Investigator mysteries. Her latest is *A Scarlet Death.* Elaine also wrote *Deal with the Devil and 13 Short Stories.* She's won the Agatha, Anthony and Lefty Awards. Elaine will receive the Lifetime Achievement Award at the Malice Domestic Mystery Conference April 2024.

The Last Dance

By Josh Pachter

Ghent, Belgium

Behind the wrinkled parchment of her eyelids, the old woman watched herself dancing with her beloved Alexander. It was 1917, but in her mind it was always 1859, almost sixty years ago, when they were both in their twenties, still practically children. The polka mania had reached Ghent by then, and the night before Alexander set off for Lombardy to offer medical assistance to soldiers wounded in the Austro-Sardinian War, they celebrated his impending departure by attending the Freemason's Ball in the sixteenth-century Guild Hall opposite the St. Nicholas Church.

For many years after that last happy evening, her daydream would give way to a vision of the terrible Battle of Solferino, in which some forty thousand soldiers on both sides died or were wounded, a battle whose devastation led Swiss businessman Jean-Henri Dunant to found his International Committee of the Red Cross.

It was during that battle that Alexander—her fiancé, a noncombatant— had paid the ultimate price for his altruism. He had been her one true love, and following his death there had been no one else. At last, though, she had tamed her mind, taught it to remain inside the Guild Hall, where she and Alexander twirled gaily across the hardwood floor, young and happy in the foolish belief that upon his return from Italy they would spend the rest of their lives together.

"Mam'selle Caekebeke?" a nurse whispered, laying a gentle hand on her shoulder. "You have a visitor."

The old woman opened her eyes and blinked at the daylight streaming in through her room's one window. "A visitor?" she said. "For me?"

"Yes, mam'selle. It's that reporter again. You remember, you spoke with him several months ago?"

A smile flickered across her lips, and her rheumy eyes twinkled for just a moment. "Ah, yes. He asked me about Dr. Guislain and the murder at the Hospice."

"I did," the journalist confirmed, stepping out of the direct sunlight so she could see his face. "My editor was very pleased with the article I wrote, and we've had letters from readers asking if you might perhaps have more stories about the doctor to tell."

The pale pink tip of the old woman's tongue emerged from between her chapped lips and licked them, top and bottom, side to side. "More murders, you mean?"

"That would be too much to hope for," the journalist smiled. "But anything you might remember about Dr. Guislain in the days when his hospital was new would be welcome."

She closed her eyes and sat motionless for such a long time that the journalist began to fear she had slipped back into the reverie from which his arrival had aroused her.

But then she looked up at him again. "Well," she said, "there were no other murders, I'm afraid, but there was a theft, a most mysterious theft, what Mr. Chesterton's Father Brown might perhaps call a locked room within a locked room within a locked room."

The journalist pulled up a chair and took out his notebook and pencil. "That sounds like just the sort of thing I'm looking for," he said eagerly….

* * *

"Amandine," said Dr. Guislain, removing his ornate half-hunter from his vest pocket and checking the time. "You're a little late today, are you not?"

This was no great feat of deduction on his part. I always arrived at the Hospice Guislain—the first and, in 1859, still Belgium's only hospital devoted to the care and treatment of men who had been diagnosed with an assortment of mental disorders—fifteen minutes before the doctor, so that I could air out his office for him and put water on to boil for his morning coffee.

As he selected a key from his ring and swung open the large oak door that led from the graveled parking area for carriages to the hospital's interior, I put away my own keys and nodded meekly. "I'm afraid I was out rather late last night, Dokter," I acknowledged.

"Yes, of course, you and your young man were at the Freemasons' Ball." He chuckled, and it was clear that he was not disturbed by my tardiness. But then his kindly expression turned somber. "He leaves for Italy today, if I remember correctly?"

I sighed. "Yes. I don't know when I will see him again."

The doctor ran the backs of his fingers contemplatively down the length of his fashionable side whiskers. "Well, my girl, we'll just have to keep you busy here, then, to take your mind off your loneliness."

As he spoke, we strolled side by side beneath the brick archways that lined the four sides of the hospice's central courtyard, where the yellow-green leaves of the pollard willows filtered the early-summer sunlight and helped keep the air refreshingly cool, though later in the day the heat was sure to be oppressive.

Dr. Guislain unlocked the door to his office and gallantly stepped to the side to permit me to precede him within so that we could begin our day.

It was that afternoon that Paul Claeys, one of our orderlies, reported that Stijn De Meester, who had been remanded to our care a week earlier, was having another of his 'episodes.'

As a rule, the Hospice Guislain's patients gave the staff very little trouble. Though each of them suffered from some sad psychological affliction serious enough to require hospitalization, they were for the most part quiet, withdrawn, and well-behaved. But there were occasional exceptions, and at times it was necessary to administer a drug to put an end to a spell of violence.

The drug we used at the Hospice Guislain was morphine, an alkaloid compound first isolated from the resinous gum secreted by the opium poppy by a young German pharmacist's assistant in 1805 and named after Morpheus, the Greek god of dreams, because of its tendency not only to relieve pain but to cause sleep.

Our supply of morphine was kept in a locked metal strongbox, and the strongbox resided within a wall safe in Dr. Guislain's office—

* * *

"And you've said that the office itself was locked," the journalist interrupted the old woman's narrative. "Therefore, a locked 'room' within a locked safe within a locked office."

"Precisely," she nodded. "And you can surely guess what happened next."

"When the doctor opened the safe and the strongbox," the young man ventured, "some of the morphine that *ought* to have been there was missing."

"Not 'some,'" she corrected him. "*All* of it, perhaps enough for thirty doses."

* * *

"Mon Dieu!" the doctor exclaimed. "Amandine! Come here at once!"

I hurried from my little anteroom, which adjoined Dr. Guislain's office, and found him staring, horrified, into the strongbox, which he held open in trembling hands.

"The—the morphine," he stammered. "It's gone!"

"Impossible!" said I.

"And yet," he returned, "see for yourself!"

I followed his gaze—and, yes, the box was empty. The three of us—the doctor, Paul Claeys, and I—stood there gaping at its bare interior.

With a great effort, Dr. Guislain recalled himself to the immediate problem at hand. "Paul," he said, "you'll have to try to calm De Meester down some other way. Hurry now, before the poor soul does himself an injury."

The orderly scurried off, leaving my employer and me to consider the confounding mystery of the vanished drug.

Explaining how a thief could have entered the doctor's locked office was the least perplexing element of the crime. There were numerous keys in circulation: Dr. Guislain had one, naturally, as did I, as did the director of the hospice's cleaning crew, and it seemed quite possible that there were others, as well.

But only the doctor knew the combination to his wall safe, and only he had a key to the strongbox.

For the next several hours, Dr. Guislain interrogated members of the staff, but no one acknowledged having seen anything, having heard anything, during the course of the previous evening. He summoned the night shift from their beds, but they too had nothing to contribute. Nights at the hospice were generally uneventful, and the few orderlies on the premises rarely had occasion to leave the staff cafeteria, where they were more often than not free to pass the quiet hours reading, playing cards, dozing.

I proposed calling in the local police to investigate the theft, but Dr. Guislain quickly vetoed that suggestion. "And let it become public knowledge that a quantity of morphine has disappeared from my care?" he said, making the very thought of such a revelation sound absurd. "No, Amandine, if we cannot solve this mystery ourselves, then I'm afraid it must remain a mystery for all time."

* * *

The old woman stopped talking, and, as the silence lengthened, the journalist looked up from his notes. "Well?" he demanded.

She chewed abstractedly at her lower lip.

"Come, now," the young man said. "What happened next?"

She shrugged. "Nothing."

He laughed nervously. "You can't be serious!"

"I am perfectly serious," she replied. "We never learned who stole the drug. The doctor was right: the mystery remained a mystery."

"But I can't write a story without an ending," the journalist expostulated.

"The story *has* an ending," the old woman said. "Dr. Guislain had the safe replaced and added a second lock to his office door, he replenished our supply of morphine, and there were no further thefts."

"That's not an ending."

"It's not a *resolution*," the old woman acknowledged. "But it is an ending. It's the way this story ends."

Suddenly, the expression on the young man's face changed from anger to understanding. "I have it!" he said. "You're covering up for your employer. The doctor must have taken the morphine for his own use. He knew the combination to the safe, and he obviously had the keys to his own office and the lock box."

The old woman shook her head stubbornly. "No, no," she said. "You mustn't write that. It's not true, I'm absolutely certain of it. The doctor disapproved of drugs. He administered them to patients only very occasionally, when nothing else seemed capable of calming them, but he would never have experimented with them himself."

The journalist glared at her in frustration—and, after numerous failed attempts to get her to admit that there *was* in fact more to the story, he gave up and went away, grumbling at the waste of his valuable time.

The old woman watched him go.

Perhaps, she thought, she shouldn't have teased the boy with her tale of an impossible crime lacking the sort of resolution that Englishman, Conan Doyle, provided for *his* readers. But she had been unable to resist. Other than her daydreams, there were so few pleasures left to her anymore.

When he was gone, she permitted herself to think back to that fateful night, when she and Alexander returned to the Hospice Guislain after what would turn out to have been their final dance.

It was two in the morning when they got there. The patients were long asleep, most of the staff had left, the night shift were dozing at their posts, the cleaning crew would not arrive for another hour. She had keys to the hospital's main entrance and Dr. Guislain's office, of course, and she knew full well that he kept the combination to the safe scrawled on a slip of paper and hidden away in a drawer of his desk—along with the key to the strongbox, which he saw no reason to carry around on the ring of keys he used every day—so she'd had not the slightest difficulty admitting them to the office and opening both the safe and the locked box within.

In the course of their last evening together, she had asked Alexander what he knew of the conditions he would find in Lombardy. He had told her what he himself had been told of the hardships experienced by the combatants on both sides of the Austro-Sardinian War, of the lack of supplies that made care for the wounded so much less effective than it *could* be if only the volunteer medical personnel were better equipped. She had told him of the morphine locked away in Dr. Guislain's office, and he had begged her to turn the drug over to him, so that he might use it to alleviate the suffering he was sure to encounter on the battlefield. And how could she deny him, the only man she had ever loved—the only man she *would* ever love?

She had felt terrible about betraying the doctor's confidence in her, but she knew that he would never agree to *give* her the morphine—and that he would believe her when she told him she had no idea who might have taken it, how an unknown thief could have managed to penetrate the locked box within the locked safe within his locked office.

Some stories, she thought, end without a resolution—or at least without a resolution known to the world at large.

She had always wondered whether or not the doctor had finally realized that the only person who could possibly have taken the missing morphine was she herself, Amandine Caekebeke, his trusted assistant. But less than a year later—on the first of April 1860—he was dead, at sixty-three an elderly man in the Belgium of that time. The hospice that bore his name was turned over to a new director, who brought with him an assistant of his own choosing. So within the space of a single year, she had lost her fiancé, her employer, and her career.

She had carried on, though, had found another position in another of Ghent's hospitals, had worked for many more years, had done much good in the world.

But she had never found a man to replace her poor Alexander, so in a sense *her* story, too, was a story without a resolution.

Today, outside her tiny sanctuary in one of the city's smaller nursing homes, the Kingdom of Belgium remained occupied by the German Kaiser's army. But the view from her window was peaceful: a garden, lovingly tended by the staff, though this deep into the autumn the chrysanthemums and dahlias and majestic sunflowers struggled to retain their color.

Inside, alone in her room, the old woman rested her head against the back of her chair and closed her eyes and returned once again to her last dance with her beloved Alexander.

* * *

AUTHOR'S NOTE

The Hospice Guislain is a real place, founded in Ghent in 1857 by Dr. Joseph Guislain (1797-1860) as Belgium's first psychiatric hospital. It still exists today, serving as a museum of psychiatry.

The Austro-Sardinian War (also referred to as the Sardinian War, the Franco-Austrian War, the Second Italian War of Independence, and the Italian War of 1859) was brief but deadly, lasting from April 26 through the signing of the Armistice of Villafranca on July 12. As noted in the story, some forty thousand soldiers on both sides were killed during the climactic Battle of Solferino on June 24. Following the battle, Swiss businessman Jean-Henri Dunant visited Solferino and was inspired to take political action that eventually led to the adoption of the Geneva Conventions and the founding of the International Red Cross.

All other characters and incidents described here are fictional.

***

Josh Pachter is the author of more than a hundred short stories, the translator of sixty stories and novels from Dutch to English, and the editor of twenty anthologies. As *Mystery Most International* goes to press, his first novel, *Dutch Threat,* is a finalist for the Agatha and Lefty awards. His first book for young readers—*First Week Free at the Roomy Toilet*—is due this year from Level Best.

No Escape

By Robert Lopresti

Barcelona, Spain

"Shut the door," said Walsh, leaning back in his office chair. It was big enough to hold three of him. A battle with cancer two years earlier had left him bone-thin. The brass had given up on trying to convince him to retire. His eyes were dead-flat, but that had been true long before he got sick.

Simington was surprised to see Vazquez already slumped in a chair. He had never worked with him, but the kid had a good rep in the unit.

"What's up, Lou?"

Walsh popped a piece of nicotine gum into his mouth. "Jimmy Bernhart's been seen."

"Who by this time?" asked Simington. "A psychic? A cub scout?"

He sat back in his chair, trying to match Walsh's calm. The reward had brought out a flock of loonies.

"A cop in Spain, a member of the—" He squinted at a piece of paper. "The *Guardia Urbana* named Putro."

"That sounds good, right?" said Vazquez, grinning. "How sharp are the Spanish cops?"

"You're about to find out," said Walsh. "I'm sending you to make sure we bag that skunk."

The kid's eyes went wide. "We're going to Spain?"

"Bernhart's wife was murdered almost two months ago," said Walsh. "Are we waiting for the rich clown to take a world tour? Go nail him."

"I will," said Simington. "But why are you sending the rookie?"

"Hey," said Vazquez, sitting up straight. "Maybe you haven't noticed but I've been on the job here almost two years."

"And you've made a hell of an impression," said Simington, flatly.

"He's going because you need someone who speaks the lingo," said Walsh. "You have the rest of the day to pack a bag."

Outside the office Simington asked "Since when do you speak Spanish?"

Vazquez grinned. "Since it gets me a free trip to Europe."

"Caramba."

* * *

Before heading home to throw some clothes in a suitcase, Simington called the *Guardia Urbana* in Barcelona. After identifying himself as the chief detective investigating the Sylvia Bernhart murder, he was put through to Officer Putro. Miracle of miracles, Putro spoke English, did not oversell, and didn't sound like a man who imagined things.

"It is the rich man, sí. Bernhart. He wears a disguise, but I am good with faces."

"You didn't send a photo."

"I'm a police officer, not a cameraman. You want me to ask somebody—"

"No, you're right. The more people know about it the faster someone will clue the joker in."

"Anything else you want?"

"Just keep an eye on him."

Putro laughed. "Both eyes."

* * *

"This place is crazy," said Vazquez. He was looking out the taxi window.

"What's the problem?"

"I used the ATM at the airport, get some of those Euros? I had to go to a second screen to find English. The first screen had four other languages."

"Well, we are in Europe. Spanish, French, German…"

"No! Most of them were languages I never heard of. Something like *Catalog.*"

"Catalan. They must have been Spanish regional languages. We're in Catalunya."

"I thought this was Barcelona."

Simington sighed. "Hey, señor."

The taxi driver looked at him in the mirror. "Sí?"

"What part of the country are we in?"

"Catalunya, señor."

"And you have your own language?"

"Sí, señor. And soon our own country."

Simington nodded. "Yeah, I read about the independence movement."

Vazquez eyes went wide, and his voice went soft. "You think that's why Bernhart came here? He's hiding with the rebels?"

"It's a political movement, not terrorists." He shrugged. "Mostly. Besides, Bernhart doesn't need them. Billionaires have friends anywhere they go."

* * *

They stored their luggage in their hotel in a neighborhood called Sants-Montjuic and then called Putro. He met them at a café.

The Spanish cop was a tall, thin man in his thirties with jet black hair and a big smile. He wore a civilian suit of good quality. "The American investigators! We meet at last."

After introductions they ordered espresso and Putro filled them in.

"Your rabbit is staying in a very expensive hotel in Eixample."

"Example?"

Putro corrected him. "A very nice part of town. It was the center of the Modernism movement. Miró. Gaudi."

"We're not tourists," Simington said. "How sure are you that this guy is Bernhart?"

"Very confident. He has changed his appearance but not his walk. And, as I said, I have an eye for such things."

"I hope you do. When can we see him?"

"He takes the stroll down the Ramblas every day around 2100 hours." Putro smiled."With two bodyguards."

"Twenty-one," said Vazquez. "Nine P.M. About three hours from now."

Simington nodded. "So, about the crew I asked you to put together."

"They will be ready tomorrow morning. I assume you aren't going to move on him tonight."

"Nope. For now we just want to confirm the target."

* * *

They were set up at one side of the Plaza in plenty of time to watch a white SUV pull up and see a lanky man climb out, accompanied by two gorillas.

It took Simington half an hour to make up his mind. Bernhart had cut his hair and bleached it. He had a straggly beard and wore oversized sunglasses under a floppy hat.

But Putro was right. The gangly loose-limbed walk was a giveaway. And when he passed the bright light in front of a restaurant, Bernhart felt certain.

"That's our boy," said Vazquez. "Let's move."

"No. Look at those bodyguards. That's why we need backup from Putro's people."

"What if he gets spooked and disappears?"

"Then Walsh is going to hand me my walking papers. Among other things."

* * *

Vazquez wanted to go out and see the sights.

Simington laid down the law. "We need to be at our best tomorrow. If you show up with a hangover, I swear I'll get you canned."

"You aren't any fun."

"So both my ex-wives told me."

* * *

They slept late, getting over jet lag, and then spent the afternoon coordinating with Putro's people. They all claimed to speak English, but Simington had their man translate everything, just to make sure.

Everyone was in place an hour early. Simington was sure they had prepared for every foreseeable possibility.

He also knew you can't foresee everything.

By nine P.M. Vazquez was vibrating with nervous energy, like a man who had slammed a triple espresso on an empty stomach."Where the hell is he?"

"Just stay cool."

"If he took off—"

"Look. The white SUV. The same one he arrived in last night."

The vehicle was circling the Plaza de Catalunya. It stopped a hundred yards away. Two big men climbed out of it.

"His gorillas!" said Vazquez. "Come on!"

Simington grabbed his arm. "If they see us, he won't get out of the car."

"Oh. Right."

The bodyguards apparently decided there was no danger. One of them thumped a heavy hand on the roof of the vehicle.

And out he came, wearing a different hat from the night before, but demonstrating the same gangly stroll.

"Gotcha," said Vazquez.

Simington found himself relaxing. "At last. Now we're gonna get some answers. Let's— Hold it! Who the hell is that?"

A woman was stepping out of the SUV, long shapely legs first. She was almost as tall as Bernhart, built like a swimsuit model.

"Man," said Vazquez "He didn't waste any time."

"Apparently not."

"Do you think she knows how her boyfriend's wife died?"

"We'll find out. Come on, they're moving."

The Ramblas was a wide pedestrian street that meandered downhill from the plaza to the harbor, most of a mile. All the way it was crowded with tourists looking at the restaurants, shops, vendor carts and entertainers.

"When do we move?"

"Take it easy." Simington was watching the crowd, looking for the perfect moment, when no tourists would be in the line of action.

It came as the couple and the bodyguards passed the open-air meat market. Apparently Bernhart's lady friend found the sight unappealing and hurried to the other side of the street. Bernhart followed, leaving his guards momentarily behind.

"This is it," said Simington. He raised an arm as if he was waving at someone.

There was a loud shout. Two men a few feet behind Bernhart's party had squared off for a fight. The taller man pushed the other one, who came back with both arms swinging wildly.

Most people, bodyguards included, turned to watch.

Simington stepped forward. He could only hope Vazquez was in position, too, because he didn't dare take his eyes off the target. "Hey, Jimmy!"

Bernhart spun around to look at him, slack-jawed.

Simington grinned at him. "Your wife's lover confessed to strangling her. Is there anything you'd like to say to him?"

Bernhart scowled. "Who the hell are you?"

"Tru-Krime TV. Is that your new girlfriend, Jimmy? What's her name?"

The billionaire took a step forward. "Why the hell won't you people leave me alone?"

"The people have a right to know."

Bernhart raised his fists. "The people can go screw themselves!"

And then the bodyguards arrived, finally. One of them shoved Simington backwards, while the other made a grab for Vazquez's video camera.

Fortunately, the kid had already turned and made a run for it, straight down the hill.

The bodyguard rushed after him, but Officer Putro appeared in front of him, badge in his hand, ordering him to stop.

Beautiful.

The girlfriend, if that's who she was, had disappeared into a café. Bernhart was following. The guards, humiliated and thoroughly ticked off, blocked the door. Simington didn't even try to approach them.

They had what they needed.

* * *

After uploading the files to the network, they celebrated at what Putro assured them was the best tapas bar in the city, far from the tourist traps.

Putro himself had gone off to the police station to explain his absence from post that day. He would have some trouble with his bosses, but he had a fat pile of euros to comfort him.

Simington was tapping on his phone. "You saw the texts from Walsh?"

"No. What's the mighty news boss have to say?"

"He's thrilled to bits. Apparently you remembered to take the lens cap off."

"Yeah, and you pointed your mic the right direction. How grateful is he?"

"He's talking about raises for both of us."

"I can use one." Vazquez nibbled a piece of ham. "You think it's worth it?"

Simington made a face. "You haven't had enough wine to get philosophical yet. We're the press. The Constitution gives us the right to tell the people the truth. The fact that the only truth they care about is gossip about celebrities is not our fault."

"Nah." Vazquez shook his head. "Not what I meant. Look."

He pointed to the computer screen. "We got five minutes of prize footage. Maybe ten minutes of B-stuff of the billionaire strolling with his mystery girl."

"So?"

"So is that worth what the network paid for it? Our expenses, the rewards, the bribes."

Simington's eyebrows shot up. "You kidding? Your film is going to be the lead on every gossip show in the world tomorrow, with the Tru-Krime bug running in the corner. It's the biggest scoop of the year. Great clickbait. Our website will catch millions of eyeballs."

"Yeah, I guess so." Vazquez waved at the waiter. "Too bad Bernhart didn't say the F-word. You know? 'The people can go screw themselves.'"

"No problem. The network will bleep out the word and people will assume the worst."

"I guess." Vazquez tapped the keyboard, freezing the screen with Bernhart. red-faced and gaping-mouthed, glaring at the camera.

"Look at the rage on that guy! You know, it's a shame he's not guilty of something."

Simington chewed on a shrimp. "Well, consider this. The next time Bernhart steps out of his hotel there'll be a hundred photographers waiting for him."

He grinned. "Maybe he'll assault one of them."

* * *

Robert Lopresti is a retired librarian who lives in the Pacific Northwest. His hundred-plus stories have won the Derringer and Black Orchid Novella Awards and been reprinted in *Best American Mystery Stories*. His novel, *Greenfellas,* is a comic caper about the Mafia trying to save the environment. He blogs at SleuthSayers and Little Big Crimes. Roblopresti.com

Death on the Nile

By Jeffrey Marks

Nile Cruise, Egypt

I awoke in time for happy hour on the small ship's weather deck. The seven-time zone difference had made naps at any time seem reasonable.

I stepped into the brilliant sun, stopping to wave at a few people. The murky waters of the Nile sparkled as I glanced over the rail. I had come to Egypt to take the cruise featured in *Death on the Nile*, one of Agatha Christie's best novels. I had toured Cairo, then caught an overnight train to Aswan. I was returning to Cairo to fly home, courtesy of our small ship, *Ma'at*, with approximately thirty passengers.

While I'd come here alone, I'd made friends quickly. Last night featured a murder mystery party with clues and one passenger playing the victim. I solved the 'crime' in under twenty-five minutes.

In fairness, the case had been simple. The two clues pointed to the same person, and the motive ran as wide as the Nile. However, I seemed like a great detective to the passengers, who appeared not to have any clue at all.

I had barely sat down at a table with Valerie and Jesús when she asked, "Have you heard the news?"

Valerie and Jesús had chosen this trip for their honeymoon—a choice I thought tempted fate, given the *Death on the Nile*'s storyline. She was

Egyptian; he'd been born in Spain.

They had adopted me, a quirk I'd encountered with other recently married couples. I had left one such pair behind in Cincinnati and didn't want another.

I looked from one to the other; Valerie seemed more interested in telling me the story. She hadn't spent much time on her outfit, a turquoise cotton blouse that had seen better days. A few loose threads were pulled from the fabric. Her hair danced in the breeze, but her eyes were bright.

"I went to bed early," I said truthfully. Valerie poured me a glass of wine, white, despite my preference for red. I didn't complain as she had expensive tastes.

"A passenger was murdered."

The glass paused halfway to my mouth. While I wanted my vacation to follow the itinerary of the novel, I did not want an actual reenactment. "Who died?" I asked, hoping that this was another onboard game.

"The girl who came with her boyfriend, and future mother-in-law? She was stabbed, like Glenda in your book."

My head ached. There were no stabbings in *Death on the Nile*—and no Glenda. Valerie managed to get both the plot wrong and the victim's name. I began to think about the murder in silence.

"You've seen the Chisholm family?" Valerie asked.

"The older woman with the son and his betrothed," Jesús prompted, though I had known their names.

"I've gone to a few sites with them," I conceded. "They're very knowl-edgeable."

"According to another tourist, Amy was murdered—stabbed. The steward found her. The son and mother have alibied each other, claiming to have been on the weather deck," Valerie added.

If the young woman had been murdered, shouldn't Mrs. Chisholm have found her? Indeed, the older woman would be the most likely suspect since they'd shared a cabin.

* * *

I was only a few pages into my reread of *Death Comes as the End*, another Christie set in Egypt, when I realized Marwan was standing over me. He was also a guest on the tour, one of those tourists who had lived in a region his entire life but had never seen the sites. He was younger than most of the passengers and a bit flirty, which I found disconcerting given Egyptian laws.

"What are you reading?" he asked with a knowing smile. I was sure that he recognized the book.

I explained the book and its premise of life being much the same in ancient Egypt as it was today. Greed, lust, and fear still led people to kill—then as now.

He laughed at my speech. "Things have changed. Do you think there were ships like this four thousand years ago?"

Before I could speak, he grew serious. "Some things were as dangerous then as they are now, my friend. Be aware of that." His eyes met mine, and I felt flustered, unsure of what he meant.

He stood up abruptly and walked away.

Marwan had just walked out of sight when Valerie approached me. She held a key between her forefinger and thumb.

"I thought you'd like to view the cabin," she said. "I tipped housekeeping well, and I got a favor in return. I want to see how you solve a case. Bring your book if you want." The last sentence was said with a boredom recognizable in any language. I couldn't understand why she would encourage my visit if she disapproved of my reading material. She preferred real murders to fictional ones.

I followed her two levels down to the middle passenger deck.

I looked down the hallway toward my room, but my eyes were drawn to an open door in the other direction. The door to Amy's cabin was slightly askew and off its hinges.

"Who broke in?" I asked, trying to sound calm and yet interested.

"The steward. The future mother-in-law who shared that room couldn't open the door without assistance." Grant, the fiancé, slightly built and possibly 5'9", couldn't have broken down the door either.

"The door was locked from the inside?" I asked, taking steps to the door.

Valerie warned me, "Do not touch anything. You don't want your fingerprints on anything. The police could think that you did it."

I examined the door. A lock protruded from inside the knob. The ship had added extra protection against intruders. But the deadbolt lock hanging from the door didn't offer much help. In my room, the lock moved the bar horizontally via the twist of a knob only found inside the door. I investigated the deadbolt, which had been covered with adhesive. A sloppy piece of duct tape held a thick section of rope. So the question was, how did someone get out of the room?

The frame was shattered, and I could barely distinguish the bore in the door jamb.

A locked room. *Death on the Nile* had held no such impossible crime.

The far wall had a single porthole. The opening was small, certainly not large enough to accommodate Mrs. Chisholm's size. In fact, it was too small to fit all but a very few of the passengers.

The ship had been generous with their portions on this trip, and I looked down to see what a full English breakfast could do to a guy. I would be excluded from the list of those who could escape via the porthole. But Grant could have squeezed through.

I looked out the porthole. The outside of the ship was metal, with nothing to grasp. I wasn't sure how someone could have made it out the window without help. The killer could have grabbed a rope and climbed to an upper deck. It would take strength, more than I had, but it might be done.

Just below the window, I saw the black scuff marks of a shoe. Of course, I couldn't tell if the marks had been made recently or on a trip up the Nile three years ago.

Valerie cleared her throat as if in a stage play. I turned around and found Grant standing in the doorway.

"What are you doing in here? This is a crime scene," he said, his tone rising. He took a deep breath. "Have you come to any conclusions? Do you know who killed Amy?"

I was puzzled. Accusing me of the crime one minute and now asking for my assistance?

"Not yet," I said, trying not to sound like I had no idea what was happening. I didn't understand the expectation that I could solve an actual case in minutes.

I turned away. A cake and two glasses sat on the edge of the sink in the room. The white icing with multicolored decorations made me wonder who was being feted by the ship. I had heard no singing or clapping.

"What's this from?" I asked.

"Yesterday was Amy's birthday. We ordered cake and champagne to celebrate. We just never had a chance before—she was gone." I did a quick inventory: forks, small plastic plates, a plastic stopper for the champagne, definitely not to Valerie's taste—no knife and no bottle.

I decided to change the subject, not wanting to see him cry.

"Have you gone through her things? Has anything been stolen?" I pointed at the suitcase on the floor by the bed.

Grant shook his head. "Help yourself," he said with a flourish of his arm.

Without another word, Grant left the room. I was there alone with Valerie, even more baffled. His trust level seemed inappropriate.

Valerie looked through the suitcase and bags by the twin bed. "A galabeya is missing. I saw her at the market yesterday. She looked at several before she bought one."

The galabeya could have been used to protect the killer from the bloodstains. Stabbing would be messy. Throw the galabeya out the porthole, and no one would likely know that a crime had been committed.

I examined the lock again. In a mystery novel, the killer manipulated the deadbolt so that it would appear locked before the person left. Was it as simple as the tape and a rope? A sharp tug on the rope would have drawn the lock into place. I used small scissors from the table abutting the mirror to snip a two-inch end piece from the rope. I would try it on my own door later.

But there were two possible ways to have left the room. The porthole could be used, but a thin person would need to scale the side of the metal hull without help. The door could have been used, but locking the deadbolt would require specific skills. And I had no explanation for why the door jamb's bore had been smashed so thoroughly. What was the door's lock hiding?

The porthole still intrigued me. Its use limited the suspects to two or three travelers. It was an exit, but its use would mean a co-conspirator helped the killer scale to the next level of the ship. How many people could have been involved in this? I looked out the circular egress and watched the Nile float by. Had someone left the room in this manner?

I walked back to my room. One of the nice things about being observant and particular was in my first moments through the door, I could see that someone had gone through my things. I rummaged through the clothes still in my suitcase and the numerous souvenirs in the corner by the sink.

I rifled through everything twice, but nothing was missing. My cash was in my pants pocket, and my passport was where I had left it. What had the burglar wanted from me?

I needed to get ready for cocktails before dinner, but I took a few minutes to press the snipped rope between the door frame and the door. It refused to shut. I pushed harder, but even the small amount of rope I'd found on Amy's door could not fit. I'd verified that my deadbolt was the same as hers. The rope hadn't been used for locked room shenanigans.

Someone had wanted to make me believe that the string had been used to close Amy's door. I wondered who was clever enough to create such a red herring—and knew that I would be looking into the matter. No one else had expressed a fascination for mystery fiction—except me.

* * *

I looked around the cocktail party and found Marwan. He greeted me with a grin. "How goes the trip?"

I nodded and sipped my drink. "The trip is great. I'm nervous about the murder and the solution. I'm not sure if I can solve this."

"If not, it's no sweat, right? The police will come in and take over soon. Then we'll learn what happened."

Mrs. Chisholm was holding a drink as she approached me. "Have you discovered the killer yet?" she asked in a shrill voice that carried around the party. I had already excluded her from suspicion, but her conviviality made me wonder how much she had liked Amy.

"Not yet," I said, marveling at how fast she had recovered. "Where were you the night of Amy's death?" I asked, feeling like I needed to play the part.

"Well, you saw me up at the mystery game. The ship has so many things to do!" She paused, then continued, "After that, most everyone left, and I stayed to watch the Nile. It's been traveling the same path for thousands of years. The people who died under the pharaohs are long forgotten."

"So you didn't see Amy back in the room?"

She smiled. "Not at all. She left long before I did. I assumed she went to Grant's room. That's why I didn't think about the time."

I nodded and looked around for Grant but didn't see him. "Where's your son?" I asked.

She took a healthy swig of her drink and wandered off.

Valerie came up next to me. "Stop asking questions and enjoy the trip," she suggested. "It's like Poirot on that Caribbean mystery."

I thought about correcting her but decided against it. I'd already set a precedent of ignoring her mistakes.

* * *

Jesús joined me at an early breakfast, where I was eating toast. He had a cup of coffee. "Is that enough for you to eat?" he asked, using that paternal tone.

I nodded. Valerie joined us, and we headed to the Edfu Temple.

Ptolemy III Euergetes had built the temple as a tribute to Horus and Hathor, with inscriptions indicating the origin of the earth. Ptolemy, who had returned to Egypt to squelch an uprising, focused on raising buildings and temples that represented his Greek and Egyptian roots. Over the centuries, the edifice has been renamed more than a Gabor.

But I wasn't focusing on the temple. Grant Chisholm was talking with a woman dressed in a galabeya over trousers and a headscarf.

"He sure got over that quick," Valerie said, watching them walk together.

"I don't think his mother approved," I added.

Valerie laughed. "My parents didn't want me to get married but look at us."

"Is she wearing Western clothes?" I asked, wondering if the woman was someone we might know.

"It's common to wear a traditional layer of clothing over the more modern clothes. I think you call that layering?" Valerie asked.

I nodded, strolling and thinking. Despite the beautiful walls and the falcon statue representing Horus, I wanted to return to the ship.

Valerie said something in another language, and after a long laugh, Jesús replied. I looked from one to the other, but they didn't elaborate.

The rest of the tour that morning was quiet. Valerie and Jesús walked ahead of me, arm-in-arm. I finished the tour and left, wanting to get to the ship ahead of everyone else so I would be undisturbed.

Amy's room was just as it had been the previous day. The door was propped against the wall. I looked for something sharp.

I snatched a plastic fork by the cake. Slowly and carefully, I used a tine to peel the tape from the lock. I found a string under the tape, nearly invisible. A thin piece of cotton could move the deadbolt into its slot. I deduced that the string must have broken before it had forced the lock into its place.

I held it up to the light and noticed the slight turquoise color. I knew where I'd seen that string.

I heard a noise at the door before I could put the string back behind the tape. I looked up and saw the steward standing there, watching me.

"May I help you, sir?" He watched my movements closely.

"No, I was just looking for something here," I said almost truthfully. "I'm done now." I was concerned. The steward had smashed the jamb to hide something. He had physically forced the door open, and now I worried he might use that force against me.

"Please let me know if you need anything," he said, standing aside so I could pass.

I knew three things: who had the turquoise string; the steward would ensure the thread was gone by morning; and he would tell someone else what I'd found.

* * *

I returned to my room after lunch. Jesús was already there.

I saw no reason to beat around the bush. "You took a thread from Valerie's blouse. You used that to pull the deadbolt into place. It was fortunate that the smaller thread broke, and the thicker piece you'd used as a red herring did not break." I wanted to sound confident, especially since I had no proof. As predicted, the thread had been gone this morning.

"That's a strong accusation," Jesús said, closing the door. "Do you have any proof?"

"Two people ate the birthday cake. Two forks were missing, and the knife. The champagne had been opened. Amy could have downed the champagne herself, but no one uses two forks to eat cake."

"Maybe she asked the captain or a friend or her fiancé." Jesús grinned as though he held all the cards.

"Two people eating cake and drinking together seems rather intimate. It would imply that she's involved with someone—but her fiancé and his mother were up on the weather deck. So who could it be?"

"Like you know anything about intimacy. I know who you are, and I'd happily share it with everyone here." His face reddened, and he paused for a moment. His voice grew soft. "That leaves about twenty-five people onboard who could eat cake."

"Except that string came from Valerie's shirt. The day she told me about the murder, she wore a blouse that color, with gaps where threads had been pulled loose. Your fingerprints will be all over the place. Then you'll have to explain why you were in Amy's room."

He held up a soft cloth. "Not anymore. I wiped everything clean before I came here today. I say again, you have no proof."

415

I looked around my room, glad I'd stored the plastic cork from the champagne bottle and the plates in Marwan's room before coming here. I'd suspected Jesús would be here, wanting to take care of me as a loose end of another kind.

"That won't work. I took the plastic champagne cork," I said, keeping mum about the plates. Even if something did happen to me, there would be evidence he wouldn't be looking for.

"It was Amy's fault. She followed us onboard the ship. She wanted me to leave Valerie. We had just married, and she wanted me to break it off. She told me she would tell her everything unless I got an annulment. Amy had some idea of a big church wedding—as if that would ever happen. I had no choice. It was a *crime passionnel.*"

I knew he was lying. "If you'd stabbed Amy and left, perhaps, but the locked room had to be planned. You had to get a piece of rope, tape, and a string from Valerie's blouse. You even took a galabeya to cover your clothes. You had a plan, and you followed it to the end."

He took three steps towards me and stopped. I didn't back away, and I didn't flinch. Then he turned around and walked to the wall. I had been right; he was thin enough to push himself through the porthole.

* * *

Valerie wouldn't speak to me when we disembarked. She saw me walking down the gangway and pushed ahead of a few people. The police had been contacted after the second death, and they'd found Jesús' body in shreds. Marwan had told me crocodiles in the Nile grew to sixteen feet in length and weren't shy about eating humans for dinner. He wished me well as he returned to his job, and I headed back to Cincinnati.

* * *

Jeffrey Marks is the Edgar, Agatha, Anthony and Macavity nominated author who has written prolificly about mystery authors of the 1940s and

1950s, including *Who Was That Lady?* and *Atomic Renaisance*. He is currently working on a biography of Erle Stanley Gardner and a dual biography of the two men who wrote as Ellery Queen. In his "spare time" he is the publisher for Crippen & Landru, Publishers.

Death Comes to Coakley

By Shawn Reilly Simmons

United Kingdom

UKStays.com Customer Reviews: **COAKLEY MANOR B&B**

Nicole (US) Rating 8

Pro: The hosts were gracious and welcoming, a warm comfort after our long journey. The staff at the inn were a bit frantic getting ready for SummerFest, but we were given a key and told how to find our room with little fuss and were able to settle in for the night.

Con: We were told not to touch the temperature knob in the shower, and the water was a bit cold, but that's to be expected in an inn dating back to medieval times.

David (UK) Rating: 9

Pro: Our friendly hosts and their extraordinary knowledge of the history of the inn and surrounding village.

Con: Our room could have used a good dusting, but overall, it is a nice weekend getaway spot.

Rowena (ITL) Rating: 1

Pro: Not a lot

Con: Alcohol on the breath of the host as we arrived, as if we'd interrupted a night out at the pub instead of checking into our lodging for SummerFest. The room had not been cleaned in weeks, and there was no door to the bathroom. After noticing rodent droppings in the room, we packed our things and headed out. The host refused to refund our fee. While a financial loss, the state of the property left us no choice. This inn is not fit for habitation and should be avoided at all costs.

Property Response: Lord of the Manor: Dear Rowena, When booking through UKStays.com, you agree to the terms of service, which state no refunds are granted once the guest checks in to their stay. As to your opinion about the inn being fit for habitation, please refer to the thirty-plus positive reviews on this website. Bottoms up.

Anonymous (US) Rating: 5

Pro: Location

Con: Two withdrawals were made from our account for just one room, which we discovered after we'd arrived home. We've left several messages at the inn with no reply. The room had dirty coffee mugs left over from previous guests.

Property Response: Lord of the Manor: Dear Anonymous, You and your betrothed booked two rooms under two different names and two different bank cards. We sat up late, waiting for a no-show guest, as this technically turned out to be, and were unable to re-book the extra room you reserved in error. We didn't realize your mistake until you'd gone. In the future, we suggest you hang on to confirmation emails when you book stays or simply reference your UKStays.com history to avoid double booking yourself again. As a show of good faith and a wedding gift, we have emailed you a gift certificate good for any starter at our pub, The Coakley Arms. Restrictions apply, including not being valid during SummerFest.

Jason (UK) Rating: 10

Pro: Our excellent hosts! SummerFest at Coakley was the very best way to celebrate midsummer. The fete was one of the most fun I've ever attended. The Coakley Arms, sundries room, and the crafts market were conveniently on the property grounds, so there's no need to go into town for anything—a good thing since I forgot my toothbrush!

Con: Not a thing! Can't wait to get back here for a longer stay.

* * *

"This is one of those places you'll have known about your whole life, but never have the chance to see the inside of for yourself," PC Hanker said, peering through the windscreen at the historic manor house in front of them. Gravel crunched under the patrol car's tires as they crept into the shadow of the medieval-era manor home. "Until someone calls about a dead body."

Sergeant Mallory, in the seat next to him, grunted a noncommittal reply.

"Have you been to the estate before?" Hanker asked.

Mallory sighed. "I have. I brought the kids to SummerFest years ago, back when they still wanted to do things with me. I've never stayed the night, though. It's a bit too rich for my wallet, if you know what I mean."

"I don't know why you'd want to stay here anyway. It's all a bit…old." Hanker parked the car and opened the door.

Mallory hefted himself from the seat, straightened his vest, and gazed at the moldy tiles over the front door. "Age is not the problem. It's staying ahead of decay."

"I'd bet my next paycheck this isn't the first dead body found at Coakley Manor. There are probably dozens going back hundreds of years," Hanker said, eyeing the twin brick chimneys. A crack that had been patched with plaster some time ago ran down the left one. "It's wild the place is still standing."

"This was a showplace when it was new, the home of a noble family eight hundred years ago," Mallory said. "Decay creeps up on you, takes its time. And then one day, you're surrounded by it."

* * *

"When did you find her?" Mallory asked, squinting at the woman at the bottom of the stairs. She was face down on the concrete floor of the dimly lit cellar, a pool of dried blood under her head and her one arm bent at an unnatural angle.

"First thing this morning." Miriam Weatherby's voice was hoarse. She sat at the scarred wooden table in the center of the kitchen, her red, chapped hands folded in front of her. "I was heading down to get some champagne for breakfast. Mimosas for the honeymooners upstairs, you know. I took one look, slammed the door, and called for Charles."

"The guests aren't supposed to be in this part of the house," Charles Weatherby, her husband, said. He stared down at the table, sitting opposite his wife. "Only staff. And by staff, I mean her and me, the sole proprietors. Sometimes, the pub chef comes through the kitchen to get supplies, but he never turns up before noon."

"Did you touch the body at all?" Mallory asked.

"Of course not," Charles nearly shouted. "I took one look at the state of her, closed the door, and called the station. I'm hoping we can get this worked out before the festival kicks off tomorrow. We've sold a lot of tickets."

"Do you recognize her? Is she one of your guests?"

The Weatherbys shrugged in unison. "I can't be sure, but I don't think she's been a guest at the inn," Miriam said. "It's a bit of a madhouse around here this week, though, with the festival and all. Lots of visitors coming and going, special deliveries, festival staff setting up and milling about."

"We've got a full house booked this weekend. Thank the lord for the cash," Charles said. "People are coming back to things after lockdown. And acting differently, if you ask me." He shot a glance at the cellar door.

"Go down and get a look at her, see if she's got ID," Mallory directed Hanker. "I'll get the medical team out."

* * *

As the stretcher made its way up the stairs and through the kitchen, Mallory directed them to stop. He glanced at the woman's face. Dried blood matted her dyed-black hair. Her makeup was perfect, and she was stylishly dressed in an expensive-looking blouse and linen pants.

"She had this," Hanker said, handing Mallory a small purse. "Lydia Beauregard is her name." He handed Mallory a business card he'd taken from the bag with the dead woman's smiling face in one corner. "Estate agent at Manor Homes Specialists. Her phone is smashed, but we might be able to get something off of call records."

The Weatherbys had stepped outside as the medics did their work. Mallory glanced out the leaded window at them, standing at opposite ends of the wide back porch.

"Interesting," Mallory said, rubbing the edge of the card with his thick fingers. "Maybe they were looking to sell."

"What would you ask for a place like this?" Hanker asked, toeing a loose tile on the kitchen floor.

"That's a good question," Mallory said. "Millions, I'd think, for the property alone."

The coroner team zipped up the bag and brought the body through the kitchen toward the front door.

"It feels like you need a million dollars to buy any home these days," Hanker said.

Mallory braced himself for another long-winded story about the state of the housing market in their part of the world. Hanker and his fiancee had been searching for a home for months and weren't having much luck. Mallory listened with mild irritation to the Monday morning stories about the previous weekend's house-hunting missions, unsuccessful bids for properties, and bitter diatribes about interest rates and down payments. It seemed to Mallory that Hanker and the Hankerette were aiming for their end-of-life home while still in their twenties, not considering anything less than showstopper properties. Mallory lived in a two-bedroom flat over an Indian takeaway restaurant fifteen miles from his previous home where he raised his children, one mile for every year of marriage. The second bedroom was for the few times a year the kids would come and stay. His ex got the house along with his faith in humanity in the divorce many years ago. He was happy to let her deal with the grief and aggravation of home ownership and eat curry as many times a week as he could manage.

"She was wearing a wedding ring," Mallory said. "Get in touch with the husband." He opened the kitchen door and motioned for the Weatherbys to come back inside.

"We've got guests to tend to," Miriam reminded him.

"How many people are here right now?" Mallory asked.

"One of the rooms is occupied," Charles said. "Young honeymooners in the largest bedroom. We've got more checking in today. It's traditionally one of our busiest weekends each year."

"Where is the rest of the staff?" Mallory asked.

"You're looking at the staff," Charles said. "She and I do it all. Have for years. Cooking, cleaning, managing the inn, dealing with—"

"We took over from my parents," Miriam said, cutting him off. "When my mother died, I inherited the estate."

"We've only been away from this place together three nights in the last twelve years," Charles said.

"So it's just the two of you living here full-time, then?" Mallory said.

"Our son Simon visits when he can, but he's working in London now," Miriam said.

"Work," Charles said with a sharp laugh.

Miriam gave Mallory a tight smile and said, "He's a musician. He works hard at it. The band he's in…"

"And lives with—" interjected Charles. "Like a pack of stray dogs wandered away from home."

"…put on performances most weekends," Miriam finished. "They're playing SummerFest again this year. He's known one or two of his mates since they were boys. That they've stuck together is nice."

"They're playing gigs at bars till all hours of the morning. Calling them performances makes it sound like he's the first chair flautist at the Royal Albert. At any rate, he's not interested in hospitality," Charles said to Mallory.

"Do either of you know Lydia Beauregard?" Mallory asked. "That appears to be the name of our victim."

The Weatherbys stood silent, staring at him.

Finally, Miriam said, "We've had so many guests, it's hard to remember everyone you meet."

"She was an estate agent," Mallory said. "Were you looking at selling the place?"

"Of course not," Miriam said. "This is not just our home; it's our livelihood."

* * *

"Our victim's husband, one Daniel Beauregard, has been away on business," Hanker said, ending a phone call. Mallory had joined him out front of the inn, and they stood next to their patrol car on the gravel drive. "He's pretty distraught about his wife. He's catching the next train back from Manchester."

"The Weatherbys claim they don't know her. So why was she here?"

"I know someone from the agency where she worked," Hanker said. Mallory thought he probably knew someone at every estate agent in the area. "I called her office to see if there was a connection to Coakley Manor. The office administrator said there was nothing in Lydia's files about this place."

"Hm," Mallory said. "The wife says they weren't looking to sell."

"It's not listed for sale," Hanker said, glancing at his phone. "The last transaction on this property was back in the seventies. It was bought piecemeal, one building at a time, until eventually..." He swept his hand, indicating the home, grounds, and pub behind them.

"While it's a public place, in a way, it's a private residence too," Mallory said. "But she could have come here to meet one of the guests, I suppose. A romantic entanglement?"

"You think a young man on his honeymoon would invite a local estate agent for a bit of fun...here?"

Mallory eyed him and relented. "Yeah, that's not the most obvious scenario, is it?"

"I mean, she's a lot older than the honeymooners."

Mallory figured Lydia was in her fifties, which probably did seem ancient to Hanker's generation. Mallory might have considered dating someone like Lydia, if he ever thought about dating again.

"She's closer in age to the Weatherbys," Mallory said. "Maybe she was here for Charles?" Mallory couldn't imagine why any woman found any man attractive, but even so, Charles Weatherby could take the cake as the most unattractive man he'd met. Mostly due to his attitude and demeanor.

"I'm not pegging him as a playing-away kind of guy," Hanker said doubtfully. "He's unshaven and unkempt. Not prepped for a romantic liaison."

"Then why, and why here?" Mallory said with a shiver, pondering Charles Weatherby being the object of anyone's desire.

"Trust me," Hanker said, "it's not like anyone needs an extra reason to kill an estate agent."

***

Lydia Beauregard's husband opened the front door of their sleek, modern home before Hanker and Mallory had gotten out of the patrol car. He looked like a man who hadn't slept, his distraught expression hardening his otherwise doughy features.

"When did you arrive at home, Mr. Beauregard?" Mallory asked, making his way up the front steps from the circular driveway. Hanker trailed behind, shooting glances at the home and property as he followed, either searching for clues or sizing up the curb appeal of the Beauregard homestead.

"Just a few minutes ago," Douglas said. "I shot back from my conference as soon as I heard."

"We know it's a difficult time," Mallory said in what sounded like practiced speech, "but we must ask some questions."

"Sure," Douglas said. "I expected as much." He led them through to the kitchen at the back of the house. The home was well-kept and expertly decorated, like a scene out of an upscale home magazine, or staged as if perpetually ready for selling.

"When did you last see your wife, Mr. Beauregard?" Mallory asked, his bulky, uniformed frame appearing out of place in the kitchen's white and silver gleam.

"Yesterday morning," Douglas said. "I left for the station first thing. We had coffee together at sunup, and then I was off to Manchester for a weekend conference."

"Are you also in real estate?" Hanker asked, standing behind the center island. The top of his head was level with the pans that hung from a decorative rack suspended from the ceiling.

"In a way," Douglas said. "I'm a developer. I work more on the commercial building end of things."

"And how long have you been married?" Mallory asked.

Douglas put his hands on his hips and closed his eyes for a few seconds as he thought. "Two years. From the first night we met, we hit it off and found we had a lot in common. We married six months later that same year. It was during lockdown, so it was just us at the registry office in town."

"Is this your first marriage, Mr. Beauregard?" Mallory asked.

"No, it's the second for both Lydia and me," Douglas said. Hanker jotted a note on his pad.

"Any children?" Mallory asked.

"I have two grown girls. They've lived together in New York for the past six years, working on their artistic and acting dreams. Still mostly waitressing and relying on the Bank of Dad."

"How about Lydia?" Hanker asked, still scribbling.

"Lydia doesn't have children," Douglas said.

"Have you met Lydia's ex?" Mallory asked.

"That would be difficult," Douglas said, shaking his head. "He's dead. Committed suicide, sadly enough. My ex-wife has passed away also. Lydia and I met at a grief support group for people who have lost their partners."

Mallory's eyebrows pushed the wrinkles farther up his forehead. "Why the rush to get remarried?"

"When you've been married a long time," Douglas began, "it feels strange not to be. When you find someone who matches you again, why wait?"

Mallory stared at him for a beat, then asked, "Do you have any idea why your wife would have been at Coakley Manor late last night or very early this morning?"

Douglas shrugged. "I imagine for her work somehow, except she never mentioned the manor to me. She did admire historical properties, although she'd never live in one. Lydia liked shiny new things." He glanced around the kitchen as if to prove his point.

"Was anything bothering her lately?" Mallory asked. "Would she have any reason to...hurt herself?"

A brief expression of surprise, then disbelief, crossed Douglas's face.

"Not that she shared with me. The counseling we went through did help. But, well, you probably know that real estate professionals faced a number of challenges during the pandemic. Sales, finance, and builders were in a virtual stoppage. We're all still recovering from two and a half years of not being up to full speed for both income and morale. Luckily, a few commissions have come in for me in recent months. I mean, I was fine and would continue to be for a long time, but Lydia was still struggling to rebuild her business. Things are starting to look up, though, and she was encouraged of late. Are you suggesting she might have done this to herself?"

Mallory put up a hand in a placating gesture. "We're investigating an unattended death and considering every possible scenario." His phone buzzed from his pocket and he pulled it out, glancing at the screen. "Excuse me one minute."

"How many active listings did your wife currently have on the market? Anything similar to his home up for grabs?" Mallory heard Hanker ask as he headed down the hallway. He rolled his eyes and dialed the number that had appeared on his screen. A few minutes later his jawline hardened as he listened to the coroner on the other end of the call.

* * *

Mallory and Hanker left a stunned-looking Douglas Beauregard standing in his kitchen after informing him that his wife Lydia had, in fact, been murdered. The coroner had found strangulation marks around her neck, indicating she'd been choked first, then flung down the cellar stairs. They were running toxicology reports, which would take a while, but it didn't appear Lydia had been impaired in any way.

"What do you make of him?" Mallory asked as they pulled away.

"Nice enough," Hanker said with a shrug. "A bit snobbish, you ask me, but he's got the funds to back it up. "

"Did he seem distraught to you?"

"I think he's stunned," Hanker said. "But more tired than anything. I suppose that amount of shock and adrenaline can do that to you."

"Maybe," Mallory said. "He did look like a man who hadn't slept."

"Being away at a conference, I suppose it's not like being in your own bed," Hanker agreed. "I imagine they have a pretty nice one upstairs."

"Your own bed," Mallory mumbled. "Check around to that conference. Whatever one he said he was at. Check the train station, too."

"You think he killed his wife? At Coakley Manor?" Hanker asked. "Why?"

"I don't think anything," Mallory said. "We're checking out his story. That's what you do in murder investigations. What are they teaching recruits now, to take everyone at their word? It's been a long time since I've been in training, but it can't have changed that much."

"All right, all right," Hanker said with a sigh. "Anything else to check on?"

"Yeah, find out if he had a suitcase with him. I didn't notice one in the foyer. If he was going to be gone several days, surely he'd pack at least an overnight case."

"Got it," Hanker said. "Anything else?"

"Yeah," Mallory said. "Find out what happened to wife number one."

* * *

The sound of shouting emanated from the back of the manor house as Mallory and Hanker entered the front door the next morning. SummerFest preparation was in full swing and dozens of people rushed around performing various tasks related to the fete. They made their way to the kitchen, following the voices.

"I don't have to play here every year, you know," a young man was shouting as they entered. "I had to turn down three gigs to do you this favor."

"Don't do me any more favors," Charles shouted. The young man was clearly the Weatherbys' son. He was a mixed pot of both of their features, but he lucked out and was tall and lanky compared to their short, squat frames.

"Charles, enough," Miriam said, cutting between the men.

"Excuse us," Mallory said.

The family of three froze and set their gaze on the pair of policemen in their kitchen.

"You must be Simon Beauregard," Mallory said.

"I must be," Simon said. "No choice there."

"Stuff it," Charles warned.

"When did you arrive in town?" Hanker asked in a too-lighthearted tone, as if he'd just bumped into an old friend on the sidewalk. He was obviously uncomfortable with the tension radiating off the family.

"An hour ago," Simon said. "I caught an early train." His hair was dyed dark blue, and a thin gold ring hugged his nostril.

"We're so glad you could come," Miriam said happily. "Simon always brings his band to play for the festival. It's a big draw for our guests."

"Yes, they come far and wide to hear The Pudding Riots yell into microphones for three hours," Charles said, matching her happy tone.

"You know I'm in a different band now, Dad," Simon said, mimicking their joyful way of speaking. Mallory wondered if this was some shared Weatherby game meant to make outsiders uneasy. "We're the Royal Pains now. You remember, don't you, Dad?"

Hanker slid a nervous glance to Mallory before asking, "Did you know the woman your parents found at the bottom of the stairs? Lydia Beauregard?"

Simon shook his head and chewed his lip as he looked at his parents. Mallory saw a flash of concern cross his face. "Not that I can say. How do you know a maniac isn't running around the grounds, sneaking up and pushing people down stairwells? My parents aren't safe in their own home. It's not like the security around here is current to this century."

"We've had no problems up to now," Miriam said a bit defensively, the first time she'd been anything but glowingly supportive of her offspring.

"Times change," Simon said.

"That might be the only thing my son and I agree on," Charles said.

* * *

Mallory lingered near the stage in the large field behind the manor home as the band set up. Dozens of tables had been staged on the lawn, featuring various vendors from the area hawking their wares to celebrate the height of summer. Simon appeared to be the lead vocalist. He had a blue guitar strapped to his back, the same color as his hair, as he spoke on the phone to someone.

"It's late notice, but we need you out here for this gig," Simon said in low tones beside the back curtain. Mallory paused his pacing to listen. "Kit…isn't well. We need a drummer fast. I'd owe you one, man. It's the farewell performance. Celebrations after. You still live in town, so I thought you might be free."

Mallory strolled back to the back of the manor, pulling out his phone and making a call.

* * *

"What would you call this kind of music?" Hanker shouted to Mallory over the din of electric guitar. A crowd had gathered before the stage and bopped to the sound, apparently recognizing the song.

"Says right here it's glam metal," Mallory said, showing Hanker a website on his phone. "This guy didn't make it." He pointed to the drummer in the photograph. "They got a last-minute fill-in. A friend of Simon's from school."

"How did you figure that out?" Hanker asked.

Mallory smiled, a rare experience that always thrilled Hanker. "I figured out some other things, too. Did you find out what happened to the first Mrs. Beauregard?"

"Cancer," Hanker said. "She went quickly, from all accounts. And Mr. Beauregard's story checks out. He was at that conference and on the first train back this morning."

"Let's go inside. I've had enough of the Royal Pains. And I need you to make one more call for me."

* * *

Charles and Miriam Weatherby were in the kitchen drinking lemonade, their exhausted faces shiny from exertion and the heat of the afternoon.

"Enjoying the fete?" Miriam asked hopefully as the policemen entered the room. The muffled music from the stage ended, and a round of applause and shouts followed.

"Quite," Hanker said. "It's a nice turnout."

"You?" Mallory asked.

Miriam glanced at Charles before replying. "We always do. Could have done without the bother from yesterday, but it's all going to be fine now."

Charles remained silent, focusing on his lemonade.

"Speaking of the bother," Mallory said. "You're sure you'd not met Lydia before?"

Miriam smiled. "I think I said I may have met her but couldn't remember, since we meet so many people."

"Hm," Mallory said with a nod.

"And your son arrived on the first train this morning from London?"

Miriam hesitated briefly, then the smile again. "Yes. Why?"

"He wasn't on the morning train," Hanker said, checking his notes. "The station manager says the guys from the band came in last night. He remembered them holding the doors open and setting off the buzzer, trying to get the drum kit out."

"But the drummer couldn't make it today," Mallory said. "Why drag drums up from London and then not play?"

"What's going on?" Simon entered through the kitchen door and went straight for the lemonade.

"Nothing, dear, just more about that poor woman," Miriam said. Charles remained still and silent.

"Why did you lie about when you got to town?" Mallory asked.

Simon took a sip of lemonade and set his glass down. "When did I lie?"

"When you said you arrived on the early train this morning," Mallory reminded him. "When you and your mates actually arrived last night."

"No reason," Simon said. "I blame the shock of my parents discovering a dead body in their kitchen cellar."

"Lydia Beauregard was her name," Mallory said. "You also lied about not knowing her."

"You called her office four times," Hanker said, eyes on his notes. "All in the last week. And also her mobile yesterday."

Simon looked down at his boots, then at his father. "Okay, so? Doesn't mean I killed her."

"Lying to the police in a murder investigation is a crime in itself," Hanker reminded him.

"He's not lying," Miriam said. "He just forgot to say some things."

Charles scoffed. "Don't make it worse, Miriam."

"Where were you last night? And why had you been in touch with Lydia? I'd advise you to stick to the truth this time. Lying to us again won't help you in the least."

"I called her," Miriam interjected before Simon could speak.

"Except there's no record of that," Hanker said, flipping through pages on his notepad. "Only Simon."

"Mom, it's fine," Simon said. "Yes, I called Lydia. I knew she did real estate here and…well, this place is killing them." He glanced at his parents with a pleading expression. "My dad's miserable. He hates it here, and I thought if they could break free of all this responsibility and work, this generational obligation, they might have a chance to be happy again. To stop hating…things."

"Oh, dear," Miriam said. "We're not selling. This is your inheritance."

"But I don't want it," Simon hissed.

"And you don't want the responsibility of taking it over," Mallory added. "So it would also benefit you to not have that obligation hanging over your head."

"No way he could manage it anyway," Charles mumbled.

"So, what happened? Did she tell you this place couldn't be sold?" Mallory asked. "How did she end up at the bottom of the stairs?"

"I have no idea," Simon said. "We agreed to meet at the manor late, after my parents had gone up. I was only going to show her a few things, walk the grounds, get a general sense of what she thought the property might be worth. I waited a half hour, and she didn't show up. I left to meet my bandmates at a bar in town."

"Including your drummer, Kit, who didn't play today," Mallory said.

Simon looked nervous. "He…had some things going on."

"Like dealing with the death of his estranged mother?" Mallory pressed. "Her picture was on the front page of the local paper this morning."

"Sir," Hanker said under his breath, flipping to a note. "Lydia had no children. Her husband told us."

"None that she acknowledged anymore," Mallory said. "Even to her new husband. A son that she cut off years ago, living a lifestyle she didn't approve of in London. A son she blamed for her husband's suicide."

Miriam gasped and sank into the nearest chair.

"So why would she agree to help her son's friend sell his parents' estate?" Hanker asked, confounded.

"Money talks," Mallory said. "A big commission like this would melt any icy heart."

The Weatherbys stood silent, staring at each other.

"Kit gave me the number to her office," Simon admitted. "But I didn't kill her."

"Simon Weatherby, I'm placing you under arrest—"

"Wait!" Miriam said. "I killed her. I did it!"

"Don't be stupid," Charles sighed. "I killed the nosy woman. Caught her poking around in here where no one is supposed to be. Came down for a nightcap and found a woman in the kitchen. Said she was looking for Mr. Weatherby. That's me, isn't it? But she meant Simon, I guess."

"So you strangled her and pushed her down the stairs?" Mallory asked.

"What would you have done?" Charles asked defiantly.

Everyone in the room stood silently stunned.

"She was waving a card around, saying she could sell the place as-is. As-is? The silly woman was trying to undercut us, trick us into thinking she'd be doing us a favor by taking on the listing. What made her opinion matter, anyway? I may be a fool, but I wasn't born yesterday. I know the value of this place." He pulled a business card out of his pocket, Lydia Beauregard's smiling face in the corner.

"But, Dad," Simon said. "You hate this place, your life, me."

Charles sighed and tossed the card onto the table. "That's where you're wrong, son. I don't hate anything."

Douglas (UK) Rating: 1
Pro:
Con: The Lord of the Manor murdered my wife.
UKStays.com reply: This property is currently unavailable for bookings.

* * *

Shawn Reilly Simmons is an Agatha and Anthony Award-winning author and editor. She's written eight novels in her Red Carpet Catering mystery series, and over twenty-five of her short stories have appeared in various anthologies. She is co-owner of Level Best Books and serves on the Bouchercon board of directors. Shawn is a member of Sisters in Crime, Mystery Writers of America, the Crime Writers' Association, and International Thriller Writers. She lives in historic downtown Frederick, Maryland.

http://www.shawnreillysimmons.com/

Facebook: @ShawnReillySimmonsAuthor

Twitter & Instagram: @ShawnRSimmons

About The Mystery Patrons

The Mystery Patrons were founded to assist members of the mystery writing and fan community through grants and scholarships to conferences, conventions, classes, memberships, and other activities where costs might impede attendance. Our mission is to offer financial support to members of the mystery community in an effort to grow and enrich the community. All projects published through the Mystery Patrons will benefit our established scholarship fund.